The HOLIDAY GRUMP

ENNI AMANDA

Welcome to
HIDEAWAY HARBOR

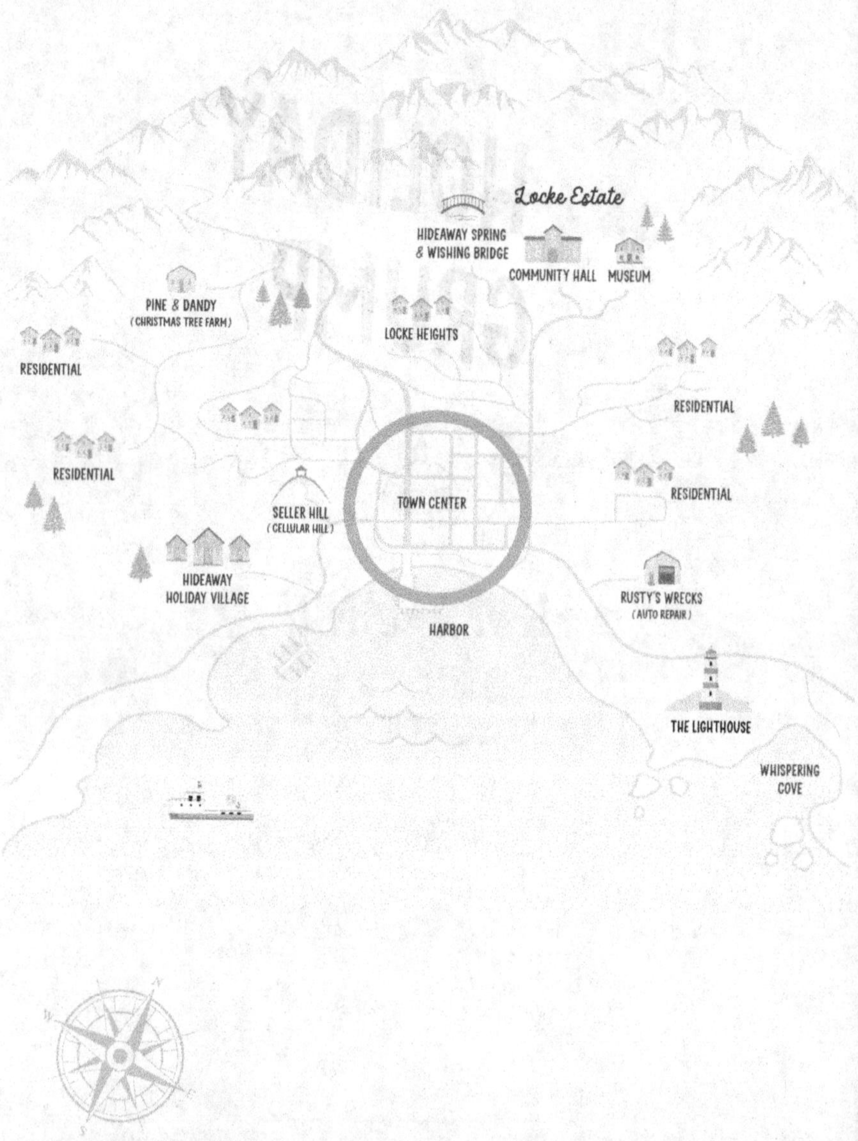

Locke Estate

HIDEAWAY SPRING
& WISHING BRIDGE

COMMUNITY HALL   MUSEUM

PINE & DANDY
(CHRISTMAS TREE FARM)

LOCKE HEIGHTS

RESIDENTIAL

RESIDENTIAL

RESIDENTIAL

TOWN CENTER

SELLER HILL
(CELLULAR HILL)

RESIDENTIAL

HIDEAWAY
HOLIDAY VILLAGE

RUSTY'S WRECKS
(AUTO REPAIR)

HARBOR

THE LIGHTHOUSE

WHISPERING
COVE

The town center

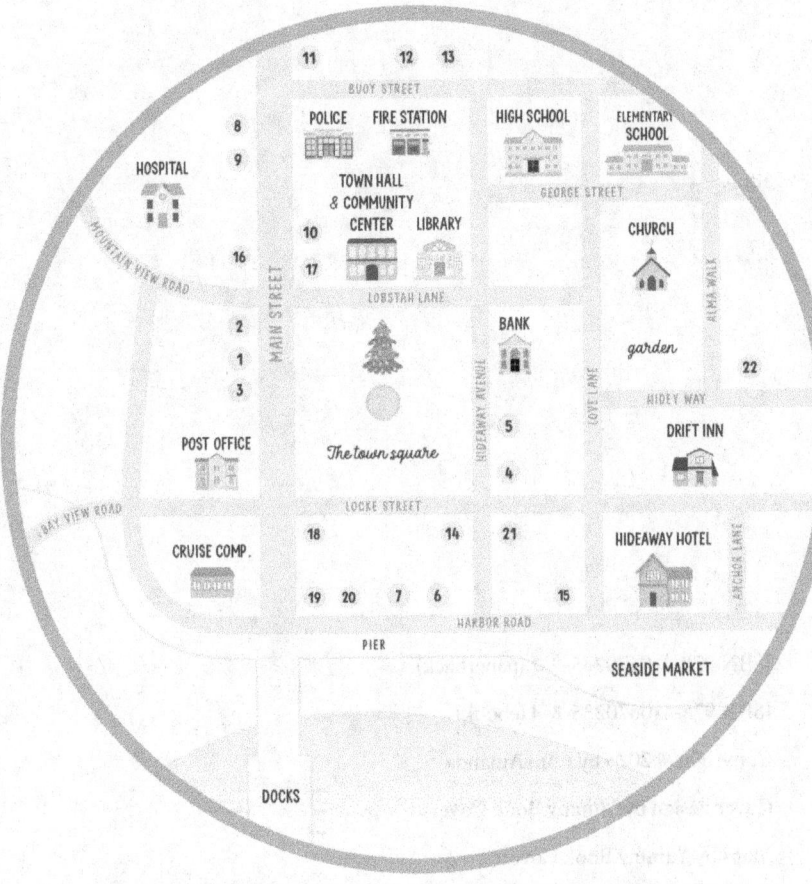

1. LOVE AT FIRST SIP (CAFE)
2. HIDDEN ITALY (RESTAURANT)
3. MAKING WHOOPIE (BAKERY)
4. HARD TO FIND (BOOKSTORE)
5. CHRISTMAS WONDERLAND (POP - UP STORE)
6. HOOK, LINE AND SINKER (RESTAURANT)
7. THE SHORE THING (BAR/RESTAURANT)
8. THE PERFECT PACKAGE (ADULT TOY STORE)
9. SCENTS AND SENSIBILITY (PERFUME SHOP)
10. TONIC ROOM (HERBAL SHOP)
11. HIDEAWAY GROCER (GENERAL STORE)
12. LOBSTAH LIFTS (GYM)
13. HIDEAWAY CLINIC
14. HIDEAWAY TREASURES (GIFT SHOP)
15. THE CHOWDER HOUSE RULES (RESTAURANT)
16. ALMANAC (TOWN PAPER)
17. KIPPIS (SMALL BAR)
18. THE SWEETEST THING (CANDY STORE)
19. BEAUTY PARLOR
20. THE MASTER BAITERS (BAIT & TACKLE SHOP)
21. HAMMERTIME HARDWARE
22. OFF THE BEATEN PATH (ADVENTURE COMPANY)

ISBN 978-1-0670235-9-1 (paperback)

ISBN 978-1-0670235-8-4 (ebook)

Copyright © 2025 by Enni Amanda

Cover design by Yummy Book Covers

Maps by Yummy Book Covers

Editing by Jenny Sims / Editing4Indies

For all the drifters, dreamers and adorable misfits—
welcome home to Hideaway Harbor!

CHAPTER 1

Noelle

The moment I stepped off the bus, I realized my brilliant plan had one fatal flaw. How could I skip Christmas in a town that was obsessed with it?

After a topsy-turvy ride over a mountain range, I'd landed in the middle of a shimmering tinsel dream. Giant wreaths hung from every lamppost, and the cute houses lining Main Street were strung together with a canopy of lights. Playful snowflakes drifted as if in slow motion, completing the storybook scene.

"It's Christmas already?" I blinked at the twinkling lights.

"It's late November, dear. At Hideaway Harbor, we start right after Halloween." Ida, a gray-haired lady I'd met on the bus, beamed with pride as she negotiated the wobbly bus stairs.

I offered her a hand down to the icy sidewalk. Maybe it

wasn't that early, but fresh off a Mediterranean cruise, I felt like I'd slipped through a wormhole.

Ida smiled at my slack-jawed expression. "It's that way to the harbor restaurants. Off you go. Get yourself some dinner and put some meat on those bones." She pointed toward a slice of dark ocean peeking between the decorated buildings.

"Thank you! And thank you for the lesson. I promise to practice!"

She'd taught me to crochet on the bus trip, and I couldn't wait to try my hand at the gorgeous flowers she produced with ease. Finally on dry land, with access to shops and an apartment of my own, I was itching to create. Yarn, fabric, beads. I wanted to try it all.

Ida patted her oversized tote, which I now knew was full of yarn. "The crochet club meets every Tuesday night at the Sip. Come along!"

"Sure thing." I had no idea what the Sip was, but I'd find out.

I drew in a lungful of crisp winter air and adjusted the heavy backpack on my shoulders as I headed down the road.

Hideaway Harbor. Despite the over-the-top Christmas cheer, it still felt like a good place to lay low. A hard-to-reach coastal town with a name to match, where I didn't know anyone and nobody knew me.

As I reached the harbor, icy wind pinched my cheeks, and I followed the noise to the nearest bar. White lettering on the window welcomed me to The Shore Thing. Was it some sort of hookup place? I sighed and pulled at the door. I was too hungry to care. If this were the local meat market,

I might as well present myself with unwashed hair and a layer of travel sweat under my coat. Consider it a public service announcement that I wasn't on the market.

A pop version of "White Christmas" met me at the door, along with the scent of pine and beer. I took a deep breath, adjusting to my new reality. Just a week ago, I'd been at the Port of Skala outside Santorini, watching retirees roast in lounge chairs and knock back ouzo. Christmas hadn't crossed my mind, especially since I'd planned to skip it this year.

It wasn't an easy choice because I loved Christmas. My whole family did. Mom watched holiday movies year-round and had named me Noelle and my sister Holly. We used to joke about an imaginary brother named Rudolph. My decision to stay on a cruise ship to work through the holidays had been a bitter pill for them to swallow.

Fate had other plans. The ship's engine failed, leaving us stuck on home turf six weeks early. I needed work, both for money and distraction, so I'd taken the only job offer available: selling Christmas decorations at a pop-up shop. Which begged the question, was it even possible to skip Christmas while peddling fairy lights and plastic Santas?

Either way, I couldn't go home, so this was it.

I stepped into the bar, ducking under a low-hanging garland. A handful of older men nursed beers, eyes glued to the blond bartender. The tables and booths were filled with younger people enjoying drinks, chowder and lobster rolls. Apart from the seasonal touches, it felt like the ship again, noisy and boozy with vacation energy. The interior had the charm of an English pub decorated with Maine fishing paraphernalia. Lights with stained glass lampshades hung over weathered tables, and framed pictures, anchors and ship wheels crowded the walls. By the window, an impressively tall potted cactus tried in vain to blend into the nautical theme.

I rushed to grab the one empty table by the cactus. The bartender appeared with a smile and a notepad. "What can I get you? We've got a two-for-one Black Friday deal on lobster rolls."

That explained the crowd. I studied the menu and ordered a turkey sandwich. When she left, I checked my phone.

> Grace: Everything okay? Call me!

> Mom: How's the Caribbean?

I sucked in a sharp breath, staring at the screen. I typed a quick reply to Grace, my Korean stewardess friend, but it bounced back within seconds.

No network connection.

That was just as well since I had no idea how to reply to Mom. She didn't know I was back in Maine and only two hours away. If my parents found out, they'd drag me home. And Spencer would hear I was back.

He would find me.

I briefly considered asking Mom to keep my whereabouts a secret, but she'd have to tell Dad, the family blabbermouth. Besides, everyone loved my ex-fiancé. Everyone, including me, thought I'd lost my mind. Who left New England's number-one bachelor at the altar? He was wealthy, generous, and handsome. I was a college dropout who liked upcycling clothes.

Marrying Spencer Alford had made perfect sense to everyone. Running away to work on a cruise ship barely made sense to me. I'd been trying to come up with an acceptable explanation for a full year, and I still had nothing. Which is why I kept my updates short, sweet, and future-focused.

How could I tell my loving, devoted parents that I didn't want financial security and happiness as Spencer's wife? That I didn't want the huge house in Bangor and the summer place on Martha's Vineyard, where my whole family would always be welcome? I'd torn up their dream, wasted every penny they'd sunk into deposits in a desperate attempt to match the Alfords' wedding budget. Of course, I'd also wasted an obscene amount of Alford money, but I cared less about that than about my parents' meager savings.

No. I couldn't let Mom know I was this close to home. But I had to send her a picture, something convincing. My gaze landed on the cactus, and it gave me an idea. If I framed myself against it with a tropical-looking cocktail, maybe it could pass for Port Canaveral, the first stop on my canceled Caribbean cruise. Just another terrible holiday shot by a terrible photographer, which everyone knew I was.

I hurried to the bar. "Hey, can I order one more drink? Anything tropical looking, maybe with a straw."

"O...kay. Alcoholic? Any flavor preference?"

"Any juice, really, with lots of ice. It's a photo prop."

She gave me a slow nod, eyebrows raised. "I'll whip up something."

I returned to my table and undressed until I was slightly

5

shivering in my T-shirt. I rubbed my arms, but the goose bumps remained, teased by the cold air leaking in through the windows. I put my jacket back on, trying to think of a solution. Burpees!

The other bar-goers didn't seem to be paying any attention, so I cleared enough room between the chairs and dropped onto the floor. Push-up, jump, push-up.

By the time the server arrived with my orange drink and a little umbrella, I was sweaty and out of breath.

"Just warming up for the pic," I explained, scrambling to my feet. "That looks perfect."

"Good thing I mopped yesterday." She shook her head, laughing.

I posed with the drink and the cactus, snapping a smiling selfie. It looked good, except for the frost on the windows, which screamed "Maine," not "Florida."

I edged closer to the cactus to crop out the background. That was when I noticed the thick layer of dust on it. Would a cactus in Port Canaveral look like that? Maybe, but I had a feeling Mom would comment on it. Sighing, I dug a makeup brush from my bag and got to work.

Yes, I was dusting off a cactus in public.

Once it looked a little shinier, I tried again. Perfect.

I restarted my phone, but *connection error* popped up again. My eyes drifted around the bar, and I noticed something strange. Nobody else was on their phones. Not one. There were no glowing screens or scrolling thumbs. Everyone was talking and laughing over the music.

This was what life must have looked like before the internet. Conversation. Happy smiles.

And… a scowl.

I turned and found myself caught in a stare. Deeply confused and borderline judgmental. The unsettling pair of eyes belonged to a beautiful man with the wildest hair I'd ever seen, like a tuft of grass that had never seen a lawn-mower. His sculpted jaw was covered in a stubble so long it was almost a beard. He wore an old-fashioned tweed coat over a flannel shirt so crumpled I wondered if he'd hung it after washing. It made him look both outdated and neglected, like he'd been cast in a period drama, but the wardrobe department hated him. He had a bottle of beer in front of him and a leather-bound book in his hands.

What was it? A dictionary? A Bible? Who read that kind of book in a bar by himself?

He turned back to it, shaking his head like he couldn't believe his eyes. Had he been watching me? Judging me? When someone did something silly, people usually laughed. At least people who were out in a bar, drinking alcohol. What was this guy's problem?

My curiosity kicked in like a drug. I'd always been fasci-nated by anything a little different. Spencer had told me I needed to reel it in. It was fine to be sociable, but I wasn't supposed to bombard people with invasive questions. His mother had trained me for weeks, the way I imagined someone training a commoner who was about to marry into royalty. She'd said I had the makings of a wonderful conversationalist, if only I learned proper decorum.

Decorum, schmorcorum.

Spence was not here, and neither was his mom. If I wanted to find out what this stranger's deal was, I would do exactly that.

CHAPTER 2

Fredrik

Before that Friday night, the craziest thing I'd seen at The Shore Thing was my friend Jackson tipping with a fifty-dollar bill. And he was a trust fund kid who occasionally got far too drunk, so it wasn't that out of the ordinary.

That was until I saw a woman approaching a cactus with a makeup brush. Moments earlier, she'd dropped to the sticky floor to do some sort of push-ups. It was hard to tell since she was wearing a fluffy, peach-colored overcoat that made her look like a baby chick. I was good at minding my own business, but when she took out a toiletry bag to attend to a cactus, even I couldn't look away.

It wasn't my intention to gawk at anyone or, God forbid, catch their attention. I despised chitchat and avoided it at all costs. According to my sister, that defeated the purpose of going to a bar, but I liked the soundscape—talk and laughter blending with music. Upbeat, meaningless noise that drowned out my darker thoughts.

Except now my meditative Friday night buzz had been replaced by jittery nerves. The strange woman at the nearby table had noticed me watching her, and she had questions. I could feel them in the air as she regarded me with open curiosity.

I kept my gaze on the book, but she shuffled closer, flashing a sunny smile. "Hey! Can I ask you something?"

I reluctantly lifted my eyes off the page. "What?"

"What's the deal with the internet?" She raised her phone, turning it in her hand.

I lowered the book by an inch. "Bad signal."

"Is it a satellite connection?"

"No. There's a tower, but..." I sighed and lowered the book in defeat. "It's not close enough, and we get some odd weather events, like temperature inversion. And if anyone tells you anything else, don't believe them."

Her eyebrows traveled up. "Like what?"

I cast a weary look at the ceiling. "Evil spirits. Government experiments. None of it's true. The government doesn't give a rat's ass about us. There's no conspiracy. Only gradual decay and entropy. And eventually, death."

She nodded solemnly, her eyes exaggeratedly wide. "I can tell you're fun."

Better that she found out right away. And left.

Except she wasn't leaving. Instead, she leaned forward.

"What do you do when you need to call someone?"

"Use the landline. Or go up Cellular Hill." I picked up the book again, signaling the end of the conversation.

She let out a bubbly laugh like I'd cracked an exceptional joke. "Cellular—"

"Yeah, hilarious." I angled myself away from her and resumed my reading.

"I didn't mean to make fun of… anything. It's an odd name, that's all."

Clearly, she wasn't going to leave me alone. I lowered the book again.

"The official name is Seller Hill. It used to be where the market was held, before they built the town square in 1862."

She stared at me in awe. "Wow. You must be amazing at trivia nights."

I pushed out a flashback from my old life.

"Trivia is useless," I muttered, flipping a page I couldn't focus on.

She scooted to the edge of her seat, her knees nearly touching my satchel. I used it as a barricade, making sure not even the densest idiot thought the seat beside me was vacant.

I heard the smile in her voice. "So… are you like a history buff or…?"

"Do you mind?" I nodded at the book.

"Ah, sorry." She finally retreated to her table just as the bartender, Summer, arrived with her food.

"Thank you so much!" she beamed.

Summer threw me a reproachful glance. "I apologize for whatever Fredrik said."

"Oh no!" The woman waved her hand. "He was very helpful—"

"No, he wasn't." Summer glared at me. "He was an ass,

and he's sorry. This is not how we treat visitors in this town."

I harrumphed behind my book.

"Where are you staying?" Summer asked, ignoring me.

"I'm here to run a pop-up shop on the town square. I haven't even seen it yet. I was too hungry. But I hope it's nice. There's an apartment at the back I can stay in, so it's a great deal."

Summer brightened. "A shop? Really? What do you sell?"

"Christmas decorations, apparently."

"Wow. Didn't know we needed any more of those." Summer laughed, glancing at the pine garlands hanging from the ceiling. "But that's great that you got yourself a job."

The woman nodded enthusiastically. "I'm so grateful I don't even care what I'm selling. I got off a cruise ship this morning, and it's so amazing to be on dry land for more than two hours and, you know, out at night."

She sounded so perky. Full of excitement. Where the hell did they breed her kind? I'd long ago stopped pretending to read and was now shamelessly listening in. She knew it, too, raising her voice just enough for my benefit.

Summer threw me a dirty look and aimed her honeyed voice at the newcomer. "Sounds like a special occasion."

"You have no idea. Excuse me, I'm starving." She took a bite of the sandwich, smiling apologetically.

Summer laughed. "I'll let you eat. But you must tell me all about the shop later. I'm Summer."

"Noelle," she said after chewing and swallowing her food.

Summer gave her a thumbs-up and headed back to the bar, weaving between the tables.

Noelle. Her name was Noelle, and she was here to sell Christmas decorations. *More than a little on the nose*, I thought, shaking my head. But I memorized it anyway. I might bump into her again.

I wondered where her shop was located on the town square. I knew the place like the back of my hand. A couple of empty shops remained—one next door to mine—but that space was too big for something so frivolous. It didn't make sense.

As she ate, I enjoyed the silence. She wasn't a talk-with-her-mouth-full type, thank God, even if she kept glancing my way between bites. No doubt she was gearing up for another question with that head tilt and those giant anime eyes, expecting me to dazzle and entertain her.

She was barking up the wrong tree. I was as dazzling and entertaining as that cactus she'd been putting makeup on.

My shoulders dropped with a heavy exhale as I took a sip of my beer. It had turned warm and flat an hour ago. Mostly, I used it as a prop. Summer knew better than to push alcohol on me. I was a cheap, lousy drunk, once voted "Most likely to fall asleep in public." I didn't care either way. I'd long since stopped feeling embarrassed over things I couldn't control.

I didn't deal in secondhand embarrassment, either, so watching this woman in a baby chick coat exercise and brush a cactus didn't bother me. Her incessant questions did.

"What are you reading?"

I lowered the book, giving her a tired look. *"How to Keep People at Bay*. It's self-help."

"Self-help?" Her lips twitched like she wasn't buying my bullshit. "Can I see?"

She reached for the book, but I slipped it into my bag, committing to said bullshit. "It's annotated. Very personal stuff. I can't risk showing it to a stranger."

Why was I encouraging her?

She was smiling now. A pretty smile that made her brown eyes glint. "You shouldn't write anything that sensitive in the margins. What if someone comes to visit and starts browsing through your book?"

"Well, then, the writer has failed to help me keep people at bay. She'll get a scathing review." I gave her a stern look, which did nothing to discourage this muppet.

"Who's the author? I'll look it up." She batted her eyelashes like a cartoon character, leaning in to peek into my bag.

I closed the flap in her face, and she giggled.

"Come on! If it's about keeping bad people away, I need that book." Her laughter fizzled, and something dark crossed behind her eyes. She hid it well, keeping that smile on her lips. But I'd already seen it.

"Do you have trouble keeping bad people away?" I asked despite myself.

As much as I wanted to return to my peace and background noise, I couldn't ignore the red flag.

Noelle jerked back a little. Her gaze flicked to the door before she smiled again. "No trouble. I just keep moving."

"You keep moving?" I told myself to drop it, but my mouth didn't listen. "Is someone after you?"

Her head twitched like she was about to look at the door again. "Nobody knows I'm here, and there's no cell signal, so I'm good." She grinned, but I saw through it. She was running from something. Or someone.

As much as I wanted to dismiss her and the rest of the world, I couldn't shake the unease. If there was any chance that she was in danger, if she kept bothering me because it made her feel safer to have a man nearby, I couldn't ignore it.

I waited for her to elaborate, but she bounced up, pulled on the fluffy coat, and hoisted a huge backpack onto her shoulders. "Well, it was nice to meet you," she chirped, heading for the door.

What was I supposed to do?

Cursing, I gathered my things, threw money on the table, and followed her.

CHAPTER 3

Noelle

I couldn't believe my ears when I heard Fredrik behind me. He muttered something, then rushed past to open the door. He'd made it clear he had no interest in talking to me, and I'd already exhausted my willingness to be humiliated. No matter how much it fed my curiosity, I was done.

"I'm not in any danger," I insisted as we reached the foot of the stairs, icy wind whipping in from the harbor. "You can go back to your... self-help. I'm sorry I bothered you."

He shifted uncomfortably, adjusting the bag on his shoulder. "I... I'm sorry I was rude, but I don't come here to talk." He swallowed. "Where are you going? I'll escort you."

Who even used words like that? I stared at him, not sure what to make of my reluctant, bookish bodyguard. "Why?"

"To be on the safe side."

"Is it particularly unsafe out here?" I glanced at the empty pier. The faint sound of "It's Beginning to Look a Lot Like Christmas" drifted from the bar. The most dangerous thing out here was probably the icy sidewalk, and my boots had a pretty good grip.

He shrugged. "Humor me?"

It was the friendliest expression he'd managed so far, almost like a smile.

I narrowed my eyes. "What if *you're* dangerous?"

He gave me a solemn nod. "That's the risk you'd be taking, obviously."

"Can you even protect a woman? Do you have muscles? Do you carry a gun? Do you know Krav Maga?"

He looked at his feet. "I can deadlift a box of encyclopedias."

"What do you do?"

"I'm a bookseller." He gestured down the street to get us moving, but I planted my feet.

"And your name is Fredrik?"

"Yes."

"Can I call you Freddie?"

"No."

"Ricky?"

His forehead wrinkled in frustration. "I don't do nicknames."

"Not even when you were young? What did your classmates call you at school?"

He blew out a breath, steam curling in the cold air. "Nerdrik. Happy now?"

I beamed. "Yes. Let's go, Nerdy." I gestured toward the street.

16

He mistook my raised arm for something formal and took it, escorting me like a duke. An unexpected laugh burst out of me, but I decided to roll with it. It wasn't every day you got escorted by a bookseller. I loved reading, so in my mind, he was basically a drug dealer.

We walked a few steps toward Main Street before I halted. I had no idea where I was going. "Wait. My shop's supposed to be by the town square, at 51C Hideaway Avenue. Do you know where that is?"

He stiffened. "It's 51C? Are you sure? There's only 51."

"I'm pretty sure."

"Okay."

We turned and headed in the opposite direction, down a small side street that opened into the town square, glowing with what looked like thousands of fairy lights. Two dog walkers in scarves and wool hats passed us, nodding at Fredrik and sneaking long looks at me.

The shop windows were so elaborately decorated that it took me a minute to spot the business names. I spotted a gift shop and a hardware store.

"Do you know where the Sip is?" I asked.

"The café? It's over there." He pointed diagonally across the square.

"It's a café? Great! That's where the crochet club meets!"

He frowned. "How do you know about that?"

"This old lady I met on the bus. She taught me how to crochet these super cute flowers and invited me to join the group. I think her name was Ida."

"Ida Kallis," he gave a slow nod. "She's obsessed with yarn. Watch out for Eileen, the café owner. She'll set you up with anyone single with a pulse."

I chuckled. "She'll give up when she finds out I'm only here for the holidays."

"I wouldn't be so sure."

I let Fredrik lead the way. When we stopped at a door with the right number, he jerked back. "Wait... what?"

"This is it. It's 51C!" I pointed at the small shop window with a familiar name, *The Christmas Wonderland*, spelled out in brand-new vinyl letters, along with the address. The shop front had been painted red, but ironically, the window display was the dullest on the square, a single string of garishly blinking rainbow lights. I'd fix that first.

"When did they put a door in here?" he grumbled. "They were renovating, but this is insane."

"What's insane?"

I scanned the doorway, and I spotted the lockbox. I knelt to open it with a code I'd memorized and pulled out the key with a triumphant flourish. "Look!"

He watched in silence as I unlocked the door and stepped into the dark, stale-smelling room. Relief washed over me. I'd made it somewhere safe for the night.

"In or out?" I asked as Fredrik lingered in the doorway, letting cold air in.

He stepped inside and shut the door.

But when I flipped on the light, my rosy expectations clashed with reality. The narrow room was crammed floor to ceiling with cardboard boxes and smelled like a recycling facility. The owner had told me some setup work was needed, but I hadn't pictured this.

"Holy shit," Fredrik said, staring at the wall. "They must have split this off from the main office. It used to be a real estate agency."

"Well, now it's a Christmas shop!" I announced, going for confidence. "I just need to do a bit of unboxing."

"Yeah. A bit." He eyed the boxes with horror. "Did you say there was an apartment?"

"Yes, at the back."

Dodging boxes, I headed to a closed door. I'd spent the past year in windowless cabins in coffin-like confinement, so I was ready for anything. Still, my heart thudded as I turned the knob and flicked on the ceiling light.

I gasped. This wasn't an apartment. It was a room, and nearly as small as my cabin. The bed looked like it belonged to one of the Seven Dwarfs, and a small desk was wedged so close there was no room for a chair. Not that it mattered, since the desk was already buried under boxes.

"You can't live here," Fredrik said flatly.

I hadn't noticed him behind me and jumped a little at his voice. "Of course I can!" I said brightly, pushing inside.

My back twinged, and I dropped my heavy backpack onto the bed. The springs groaned in protest. Then I spotted a silver lining: a window with a latch. I muscled it open, sucking in the cool night air. This wasn't so bad.

"This isn't legal," Fredrik grumbled from the doorway, his face set in a deep frown. "They can't rent out a place with no kitchen or bathroom."

"Technically, they're not renting it. They just said I could use it. And I can't afford a hotel. Not for long. Do you know what it costs this time of year?"

He took off his hat and dragged a hand through his wild hair, making it even wilder. "Christmas is high season here. You probably wouldn't find anything available, no matter what you pay."

I nodded. "Well, there you go."

"But you can't live without a kitchen or a bathroom," he insisted, squeezing the hat inside his fist.

Something about his stance made me think of his comment about lifting encyclopedias. Maybe there was more muscle under that mad-professor outfit than he let on. He didn't stand like a sluggish man. Not like Spencer, who'd been the privileged kind of languid—used to such a level of convenience that muscle was only desired, and acquired, for cosmetic reasons.

Looking for a counterargument, I scanned the room. Under the desk, I spotted a microwave and a small Nescafé machine with a handful of pods. "Look!" I crouched down, triumphant. "I can buy bottled water and make coffee. And cook noodles in the microwave. That's basically a kitchen." I held up a coffee pod, forcing a smile.

He stared at me in disbelief. "And then you pee in a bottle and toss it out the window?"

I froze. "Are there any public bathrooms? A library, maybe?"

"Across the square."

"I'll just close the shop and walk over. Or maybe there's a gym? I'll get a membership. Then I can shower there too."

"The gym's two blocks away."

I turned back to the window so he wouldn't see the panic creeping in. I was used to discomfort and could make this work. But my dreams of crafting and enjoying life on dry land were slipping away. There was no room for hobbies in this tiny room. I'd be in survival mode, hunting bathrooms and planning microwave meals that didn't give me scurvy.

I poked my head out the window. The back alley was dark and quiet, just garbage cans and a lone cat prowling a box. A few windows across the narrow drive glowed behind drawn curtains. Mine had no curtains. I'd have to change on the floor. A lump rose in my throat.

"I have a bathroom in my shop next door." Fredrik's voice cut through my thoughts. "You're welcome to use it."

My head whipped around. "Are you serious?"

"It's nothing grand," he clarified. "And it doesn't mean I think you, or anyone, should live here. But if you have no other choice…"

"Can I use it now?" I asked in a small voice. "Before you go?"

I hated depending on him, but I'd just downed a soda and a mango mocktail. There was no way I'd last the night without peeing somewhere.

"Sure." He pulled a set of keys from his pocket. "Let's go."

"What time do you open tomorrow?"

"Ten o'clock."

"Damn. I'll have to limit my fluid intake." I grimaced.

He didn't laugh. Instead, he gave me a look that was equal parts concern and judgment. I felt like I was in the principal's office, explaining why the gym teacher's pants were flying from the flagpole. Spencer had always said my sense of humor needed "fine-tuning." I'd never learned to stop before crossing the line.

I swallowed. "I know I was an idiot to accept this job, but I have nowhere else to go."

"Where're you from?"

"Bangor."

"That's two hours away," he stated.

I looked away, feeling the burn of shame on my face. "I know. But I can't. Trust me."

To my relief, he didn't push. He just turned, kicked a box out of the way, and headed for the door.

I locked up and followed him down the street. Fredrik stopped next door at a darkened shop I'd completely missed earlier. In contrast to the bright and festive displays around it, the window looked like a black hole. Only when I drew closer to the glass did I make out shelves crammed with books, stacked so tightly they formed an impenetrable wall of literature.

Fredrik unlocked the door. As we stepped inside, a buzzer doorbell screeched overhead, a sound that instantly made me think I'd failed a test. The air smelled of books and dust. In the dim light, the tall shelves loomed like an ancient forest. I hugged myself, terrified of bumping into one and starting an avalanche.

I loved bookstores. I'd seen my share of crammed little stores, but never anything this... grim.

Fredrik vanished behind a shelf, and a light flicked on at the back, throwing long shadows across the floor.

"The bathroom is upstairs."

I followed his voice to a narrow staircase. Upstairs opened into a cramped hallway. The bathroom was old, but to my surprise, it had a shower stall.

"This used to be the shopkeeper's quarters." He gestured down the hall. "Now it's... storage."

I didn't linger even though I wanted to. I could always brush my teeth later with bottled water. I was resourceful when I had to be.

Still, I couldn't resist grabbing a clean towel from a shelf, wetting it, and giving my armpits a quick wipe. Oh, the bliss.

I rinsed the towel and came out, dabbing my cheeks. "I borrowed a towel. I hope that's okay?"

He gave me a quizzical look. "Sure."

"I really need a shower, but that's okay. I'll find the gym tomorrow. Where did you say it was?"

"On Buoy Street, past the library and fire station. But it might not be what you're picturing. I've never seen a woman there."

"I'm not fussy!"

"No, you're right. It's probably better than a bar for push-ups," he said dryly.

I muffled my laughter in the towel. "I was taking a photo and wanted to look a bit warmer."

He nodded, and for a moment, it looked like he'd drop the subject. But as we reached the stairs, he turned back. "Why?"

I could tell it bothered him, and I felt a sudden bout of glee. I'd managed to crack that carefully curated act of disinterest. Because it was an act. I was sure of it.

He wore no ring. He sat alone in a bar on a Friday night. He'd warned me about a matchmaking lady. All signs pointed to being single. Yet he acted like he wanted nothing to do with anyone. Why sit in a bar, surrounded by people, if you didn't want to talk?

I'd never met anyone like him. Guys like this didn't end up on cruise ships, though, so maybe it was a case of sampling bias.

I didn't think I was stunning, but I was cute enough to get by. I could tell he felt responsible for me in some old-fashioned, chivalrous way. But he hadn't looked at me with even a flicker of interest.

Except now. Now, I *bothered* him. It wasn't exactly the stuff of daydreams, but it felt like a victory.

A smile tugged at my lips, and I met his gaze. In the low light, his eyes were almost black. "I'll tell you, if you first tell me why you read in a bar."

CHAPTER 4

Fredrik

I stared into a pair of twinkling brown eyes, trying to ignore the itchy warmth under my collar. I told myself I wasn't that curious. I'd let her use the toilet and borrow the towel and whatever the fuck she needed to be okay. This was all for public health, to stop her from peeing in bottles. Could women even do that?

There was no need to know the secrets of a woman who was here for a few weeks to sell tinsel. Not unless she was in danger and those secrets were about to rock up on my doorstep.

But I must have managed to get a little more beer in me than I usually did because I found it harder to ignore the niggling questions. *Was* she in danger? Why couldn't she return to her hometown? My sister would have regarded this as a prime opportunity for gathering information. A chance to be neighborly. Felicity had a lot of euphemisms for gossip.

I took a breath, weighing my words. "If I read at home, nobody brings me food or beer."

"You weren't even drinking the beer. You were nursing it like it was on death's door."

"Nice simile."

She stuffed the towel into her pocket even though it didn't fit and shot me a look. "Nice English degree."

She had me there.

"Yeah, it's pretty useless," I admitted, following her down the stairs.

"Just like trivia, eh?" Noelle threw me a look over her shoulder before heading for the door, turning sideways to glide between two shelves as if the gap was too narrow to walk through normally.

I turned off the lights and felt my way out of the shop. I'd had years of practice navigating its tight corners. Everything about this room felt familiar. So familiar that I'd long ago stopped wondering what it looked like to other people.

Was it too crowded in here? It was a bookstore, not a gallery. Surely having a wide selection of books was preferable to empty shelves or pretentious display tables. The lack of floor space was my go-to excuse for not being able to host signings or other tedious events. Instead, I stocked all the hard-to-find gems.

"Oh no!" The rumble of falling books followed Noelle's panicked voice.

I rushed to her and found her by the front door, scrambling up from under a pile of Russian classics. I'd secured the shelf to the wall at the top, but she'd somehow managed to knock the bottom, causing the books to tumble down.

She got up to her knees and tried to straighten the shelf. "Sorry! I tripped on something."

I could barely see her in the faint glow of streetlights and Christmas lights behind the window. No wonder she'd tripped. Why had I turned off the lights?

Berating myself, I helped her to her feet, then picked up a fallen Dostoevsky. She busied herself picking up the rest of the books, setting them back on the shelf, and turning each slightly to face the door.

"That's okay. I don't think they were that strategically placed."

"Tolstoy," she said, staring at a copy of *Anna Karenina*. "Do you sell anything... recent? Maybe romance?"

"That *is* a romance."

She turned the book in her hands, giving me a dubious look. "Does it have a happy ending?"

"She throws herself under a train."

She gave me a long, assessing look. "So not a romance."

I held back a scoff. "I focus on collectors' items."

"I know lots of people who collect romance. Special editions and all that."

"Special editions? What do they do? Put gold foil on the guy's nipples?"

She put down the Tolstoy, staring at me in amused disbelief. "Have you seen a romance book lately?"

I folded my arms. "I stock some for the crochet club ladies, but they won't touch the cartoon covers. Needs to have abs or something."

She cocked her head, grinning. "Well... abs are nice. But

I like the other styles, too. I can give you a list of my favorites if you want to give them a try?" She scanned the room. "But you might have to make some room first. Sell a few books or something? That brown bookshelf at the window blocks the view into the store. And why is it painted brown? It looks like it's wooden."

"You don't like my shelf?"

"It's just big and bulky and... so ugly." She clamped her mouth, horrified. "Sorry. I meant, it's big. It makes the room so dark."

"Tell me what you really think," I mused.

What the hell was wrong with my shelf? It had always been there, doing its job. Which was to block the view into the store.

Sure, the store was barely getting by. But so was I. We were both in survival mode. It had been nearly two years since the worst tragedy of my life. For the first twelve months, everyone had been supportive and understanding. During my first Christmas as a widower, nobody had asked me to put up lights or redecorate. They'd given me space and made excuses for me. They'd bought books to support me. But now it seemed the grace had run out, and everyone was out to give their two cents on the store, my appearance, and my lack of dating efforts. Was two years some sort of cutoff for moving on?

Of course, tourists made comments and asked stupid questions, which earned them stupid answers, but it was different when it came from people I knew. And now, from a woman who lived without a toilet or kitchen.

"Thank you for your feedback," I said, yanking open the front door.

I needed her out of here, confusing me with those giant brown eyes, challenging the way I chose to live my life. I couldn't entirely ignore my mother or sister, but I could ignore this one.

"I didn't mean to offend!" she piped as I guided her down the steps. "I'm just saying if you wanted to move more copies, you could try to spruce it up a little and add some new titles."

Irritation coiled in my gut. "I specialize in classics. There *are* no new titles."

"Maybe you could mix it up a little? To get more customers."

I'd spent most of the day behind my desk, doing a crossword puzzle, watching tutorials for making things I was never going to make, browsing an old poetry book, and snacking on a platter of dried fruit and nuts Felicity had dropped off when picking up her daughter. My niece, Kailee, hung out at my store after school. My sister said it was good for her to "get out of the house and hang out with people," but the girl mostly sat in the corner reading her dragon books. We coexisted in silence, which suited me just fine.

"Are you going to be okay?" I asked, diverting attention back to her. "I'll be back before ten o'clock tomorrow."

She smiled, and the reflection of streetlamps danced in her eyes like fireflies. "I'll probably be waiting for you out here. Cross-legged."

I took a deep breath. "I can give you the key." I pulled my keys from my pocket and started detaching the right one. "There's an alarm system, but I hardly ever turn it on. It's off now."

"Why?" She narrowed her eyes.

Because I don't care if I get robbed.

I shrugged. "I'm lazy."

"If you show me how it works, I'm happy to use the alarm system."

"Just use the key," I said, thrusting it into her hand.

"Are you sure?" Her baffled eyes peered at me from under the rim of a pink beret.

Steal everything. Burn it to the ground. Put me out of my misery.

I nodded. She couldn't put me out of my misery. Nobody could. But she needed to pee, and I needed to make sure she didn't pee in the street.

Still, her grateful smile made me feel something. Like a shot of whiskey on an empty stomach. A lingering warm glow.

"Thank you so much! You have no idea what this means!" She held the key with both hands ceremoniously, like accepting a tiny award. "I promise I won't knock over any more books. I'll move through your store like a ninja. Or like a ghost."

"Just turn on the light. There's a switch by the door."

"No! I don't want to draw attention. I'll use a flashlight or something. I think my phone has one."

"Okay."

"Thank you, Fredrik. I've only been here for…" She took her phone from her pocket. "Three hours, and I've already made a friend! Can I hug you?" She was already hugging me, her arms wrapped around my waist, her woolly hat tickling my nose. Something smelled of raspberries and vanilla, like a dessert.

I patted her shoulder rather awkwardly and staggered backward. "It's nothing. Good night!"

The last thing I saw was the little bounce she did, waving the key in her hand. I'd probably made a huge mistake, but it had been a long time since I'd seen that kind of excitement. It felt good. For the first time in weeks, I felt like smiling.

I'd made it around the corner when I realized she'd evaded my question. I still didn't know what she'd been doing at the bar.

CHAPTER 5

Noelle

J couldn't sleep. The bed was so short I had to curl my legs, which would've been fine if the springs didn't squeak every time I moved. And I was a very mobile sleeper. I knew this from all the times Spencer complained about being kicked. After a few fitful hours, I sat up, staring at the dark room. A glance at my phone told me it was 3 a.m. I was exhausted yet too wired to fall asleep.

I pulled on my jacket. Everything in this tiny storage room was depressing, but outside was a winter wonderland. Maybe I could take a stroll, admire the lights, and get some fresh air. Then I'd come back and try sleeping on the hardwood floor. At least that didn't squeak.

Bundled in a wool beret, scarf, and mittens, I braced against the freezing air. Snow had kept falling all night, covering the ground like a diamond blanket. I headed toward the bookstore, fingers fumbling for the key Fredrik had given me. I didn't even need to use the bathroom, but I wanted to take a look around.

I was curious about Fredrik. He dressed and talked like an old professor or a hermit buried in books, but he was too young for that. Like he'd put on a Halloween costume and never taken it off. He was the hottest mad professor I'd ever seen, though, with dark lashes and a sculpted jaw. And maybe, just maybe, I had a little thing for elbow patches.

I worked the key into the lock with half-frozen fingers. The bookstore, dusty and crowded as it was, instantly calmed me. It had to be the smell of books, steady and loyal, faithfully holding all the thoughts even the writers had long ago forgotten. Books were keepers, and I felt adrift, like nothing was keeping me.

My eyes fell on the Russian classics shelf. Had Fredrik really read them all? He probably had. I loved reading, but I'd never picked up anything without a fun, colorful cover. Why choose an author you couldn't stalk online or buy merch from?

I grabbed Dostoevsky's *Crime and Punishment*. Maybe if I read one of Fredrik's favorites, I could figure him out. What else did I have to do in this town, with no friends and a squeaky bed?

Carrying the leather-bound brick, I wandered to a corner where two wingback chairs had been squeezed next to a shelf of category romance. He hadn't lied. This was the entire romance section, featuring endless medical-themed titles: doctors, surgeons, and nurses finding love in small towns, many of them with secret babies. I wondered if the ladies from the crochet club placed special orders.

The green velvet chair was dangerously comfortable. More comfortable than my bed. But instead of putting me to sleep, the book pulled me in. Sonya was no spunky romance heroine. She was an oppressed doormat, which bothered me enough to keep turning the pages.

Eventually, exhaustion crept up. I'd never really thought about what those "wings" on a wingback chair were for, but when my head lolled to the side and was caught in one, I sighed in relief, and sleep claimed me.

I WOKE to the alarming sound of the door buzzer and shot upright. The five-pound book slid from my lap and hit the floor with a thud.

Shit.

I scrambled up, smoothing my hair and brushing at my clothes. The morning light seeped through the window. If Fredrik caught me here, I'd pretend I'd come in to use the bathroom. I'd even buy this stupid book.

But it wasn't Fredrik. A tall woman in a bright blue overcoat rounded a shelf, took one look at me, and screamed.

"I'm so sorry!" I blurted, hands in the air like I was under arrest. "Fredrik gave me the key to use the bathroom. I just moved next door to run the Christmas pop-up shop, and there are no facilities, so I'm trying to figure it out." The words tumbled out in a frantic rush.

She steadied herself against a shelf, eyes wide. "Fredrik gave you a key? Holy mackerel."

Only then did I notice the bucket of cleaning supplies in her hand.

"Are you his cleaner?" I asked.

She plopped the bucket onto the counter. "Yep. But I'm also his sister, which is the main reason I'm here."

I tucked the Russian brick under my arm and stuck out my hand. "I'm Noelle. Nice to meet you."

She tugged off a glove and shook my hand. "Felicity. Owner of Sparkle & Shine. And your new admirer." Mirth danced at her lips.

"My what?"

"My brother hasn't been in a good place for... a while. The fact he gave you a key is a big step." She peered over my shoulder, eyebrow raised. "And I see you've made yourself very comfortable?"

I turned and stifled a yelp. My pockets had spilled their contents across the velvet armchair: phone, packet of mints, three scrunchies, and a menstrual cup. A grotesque still life of disorganization.

I lunged, scooping everything up. "I'm so sorry. I fell asleep reading." My lip wobbled. "The bed in my place squeaks, and I couldn't sleep, so I came here. Please don't tell Fredrik. Please."

Felicity laughed kindly. "I won't."

I eyed the cleaning bucket. "Can I help?"

She tilted her head. "I don't need help, but you'd probably feel better if you did something. Right?"

I nodded eagerly. *Crime and Punishment.* I lifted the book.

She chuckled, tossing her coat on the chair behind the desk and snapping on latex gloves. "What kind of punishment? I usually just empty the trash, vacuum, and wipe the desk. But yeah, this place could use some dusting."

"Anything," I said, grabbing the duster.

"Fredrik sort of lost interest in looking after this place a couple of years ago," Felicity said as she spritzed a cloth. "We made a deal. He watches my teenager after school, gives her something to do, and I come in once a week to stop him from descending into total chaos."

"Sounds like a good deal." I tackled the Russian classics.

Books sure gathered dust fast when they didn't fly off the shelves. The fluffy duster barely made a dent in the grime between the spines. I googled a solution.

"Does that have a brush attachment?" I asked as Felicity wrestled the R2-D2-looking vacuum cleaner down the stairs.

"Maybe. Check the upstairs cupboard."

I rushed up the stairs and followed the dark hallway, finding the cupboard right past the bathroom. When I opened it, a toothbrush and cup toppled out. I set them back on the shelf beside the shaving cream and a pair of boxer shorts I could only pray were clean. Fredrik must have spent nights here. Where had he slept? Surely not in the armchair.

Curiosity took over. After digging out a likely brush attachment, I noticed another door. With the vacuum roaring downstairs, I risked a peek.

It was an office. With a bed.

The space was twice the size of my shoebox room and strangely bare: just a desk stacked with books, a checkered spread on the bed, and heavy curtains drawn tight. The air was stale. Clearly not one of the rooms Felicity regularly spruced up.

I backed out, closing the door and wiping the knob with my sleeve like the worst burglar ever.

Back downstairs, Felicity had just finished vacuuming. "You want this?" She handed me the vacuum cleaner.

"Yes, please."

I spent twenty minutes vacuuming the display books while she emptied trash and wiped down surfaces.

"So... what happened two years ago? I mean, what happened to Fredrik?" I asked, unplugging the cord. The question had been burning inside me, and I couldn't hold it back anymore.

She gave me a long, assessing look. "Trust me, I'm normally delighted to pass on information. I'm even happier to gather it. For example, I'm not going to let you leave before you tell me your story." She threw me a wicked smile, then turned serious again. "But I feel like maybe my brother could connect with you, and God knows he needs a friend. Which is why I think it's best that he tells his own story."

I nodded, though I didn't get it. "But... it's nothing illegal, right? He's not fresh out of prison, or... dying?" Horror flooded me. I slapped a hand over my mouth. "Sorry! I don't mean I wouldn't be his friend if he were dying or a criminal, I just—"

I was just a pathologically curious nutjob with zero filter.

Felicity laughed. "Relax. He has no criminal record. He's never even been in a fight. Fredrik is an expert at avoiding conflict. I'm not selling him, am I?" She shook her head, and her laugh fizzled out. "I mean, he's a stand-up guy with a finely tuned moral compass. And as far as I know, he's in perfect health. He's just... he's a widower."

The word landed heavy. My mind filled with follow-up questions, but Felicity held up a finger. "Nope. Not saying anything else. Talk to him."

"Okay." I drew a breath, trying to quell my quest for knowledge. "I was invited to join the crochet club, though. What if I hear it from them?"

"Well, that's a real concern." She paused, fighting the trash bag into a tight knot. "I'll talk to those ladies," she finally said. "Now, what brings you to Hideaway Harbor?"

CHAPTER 6

Noelle

Felicity beamed at me, blocking the doorway so I couldn't escape. Not that I wanted to. I liked her. She seemed like the type who spoke her mind but also cared. She reminded me of my sister even though they looked nothing alike. Holly was shorter, blond, and delicate, while Felicity was tall and dark with expressive eyes. But they shared that same energy.

Holly had gotten me onto my first cruise ship, jumping into action when I'd been frozen in terror. What were you supposed to do as a runaway bride? There was no protocol for jilting the great Alford family. I was forever grateful to my sister, which reminded me that I needed to send her a message.

"Can you point me toward Cellular Hill?" I asked Felicity. "I really need to send some messages."

"You think you can change the subject on me?" She gave me a reproachful smile.

My shoulders slumped. Ah, yes. My life story. There was no point trying to dodge it, or even to polish the ugly truth. Felicity seemed like someone who'd see straight through me.

"I ran away from my wedding and worked on cruise ships for a year. And now I'm back, but I can't return to Bangor. I haven't exactly tied up loose ends." I swallowed hard.

She cocked her head. "You think if you stay away long enough, everyone will forget?"

Her words hit me hard, mostly because she was right. That's exactly what I'd been secretly hoping—reaching some magical threshold of time, after which my sins would expire, and no one would even remember.

But of course they remembered. I'd humiliated the most powerful family in Bangor. Updates from Holly and Mom had given me glimpses: how they'd eaten the wedding cake over two weeks (Holly swore she gained two pounds because of me) and that they'd sold the floral centerpieces (my family's contribution) on eBay. But just because my family had stopped talking about it didn't mean the rest of the town had.

And they didn't know where I was, which probably made the gossip even juicier.

"I don't know if time will fix it," I admitted. "And I don't know how much time it would take. But I'm scared to go back. My ex-fiancé's family is influential. If Spencer finds out I'm here..." I shuddered.

Felicity's eyes widened. "Spencer? Spencer Alford? You're the Missing Runaway Bride?"

Cold dread seized me. "Missing Runaway Bride?"

She whipped out her phone, pulled up an article, and shoved it at me.

Young Bride Cracks Under Pressure—Where is Spencer's Fiancée?

My heart thumped as I scanned the article. It was an interview with Spencer, painting him as the long-suffering fiancé who still held a candle for me.

"I'm so worried about her, I can't sleep. I want my girl home, no matter what," a pull-quote declared.

Worried about me?

I read on, and there it was, hidden between the lines: I'd lost my mind.

He never said it outright, of course. It was dressed up as care and concern. He talked about stressors. Signs he'd missed. How he was disappointed in himself for failing to get me the "help I needed."

I checked the date. The article had been published five days ago.

I shivered.

"Has everyone seen this?" My voice cracked.

Felicity frowned, probably trying to figure out what I meant by *everyone*. "It's online. But maybe it'll blow over."

"Please don't tell anyone." My voice rose to a plea. "Please."

"I won't." She scrolled through the article. "It only mentions your first name a couple of times. There are no photos of you."

Instead, there were plenty of photos of him. Spencer in front of an antique fireplace. Spencer holding a framed photo of me, the camera focused on his hands instead of my face. Relief trickled in. As long as no one connected me to the story, I was safe.

"So... I get the feeling this is bullshit," Felicity said, peering at me, her finger pointed at the article on the screen.

My stomach knotted. "It's true I was engaged to him. And that I ran off without saying where. I couldn't risk him finding me. But the rest..." I shook my head. "I was a project for him and his family. They coached me to be like them, but I'm uncoachable. I never lived up to their expectations. He always said it was fine and that I didn't need to apologize."

Felicity blinked. "Apologize for what?"

"Just... all the wrong things I said. When I made someone uncomfortable or missed a social cue. I do that."

It was better she knew. If I could wear a sign around my neck that said *I will say the wrong thing, please forgive me*, I would.

Felicity harrumphed. "They sound like a bag of pious dicks."

Part of me wanted to laugh, but I couldn't. "The Alfords are very influential. If they find out I'm here—"

"I get it." She squeezed my arm and opened the door. "I won't tell anyone. I have to get to work, but I'll come see you later. Where's your shop?"

"Right next door." I dressed up and followed her outside, pointing at my little shop.

"Is that where the real estate office used to be? That space is huge."

"They split it into three shops. Mine's tiny."

Her jaw dropped. "And no bathroom? That can't be legal!"

"I wasn't supposed to live there full-time," I admitted. "But I don't have anywhere else to go, so I figured I could make it work since they said there was a bed."

She gave me a sympathetic smile. "Not like you had a lot of choice. The town's booked solid for the holidays."

"My cruise contract ended early, and I had to find something fast. A friend knew the owner…" I gestured helplessly in the direction of my cardboard-box palace. Then I remembered. "About Cellular Hill—"

"Walk towards the harbor and take a right. You'll see it. There's a little gazebo at the top."

"Thank you!"

My muscles were sore, and my stomach growled as I tugged on my mittens. "Maybe I'll see you later?"

Felicity grinned, her brown eyes sparkling. "You sure will."

She was a lot friendlier than her brother. Easy to talk to, quick to smile. I could only pray she'd keep her promise and not tell anyone about my past. If word got out, Spencer would find me. Apparently, he was already looking.

I headed to the harbor. First, I'd send my messages, then buy coffee and breakfast. After that, I'd tackle the cardboard boxes.

The snow had stopped falling, and the early morning sky

curved above me in shades of warm pink and blue, stars already fading. It was going to be a beautiful day, and I'd already made a friend. I wasn't about to let anything bring me down.

CHAPTER 7

Fredrik

I arrived at the store half an hour earlier than usual. Not because I was hoping to catch Noelle, I told myself. I'd simply woken up early and couldn't go back to sleep, so I was following my usual routine a little ahead of schedule.

In all honesty, my usual routine didn't make any business sense. The bookstore wasn't making money. I could have sold my assets and lived a quiet life for the rest of my days, taking no part in anything. But I knew Kailee needed somewhere to hang out in the afternoon, so I showed up. I was a sucker for being needed.

On my way to work, I picked up a black coffee from Love at First Sip.

"You're looking worse for wear," Eileen remarked, handing me my order.

"Gee, thanks."

"It's the dark circles." She waved a finger around her eye, accidentally tapping on her oversized glasses as she peered over the rim at me.

"I didn't sleep well. Hence the coffee." I raised the cup, hoping this bit of information was enough to satisfy her curiosity.

"What are you losing sleep over?" She leaned forward, her flowery top brushing a tray of cinnamon buns.

I was actively ignoring their tantalizing smell. If I started using butter and sugar to medicate my sour moods, Hide-away Harbor would run out in a week.

"I, um…" I tried to gather my thoughts.

I could have sworn the background noise of the café dipped by several decibels, as everyone listened in. Hide-away's favorite son, Ralph, set down his pie and turned around, staring at me expectantly. He must have been between his many temp jobs and business ventures, idling at the Sip, waiting for inspiration. Or good gossip.

"Is it a girl?" Eileen whispered, her voice brimming with hope. "I heard there's someone new in town. A pretty one. Colorful clothes."

Of course she'd heard.

"A girl is selling Christmas ornaments. It's a temporary job."

"Have you found out her name? I've been asking—"

"She said it's Noelle."

Eileen gasped, and her hand flew to her mouth. "You've met her? Oh, darling! Tell me everything!"

She circled the register and pulled me aside, much to Ralph's disappointment. We ended up by a giant calendar advertising the upcoming December events. My gaze snagged on "Peppermint Hot Chocolate Appreciation Day," and I nearly groaned out loud.

Who needed all this?

"There's nothing to tell," I assured Eileen. "She arrived yesterday. She'll sell some plastic crap, then leave."

"Where is she staying?"

I swallowed. "At the back of her shop."

"Is it that Christmas store I noticed them setting up earlier? It's right next door to yours!"

I nodded, looking at her blankly.

"You're neighbors!" She exclaimed. "You need to be neighborly."

"I am." I almost told her about our bathroom deal, but Eileen didn't need more fuel for her fantasies. They were already out of control.

"Good," she said, letting out a breath. "But I'll need updates."

"I'll keep you updated," I promised half-heartedly, and we returned to the cash register.

I handed her a twenty-dollar bill. "Keep the change."

"This is way too much."

"It's for my coffee and your discretion."

"Men," she harrumphed good-naturedly. "You gave me nothing I couldn't get from Summer. Less, actually. She said you were acting rude at the Shore Thing last night."

I rolled my eyes. Why was she questioning me on the things she already knew? Was it a new interrogation technique?

"Noelle has a microwave under her desk," I offered. "And her shop is full of cardboard boxes. I think she'll need help

47

with unpacking and setting up. Otherwise, it'll take a week, and she'll lose sales."

"Noted." Eileen tapped on her nose. "We'll find some hands on deck."

"I'm sure she'd appreciate it," I said noncommittally, but I couldn't deny it felt good.

Hideaway Harbor might have been the quintessential, nosy small town, but our people always came through. And a small part of me wanted Noelle to see that. Not that it mattered. She was a fleeting visitor and would soon be on her way, most likely on another cruise ship, sailing somewhere exotic. I couldn't sell her on this place any more than I could convince her to take a chance on a hermit like me. *I* wasn't even betting on myself.

Yet I couldn't stop thinking about her. Every time I'd woken up last night, I'd been blinking away an image of her. Noelle in that funny, fluffy coat and pink beret, with a smile so warm it could melt snow.

Maybe it was healthy for me to have a little crush. I'd felt so bereft of any joy lately that even a gentle, brewing sensation in the pit of my belly felt like a miracle. After everything, I still had life left in me.

When I approached my store, I observed it for any signs of life, but it was dark and quiet. I unlocked the door, trying to ignore the pang of disappointment.

The air smelled fresher. Felicity must have stopped by. She didn't usually clean this thoroughly, though. The Russian classics shelf looked different. All the surfaces were clean and empty, with a pile of books stacked on my desk.

I sat down with my coffee and fired up my old laptop. With no distractions around, I might be able to focus on my bookkeeping. I could at least pretend to be a proper business owner who gave a shit.

After twenty minutes of staring at depressing numbers, with only the dregs of coffee left in my cup, I was ready to admit I needed to check on her. Just to make sure she'd survived the night.

I pulled on my jacket and gloves, then flipped the sign on the door and headed to the Christmas Wonderland.

The lights were on, and the door was unlocked. I pushed it open and froze in the doorway.

Holy shit.

Every single cardboard box had been opened. Even boxes that had been stacked against the wall were now spread across the floor, covering every available square inch. Noelle stood in the middle, dressed in a pair of green overalls, her hair up in a lopsided ponytail, holding a utility knife.

"Fredrik!" Her face lit up with a smile that ignited a warm glow in my chest.

"What are you up to?" I scanned the chaos around me.

"I wanted to see what I'm dealing with."

"So you opened *everything*?"

She laughed like this was the best fun ever. "It's like Christmas morning!"

"But... wouldn't it make more sense to deal with one box at a time? So you could still, you know, *walk*?"

She looked around like she was only now noticing the utter mayhem around her. "Ah... maybe. But I needed to see what it all was so that I could decide where it goes. What if I gave the most prominent spot for these blinking Santas, for example?" She lifted a garish Santa ornament that, indeed, blinked. "And then I opened another box and discovered something *awesomer*, like these blinking Santa hats." She dove into another box and balanced a pointy red hat on her ponytail. The white fluff ball at the end pulsated in the entire color spectrum.

"*Awesomer* is not a word."

"It is when you find a blinking Santa hat that plays music." She squeezed the white pompom, and a tinny, digital version of "Jingle Bells" hit my ears. "It's like those musical greeting cards, only it's a hat."

Was she genuinely excited about this gaudy shit or just enjoying my reaction to it? I couldn't stand mass-produced crap, and my face probably gave it away in full volume.

Noelle silenced the hat and hopped over two boxes, landing on a small clearing in front of me. "It's not all that bad. There are some basic ornaments, baubles and stars and bows and lots of fairy lights. There's even a box of some heavy-duty lights. You know, the ones that look like light bulbs. They're quite nice."

"Okay."

I didn't really care. But she smelled of vanilla and raspberries again, and it was making me feel funny. Or maybe just hungry. I'd skipped breakfast, mostly because I hadn't bothered to go shopping. And fasting was good for the gut, right? When I got into the zone, I could go on for hours without thinking of food. But this morning, the cravings were hitting me hard.

"Have you eaten?" I asked. "There's a nice bakery—"

"Making Whoopie!" she exclaimed, her eyes sparkling. "I saw it earlier on my way back from that Cellular Hill, and I promised myself a coffee and a whoopie pie. But then I decided to open a couple of boxes first. To really earn it, you know? Delayed gratification."

"I was on my way there," I lied. "I can pick you up something."

"I'll come with you!" she announced. "Let me get my jacket."

Great. Nothing fueled rumors like us getting pies together. But she was already on her way, hopping over boxes like she was playing floor is lava in reverse.

It was only ten thirty in the morning. If she'd already climbed the hill and managed to open and investigate fifty boxes, maybe she didn't need outside help. She made me think of a hurricane. Something that moved fast, tore up trees, and inspired awe.

"Did you... use the key I gave you?" I asked when we made it outside.

"Are you asking me if I've gone potty?" She chuckled.

I coughed. "No, I mean, did it work? Is everything working okay?"

"Your toilet works fantastically."

I sighed. "Great."

She shoulder-bumped me so hard I nearly lost my footing. "I'm just messing with you. Thank you so much for the key. I went in this morning and met your sister. She came in to clean the store." Noelle raised her eyebrow at me.

"We have a deal. She does my weekly cleaning, and I watch her kid after school. She's fifteen and mostly sits there and reads, so it's a pretty good deal."

"You really don't like cleaning, huh?"

"Or maybe I don't care enough."

I meant it as a lighthearted comment, but she stopped in

her tracks, like running into an invisible wall. "Are you depressed?"

I stopped, too, turning to face her. "I don't think you're supposed to ask that."

Color drained from her face. "Oh. Is it too personal?" She squeezed her eyes shut, grimacing. "I'm sorry. I've been told I do this. I'm sorry."

"It's no big deal," I said, a bit thrown by her reaction. "I've been told I deflect to avoid hard topics. It's probably a me issue."

Her face relaxed. "No, it's definitely a me issue. But thank you for saying that."

We walked in silence as I searched the corners of my mind for something to say. "According to some studies, probiotics can be as effective, or more effective, than anti-depressants."

Great. More useless trivia.

"Are you taking probiotics for depression?" She peered at me with open curiosity, and I regretted opening my mouth at all.

"I'm saying I've read a lot of studies. I—"

"You collect trivia." She gave a firm nod and resumed walking.

I had been taking probiotics, just in case, and almost felt like telling her to see what she'd say. I'd never met anyone as guilelessly direct before. I could tell she wasn't *trying* to make me uncomfortable. This wasn't a power play. She simply spoke without thinking, the words bursting out of her like an uncontrollable sneeze.

Maybe I needed to throw some questions back. To catch her off guard in the same way to see what happened. We crossed the square, navigating around the winterized fountain with a giant Christmas tree, passing snow-laden benches and shrubs. I could already see the line outside the bakery. So many people.

"You never told me what you were doing in the bar," I said, slowing down before we crossed the street and got too close to the crowd. "Why did you put makeup on the cactus?"

She burst out in laughter. "I wasn't putting makeup on it! I was dusting it!"

"Because *that's* totally normal?"

We reached Main Street, and she halted there, smiling. "It made sense at the time."

"You're not going to tell me?"

"You didn't tell me why you were reading in there. Not really."

"What kind of explanation are you after? People read in various locations. It's pretty mundane."

She tilted her head, assessing me from head to toe. "No. What you've got going on here is not mundane. It's like a... statement. Like you're trying to say something."

I frowned in confusion. "Like what?"

"Like... 'I played Freaky Friday with my grandson and now I'm an old man trapped in a young man's body.'"

"Wow. Thanks."

She slapped her glove over her mouth, eyes wide. "I did it again," she mumbled. "I'm out of control." She looked up at me pleadingly. "If it helps, I'm really into the sexy elbow patch look. I think I have a thing for professors, which makes no sense because I dropped out of college."

I stopped breathing, suddenly feeling both hot and cold.

She was *into* me? Or... into my jacket? I'd heard plenty of shit about my wardrobe, but no one, and I mean no one, had ever called any part of it sexy. I didn't go shopping for clothes, and I'd been gifted quite a few items by my grandfather, who positively lit up when I wore them. Elora had hated every single thing. She'd refused to be seen with me until I changed into something contemporary that she'd bought. But she wasn't here anymore, so I was free to look as outdated as I liked.

Underneath the vintage parka, I was wearing the same 70s blazer as last night, but I'd showered and changed my shirt. It may have still had a day of wear left in it, but I didn't want to risk smelling bad if she suddenly hugged me again.

"Please don't make this weird," she finally said, eyes widening in panic as I simply stared at her, my mouth hanging open.

I should have said something. I should have flirted back or embarrassed myself to even the score, or whatever normal, *fun* people did. Instead, I looked like a fucking fish.

"What did you study?" I finally asked. "Before you dropped out."

"Fashion design."

"So you know your way around elbow patches?"

I wanted to bite my tongue. Looking like a fish was better than fishing for compliments. But Noelle didn't seem bothered.

"Yes! I love upcycling and vintage clothing, but the fashion industry is so competitive, and I realized I could never afford to do unpaid internships. And that's how I ended up working at The Gap instead."

"And... then on a cruise ship?"

She did an exaggerated eye roll. "The navy-blue uniforms were so cute I couldn't resist."

We crossed Main Street and joined the line. The chalk-board sign advertised a three-for-one deal. No wonder there was a crowd. After a moment, we made it to the door, and an older couple exited. I recognized the woman. She was friends with my mom and greeted me excitedly, her eyes lingering on Noelle as her husband held the door for us to enter. Noelle skipped inside, but I held back, inhaling the thick scent of butter, sugar, and spice. I could feel the eyes of the whole town waiting for me inside. Was I ready for this?

CHAPTER 8

Noelle

Spence had been right about me. I was not fit to be in public. I asked questions like a three-year-old who could get away with it by being cute and clueless. And I wasn't that clueless. I had to learn to edit myself, especially when it came to my feelings about elbow patches or the men wearing them.

Fredrik hung on to the door for a long beat before following me inside. What was the big deal about going to a bakery? He must have been a regular here. These people saw him every day.

But as I felt the questioning gazes burning holes through my winter clothes, it hit me. They'd never seen him with someone like me. I stuck out like a clown at a funeral in my pink beret, fluffy peach coat, and olive-green overalls. Even my boots were purple.

I couldn't resist color. Sometimes the combinations worked. Other times, it was too much. Either way, colors made me happy. After a year on the ocean, stuck in a boring navy-blue uniform, I was desperate to be me. Maybe I needed something more understated this Christmas. I was here to hide, not draw attention to myself.

Making Whoopie wasn't understated, though. I'd already fallen for the deep red facade and bright blue door. Inside, the checkered floor tiles and cheerful blue counter made me inexplicably happy.

The young woman behind the counter smiled as the line moved along. She had a topknot with wild flyaway hairs, flour on her cheek, and fantastically expressive eyes. Her gaze flicked between Fredrik and me as she worked to keep the line moving.

I read the specials on the board:

A FIRESIDE THREESOME: *S'mores-inspired graham, triple fudge, and toasted marshmallow cakes with hot cocoa ganache and cinnamon spark.*

"OH MY GOD. SOLD!" I nudged Fredrik's arm. "Can you share that with me? I want to try everything!"

"Teddy!"

I didn't see the huge guy in a biker jacket before he crashed into Fredrik, giving him a bear hug that nearly knocked him over.

Fredrik regained his balance, surprisingly unbothered. "Are you drunk? It's not even noon."

The guy ran a hand through his dirty-blond hair and grinned. "No! I'm just expressive with my love."

"Did he just call you Teddy?" I asked. "I thought you didn't do nicknames?"

Fredrik sighed. "Some people choose to ignore my preferences. One of them is Jackson." He turned to his friend. "Meet Noelle. She's running a new Christmas shop on Hideaway Ave."

There was affection in his voice beneath the scorn. Jackson had earned his nicknaming rights.

"Lovely to meet you, Jackson." I offered my hand, but he spread his arms wide. I gave a startled shrug, which he took as consent, squeezing me so tight my boots lifted off the floor.

"So good to meet you, Noelle," he whispered into my ear.

I laughed breathlessly, grabbing the glass cabinet of pies to stay upright.

"Don't even think about it." Fredrik snapped his fingers in front of Jackson's face as he kept staring at me with an exaggerated, love-drunk expression.

Jackson's smile was gorgeous, his ice-blue eyes playful. Everything about his outfit seemed carefully chosen, from his leather boots to an expensive watch.

"But she's so pretty," Jackson protested, still looking at me. "And she's dressed like a rainbow candy cane."

My cheeks heated, and I shoved my beret into my pocket.

"Jackson. Behave." Fredrik's voice dropped into a low growl that sent shivers down my spine.

"Apologies." Jackson smiled at me, dropping the act. "It's

not every day you meet a beautiful young lady... willingly spending time with our Teddy." He elbowed Fredrik.

"What are you even doing here?" Fredrik asked.

"Three-for-one whoopie pies!" He grinned, gesturing at the cabinet.

I began to understand Fredrik's hesitation. He hadn't invited me to join him. He'd offered to *bring* me a pie. Big difference. I'd attached myself to him without realizing it. I only wanted to see the town with a local guide. Okay, maybe I wanted that guide to be Fredrik, with his signature frown and sexy elbow patches, but still.

We finally reached the counter and bought our pies: three sweet ones to split, plus chicken pastries for lunch. Before I even reached for my wallet, Fredrik had paid for everything.

"Thank you," I said as he handed me the bags. "I'll pay you back."

"I'd love to check out your shop," Jackson said as we stepped away.

"It's not open yet. Maybe tomorrow."

Fredrik gave me a doubtful look.

"Okay, maybe in a couple of days," I corrected. "I tend to be overly optimistic about what I can achieve in a short time."

"Me too!" Jackson echoed. "I thought I'd get a new floor down in one of our properties today, but... eh. Maybe tomorrow."

"Jackson's family renovates old houses," Fredrik explained.

"Lovingly restores," Jackson corrected. "We specialize in

historical buildings." He slipped me a gold-foiled business card, wiggling his eyebrows.

I stared at it. "I don't own any historical or other—"

"She doesn't need your services." Fredrik plucked the card from my hand. "Her employer might, though. You should see the shoddy job they did on her shop. Remember that real estate agency on Hideaway Ave? They split it into three units. Hers doesn't even have running water."

"What?" Jackson looked appalled.

"They said it's coming," I added quickly. "They just haven't installed the sink yet. Or the bathroom."

I'd received an email from the shop owner explaining that I could use the library's facilities during the day. Clearly, he assumed I had other accommodations. I wasn't going to correct him, and I didn't need anyone else to do it either. If Jackson reported my landlord, I'd be out of both a job and a place to stay.

With our pies in hand, Fredrik made for the door but was stopped by two older ladies bombarding him with questions about his parents and the bookstore. I hung back with Jackson.

When they finally let him go, Fredrik stepped outside like he'd come up for air. I felt guilty for putting him through it.

Jackson stuffed his pies into his coat pockets and clapped Fredrik's back. "I'll come around later to work on the house." He nodded at his motorcycle, then winked at me. "And I'll see you as soon as your shop opens. I need me some tinsel."

"Sure thing!" I grinned, watching him hop on his bike and roar off.

"If he tries to give you his number again, burn it," Fredrik muttered. "He's… trouble."

I shrugged. "I do attract trouble. But he's not my type."

"No elbow patches?" He gave me a suspicious look, like he expected me to confess I'd been mocking him.

I blew out a sigh. "Not even one. Some people put in zero effort. It's sad, really."

He gave a dry chuckle. "If you ever tell him that, I want to be there. That man spends more on hair products than I spend on groceries."

"We'll make a night of it," I promised. "He'll be thoroughly scandalized."

He laughed again, shaking his head. "We've known each other since kindergarten. Jackson's always been there for me, but we live different lives. He's a lot more outgoing. Never brings the girls home."

His tone carried a warning.

"Don't worry. I stick to the elbow patches and the men who never leave their homes."

"Ouch."

I winced. "Oh no! I was joking."

"It's true. I don't go anywhere." His voice turned bleak.

"I'm sorry I brought you here. I could have picked up the pies." I glanced toward the café. "Actually, I'd love some coffee with mine. I'll do that by myself, okay?"

I nodded at Love at First Sip, its pink door beckoning me. I expected him to head back to his store, but he followed and stopped at the entrance. "I'll… wait here."

As I stepped in, the silver-haired woman behind the counter perked up. She was timelessly beautiful and surrounded by happy pops of color. Candy cane earrings dangled above her pink blouse, while matching mugs lined the counter. She quickly finished with a customer, then hurried toward me with a wide, eager smile. "Hello! You must be Noelle! Come in! Let's get to know you."

"Ye…es. How did you know?"

Her smile deepened. "Word travels fast around here. I'm Eileen, the owner."

She walked me to a table by the window, ushering a white-haired man to the side. "Scoot, Wayne. We have a special guest."

Wayne grunted, sliding his chair two inches over.

"I'm just here for coffee," I said apologetically. "To go."

"Oh no! Are you in a hurry?"

I made the mistake of glancing out the window, where Fredrik stood waiting. Eileen followed my gaze and shook her head. "That fool! What is he doing standing out there?"

I noticed several patrons had paused their conversations, sneaking glances. At least I could spare Fredrik from it.

I paid at the counter. All the drinks were named after romance heroes, so I picked a Fabio for myself and asked what Fredrik usually ordered.

Eileen bit back a smile. "I make him a special I call the Grump."

"Sounds fitting."

After promising to come back for a proper chat, I took the coffees and rushed outside.

"You didn't have to bring me anything," he said, taking the cup. "But thank you. It's freezing."

"Eileen knew who I was," I said. "How would she—"

"My sister."

"Ah." My stomach knotted. "Is she… well connected?"

"You mean a huge gossip? Yes."

Had she told Eileen about my past? The question burned in my mind as we walked. He guided me across the street, steadying me when a car passed.

"But... if your sister promised to keep a secret, would she?" I cringed at the words.

Fredrik studied my face, trying to read between the lines. "I don't think she'd break a promise."

I exhaled. "I like her."

"So what secret did you—"

"I love staying at home, you know?" I cut in, desperate to change the subject. "I totally get that feeling of not wanting to go out and be on display. It's draining."

He eyed me with suspicion. "But you seem so outgoing."

I laughed. "Maybe. But I'm also acting odd because I suddenly have all this freedom. Cruise ships are structured. You just follow the rules and the daily schedules, and you get a little institutionalized. But now I can wear my own clothes and go where I want. Being here is exhilarating!" My gaze swept across the decorated town square.

He looked baffled. "You find Hideaway Harbor exhilarating?"

We took the long way back, walking along the shops. Their facades glowed in cherry reds, sky blues, and soft pastels. It felt safe and contained, like a little universe hugging us from all sides.

"Yes. I mean, I have more freedom, but it's still small enough not to be too scary. A bit like a cruise ship."

"You mean, everyone knows your business and you can't escape?"

I laughed. "Exactly. And you go a little mad and develop ship goggles."

"Ship goggles?"

"They're like beer goggles, but you don't have to be drunk. You only have to be stuck together on a ship, and suddenly, those people start to look like viable... options."

"Who did you sleep with?" He narrowed his eyes, smiling. "The captain? The pirate with a hook?"

"For your information, pirates are hot. And what happens at sea, stays at sea." I shot him an indignant glare, thanking my lucky stars that I hadn't slept with anyone. Looking back at the selection, I would have regretted it. Working almost nonstop probably helped in keeping me out of trouble, as well as the strict rules on alcohol consumption.

"I'm going to assume it was the 100-pound deckhand with buck teeth." He looked happier by the minute, and I mentally high-fived myself for changing the topic.

"How do you know that's not my type?" I asked. "Maybe I'm weak for tiny, buck-toothed men, even on dry land."

He shook his head, and the sadness returned. "I'm quite sure your type is blond, blue-eyed, and trust-funded."

A lump rose in my throat. Because he was describing Spencer. Did he know?

He had such beautiful eyes. Soulful eyes. Like they'd been painted with layers and layers of color, so many that you couldn't really tell the original shade, like in an old student rental.

Once we were away from Main Street, I gathered my courage. "So... you know about my ex-fiancé? You've heard the stories, right?"

"I don't do gossip," he said gruffly.

"I thought, because you said blond and trust fund..." I trailed off, suddenly feeling defensive. "That's not why I fell for him, though! I didn't even know he was that wealthy until later."

"What did you like about him, then?"

His question threw me. What had I liked?

I rubbed my forehead like it was a broken genie. "He was generous..." I ran out of words. Was that the end of the list?

He'd bought expensive gifts. Thoughtful gifts. However, I had a sneaking suspicion he'd outsourced the task to his many assistants. But he'd thought I was cute and funny. Hilarious. And who didn't like adoration? Especially a college dropout in a dead-end job.

"Generous, huh?"

"Yeah. He'd pay for everyone at dinner. He donated—"

"For a tax deduction."

I forced a laugh. "You're not that cynical."

"Did he pay his taxes? Did he donate half of his annual gains?"

I glared at him. "Why would he?"

"You said he was generous."

My cheeks burned as my mind darted around, searching for the truth.

"Generosity is relative," he continued. "If you share one percent of your wealth and dodge taxes, how generous are you really?"

I thought of the prenup my parents had assured me was "standard." I'd agreed. Why wouldn't I? I had nothing to my name.

"He was patient with me," I said. "I embarrassed him and his family constantly, and he still gave me a chance."

"He told you that you embarrassed him?"

"He didn't have to. It was pretty obvious. But he guided me. He was helping me navigate that world."

"You mean he made you feel like there was something wrong with you?"

"There *is* something wrong with me," I blurted. "Nobody is perfect."

"Including him. Did you ever guide him when he did something wrong? Did he apologize?"

I froze. Why couldn't I think of a single time he had?

"Why would he? He didn't do anything wrong," I insisted.

Fredrik huffed a laugh. "So he was perfect? The one who got away?"

"No. I left him."

"Why?"

I opened and closed my mouth twice before words emerged. "Because I wasn't right for him."

"Noelle." His voice was soft. "If he made you feel like something was wrong with you, maybe *he* wasn't right for you."

"Semantics." I huffed, stomping off. "I have to get back to work."

He walked along, maintaining a healthy distance while not saying a word. When I made it to my store, I stomped inside and collapsed on the floor to catch my breath.

Was Fredrik right? Was Spencer not generous? Was he not the good guy I'd told myself he was?

For months, I'd been telling a different story. That I'd

fallen in love, but then realized we weren't compatible. He was the perfect catch, but I was too free-spirited and impulsive. Safe in my ship bubble, I'd been happy with that story. But was it even remotely true?

Spencer had been known for his generous gestures, but I'd always known my place. It was all his. The house. The cars. The family crest.

I'd told myself it was fine because I wasn't a gold digger. But if Spencer wasn't generous, what was left on my list? I couldn't name a single thing I truly liked about him, and it bothered me so much I found it hard to breathe. Even his willingness to guide me now felt tainted. Had he been guiding me, or... controlling me? He seemed happiest when I groveled and apologized. When he could demonstrate his grace and patience.

I glanced over my shoulder. The snow was falling again in big, floaty flakes. Fredrik was gone. He'd walked away, after casually calling me out on my dirty secret—that I'd fallen in love with the attention from a rich guy and agreed to marry him. I'd loved the dinners and the vacations and lapped it up every time he'd told me I was funny or cute. As his fiancée, I'd felt important.

I'd wanted that lifestyle for my hardworking parents and my sister. I'd wanted it so badly that I'd ignored every red flag and convinced myself I was in love with him.

I removed my jacket, grabbed the nearest open box, and began stacking packets of fairy lights on an empty shelf. I'd probably have to rearrange them later, but I needed something to do.

"I want my girl home, no matter what."

The line from the article echoed in my mind, now sounding vaguely threatening.

We'd parted without any closure, with me running to catch an Uber, the veil still attached to my hair. I'd been too much of a coward to face him and too paralyzed by terror to even write a note. And now he was waiting for me to come home? It made no sense.

Spencer had been running late with a hair emergency. He was so particular about his hair. I'd been left waiting at the back of the church with my sister. Holly had seen something in me that went beyond the usual jitters. She'd found a thread and pulled it.

Suddenly, I knew with absolute certainty that I couldn't go through with the wedding.

Holly smuggled me out, and within forty-eight hours, I'd boarded my first cruise ship. I changed my phone number and figured Spence would get the message. Over time, he'd realize I'd done him a favor and be grateful.

I'd carried on in my happy bubble, believing my own lies, until Felicity had shown me that article. I'd kept busy all morning, trying not to think about it. But I had to face reality. Leaving Spencer at the altar wasn't only my biggest embarrassment. It was his biggest humiliation. And men like him didn't forgive humiliation. Whether he regarded me as lost property or wanted revenge, he was on a mission.

And here I was, back in Maine, making friends, wearing bright colors, and drawing attention.

I was a fool, and I had to get back on the ocean.

CHAPTER 9

Fredrik

I wrestled open the bookstore door, cursing under my breath. I'd managed to offend her. I'd made assumptions about her ex without any solid evidence. For all I knew, she still loved the man, and my questions only strengthened that loyalty.

Maybe Felicity was right. I was turning into our grandfather. Not the nice one who donated his corduroys to me, but the crank who'd choked to death alone in his house.

"Fredrik!"

I jumped at my sister's voice. She sat behind the counter, still wrapped in her coat and wool hat, snowflakes clinging to her sleeve.

"What are you doing here?" I demanded, leaning on the doorway.

"What did you bring me?" She leaned over the table to

snatch the paper bag from my hand and peeked inside. "Whoopie pie!"

"Go ahead," I said. I'd already given the other two to Noelle and eaten my chicken pastry on the way back.

"Thanks!" She took a big bite. "I'm so mad right now. Someone stole my favorite gloves, so I had to go shopping. It's like a crime wave."

"Or maybe someone just borrowed them."

Felicity liked her things *just so*, but her staff were looser, misplacing supplies and even "accidentally" eating her lunch. Which counted as a crime wave in Hideaway Harbor.

I took off my coat and threw it over the desk.

Felicity gobbled up the pie, then eyed my window. "You need to put up lights this year. Maybe a wreath. This place looks glum."

"Why are you here?" I asked again. "I thought you already cleaned."

"Oh, I did," she said brightly. "With the help of your new, super cute neighbor. Who also happens to be a famous runaway bride."

I tried not to bite, but my intrigue flickered. *Famous?*

Felicity's eyes sparkled. "Oh, goodie. You *are* interested. Just ask. I'll tell you. I know you won't spread it, and you need to watch out for her."

She knew how to appeal to my sense of duty instead of curiosity.

"What?" I asked, gritting my teeth.

She leaned in, lowering her voice. "Last Christmas, Noelle was about to marry Spencer Alford. Biggest wedding in Maine. Huge."

"But she… didn't?"

Felicity thrust her phone at me. I skimmed an interview with a blond, blue-eyed "CEO of Alford Corporation." Not just wealthy—*obscenely* wealthy. My pulse thudded faster with each line. This guy reeked of bad news.

His account didn't match Noelle's. Not one word rang true. Noelle wasn't unstable. Unfiltered, yes. Spontaneous. Too optimistic, maybe. But he painted her as some fragile woman who'd lost touch with reality.

The man sounded entitled and delusional, but also dangerous. He was on a quest to find her, probably to prove that no woman in her right mind would walk out on him. Would he get violent? A man like that would probably use other people to do his dirty work.

"He sounds…"

"Absolutely fucking unhinged," Felicity finished, eyes wide.

"She's living two hours away from this nutjob," I barked. "She's not safe here."

My sister folded her arms. "We'll keep her safe. We'll watch out for her."

"She lives alone in the back of that ridiculous shop. No toilet, no nothing!"

Felicity sighed, like I was being difficult. "Well, obviously she can't stay there."

"Where's she supposed to go? Town's fully booked. You've got a kid and a dog in a two-bedroom."

She smirked. "Good thing you live in a mansion."

"With one habitable, heated room and an unfinished bathroom," I shot back.

She shrugged, giving me that look everyone else had

been offering lately. "And why *do* you only have one habitable room? Ever thought about that?"

My eyes drifted across the overstuffed shelves. "Because nobody buys books in the days of the internet?"

Her eyes flashed. "Not the internet excuse! Not in Hideaway Harbor, where the Wishing Bridge works more reliably."

"Technically, it's a wishing *dam*. People throw those coins all over the place. Up the stream, into the spring…"

"*Damn* you and your nitpicking!" She swung her purse over her shoulder and stormed out. Almost.

When she reached the doorway, the buzzer above the door went off.

"I hate that sound," she muttered, then turned to give me an assessing look. "You've pissed her off already, haven't you? Said something condescending or mansplain-y? And now she's never going to talk to you again."

The hurt in her voice shrank my chest. I was good at driving people away, but with Noelle, I'd been trying. And still, I'd upset her.

"I'll fix it," I said. "I didn't know about the runaway bride thing. Must be a sore point. She was defending the guy and blaming herself. It made no sense."

Felicity's face softened. She leaned on the door. "I think she's been gaslit by that psycho. Be gentle with her. She'll figure it out."

"I'm not a therapist. I can barely keep my own life together."

"She vacuumed your stupid classics for half an hour this morning, Fredrik. She seems lovely and open to knowing you. The *real* you." Tears gathered in her eyes. "You're both screwed up. Who isn't? But she still might be the best thing that's ever happened to you."

She banged the door shut on her way out.

I wandered into the store and dropped into an armchair. Felicity was wrong. There was no hidden "real me" hiding under a prickly layer. What you saw was what you got—a sad man who'd given up. Even before Elora's death, I'd been happiest with my nose in a book. How could I ever match the energy of someone like Noelle? And she was only here for the holidays. What was the point?

I drew a deep breath and noticed the chair smelled different. Berries and vanilla. Like Noelle.

Something dug into my back. I shifted and reached between the cushions, fishing out a piece of hard plastic. A credit card. I sighed, ready to toss it in the lost-and-found basket, until I read the name.

Noelle E. Clarke.

How had she managed to lose her card *in here*?

CHAPTER 10

Noelle

I woke up to a loud bang and a sudden, searing pain. It took me a moment to realize I'd hit my head on the concrete wall. I sat up, holding my throbbing temple, cursing the tiny bed that squeaked with every shift of my restless body.

I tried to lie down again, looking for a comfortable position. There was none. I was wide awake now, staring at the ceiling. This was my third night in Hideaway Harbor and so far, I hadn't managed to sleep through the night even once. I'd spent all Sunday setting up my shop, relieved that the bookstore was closed, and I could use the facilities without bumping into Fredrik. But apparently even the vigorous unboxing and hill-climbing activities didn't help when your bed was a torture device.

"Never compromise your sleep hygiene," my mom's voice

scolded from memory. She needed darkness, silence, and the new moon to get any shut-eye. I used to take pride in being an easy sleeper, but even I had my limits.

It's a good thing her lessons were ingrained in me: get up and move. Do something until you're sleepy again. Your brain should associate your bed with sleep, not tossing and turning. At this point, my brain associated my current bed with pain and suffering.

I bundled into layers and stepped outside. The cold air hit my lungs, but the sky was clear, and stars twinkled above the halo of streetlamps and Christmas lights. A giant tree in the middle of the town square glowed like a beacon, wrapped in multicolored lights. I'd watched its lighting ceremony from behind my shop window earlier that day, gawking at the costumes, humming along to the brass band playing carols. I'd recognized Amanda Willis, the Hollywood actress plugging in the lights, and even popped outside to buy honey-roasted almonds from one of the stalls. The town fascinated me, but I felt awkward and lonely, with no one to talk to, and soon returned to organizing my shop.

Under the starry sky, with no one around, I felt more at home. Free to roam about and explore without curious eyes on me. My boots crunched against fresh snow as I wandered through the quiet streets. When I reached Love at First Sip, I stopped to peer through the windows. I loved the café and its ultra-romantic vibe. Just stepping over the threshold made you believe in something better. Something that was almost within reach, like the mistletoe hanging inside its window.

The steps leading to the café looked like a slip-and-slide,

packed full of ice and snow. *Eileen would need help with the steps*, I thought. They were a hazard to her and all the customers.

A scraper leaned by the doorway, waiting for an opportunity to be useful. I picked it up, heavy in my hands, and started hacking at the ice. It fought me, but I kept going, swinging harder, each hit sending a shock through my arms. I channeled my fear and frustration into the stubborn ice until sweat slid down my back despite the cold.

When the last shard broke loose, I replaced the scraper exactly where I'd found it, smudging my footprints as I went. No one needed to know. I'd already drawn too much attention.

After the literal ice-breaking activity, blissed exhaustion flooded my body, so I dragged myself back to the store and fell asleep again, waking a couple of hours later to my usual alarm.

Every muscle in my body cried out as I stretched, throwing on a jacket to sneak into the bookstore to use the facilities. If I were quick, maybe I could shower before Fredrik showed up.

After the way I'd walked off yesterday, I felt uncomfortable using Fredrik's key. I hated relying on him and felt a little guilty over how I'd behaved. Maybe it was easiest to avoid him for a while. If he decided he no longer wanted to let me use the bathroom, he could come out and tell me. Meanwhile, I made sure to leave the bathroom better than I found it, wiping every surface after use. I even polished his partially rusted tap until it partially shone.

Feeling somewhat refreshed, I hurried back to my shop, dropped off my towel and toiletries, and strolled to the café.

It was eight o'clock and the sky was beginning to glow pink over the harbor. The bell above the door rang nonstop as the early-bird customers trickled in.

I adored the smell of freshly ground beans in the morning. Nothing was more humanizing after a night of poor sleep. I'd counted my funds again, making sure I could afford this luxury. I desperately wanted to be a regular at this café, even if it meant I had to cut back on other things, like food.

I smiled as I ascended the cleared stone steps and took my place at the end of the line, listening to the happy chatter of townspeople ordering their coffees.

I ordered The Byron, with extra cinnamon, and sat at a small table by the window—the same one Eileen had offered me last time. After a moment, Eileen appeared with a drink. It wasn't for me, though. She set it in front of Wayne, the curmudgeon I remembered from yesterday. "Here's your Romeo with extra sugar, Wayne."

"For crying out loud, Eileen. It's a black coffee."

He reminded me of a slightly younger Sean Connery, dressed as a lumberjack.

"Not in my café." Eileen raised her chin, channeling pride and defiance.

Her gaze met mine, and I smiled back.

"Next time, leave that attitude by the door before you enter," she added, setting sugar packets next to his coffee.

"You want me to leave it by that murder weapon you keep out there?" Wayne jerked a thumb over his shoulder.

"What murder weapon?" Eileen shuffled past him to peer through the window.

I realized they were talking about the sidewalk scraper.

"Nothing invites a burglary like leaving the perfect tool right by the door. You wouldn't even need to swing that hard to break the glass. A child could do it." I heard the concern under his harsh words.

Eileen cocked her head, unfazed. "Well, it worked out in my favor last night. Someone used it to clear the steps."

My heart stuttered.

Wayne sat up, frowning. "In the middle of the night?"

Eileen grinned. "Yes! We think it might have been an angel. Or an elf! Christmas is coming, after all."

Wayne stared back, his bushy eyebrows knitted. "Who would do that? It makes no sense!"

Eileen's lips quirked. "Well, that's why we're thinking an elf."

I wasn't sure if she believed in magical things or just enjoyed taunting him. Maybe it was both.

I nearly fell off my chair when she suddenly whipped around and pinned her gaze on me. "Noelle! I haven't forgotten your drink. Hang on..."

I nodded, a half-smile frozen on my face, as she rushed back behind the counter. Did she know it was me? Did the café have security cameras? I hadn't even thought of that.

"I would have cleared the steps, had she *asked*," Wayne grumbled, half to himself, half to me.

"Mmm." I nodded in agreement.

A moment later, Eileen delivered my coffee. Nothing about her behavior seemed suspicious, so I relaxed a little. Maybe I was imagining things.

Hugging the steaming paper cup to my chest, I walked back to the store. My store. It was starting to feel slightly "mine" now that I'd begun putting things on the shelves.

Everything on the ship was pretty much nailed down, for obvious reasons, so you couldn't do a whole lot to personalize your space. It was funny how the simple act of deciding where something should go could make you feel at home.

I worked all day, only stopping for some crackers and cheese from my dwindling stash. I didn't drink anything after my coffee to avoid needing to use the bathroom. In the afternoon, the store looked a lot better. The shelves were stacked, and the cardboard boxes flattened into a neat pile.

Despite my inadequate liquid intake, by the time the Christmas lights flickered on behind the window, my bladder was full. I also had a mild headache, probably from dehydration. Accepting my fate, I threw on my coat and grabbed the bookstore key. But as I reached for the door handle, I got a fright. Someone stood right outside my window. In fact, they were pushing the door as I pulled it, resulting in the door flinging open with a violent force, the bell over it ringing like an alarm. I looked up at a middle-aged Korean man with fluffy earmuffs and a concerned expression.

"Hello." The man bowed slightly and peered at the room around me.

"Hello?"

"You must be Noelle. I am In-soo Young. Good work." He nodded graciously.

Mr. Young—my boss! I'd never met him in person, only via email and phone. I sucked in a sharp breath, trying to pull myself together.

"Thank you so much for this opportunity." I backed away from the door to allow him to explore the shop. "I haven't put up all the prices yet. I'm still sorting out the best placements for everything. I didn't know you were coming."

The older man flashed me a wicked smile. "I come like a thief in the night. You won't know when..." He slowed down his movements until he came to a halt, peeking at me from behind a shelf, then suddenly jumped, eyes bulging.

He probably thought he was hilarious, but I was far too wired for this comedy show. When he jumped, I jerked like a startled rabbit, nearly peeing my pants.

Mr. Young laughed, holding his stomach. "That's right. I do spot checks. You won't see me coming."

Oh great.

I sucked in deep breaths, trying to settle my heart rate and hold the smile on my face. "Of course," I said. "It's your store."

Mr. Young explored the space, running his finger down each shelf, straightening boxes of fairy lights, and switching the order of ornaments I'd hung on a display stand. Then he pivoted on his heels and headed to the back room.

My heart pounded like I was in the middle of a proper anxiety attack. Maybe I was. It had been a long time since my last one, but I recognized the signs. I sprinted for the door and got there at the same time, but there was nothing I could do.

My boss opened the door, and there they were—my belongings, scattered across the room. There was the backpack, half open on the floor by the window, with an open toiletry bag next to it. Two sweaters teetered on top of the boxes on the desk, and the towel I'd borrowed from Fredrik hung over the edge of the bed, next to a laundry bag full of used underwear. A *sheer* laundry bag. That was where I'd stuffed my delicates, waiting for the next trip to the laundromat.

Mr. Young turned around to face me, looking alarmed. "You sleep here?"

I shook my head. "No! No. Of course not. You said it's—"

"Not allowed! Building code is for retail use only. You will get us kicked out."

Pearls of sweat gathered between my shoulder blades as my heart hammered on. "No, I understand. This is not what it looks like." I cringed at the cliché line.

Before I could explain, I was saved by the bell—The shopkeeper's bell that chimed above the front door.

"Excuse me," I said, rushing to the door.

It was Fredrik, with no hat or gloves, a dusting of snow on his hair and shoulders. He seemed agitated, with a deep crease between his eyes. Had he come to ask for his key back?

I heard the footsteps of Mr. Young and lunged at my new friend. "My boss is here," I whispered. "He saw my stuff at the back and—"

I swallowed the rest as Mr. Young reached us.

"I'm sorry. The store is not open yet. Come back tomorrow," he informed Fredrik, showing him the door.

"I'm not here for decorations," Fredrik replied, studying me with narrowed eyes.

I returned his gaze, trying to transmit a very specific distress signal.

"Fredrik is my... landlord," I improvised with a smile that likely looked desperate. "He's here to help me move to my new place." I turned to Fredrik with pleading eyes. "I'm sorry, I'm a little behind on packing. I was just reorganizing my things in there, but I first wanted to finish unpacking the shop." I gestured at the stocked shelves around me, hoping they spoke for my work ethic.

Mr. Young nodded, looking a little more relaxed.

Fredrik took a beat, then nodded. "That's okay. I'll wait." He made a show of checking his watch.

I cast him a grateful smile and ran to the back room, stuffing everything I owned into my bulging backpack in record time. When I emerged with my luggage, Fredrik leaped forward, taking it off my shoulders. "Great. Let's go."

Mr. Young stood at the door, blocking our way. "I will need your new address." He peered at me with suspicion.

"It's 55 Scenic Drive, Locke Heights," Fredrik replied. "She's renting a room from me. My name is Fredrik Hagberg."

My boss took out his phone and typed, eyebrows drawn in concentration. "Is it close by?"

"It's a couple of miles away, but she can get a ride with me. I own the bookstore next door."

"Ah! Hard to Find? I saw it! Wasn't that hard to find." Mr. Young chuckled at his own joke.

Fredrik gave him a rueful smile. "I cater to collectors."

"Very well. I'll leave you to it." My wannabe-comedian boss tipped his hat at us and opened the door. "I'll be back tomorrow to show you the cash register and other things, then we officially open the doors. Make sure you price everything. It's all in the book."

I nodded in understanding. I'd found the thick catalog under the boxes. "I'll do that first thing tomorrow. If you could come after lunch."

He flashed me a playful smile. "Okay. I make it later, but..." He flared his fingers in a gesture of surprise.

"I won't see you coming," I finished for him, forcing on a smile. "Got it."

He stepped outside, chuckling to himself.

As soon as the door chimed shut, Fredrik stepped forward, his voice low and demanding. "That nutjob is your boss?"

I sighed. "It seems so. Thanks for saving my ass."

"You can't sleep in that back room. I told you."

"Where else? I just have to get better at hiding my stuff. I didn't know he'd be making these surprise visits."

Fredrik glanced at the window. "I hate to tell you this, but he's still out there waiting."

"What?" I sidled to the window.

Yep. My unhinged boss stood a few steps down the road, hobbling on one spot, probably to keep warm. Or maybe he needed to pee, like me.

"Fine. I'll drag my stuff to your store and come back later. I need to use the bathroom anyway." I reached for the backpack Fredrik had taken off me and stored at his feet.

He lifted it onto his shoulder instead. "We can't go straight there. Not if he's keeping watch."

"For fuck's sake!" I clamped my mouth, my cheeks burning. "Sorry."

"It's okay. Let's walk to my car."

I turned off the lights, locked up, and followed him to a silver Mazda parked in front of his store. We both pretended not to notice Mr. Young hiding behind a lamppost, his collar turned up like an old movie spy. Fredrik shoved my backpack into the trunk of his car and opened the door for me. I slid inside, noting the smell of peppermint. My gaze landed on a bunch of candy canes hanging from his rearview mirror.

"Felicity," he explained, starting the engine.

"Smells nice." I watched through the back window as we drove away.

When Fredrik slowed down to turn away from the town square, I saw Mr. Young finally move toward his car.

"Just drive around the block," I told Fredrik. "He'll be gone by the time we're back."

He stared ahead, his mouth in a straight line. "I'm not taking you back to that store."

CHAPTER 11

Fredrik

I didn't care how disagreeable or obnoxious she found me. I couldn't let her live like that, hiding in a tiny storage room, in constant fear of an impromptu visit from her employer.

"How do you sleep there, anyway? The bed doesn't look big enough for you."

"It's okay," she said, her jaw jutting forward defensively as she stared out the window.

"Then you're seriously blessed in that department. I'd be up all night."

"I'm a lot smaller than you. Just take me back. I'll be fine."

"No. I have two options for you. There's a room above my store I've used as emergency accommodation before, when... um... there was a time I needed it."

"How much? I'll take it!" She let out a nervous laugh, holding her hand over her chest.

Why was her breathing so rapid? We were just sitting.

After driving around the block and seeing that Mr. Young had finally moved on, I parked in front of the bookstore again.

"Are you okay?" I asked. "You seem... anxious."

She locked eyes with me, her gaze intense. "I... I just had a mini panic attack. I'm riding it out—it'll pass." She drew in a deep breath, exhaled slowly, then added, "But I do need to use your bathroom."

"Of course."

When we got out of the car, she practically ran to the stairs. A few minutes later, she re-emerged, looking a little less agitated. I guided her to an armchair, and she sank into it with no protests, sucking in deep breaths. "I like this chair," she said.

"I know. I found your credit card inside it."

"What?" She looked up, horrified. I grabbed my lost-and-found basket and handed her the card.

"I must have... I think I sat down and was looking in my purse."

"It's fine. I find all manner of items inside that chair. It eats so many coins that Felicity nicknamed it the Slot Machine. The house always wins."

She smiled, a little relieved, and pocketed the card. "Thank you."

"You're welcome, Noelle E. Clarke."

Pink blotches rose to her cheeks. "Please don't google my name. Or do. Maybe it's better that you know. If I'm staying here and all." She twisted a strand of hair around her fingers as her gaze wandered around the room.

Was she talking about the article?

"Felicity showed me the article," I said. "I read it."

"Oh." Her gaze snapped onto mine, and she took deep breaths for a moment. "Good. You should know. Although I've been super careful. Only my sister knows I'm here. No one else in Bangor. And that article didn't have any pictures of me. So don't worry. Spencer won't turn up at your door!" She smiled, her voice forcefully bright.

"It's okay."

"And it probably helps that I don't get a signal anywhere. Only on top of that hill. So I have like no digital footprint or fingerprint or anything!"

"Maybe you need to switch carriers?" I suggested. "Mine works on most days, if conditions are favorable."

"When's that?"

"There are weather patterns that are better for it. You can check the town paper for the internet forecast." There were moments I felt proud of my hometown, and other moments, like this one, when I found myself uttering sentences so fucking weird that I wanted to bury my head in the snow. No wonder Elora hadn't wanted to live here. Always driving to Bangor for work and for pleasure. I winced.

Noelle fanned herself with a pamphlet she'd picked up from my desk. Something about Santa Speed Dating. "I get anxiety from a lot of stuff, but the patchy signal is not one of them. It helps. You stop checking your phone, and the day becomes more focused."

"I suppose."

"I loved it on the ship. Sometimes heavy clouds disrupted the satellite signal, and we lost internet access. Everyone was playing board games, talking, and drinking. Life was so contained. I had so little anxiety on the sea I honestly thought I was... healed." She blushed and hid behind the pamphlet.

A shirtless Santa with a six-pack smirked at me from the cover. Eileen had dropped off a pile of them two days ago, urging me to come along. I shuddered at the thought.

"I don't think it's something you can heal from, per se," I said. "As long as you're alive, your body will produce stress hormones. If it didn't, you'd be killed."

"Killed?" Her eyes widened. "I thought I'd be chilled."

I chuckled despite myself, feeling oddly warm. Something about her unfiltered babble put me at ease, even in her anxious state. My arms twitched with a sudden urge to hug her. I hadn't felt like that in ages, with anyone. Since Elora's death, I'd been hugged against my will so many times, forced to inhale all those old-lady perfumes.

"If you're too chill, you get killed, because your body won't alert you to danger. Stress hormones keep you safe."

"From saber-toothed tigers, maybe." She gave me a dirty look and lowered the pamphlet, now looking at it for the first time. "There's a Santa Speed Dating event at the café?"

"Welcome to Hideaway Harbor."

"Are you signing up?" she asked. "You'd look great in a white beard."

"Shirtless?" I raised my eyebrow.

"It says beards and hats are provided, nothing about shirts being confiscated. But I bet you'd look great with no shirt on!" She grinned at me, her gaze dipping to my grandpa's brown wool cardigan, which was probably the least sexy piece of clothing available on the face of the earth. Was she flirting with me? At least she seemed less agitated now, leaning back on the armchair.

The door buzzer cut my thoughts. Kailee. I'd completely forgotten about my niece.

"Hey!" she called from the door, heaving her backpack behind the register. "Do you have any snacks? I'm starving." She began peeling off her winter clothes—a black puffer coat, a gray scarf, and a black beanie. Underneath, she wore a black hoodie over baggy jeans. I suppose it was a teenage thing, hiding under a pile of oversized clothes in funeral colors.

"What took you so long?" I asked and dug up a packet of stale cookies I'd stashed under the counter.

"It's Monday. I was at the library." She glanced at me like I was stupid, adjusting her fogged-up glasses.

Noelle jumped out from behind me, giving Kailee a start. "Hi! You must be Fredrik's niece. I'm Noelle."

Kailee took off her glasses and wiped them on the sleeve of her hoodie. "I'm Kailee. You're the Christmas shop girl? Mom told me."

"In the flesh!" Noelle gave her a wavering smile she didn't return. "I came to use the bathroom. My facilities are a bit... um, lacking, so..."

"I offered her the upstairs room until she finds something better," I added, bracing for Kailee's reaction. She'd told me the best thing about my store was that nobody bothered her.

Noelle cast me a grateful glance. "And I accepted because I'm a little desperate." She pulled a face.

89

"That office room upstairs?" Kailee's gaze flicked between us as she tried to assess what was going on. "You'd have to be more than a little desperate."

"That's me!" Noelle let out a nervous laugh. "Honestly, I can't wait to sleep in the vicinity of a bathroom. It's such a luxury!"

"You're funny," Kailee deadpanned and hopped to sit on my desk, filling her mouth with a cookie.

"Are those any good?" Noelle asked.

Kailee tilted the packet her way, and she took one. "Thanks. I used to keep a stash of thin mints under my bed when I worked on a cruise ship."

"So you're used to small spaces," Kailee said.

"Very. That office room is three times the size of my cabin!"

"It's like a sealed tomb. Watch out for dust bunnies the size of regular bunnies." She shot me an accusing look.

I was almost impressed. I'd never heard a quip like that from my withdrawn niece. I'd never seen her sitting on a desk, either. Not that I was particularly thrilled that she'd planted her ass where I ate my lunch.

"Don't worry!" Noelle waved her hand. "I know where he keeps the vacuum cleaner. I will murder those bunnies!"

"You sound like my mom," Kailee muttered, but her usual eye-roll had a warm edge.

"I've met her, and I'm taking that as a compliment!" Noelle grabbed my office chair and rolled it around to sit next to Kailee, tapping at the backpack she'd hoisted on the desk next to her. "What do you have here? It looks heavy."

"Books." She said, like it was obvious.

Noelle clapped her hands. "Show me!"

To my astonishment, Kailee unzipped her bag and pulled out one of her brick-like fantasy titles, handing it over. She was drawn to Noelle, just like me, against my better judgment.

Noelle took the book and studied it, her face lighting up. "This sounds so good!"

"I'll go check the room," I said, heading for the stairs.

I doubt they even heard me, absorbed by whatever that book was about. Romance, apparently. Dragons were in a supporting role, then.

I was happy they were occupied. I had to clear the office of any personal items before I let Noelle move in. Maybe even tidy up. I'd heard enough of these jibes now, and it was true. The store had fallen into disrepair. It wasn't like I never cleaned. I kept my home in order. Sort of. Or rather, I kept it in a state of organized chaos, as I worked on restoring it with the help of Jackson. But I'd lost any passion I'd once had for the bookstore. It was just where I sat for the day. As long as I kept it open, people assumed I was coping and let me be. If I stopped showing up at work, my family would probably stage an intervention.

I gathered my personal belongings into a cardboard box and shoved the box into the hallway cupboard, coming face-to-face with the vacuum cleaner. *I might as well tackle the dust bunnies*, I thought, dragging it back to the office. This room had been my refuge during the last year of my marriage. I grimaced as the vacuum cleaner choked on a used tissue that floated from under the bed.

When I returned for a cleaning cloth, Noelle barged in, hitting herself on the cupboard door I opened.

"Ouch." She rubbed her forehead, smiling.

"Are you okay?"

"Yeah… Wait, are you cleaning?"

"Mom will never believe me!" Kailee appeared behind her, phone raised high. A camera flash momentarily blinded me.

"Give me a break." I shoved the vacuum cleaner back into the cupboard and grabbed the first cloth I could find, blinking away the purple floaters. "Your mom has seen me with a vacuum cleaner."

"Not lately." Kailee gave me an unyielding glare.

For such a quiet one, she had balls.

Noelle bit back on a grin, clearly enjoying herself.

"Nobody has slept in that room for years," I told her. "You might want to do your own deep clean. I was just clearing my stuff out of there."

Noelle's eyes widened in earnest. "I will clean it! Gimme." She took the cloth from me and skipped to the bathroom to run it under the faucet.

"I'll just do one last check…" I wandered back to the office.

"Make sure you check for stiff socks under the bed," Kailee called after me.

"Hey!" I turned to give her a piece of my mind, but she was already running down the stairs, giggling at her sudden audacity.

She never acted like that around me. It must have been Noelle's influence. Or maybe she was just growing up. I'd have to get used to that.

Noelle joined me by the desk with the cleaning cloth. "Kailee's funny."

I frowned. "She's usually so quiet. Reads in the corner for hours. I forget she's there."

"Maybe she's quiet because you're quiet?" She lifted an eyebrow as she approached the desk with the cloth.

I jumped in to help, lifting the hole punch, stapler, and pen holder out of her way.

"Thank you!" She beamed at me. "We make a great team."

It felt strange to stand so close to someone. I could hear her breathing. I felt the warmth of her body and smelled that vanilla-berry scent. What was I thinking by offering her this room? She'd be here in my space. She'd be everywhere, eating and showering and talking and making my niece talk. Everyone talking, all the time, having opinions and ideas... sitting on desks. Moving things.

I bristled.

I couldn't back out, though. If I did, I'd be left tossing and turning at night, wondering if she was being evicted from her illegal back room. She'd made her awful living situation my problem, and I couldn't escape.

It felt good, too. I couldn't deny it. Maybe I wanted to be the one to save her. The one she would run to. The one she could count on. It had been a while since anyone had counted on me for anything. And it wasn't like she smelled bad or left a huge mess in her wake. She was cleaning, after all.

Done with the desk, Noelle turned to face me, standing so close I could see the golden starbursts around her irises. She opened her mouth, as if to say something, but held there, her lips ajar, eyes soft and expectant. The berry-vanilla scent intensified, and I stopped breathing, waiting for her next move.

Was she looking at my mouth?

"Everything okay?" I asked to fill the silence that was getting loud.

"I was just thinking what it would be like to kiss you," she said casually.

I nearly choked on the little saliva left in my mouth.

Her smile was all innocence as she shook her head. "Don't worry, I won't! I know it's a bad idea to kiss your landlord."

I swallowed air, my throat now desert dry. She wanted to kiss me?

"You have a thing for bookish hermits?" I asked, covering my nerves with an awkward laugh.

"I told you, it's the elbow patches!" Her eyes were comically wide.

This was a dirty game, and she had an unfair advantage, being all cute and sexy and full of flirt.

"I'm not even wearing that jacket," I grumbled.

"But the image is seared into my imagination!" She reached around my arms to touch my elbows, and her mouth fell open.

Yes. My cardigan also came with elbow patches. I was starting to think my grandpa had them specially sewn on every piece of clothing he bought—and donated to me.

"Oh my God!" she exclaimed. "You're always ready to dramatically lean on a desk, aren't you?"

She held my elbows, and my arms flexed. I pictured myself backing her against the wall and shutting that smart mouth with mine so she couldn't say anything else. Seeing if she still had stupid jokes left.

I hadn't flirted with anyone in years. She'd forced me

into this back-and-forth, like I'd been dragged onto a battle-field with no armor.

"I use them for elbowing people away," I said roughly. "But some people are hard to shake."

"Like me?" She bit into her lower lip, smiling.

"You're the worst." My eyes assessed the straps on her overalls and the small buttons on the side. Unfasten. Undo. Unhook.

She let go of my elbows, slowly dragging her fingers back. They hovered over my chest as her eyes held mine. I could have told her to stop. I could have left the room. But I wasn't going to, and she knew it. Her touch had awakened something I thought was dead and gone. She'd coaxed out a part of me that wasn't burdened by reason.

At that moment, she held all the cards. The only form of restraint I had left was inaction. If she stepped back, I'd step back.

So I waited, completely at her mercy.

CHAPTER 12

Noelle

'd done plenty of stupid things in my life, but none so blatantly idiotic as this. As I leaned in, I could practically hear the alarm bells. This man had offered me a place to stay. Technically, he was my landlord. And I was thinking about kissing him.

The cloth slipped from my hand. My fingers curled into his ridiculous cardigan. Would he push me away? Would he bolt? He wasn't like anyone I'd ever met. Being with him felt like time travel, like I'd stumbled into a bygone era and found a man who shouldn't exist.

I should have let go. I wasn't ready for this. But my better judgment had left the building. It had probably driven out of town and fled the state. I'd been alone for so long, starving for touch—for *something*.

He held still, his breathing as ragged as mine, lips parted.

I leaned a little closer. "I'm so curious," I whispered. "It's terrible. It's like a disease."

"A disease?"

"You know, whatever it was that killed the cat. I have it."

His mouth curved faintly. "That's quite the ailment."

His chin brushed my nose, and I tilted my head, aligning my lips with his. My breath came in shallow gasps.

"We really shouldn't." A smile ghosted my lips. "It's probably better in my imagination anyway."

Still, I leaned closer, as if pulled by an invisible force.

Our lips brushed, like striking a match, and everything ignited. His hands cupped my face, and he brought our mouths together.

Oh. My. God.

I hadn't expected *this*. Not the rush, nor the intensity. His mouth landed on mine, and he grabbed me like he'd been waiting his whole life. One of his hands slid under the back of my overalls, tracing a slow path up my spine, and my skin erupted in goose bumps. I let out a small, broken sound into his mouth, and he backed me against the wall. Our tongues met, and a bolt of pleasure shot through me.

It felt so much better than I'd ever imagined. Fire and sugar and spice. My whole body hummed on a higher frequency, my heartbeat settling between my thighs, amplifying the hunger I couldn't hold back or hide.

I grasped at his cardigan, pulling him closer, scared this moment might vanish. That he might come to his senses and step away. The kiss deepened, turning raw and hungry. For a moment, nothing else existed. Only a white-hot, pulsing need. A desperate desire.

And then—

He jolted. His hands fell away, and he stumbled backward.

"I can't."

I blinked, dazed. "You can't?"

"I'm not the right guy." His voice was taut, frustrated. "If you're looking for a small-town fling, try Jackson. Try the Cafiero brothers. Anyone but me."

"I'm sorry," I whispered, mortified.

"It's okay." The fury in his eyes faded, and he cleared his throat. "We'll pretend it never happened."

I nodded. Sure. Pretend. Except the kiss was already branded into my long-term memory. I'd kissed him with reckless abandon, ready to offer him anything. And he'd kissed me back like a drowning man who'd just found air. I'd been lonely for a year. How long had it been for him?

I steadied myself against the wall. My knees still felt like Jell-O.

"Never happened," I said, my voice ringing with forced cheer. "We were just cleaning up and talking about... what did we talk about?"

He frowned. "I don't think we need a cover story."

"Right." I picked up the cloth I'd dropped and escaped to the bathroom, rinsing it until my hands were raw.

I couldn't act normally around him. I said the wrong thing and did the wrong thing. Spencer was right. I had no impulse control. I couldn't be let loose in a town like this. I'd been safe on the ship, with its monotonous routines, strict rules, and protocols. Now, I was roaming free, improvising... And it was dangerous.

"You okay?" Fredrik appeared at the doorway.

I looked up and saw his concerned eyes in the mirror.

"I'm just angry with myself," I said. "I should have never... I don't know why I..."

"Nothing happened."

"Okay, but—"

"There's one blanket and pillow and a set of sheets. Do you need extra blankets or anything else?"

I swallowed, trying to adjust to the tonal shift. "I can take one from my shop."

"Is it even big enough? It's a child's bed."

"No, it's just a little short."

He gave me a measured look. "Just like a child is a little shorter than an adult."

I smiled a little. "It's fine! But we need to talk about rent."

"What rent?"

"The rent you *must* charge me for living in your store."

"Absolutely not."

"But I can't sleep a wink if I'm in your debt. Especially since I already kissed you against your will!"

"No, you didn't—"

"I can't do this!" I shouted, my frustration boiling over. "I can't pretend nothing happened. That's not how my brain works." I chewed on my bottom lip as a hot tear rolled down my cheek.

He handed me a towel. "No. I meant you didn't kiss me against my will. I was very much on board. But it's not a good idea, so let's move on. I don't really know how to handle this, I'm sorry."

He looked so distressed, and my heart went out to him. "I don't know how to handle this, either. I'm sorry I kissed you. I made everything weird."

"No, you didn't… but I don't do casual. I've never been that guy."

Panic flared in my chest. *What did he think of me?*

"I don't do casual, either!" I blurted. "I don't go around kissing guys… I've never had a casual relationship of any kind. What does that even mean?"

"I don't know. Ask Jackson."

I let out a shaky breath. "Okay. So we're both totally hopeless and should avoid kissing from now on so as not to complicate our lives. Even though I think you're cute."

He caught the tear that had reached my chin, brushing a rough thumb across my skin. "And I think you're distractingly beautiful." His voice was as rough as his touch, sending tremors down my spine.

I held still, listening to blood whooshing in my ears, until he broke the spell. "You already have the key. And you know my hours."

"I'll keep out of your way! I'll set my alarm and make sure—"

He held up a hand. "Our paths are going to cross, so we better get along. As friends."

"Friends," I repeated. "Of course. And if you need any help in the store, or with anything else, I'm here."

"Thanks, but don't worry about it. Focus on your own store."

He headed downstairs, and I followed, trying to push down the turmoil in my chest. I couldn't focus on the rejection. He was doing this amazing thing for me. I had to show him I could be his friend. I could keep my hands off him and channel my energy into something productive.

"I could help you decorate for Christmas," I suggested as we passed the display window.

"That's a great idea!" Kailee piped up. She was sitting cross-legged in the armchair, a book in her lap. "I'll help, too!"

Fredrik threw us a look. "I don't need decorations."

"But your store does!" Kailee argued. "And I do!"

"Your customers would love it," I echoed.

"What customers?" His tone was biting.

Kailee sighed loudly. "Maybe they'd find it here if you had some lights. Seems to work for everyone else."

Fredrik stared at her like she'd grown a second head.

Her gaze snapped onto mine, and I smiled. Sure, neither of us had any say on how Fredrik ran his business, but right now, he was outnumbered. And this was something I could really help him with.

Shaking off any remnants of embarrassment over what had happened between us a moment earlier, I approached his desk. "Do you have a measuring tape?"

He looked up from his battered laptop, which didn't even seem to be on. "Somewhere upstairs. Why?"

"I'll plan your window display! My treat. I can grab anything from my store at wholesale prices, and I want to thank you for allowing me to stay here. Since you won't accept rent payments."

"No."

"Come on! You have to let me pay you back somehow. Otherwise, I'll…" I glanced at Kailee for help. What could I possibly threaten him with? More kissing? It was so dark and dreary in here, and Christmas was coming.

Kailee appeared beside me. "Otherwise, we'll do it

without your permission, and you have no say on what goes where."

I threw a horrified look at her. That was a little bold.

Fredrik glared at us. Kailee had slung her arm over my shoulders. She was tall like her mother and towered over me. I noticed Fredrik's gaze flick to that arm casually hanging by my ear, and again, I had a feeling this wasn't how Kailee usually acted. I was here for it, though, if she needed a girlfriend. God knew I needed one. Or five.

Fredrik drew a breath, still frowning. "Nothing that blinks. Nothing with those blue pinprick lights or purple glitter. And absolutely nothing that plays Christmas music."

"Deal!" we shouted in unison, then burst out in laughter.

Kailee let go of my shoulder, and I high-fived her. "Nice work, partner! Would you like to come over tomorrow to choose some items? I'll have the shop open until five o'clock."

"I'll come straight from school." Kailee's eyes shone. "I can stay as late as I want. Mom's going to the crochet club anyway, so she won't be home all night."

"Wait, what?" Fredrik sat up. "That doesn't mean you stay out all night. We agreed I would send you straight home after I closed."

Something occurred to me. "Your mom goes to the crochet club? I heard about it from this old lady I sat next to on the bus. Ida! She taught me how to do a basic flower and invited me to come along... What time is it?"

"At seven. My mom runs the club with Eileen."

I turned to Fredrik. "Perfect! Kailee and I can go together!"

Kailee frowned, suddenly looking a lot like Fredrik. "Do I have to crochet?"

"No! I'm sure it's fine if you don't."

"I think they also share books," Fredrik offered. "Felicity keeps ordering them for the club."

"Yeah!" Kailee gave me a grave look. "*The Doctor's Secret Baby. The Doctor Who Railed Me...* I'm surprised she can even see the doctor after reading those."

"There's no book titled *The Doctor Who Railed Me*," Fredrik corrected. "But they've gone through a lot of medical romance lately."

"It's because our new attending looks like Henry Cavill," Kailee explained.

"What's the required reading for tomorrow?" I wandered over to the corner shelf with Fredrik's romance titles.

"I'll show you the one Mom's reading right now!" Kailee browsed the shelves until she found the book and handed it to me.

The Doctor's Secret Baby.

"Great! I'll take it."

I took the book to the counter.

Fredrik handed it back. "You don't have to buy it. You live here. Read anything you like, just don't crack the spines."

"Oh, but I will! I'll highlight and underline and use little stickers to annotate. I'm finally on dry land, and I'm going to interact with physical things like there's no tomorrow."

I handed him my lost-and-found credit card, and he rang up the purchase, shaking his head like he couldn't understand a word I'd said.

"Hold it for me, would you?" I asked him once I'd paid.

"I'll go pick up my stuff so I can settle in for the night. It's been a long day, and I think I need a good reading session."

"See you tomorrow!" Kailee called after me, and I waved goodbye, rushing out the door.

I had to get out before I cracked and could no longer pretend I was fine. Because I wasn't. I'd kissed him, and he'd pushed me away. There was no other way to look at it. And as much as I wanted to forget all about it and be okay, the hurt burned behind my eyes. As soon as I stepped outside the store, my throat tightened and tears burst out. I felt the sting of rejection, but also disappointment.

Because I liked him.

Being around Fredrik calmed my frazzled nerves. There was something about him that my soul latched onto. Maybe it was the freedom to be myself, or the way he kept showing up for me, expecting nothing in return.

Yes. I was developing a crush on a man who'd already friend zoned me.

And now I was practically moving in with him.

Things were going from bad to worse.

CHAPTER 13

Fredrik

" *R* eady to do some tiling?" Jackson called from the front door.

His voice had a careful edge to it, like he was approaching an unpredictable wild animal. Was that me?

"Sure! Come on in," I called back, meeting him in the dark, cold foyer. "It'd be good to get that bathroom finished."

He gave me a hug, then a measured look. "You look better."

"I'm okay."

"No, you look alive."

"Thanks."

"Did you say you wanted to *finish* the bathroom? We're

not going to order original tiles handmade by monks on the foothills of Tuscany?"

"No. The one you showed me last time is fine. The zigzag."

"The chevron?"

"Whatever. It's fine."

Jackson looked at me for a moment longer, then broke into a smile. "Hallelujah! I'll go get my stuff before you change your mind."

He ran back to his truck. I put on my slippers and followed, feeling guilty. Was he saying I didn't want to finish the house? Maybe I'd been stalling a little, worried that I wasn't going to do justice to the historical features. It had always been Uncle Glenn's dream to restore the house to its original glory, and I wanted to respect that. However, after decades of renovations and alterations, it was hard to know what that even meant. He'd bought the place on a whim, like he'd done most things, and bequeathed it to me, possibly also on a whim. He had seen potential in everything. Buildings. Businesses. People.

He'd seen something in me.

It was dark outside, and so cold that every hair on my body instantly stood up. Maine winters were something else. I should have worn my boots and zipped up my jacket, but it seemed pointless to do so for a few minutes outside. Besides, it was probably good for me to get my nuts whipped by the icy wind. It'd wake me up for an all-nighter and get rid of the persistent hard-on I'd been sporting all day since that kiss. I had to stop thinking about it.

"Take that," Jackson said, hoisting a cardboard box into my arms.

It must have been the tiles since the weight of it nearly buckled my knees. I adjusted to it and carried it inside. I wasn't weak. Chopping firewood for myself, my parents, and my grandfather kept me from turning into a wet noodle, as did my occasional visits to Lobstah Lifts—whenever Jackson decided he needed a workout buddy. But I was getting lazy and sluggish, like my mind was stuck in some sort of tar. Not moving. Not feeling. Avoiding anything that might cause more pain.

And then she'd kissed me. Just like that, with no preamble. Or maybe she considered mentioning her curiosity a drumroll of some kind. It fucking wasn't. She'd blindsided me, slipping through a crack and tilting everything until I lost sight of the horizon.

But I wasn't feeling sluggish anymore. I wanted to move. To do something.

Jackson organized his tools outside the gutted bathroom and started measuring the walls. For a while, we worked in silence, laying tiles until the floor was ready for grouting.

"So..." Jackson said as he grabbed a bucket to mix the grout. "A little birdie told me you have a new tenant."

"Tenant?" I asked, buying time.

"The cute girl living at your store?"

I sighed. "How do you know about that? She moved in like two hours ago."

"Your sister came to clean a site we were working at."

I shook my head in disbelief. Kailee must have texted her mom immediately. The gossip gene ran in the family. Why didn't I have it? I'd never felt the slightest need to discuss other people's business. I barely wanted to discuss mine, especially with my friend observing me like that, his eyes filled with glee.

"Yeah, she's staying for a bit. Her boss came for a visit and told her she wasn't allowed to sleep at the back of her store."

"No shit! How was there even room for a bed in there? If they split the real estate office in three…"

"There's no room! It was a child's bed. Ridiculous."

"Did she turn up at your door with a sleeping bag or something?"

"No. I happened to be there and heard their conversation, so I told her boss she was staying with me to get him off her back."

"And then you had to find her a place? Because you can't help but get involved."

"What's this about? You wanna take her?"

"I would, but I have a feeling you'd bite my head off." He winked, slapping a load of grout on the floor, then handing me the float. "Can you carry on? I'll start from the other end, and we can meet in the middle, then we wash and let it dry for thirty minutes while we grab beers, then the final clean, and it's done."

I took the float and did my best to mimic Jackson's movements, happy to see a glimpse of what the finished floor would look like. No more picking my way across the ugly, gutted floor when I needed to use the bathroom. No more ruining socks walking on rough concrete. Why had I lived like that for so long?

Jackson grabbed a sponge and showed me how to wipe the tiles without pulling out too much of the grout. "Keep it light," he said. "Like you're stroking her hair, postcoital."

"Whose hair?" I grumbled.

He ignored me. "I, for one, think it's healthy that you're noticing someone. But remember what I've told you about local girls? This is someone who works next door and you'll see regularly. And now she's living in your store..." He paused for effect, giving me a careful look. "I told you, I'll take you out. A weekend in Bangor. We'll blow off some steam and find you a hot date."

"I don't need a—"

"I mean a nice bookish lady who's turned on by that whole mental patient slash professor vibe," he corrected, gesturing at my outfit.

I glanced at my fluffy slippers, corduroy pants, and bathrobe. "I was going for *The Big Lebowski*."

"See! Even your movie references are dated. At this rate, you'll end up with a menopausal woman."

"Noelle thinks elbow patches are sexy," I countered, then immediately froze, wishing I could reel the words back in.

Jackson halted, too, holding a measuring tape between his hands, like he was using it to assess the credibility of my words. Twenty inches of bullshit.

"She said that?"

I nodded.

"In actual words?"

I nodded again.

"To you?"

I groaned in frustration. "She says a lot of things. Blurts them out like a broken radio. It's not that deep."

"But she said it to you." He narrowed his eyes. "She's into you!"

"She's curious. She'll be into someone else tomorrow."

He shook his head. "No. She's into *you*. I'm sure there's a sexy dude wearing elbow patches in a catalog somewhere, but the way you do it? Nobody finds that sexy. Trust me."

He had a point.

"I guess there's just not that much to do in Hideaway Harbor."

"She wants to do *you* to alleviate her boredom?" Jackson gave me a look.

"Either way, she's only in town for the holidays."

Jackson's eyes widened as the realization took hold. "That's right! Because she sells tinsel and shit!"

I nodded because a lot of what that store contained was indeed shit.

"Stay away from her. I mean it." I couldn't help the words from flying out of my mouth.

Jackson laughed. "I'm not going after her! But you should. Have a holiday fling. Distract yourself from... you know. It's perfect."

"I'm..." I shook my head, looking for the right words. "I'm not like you."

I'll fall for her. She'll shred my heart, and I'll never recover.

"You mean you get way too serious way too fast?" He raised his brow. "I know. Life's not all or nothing, Teddy. There's a lot that falls in between. Fun weekends. Dates, you know? The girl who's fun-crazy when she's drunk and then the following morning—"

"She's just crazy," I finished for him. I'd heard this story. "Sounds delightful."

Jackson slapped more grout on the tiles, looking a little hurt. "Sorry I can't sell it to you with big words. I'm not a novelist like your other friends. I'm alive, though."

I had to laugh. "I love that about you."

We worked in silence for a while, dodging each other in the small space. Before long, we'd filled all the gaps and the floor looked a lot more finished, apart from the layer of grout sitting on the tiles. It was also sitting across the hem of my bathrobe.

"It's beer o'clock," Jackson announced, straightening his back with a groan. "And please don't throw that awful garment in the wash. Throw it *out*."

I discarded the bathrobe and fetched two cold ones from the fridge as Jackson plopped himself on the couch. He'd somehow finished the floor without getting anything on his expensive jeans. The man lived in a different reality.

I restarted the fire that had died and joined him.

"So… Bangor next weekend?" Jackson went for casual, but I heard the serious undertones.

We hadn't done anything he considered fun in two years. He'd been supportive and patient with me, but I had to pull myself out of this funk or I'd lose the last person not related to me by blood who still cared enough to turn up.

"I thought you'd be signed up for Santa Speed Dating this Friday. Eileen will be devastated if you skip town."

Jackson sat up. "Santa what? How do I not know about this?"

"Because you don't pay attention to her flyers?" I guessed. "They're all over the place."

"Okay. New plan! We both go Santa Speed Dating."

"Over my dead body."

"Would you prefer to be freshly killed or with some impressive rigor mortis? I'll try to time it right."

I could see it in his eyes. He'd never let this go. He'd drag me there by the fake beard he'd glue on my face in my sleep, thinking he was both hilarious and helpful. I needed to distract him with something. Anything.

"She kissed me."

The silence that followed made my ears ring, like I'd just heard an explosion.

"Noelle? The candy cane girl?"

"Don't call her that!" I tried to shake the mental image of Jackson licking Noelle.

"She kissed you, and..." He stared at me expectantly.

"Nothing. I told her it was a bad idea. She agreed."

"You didn't kiss her back?" Jackson yelled.

I wiped the spit spray off my cheek, huffing indignantly. "I... We made out. But I couldn't go on, could I? We were upstairs in my store. Kailee was there. I mean, not in the room, but..."

"But you told her you'd like to go on, right? You told her that she's hot and amazing and you'd like to take her out? Eat her out? Meet her later? Give me something!"

"We agreed to be friends. It's fine."

Jackson slammed his beer bottle against my coffee table. "It's not fine, you idiot! She kissed you, and you pulled some standoffish move. You humiliated her, and now she's never going to try again, and you'll die a miserable, lonely bastard."

"That's a little dramatic. We both agreed it's not a good idea. She's staying in my store. There's a power imbalance. It's awkward."

"Of course there's a power imbalance. She needs your help, and you made it clear you want nothing from her."

"Are you saying I should ask her to pay rent by sucking my dick?"

Jackson got up and walked over to my fridge, helping himself to another beer. "You owe me this," he said, opening it with the edge of the table. "For being that dense."

I was getting irritated now, but also worried. Was it possible I'd offended Noelle? She'd seemed fine afterward, joking with me and teaming up with my niece. "I don't care about any power imbalance. She needed help, and I'm helping her. I don't need anything in return."

Jackson rolled his head to loosen his shoulders and crossed the floor to join me on the couch again. "You think you're being a gentleman or something, but she's not going to see it that way. She's now thinking you don't like her, and desperately looking for somewhere else to stay."

The realization fell on me like a blanket of snow, spreading a chill down my spine. I'd rejected her. I'd probably made her feel like a nuisance. She'd only stayed because she didn't have anywhere else to go. She'd buried her feelings and joked around to make herself feel better. That was what people did.

If I wanted to really help her, I had to do better than that.

But what could I possibly do?

CHAPTER 14

Noelle

The night was my favorite kind—crisp and starry. The quiet beauty of it on top of Cellular Hill eased my frustration over not being able to sleep again. Fredrik's office room bed was a lot bigger and more comfortable, so logically, I should have been sound asleep, making up for the sleepless nights in the squeaky doll's bed.

In my exhaustion, I'd fallen asleep on the first spread of *The Doctor's Secret Baby* at seven o'clock, then woken at midnight with my heart racing. Must have been from all the excitement of the day. Anxiety didn't usually hit me in the middle of the night, but there was nothing usual about my life recently.

At least climbing the hill in clear weather had given me a signal and let me catch up on emails.

Mom had responded to my cocktail photo with a smiley

face. Scrolling back through our earlier messages, I found a picture of their Thanksgiving dinner. They'd set a plate for me, and Holly had drawn a smiley face on it with gravy. My tears splashed the phone screen, blurring the image.

Mr. Young had sent me a video about nap cafés in Korean workplaces, emphasizing that the beds were for <u>daytime use only</u>. I got the sense he didn't really encourage napping at work either.

I sat under the gazebo, fingers numb from the cold, scouring the internet for an affordable room within walking distance of my store. There weren't any—affordable or otherwise. If I wanted to keep my job, I'd have to continue taking up space in Fredrik's store, regardless of how bothersome or inappropriate he found me.

Why couldn't I behave like a normal person? Everything would have been fine if I hadn't kissed him. If I'd just held my tongue. That was it. My tongue was the root of all evil. Things I said without thinking, questions I asked... and even that moment I'd tasted him. A bittersweet zing shot up my spine. I could still feel his hands on my waist, pulling me flush against him. He'd kissed me back, probably caught up in the moment. Or had I imagined it? How delusional was I?

I pulled my mittens back on and made my way down the hill. Not feeling sleepy, I circled the town square. Fresh snow had fallen, but the temperature was above freezing, creating perfect conditions for snowballs. I rolled one, then another, and eventually built a snowman. He was a bit lopsided, but I found some sticks for arms and made him a face out of smaller twigs.

He was smiling. Maybe he'd make someone else smile.

At least he'd made me tired enough to fall asleep again.

I WOKE up to a knock on the door and clambered out of bed, groggy and disoriented.

"Good morning!" The door opened, and Fredrik stepped inside, balancing a croissant on top of two coffees.

I instinctively swiped my fingers under my eyes to catch any remnants of makeup, then glanced down at my red pajama pants and garish Rudolph sweater. Thanks to Mom, all my sleepwear was Christmas-themed.

"What time is it?" I asked. I'd fallen asleep again in the early hours. Had I even set an alarm?

"It's eight o'clock."

"But you open at ten," I said, eyeing the coffees in his hands.

"Is it too early?" He looked mortified. "I'm sorry. I didn't want to miss you."

"It's okay. Is that... for me?" I pointed at the cup, and he handed it over with the croissant.

"I wanted to apologize."

"For what?" I blinked in confusion.

The smell of fresh coffee and buttery pastry hit my nose, distracting me from his words.

"I don't think I said the right thing yesterday. I don't know if I did the right thing, either. I'm not great at this." I'd never seen him this flustered.

"This being...?"

"I mean, anyone showing interest in me. I don't know how to react."

He looked so adorably panicked that I couldn't help smiling. "But nothing happened."

He sighed. "Yeah. I know. That's one of the wrong things I said. Because you're right, it doesn't work. If I've learned anything from books, it's that the buried truth always comes out in a messy way. *Scarlet Letter. Crime and Punishment. Jane Eyre...*"

"*The Doctor's Secret Baby!*" I added, biting my lip. "I haven't read it yet, but I bet it fits the bill."

He laughed. "Exactly. Let's not do that."

"What do we do instead?" I took a sip of coffee, letting it warm my throat. "Announce the kiss in the town bulletin?"

His eyes flashed with horror. "The Almanac gossip columnist would lose their mind."

"You think they'd write about how the sad woman staying in Fredrik's bookstore tried to kiss him?"

Fredrik's mouth tugged faintly. "You didn't try to kiss me. You succeeded."

I released a heavy breath. "When I do stupid stuff, I commit. I'm sorry you got caught up in it."

He leaned on the doorway, fidgeting with his coffee. His voice was measured. Tender. "Are you confused over what happened here yesterday?"

I hid behind my coffee cup. "A little," I admitted. "I thought maybe you kissed me back to be polite, or... I don't know. I didn't sleep much, and my brain is circling the drain right now." My heart pounded as I looked up at him.

There it was again, the babbling honesty I couldn't take back. I was out of control and sick of myself.

"Noelle." He stepped closer, tipping my chin with a finger so I had to meet his gaze. "I didn't just kiss you back. I wanted to take you, right here. I lost control."

It was a confession. Full of regret. Yet my body flooded

with heat. For a moment, I drowned in his forest-green eyes, like I was submerged in a pond. I waited, too scared to move. My whole body tingled. I wanted him to touch me so that I could respond.

But after a moment, he released me. "I'm sorry. It won't happen again." He backed toward the door. "I'll... leave you to it."

To what? I screamed in my head as the door closed, and his footsteps faded away.

He'd come to tell me that, then left.

AT 3:20 THAT AFTERNOON, the bell above the Christmas store door chimed as my new friend Kailee barged in, school bag swinging on her shoulder, and a huge dog in her wake.

"You have a dog?"

The St. Bernard followed her inside, settling at the doorway.

"That's just Skippy. I bagged some bacon for him from the school cafeteria." Kailee lifted a greasy paper bag, smiling. "He wanders around town, but you can sway him with treats." She dangled a piece of bacon, and Skippy snatched it.

"He's gorgeous!" I crouched down to pet him. "Whose dog is he?"

"My mom says he's like a giant pigeon. Goes wherever he gets the best meal."

I patted Skippy's soft fur. "Don't worry," I told him. "You look nothing like a pigeon."

"You look sweaty," Kailee observed.

"I am." I wiped my forehead.

I'd hoped opening the doors with no fanfare would mean a quiet first day, but the whole town had turned up.

I'd spent the day learning on the go—figuring out the cash register, putting up missing price tags, and fielding endless questions about both the items and my background. Those I at least knew the answers to. But when it came to the stock, I didn't know what kind of batteries things required or if the singing, dancing Santa came with a warranty. My guess was no. Now I had a long list of questions for Mr. Young, who'd failed to show up despite his earlier warning.

It felt good to keep busy. Without this job, I would have been obsessing over Fredrik's words. I hadn't seen him since he'd walked out that morning. Now that Kailee was with me, he must have been there by himself. I'd never seen an actual customer enter his store. How did it survive?

Kailee and Skippy settled on the daybed with her homework until closing time, when I escorted the last old lady out of the shop, promising I'd look for the earring she'd lost somewhere inside.

"Ready?" I asked, peeking into the back room.

"Sure." She slid a tasseled bookmark into her book.

Skippy, relaxing on the bed next to her, lifted his head and lumbered toward the front door.

"I ran out of bacon," Kailee explained, letting the dog outside.

I watched the huge stray make his way across the town square, feeling an odd kinship. He didn't have a home either, but he made it work.

"Let me show you what I put aside for the bookstore." I beckoned Kailee to the counter, lifting out boxes of lights and decorations I'd stored behind it. "He said nothing that blinked, so I thought he'd like these vintage light bulbs. One color, probably called Edison. And then some red baubles and gold stars. Traditional and low key."

"Boring." Kailee browsed a rack of novelty ornaments and picked up a green Grinch figurine, hanging it off her finger. "This would be perfect! Do you have more of these?"

"We're trying to get him on board, not scar him for life."

She scoffed. "He's already scarred for life." She pressed the Grinch against my face. "This looks like Uncle Fredrik, doesn't it? Same frown."

I laughed. "What do you mean scarred...?" I swallowed a ball of shame. Why couldn't I keep my big mouth shut? "Don't tell me! And don't tell him I asked, please!"

Kailee chuckled, swinging the stupid Grinch from her finger. "You like him! You like the Grinch of Hideaway!"

"He's not the..." I could feel myself blushing. "I mean, he's helping me. That's not Grinch-like."

"Uncle Fredrik helps everyone! He splits firewood for Gramps and Great-Grandpa Charles and half the town. My mom constantly calls him to pick up something or drop off something or take someone ice fishing. He never says no. He just does it looking like this." She contorted her face to match the Grinch's expression, then burst out laughing.

Fredrik isn't like that, I argued with myself. *He'd bought me coffee and a croissant, and said...* I stopped myself from repeating the words I'd obsessed over all day. They didn't mean anything. He'd only been settling the score, admitting to feelings he thought I had so I'd feel better about myself.

The way *I'd* lost control. A nice, selfless act, like splitting firewood.

"Are you hungry?" I asked Kailee. "I'm starving. I didn't have time to pick up anything during the day. Any chance the crochet club has catering?"

She shook her head. "I don't think so, unless someone's been baking. The café closes at six, that's why they meet after."

"In that case, I need to find some dinner."

HALF AN HOUR LATER, we sat at The Shore Thing, eating fish chowder and French fries, which I'd bought for Kailee.

"This is where I met Fredrik," I told her, enjoying the way the hot soup warmed me from the inside out. "I sat right here, taking selfies with that cactus and a cocktail. And he sat—" I lifted my finger and froze.

Because he was right there. Fredrik plopped into his usual seat, undid his scarf, and reached into his bag for his book. As he pulled it out, he looked up and saw me.

He gave us his signature frown, his eyes flicking between us. "I thought the knitting club was meeting at the Sip."

"Nice to meet you, too." I grinned. "We're just grabbing a bite first."

"Hi, Grinch," Kailee said, popping a fry into her mouth. She'd taken off her jacket, letting her black top slide off her shoulder.

"You brought her to a bar." Fredrik scanned the room.

Summer waved at us from behind the bar, and an older

couple continued eating their pizzas. With no obvious predators in sight, he relaxed a little.

"It's not like I'm buying her beer," I said pointedly. "And we'll have to go in ten minutes, so you can read in peace."

To my surprise, Fredrik slid his book back into his bag, picked up his things, and moved to our table, sitting right next to me. "Is it any good?" He nodded at my food, looking hungry.

"It's perfect! So creamy. Try." I picked up a clean spoon from a holder and handed it to him.

"I didn't mean—" He raised his hand to refuse the spoon.

What was all this uptight nonsense? We were supposed to be friends, not awkwardly polite strangers who couldn't even share food. He'd told me our paths would cross and we needed to get along.

I scooped a spoonful of chowder and raised it to his lips. "Open up."

He scowled at the spoon, then at me, lips sealed. I felt a flash of irritation. So, I was supposed to accept his help left and right, but he couldn't accept a spoonful of soup from me?

I held up the spoon, not yielding. "I bet your mom had fun feeding you as a baby."

Kailee giggled. "Let me try!" She reached across the table, but I blocked her with my elbow, giving her a cheeky look.

"Wait, I have an idea."

I readied my spoon and looked Fredrik in the eye. "I think I'm falling in love with you."

His mouth dropped open, and I stuck the spoon in. A little dribble ran down the side of his face, but he managed to swallow the rest, staring at me in utter horror. Kailee cheered.

"It's good, isn't it?" I smiled victoriously.

Fredrik grabbed a napkin and wiped his mouth. "The chowder is great. You, on the other hand"—he gave me a long look, lowering his voice—"are playing cruel games."

He stared at me for a moment, his eyes dark and thunderous, and I swallowed hard. "What do you mean?"

"I get that I'm nothing to you but a small-town curiosity, but you don't have to make fun of me."

"Make fun of you?" I frowned, trying to make sense of his words, panic rising in my chest.

"I know the idea of anyone falling in love with me is hilarious, but I do have feelings."

"I'm sorry," I whispered, suddenly feeling awful. "That's not what I meant! I say the wrong thing all the time. It's like my brain is broken." I gestured to my head, blinking away tears.

"Can you both chill?" Kailee stood. "We need to go."

I got up too, pushing the rest of my soup toward Fredrik like a peace offering. "Please, finish it for me. We'll be late."

He harrumphed, but as we gathered our things and headed for the door, I saw him pick up the spoon.

CHAPTER 15

Noelle

*A*s Kailee opened the café door, a bout of raucous laughter rolled across the room. A large table at the back was piled with yarn, books, and wineglasses, with a huge plate of cookies in the middle. Around it, six ladies howled like it was male burlesque night on deck C. Kailee halted at the doorway.

I nudged her forward, raising my voice over the ruckus. "Hi! Are we in the right place?"

"My spawn!" Felicity shouted in delight. "And Noelle! I wasn't sure you'd show up. I've been trying to get Kailee to join us for months." She glanced at the other ladies. "She's fifteen, so let's keep it above board, okay?"

"I'm not a baby," Kailee grumbled. "I know you read smutty books."

An older lady I recognized as Ida from the bus stood. "Of course. We'll focus on the crafts this week!"

A dissatisfied murmur fluttered around the table.

"Oh, shush now!" Ida raised a finger. "You'll be happy when you finish those beautiful Christmas gifts. You'll thank me later!"

Felicity pulled out two chairs for us. I sat between Kailee and Ida and declined the drink they offered, hoping Kailee wouldn't feel left out if I wasn't drinking either.

Ida ran through the introductions. "You already know Felicity and Eileen, who owns this café. And this is Deidre Geiss. She owns the wellness shop down Main Street."

"Tonic Room? It looks so cute!" I exclaimed. I'd peered through the window on my nightly walk.

Deidre raised her glass, grinning. She looked well into her sixties and wore more color than I did. The Christmas bells hanging from her earlobes jingled as she tilted her head in my direction. "Next time, come in, and I'll mix you something to regulate your cycle and calm that restless spirit."

I took a deep breath, trying to look less restless. "Sounds... great."

Ida turned to the next stranger at the table. "And this is Lola Monroe. She runs a... business in town."

A woman with voluminous blue hair who looked about my age smiled, casting a tired look at Ida. "It's an adult toy store called The Perfect Package. Come for a visit! I'll give you my friends-and-family discount."

I stared at her wineglass, wondering if I'd been too hasty to turn down alcohol. "That's... exciting."

"And this is Erica Locke," Ida continued around the table.

A middle-aged woman with a sunny smile waved at me from across the table. "Lovely to meet you! Are you new in town, Noelle?"

Erica reminded me of my own mother, down to the deep dimples on her cheeks when she smiled, and I instantly felt at ease.

"She's right next door to Fredrik," Eileen added. I could almost see little hearts floating out of her eyes.

"How wonderful!" Erica's smile turned a little misty. "It's so lovely to see young people coming in. Maybe settling down... finding love." She blinked away tears.

Settling down and finding love? Did they not know I was running a pop-up shop for one month? I cast a panicky glance at Felicity, who offered an apologetic smile.

"Erica's daughter lives in Brooklyn," Eileen explained, making Brooklyn sound like the International Space Station. She patted Erica's hand. "Piper will settle down soon. I can feel it! Didn't you say she's bringing a boyfriend home for the holidays?"

Erica wiped her eyes, smiling. "We're so excited!"

"If you have any issues with the town, you can take them up with Erica. She's married to the mayor," Felicity said briskly.

Erica nodded, looking a little cheerier. "I'm more popular than the suggestion box at the town hall."

"How did you end up in Hideaway Harbor, Noelle?" Deidre asked.

Everyone leaned in, and my insides spasmed.

"I'm here to run the Christmas shop on Hideaway Ave," I said. "It opened today."

"Oh, I saw that!" Lola exclaimed. "Do you sell anything naughty? I'd love to get something with cocks, but seasonal."

I stared at her, my cheeks a little hot. "Sorry. I haven't seen any penises. It's not my store. I'm just here to run it for four weeks. Then… I'll be off."

It was better that they knew the truth—that I was a rootless, lost soul and not the future of Hideaway Harbor. I cast a nervous glance around the table. Would they ask me to leave?

The older ladies nodded in unison, smiling like they were in on some big secret.

"Of course, dear." Eileen shrugged oh-so-innocently. "Unless love throws a wrench in your plans." She gazed out the dark window. "You might end up staying for forty years. I can usually sense these things, and I have strong—"

"Maybe she'll stay with us for the next two hours if you all behave," Felicity shot back, then turned to her daughter. "Did you have fun with the Christmas decorations earlier?"

Kailee pulled a Grinch ornament from her pocket. "I found this guy who looks like Uncle Fredrik."

"You took that?" I tried not to sound too panicked. "I need to write down everything I'm taking from the store."

Kailee's lip wobbled. "I was gonna bring it back."

Felicity shot her daughter a stern look. "Did you take anything else? It's not like Uncle Fredrik's store. She needs to account for every item."

Kailee pouted. "I only borrowed this because I thought it was funny."

Why didn't Fredrik account for every item? Why was his

store different? My curiosity ramped up at an alarming rate, making my mouth twitch.

Eileen leaned in to examine the Grinch. "That does look like him! He made that exact face when I stopped by to invite him to the Santa Speed Dating. Which reminds me, I had more flyers printed. Here..."

She passed around the same flyer I'd seen in Fredrik's store, the one with the shirtless Santa.

"You invited Fredrik to this?" Felicity's eyes rounded in disbelief. "That's optimistic. Last time I asked, he wouldn't even go to the trivia night, and that was odd—"

"Because he's full of trivia!" I blurted out like a kinder-gartener with the right answer.

Everyone looked over, and my face flushed with embar-rassment. Why did I have a mouth?

Felicity reached across Kailee to grab my arm. "He told you about trivia nights? How he used to compete every week? How he was unbeatable? How he'd study... read every book and obsess over the most obscure details?"

I shook my head apologetically. "Not in so many words."

"But he talked to you? He... shared?"

My eyebrows knitted together so tightly my face hurt. "He said trivia is useless."

Felicity's face fell, and she pulled away. "Well, I guess it's still good that he's talking to someone."

Eileen cast her eyes heavenward. "I have a good feeling about this Christmas! Time heals all wounds, and even Fredrik will come around. He'll change his tune, you'll see."

I noticed subtle eye rolls, but Eileen didn't seem to mind. Her faith in all things love was unshakable.

"He made this face when we suggested he should put up

Christmas decorations." Kailee's voice held a hint of defiance, the ornament still dangling from her finger.

"He needs to step up," Deidre muttered. "That store is an eyesore."

"It's true," Felicity agreed, draining her wineglass. "That store drives tourists away. I can only do so much with my weekly cleaning."

"But Mom! He agreed to let us decorate!" Kailee protested. "Sort of."

"You and… Noelle?" Eileen's eyes lit up. "Oh! This is very good news! He's warming up, just like I saw in my vision. Poor Fredrik. He has such a good heart under all that…" She floated her fingers like a daydreaming choir conductor. "He deserves a second chance. Especially since—"

Felicity cut her off with a sharp noise. "No gossip about my brother, on the off-chance that he connects with Noelle. It'd be much better if he shared his own story. He hasn't talked to anyone about what happened."

"Not even Jackson?" I blurted, swallowing the question I really wanted to shout, which was *What happened?*

I'd told Felicity I was okay with not knowing, but I wasn't. Not really. This was torture.

"According to Jackson, no." Felicity sucked in her lips and reached for a pile of printouts on the table. "But let's get on with the evening's program before Ida loses her mind."

Ida flashed her a grateful smile and passed out the papers. "Thanks for printing these out for me! We have a lovely, seasonal pattern this week. A Santa hat!"

"There's also an extra one on the reverse side," Felicity said, biting her lip. "A wild-card option if you don't feel like committing to a hat."

Papers rustled as everyone flipped their printouts.

Lola waved her hand. "It's me! Last time, Ida told us you can crochet practically anything, so I looked up this—"

"Lobster trap?" Deidre rotated the paper, trying to make sense of it.

"I think it's a vagina, Deidre," Eileen said.

"A *vulva*," Lola clarified. "I found the instructions online."

Ida frowned at the page. "This isn't what I'd usually—"

"But I knew you'd be able to pick it up on the fly and help us out if needed," Felicity said firmly. "We've done so many flowers already. All those lilies for that fundraiser. This is not that different."

Ida gave her a dirty look. "You never finished a single flower."

Felicity shrugged. "I'm more of an administrator."

"And how is this keeping things above board for your young daughter?" Ida demanded, her voice a low hiss as if they were having this unseemly conversation far from Kailee's ears, which were about two feet away.

Kailee huffed. "It's a body part! Relax."

Felicity glanced at her daughter, simultaneously proud and surprised. "Also, Lola has agreed to buy any vulvas we create for her shop. The money goes toward our weekly yarn purchases and Ida's bus tickets for her yarn shopping trips, which we happily subsidize. If anyone has a problem with that..." She looked around the table, pausing at Ida.

"I do think it's nice we have good quality yarn and a lovely selection of colors," Ida said, pink blotches on her cheeks.

I studied the printout, feeling nervous. "Ida showed me

the basics earlier, but I haven't practiced, and this looks complicated."

"Don't worry, dear! I'll show you!" Ida scooted closer, looking as pleased as she'd been on the bus.

A collective sigh passed through the room, and everyone settled into choosing yarn colors and reading the instruction sheets, swiping the occasional cookie off the plate.

I chose the vulva pattern. It was a lot smaller than the Santa hat and seemed more achievable.

I made sure Kailee, who sat on my other side, saw everything we did. She eventually took the hook and some yarn and copied my movements to get started. "By the way, I'm not taking this home with me."

Eileen turned to Deidre. "How's your daughter?"

"Still single." Deidre sighed.

"Don't worry! I was praying to St. Anne. She's the patron saint of single ladies," Eileen said reassuringly.

"Why are you praying to the saints? You're not Catholic," Felicity asked.

Eileen huffed. "Pastor Jeffrey said I should stop bringing up the single people in town. I was trying to pray for everyone."

"You were writing their names on the prayer cards and pairing them up on the bulletin board," Ida pointed out.

I exchanged a glance with Kailee, who suppressed a giggle. She seemed more relaxed now.

We kept working on our crafts, and after a while, the group split into smaller conversations, filling the room with a comforting cacophony of laughter and chatter. I could tell that the oldest—Eileen, Ida, and Deidre—went back decades and had about 200 mutual friends.

Felicity got into a deep conversation with Erica while Lola tried to coax more out of Kailee.

I'd never seen anyone's hands move as fast as Ida's. While the rest of us completed a few rows, she finished her first Santa hat, and Felicity decided it was time for the book club portion of the evening.

"First of all... how many of you actually read the book?"

Erica, Eileen, and Lola raised their hands.

Felicity gave them a guilty smile. "I admit, I got halfway. It's been a busy week."

"I finished right before my doctor's appointment," Lola said.

"Dr. Handsome?" Eileen asked, eyes sparkling.

Erica sighed. "He's so dreamy that I'm convinced he's secretly starring in some medical drama."

"I keep requesting him, but they always tell me he's not available!" Deidre grumbled. "The receptionist gave me a dirty look."

"The new doctor who started at The Hideaway Clinic is unfairly good-looking," Felicity explained. "Kind of like the guy on that cover."

I set down my painstakingly crocheted bottom layer of a vulva and picked up the book. "I started reading this last night, but I didn't get far."

"Just move on to the next one," Ida muttered. "You won't miss much."

"Ida would like us to stick to crafts," Felicity continued in her narrator voice. "But some of us are not that gifted with yarn, so we try to balance the scales with books and wine."

"I'm particularly gifted with wine!" Lola took a drink, grinning.

"Maybe Noelle should pay a visit to the clinic," Erica suggested. "We've done some detective work and concluded that Dr. Handsome is single."

Lola pulled out her phone, tapped, and handed it over. "Dr. Handsome."

I stared at the photo of a striking man in a white coat. "He looks like a cross between Superman and Superman."

"Exactly!" Lola enthused. "What small-town doctor needs cheekbones like that? He should be on billboards!"

"Maybe I need to break an arm or leg soon," I mused.

Felicity's reaction to my words was subtle, like a cold draft sneaking in through a crack. Was she jealous because I was expressing interest in someone other than her brother?

"He's going through a messy divorce," Felicity said under her breath. "In case that makes any difference to any of you."

"Have you been snooping through Dr. Handsome's trash cans?" Erica peered at Felicity like a schoolteacher with a twinkle in her eye.

"My company may have been cleaning his offices," Felicity added nonchalantly, clearly enjoying herself.

Even Ida leaned in, ears perked.

Lola grabbed a cookie. "Tell me more! Does he donate to charities? Pay his bills on time? I must know! Purely for research purposes, of course."

Felicity's mouth stretched into a salacious smile. "Well, for research purposes... I heard he overuses breath mints and never finishes a sandwich."

"That'd drive me nuts!" I said without thinking. "Such a waste."

Felicity gave a slow, approving nod. "Right? Fredrik licks the crumbs off his plate. Just saying. And the breath mints could be a sign of halitosis."

"Uncle Fredrik sits in a bookstore and has like one customer per day," Kailee pointed out. "He has enough time to eat every meal twice."

"Excellent point, Kailee!" Erica praised, making Kailee blush. "Maybe Dr. Handsome finishes sandwiches at home."

"Well, if I ever break my arm, it'll be the first thing I ask, right after I sniff his breath," I promised.

Everyone laughed, and I chuckled along with them. The level of matchmaking in this town was insane, yet I felt at home. These ladies were as curious as I was and not shocked by my unfiltered comments. Instead, they were entertained. They saw me as someone worthy of being matched with these men... even a doctor. Felicity, who was aware of my past, still seemed to like the idea of me being with her brother.

To my surprise, I managed to finish one vulva, which resembled the picture on the printout somewhat. We all helped clear the table, packing the yarn into bags Ida had lined up for us.

"Thank you, ladies!"

She beamed as we displayed our half-finished Santa hats and multicolored vulvas, then pulled on our winter coats and tumbled out the door. Oddly enough, I felt as tipsy as most of them looked as they staggered down the icy steps, holding onto each other. Even with my hard work the other night, every surface outside was uneven and slippery.

I'd come back another night, I decided. After I built

another snowman and did some other good deeds. I had ideas.

"Come back next week!" Ida urged. "You're making great progress. I think you're ready to try your hand at the Santa hat. Take some red yarn." She shoved a tightly coiled ball into my bag.

"Please do!" Erica echoed. "Hideaway holds the world record for the largest crowd caroling in Santa hats, and we're determined to keep it. We need every hat we can get!"

"I'll try my best," I promised.

A soft buzz went through my body. Tonight had felt good, like finding something long lost. Maybe it was a dry-land thing, this sense of connection. Like things were more permanent and meaningful, not fleeting.

But you're not here to stay. You're the fleeting one.

"Thank you so much for inviting me," I said. "You've made me feel... at home." I wasn't sure why I was suddenly fighting tears, but within seconds, I was at the receiving end of a barrage of hugs and kind words.

"I love your colorful style!" Deidre bellowed, tossing her rainbow scarf over her shoulder.

Erica's hug was so warm and tight that it transported me back home. "Welcome to Hideaway Harbor! I hope you find your forever home."

Kailee slipped the Grinch ornament into my mitten. "Sorry I took it."

"It's okay." I spread my arms, and she jumped in for a hug, too.

Eileen held my face between her fluffy pink mittens for a weighted moment. "She's as cute as a button! Fredrik would be crazy not to take a chance. The same goes for Dr. Handsome, but my money is on the Grump."

Felicity pulled me into an awkward side hug. "You want a man who knows how to finish… a sandwich."

With my heart permanently lodged in my throat and their laughter still ringing in my ears, I walked across the square, all the way to the bookstore.

It was the strangest feeling, falling in love with a town. I'd seen so many gorgeous, breathtaking ports. So many that they blurred in my mind into a generic holiday montage. I'd always thought a place somewhere might hit me with its beauty, and I'd feel that tug to settle in and make a home.

But it wasn't the snow-covered streets and Christmas lights that tugged at my heart. It was the people. It was the sense of meaning they derived from life around here, like it meant more than anything else that went on anywhere else.

How did they do it? How did they create this sense of meaning?

Maybe I hadn't been ready for it until now. It was safer to keep moving, letting people pass by and new people take their place, like ever-changing weather.

I'd never meant to settle so close to Bangor. It was too close to the past I was desperate to avoid. I would have been better off falling in love with Reykjavík or Key West. Anywhere else, really.

This was a dangerous path.

I unlocked the bookstore and stepped in, inhaling the scent of dust and ancient knowledge mingling with cinnamon. Where had that come from?

I'd get over this crush. But first, I'd hang some Christmas lights and crochet a few Santa hats.

CHAPTER 16

Fredrik

$\mathcal{I}$ saw the lights in broad daylight before I even parked my car. I was used to my store looking the way it did, a slice of sanity nestled within the obnoxious display of holiday cheer. A safe space for anyone who wanted to skip the season, like me.

And now it was ruined.

I'd noticed Noelle and Kailee whispering in the afternoons. They'd become very buddy-buddy since that crochet meeting. My niece had begun hanging out at Noelle's store instead of mine. I wasn't sure how Noelle had energy for her. I was watching a steady stream of customers pass my door on the way to hers all day long.

My store had seen a grand total of five customers since Monday, all looking for Christmas presents for people they didn't seem to know at all, and mostly buying nothing because I didn't have that one bestseller they thought was a safe bet.

On Friday morning, a day ahead of her usual schedule, Felicity had arrived for her weekly cleaning. She'd ordered another book for their book club titled *His Runaway Bride* and asked me three times if I was being nice to Noelle.

She was concerned about the stranger I was allowing to live in my store, rent-free. How much nicer could I be?

I stayed out of Noelle's way, arriving in the morning after she'd left and leaving before she returned so our paths didn't cross. I wanted her to have a home. A safe space she could return to after a long day at work without having to deal with another person.

It was a win-win, really, since I also needed to avoid temptation. If I was going to honor my promise and keep my hands off her, I couldn't be around her in a closed bookstore after dark. I was already allowing this woman to infiltrate my thoughts on a regular basis. She was the star of my fantasies. Every time I touched myself, I undressed her. Touched her. I couldn't stop imagining things I wanted to do to her. The nicest thing I could do was to keep my distance.

To make sure she felt at home, I'd cleared away my personal clutter and brought in all the linen I'd inherited from Uncle Glenn so she could choose her own. I wasn't hugely surprised when she chose the most colorful option, featuring red poppies.

And now, apparently, I was also allowing her to make my store window look like a beacon guiding sailors through stormy seas. So yes, my niceness knew no bounds.

I stopped in front of the window, squinting at the scene.

They'd warned me, very gently, of the big reveal, but I hadn't prepared myself for the sheer opulence of it. Red baubles and glowing stars hung from a huge Christmas tree made of stacked green books. Traditional Christmas lights framed the window, and the entire ceiling was covered in fairy lights, creating a backdrop reminiscent of an Indian wedding.

As I stepped inside, a bell above the door jingled. What had happened to my doorbell buzzer?

There were also customers. Plural. They walked between the shelves, browsed back covers, sat in my armchairs, and chatted.

Any sane business owner would have been ecstatic, but I couldn't summon any excitement, no matter how hard I tried. In its place was panic, like I'd walked in on burglars cleaning out my home.

Noelle stood behind the counter, ringing up someone's purchase as Kailee slipped the book into a paper bag and handed it over with a smile.

I spotted my sister in one of the armchairs, enjoying a coffee and some flaky pastry that stuck to her black pants and the chair.

"Happy Holidays!" Noelle called after the lady squeezing past me at the door.

It closed with that jingling sound again.

"What's that noise?" I asked.

"It's your new doorbell!" Noelle grinned, stepping out from behind the counter.

She wore a short pink skirt and orange leg warmers with a reindeer sweater and some sort of homemade Santa hat, like she was filming an aerobics video in the North Pole. "Wait, there's more!"

She clicked on a remote, and "Jingle Bells" blasted at full volume from a pair of speakers installed above the door.

"I said nothing that plays music!"

"I thought you meant *decorations* that play music."

"So you thought speakers were a safe bet?"

She turned off the music, looking a little hurt. "I haven't put together a proper playlist yet. I'll find something better."

God, no. I wanted no Christmas music. None.

Fighting nausea, I backed into the only empty corner I could find, behind the counter. "Why do I need a new doorbell?"

"For holiday cheer!" Kailee answered, joining the conversation. "It sounds a lot nicer than that buzzer you had before."

"It made me think of losing a game of Operation," Felicity added, dropping her empty pastry bag into my trash. "Every time I opened the door, it was like *Errr! You nicked an artery. You'll never be a surgeon!*"

They stood around me like a gang of school bullies, unified in their low opinion of me and my store.

I glared at Noelle. "Your store sells doorbells? And speakers?"

Christmas decorations were supposed to be temporary. She'd changed my damn doorbell.

Noelle blushed. "I had to go a bit further for the speakers. And your old doorbell is still there. We didn't break it or anything. It's just silenced."

I narrowed my eyes. "Who silenced it?"

Noelle and Felicity exchanged a look.

"Jackson," Noelle said. "He installed the speakers, too."

At least they got a professional for the job. I let my eyes wander across the transformed space. It didn't look like my business. It wasn't mine at all.

I didn't know where to go or what to do. On Saturdays, I usually hid out at my store just to avoid being invited anywhere else. Everyone knew my store was struggling, so it made sense to keep it open as much as possible.

Noelle's store, on the other hand, wasn't open on weekends, possibly because her employer didn't want to pay for more hours. She'd been busy all week and sold cheap plastic at hefty markups, so the owner must have already made a killing.

"So what do you think?" Noelle asked, her eyes hesitant, like she was afraid of the truth.

Before I even opened my mouth, I knew I was going to hurt her feelings, but there was nothing I could do. I felt cornered. Figuratively and literally. My chest was so tight I could barely breathe.

"It's different," I said.

"Good… different?" She blinked.

I looked around me, and an involuntary shudder ran through me.

"Come on." Felicity yanked me out of my seat, pulled me around a shelf, and pinned me with a look that said *remember what we talked about.* "You have customers! You have enough Christmas lights to get everyone off your back. Whether you personally like it or not is irrelevant. Noelle has done all the work, and nobody is asking anything of you. Other than, maybe don't be an asshole."

"I'm not being an asshole," I hissed back. "I let her live

here. I let her decorate. I'll learn to live with a new doorbell. What more do you want from me?"

"How about a *thank you*? The poor girl was up all night building that silly book tree! She and Kailee spent two nights picking the books and color-coding them, so the tree has that gradient. Did you notice that?"

"What gradient?"

"Exactly! You didn't even look! I understand that this is a challenging time of year for you, but she doesn't know that, and it's not her fault. And if you can't act like a human being, maybe tell her why. Because I'm not sure *I* even know."

I frowned, a heavy weight crushing my chest. "You know what happened."

My sister folded her arms. "Clearly, I don't. Because when Grandma died, Grandpa Charles fell apart, but then he pulled himself together, and somehow, he wasn't an asshole two years later. It wasn't permanent."

But Grandpa Neil had been an asshole all his life. And I was equally related to him.

"That's because..." The words stuck in my throat and burned like acid.

Felicity patted my arm. "That's okay. Don't tell me. But tell *someone*. Talk to someone. I'm saying this with all the love I can muster. You're becoming unbearable."

With that, she told Noelle farewell, gathered her coat and purse, and headed out, motioning for Kailee to follow.

Noelle waved at them, then looked at me with a mix of hope and nerves, like she was still expecting an answer to her earlier question.

How could she hold on to hope with someone like me? It would have been easier if she'd stormed out like my sister. Fighting was easier. Anything was easier than this.

Noelle took a tentative step closer, eyebrows raised. "What are you thinking?" The lights gave her dark hair a coppery halo.

She was so pretty I felt ill. Like I was failing. I wanted to be a better version of myself. Someone who could have acted the way Noelle expected. The way she deserved.

But I was the real, damaged version and overwhelmed by discomfort.

I scanned the room, looking for anywhere to retreat to. Anywhere I could sit and wile away the day pretending Christmas hadn't invaded my safe space. There was none. Not a square inch of my store was left unlit or untouched by her hurricane of seasonal magic.

I took a breath. "Are there any decorations left in your store? Are they all here?"

She let out a nervous laugh. "I got a new shipment yesterday. Mr. Young was over the moon that we'd sold out of so much that he closed another store and put all his eggs, or baubles, in one basket."

"You're quite the salesperson." I meant it as praise, or at least as neutral commentary, but it came out like an accusation.

She visibly recoiled. "It's easier to sell something people are looking for. If you stocked some popular titles—"

"Then I wouldn't be called *Hard to Find*, would I?" I shot back, exasperated. "I mean... the store wouldn't be called—"

"I get it. You carry collectibles. But maybe you could do a

bit of both. Get people in the door. Then they might find the rare books, too."

"How did you get these people in the door?" I asked, glancing over my shoulder. "I don't have any popular titles."

She bit her lip, looking out the window. "I've been telling everyone to come by on Saturday to see the lights."

"So they're here for the lights, not the books?"

Her eyes flicked to an older lady who was browsing the Russian classics. She gave a subtle nod and lowered her voice. "But they're staying for the books."

Not waiting for a response, she turned around and approached the lady. "Can I help you with anything?"

I wandered across the floor and slumped into a vacant armchair. I should have been the one offering help. I'd read most of the books, and I doubted Miss Popular Titles knew much about them. But I felt defeated and out of place.

I watched Noelle gesture and smile like she'd known the woman all her life. After a moment, the lady nodded, and they moved to the counter. Noelle turned the book in her hands, looking for something. After a moment, she raised it at me, shouting across the floor. "Hey Fredrik, how much is this? I can't find the price."

Was she actually going to sell something? I forced myself up from the chair and joined them, glancing at the gold-foiled copy of Dostoevsky's *Crime and Punishment* she'd brought down from the high shelf. "This is the first English edition," I explained to the lady. "It's... invaluable."

"No," Noelle countered. "It's *valuable*. Which means it has a price. Right?"

If someone bought it, my collection would be incomplete. There'd be a gap on my shelf, and things would change. My store would change.

"This is a bookstore, and these books are for sale, right?" she pressed, tilting her head.

I took a breath, my chest tight. "Twelve thousand dollars."

"Twelve thousand?" the old lady repeated, clutching her pearls. "I... I was only thinking of something pretty for my coffee table."

"It's an investment," Noelle said firmly, without missing a beat. "A statement piece. Nobody else will have anything like this. The beloved story of..." She looked up at me, waiting for me to fill in.

"...a murderer who's plagued by guilt and the prostitute who redeems him," I said grimly.

Noelle winced at my phrasing, but the old lady's eyes lit up. "That sounds like a gripping read."

Then buy the fiftieth edition, not the first, I screamed silently. But I forced myself to nod. "It is. Very poignant. Percipient."

The lady hovered, her wrinkled fingers skating across the string of pearls. Then she exhaled with sudden resolve. "Alright. I'll take it. I'll read it as it was meant to be read, when they first printed it."

I stood frozen while Noelle ran her credit card. She wrapped the book in brown paper and string—*where had she even found those?*—and handed it over like a prize.

The lady beamed, thanked us, and swept out into the snow.

The door jingled shut.

Noelle turned to me, wide-eyed, her mouth half open. "Did you just sell a twelve-thousand-dollar book?"

I could only stare. "No, you did."

"You gave the price," she fired back. "I just helped her see the value."

"I was bluffing!" My voice cracked. "I found that copy for two thousand. I know it's worth a lot more, but... nobody buys at that price!"

"Apparently somebody does," she said, her smile equal parts astonishment and triumph.

"Excuse me?"

We turned to find another customer, a younger woman in a white puffer jacket, holding a romance book. "How much is this one?"

Noelle smiled. "I know that one! Fifteen dollars."

She charged her, and we waited for her to leave, followed by two others. I walked through the store to confirm no more strangers were hiding between the shelves. Once I knew we were alone, I marched back to the counter, my chest about to burst.

"Okay, that's enough. You've done enough." I lunged at the door and flipped the sign on it to CLOSED. "Can we turn some of these off since we're not open?" I gestured to the lights. "Do you have like a sleep setting?" I searched for a switch or a plug but found nothing.

Suddenly, the room went dark.

"Better?" Noelle asked from the far end of the room.

"Yeah," I grumbled, then grabbed my jacket and left.

My heart pounded as I walked to my car. I sat inside, freezing, windows fogging, for a long time. I could have started the engine and warmed up, but I didn't deserve comfort.

She'd done this amazing thing. She'd made more money for my business than I'd made in months. And I'd turned off her lights.

I sucked.

CHAPTER 17

Noelle

When the bell above the door stopped jingling and Fredrik's dark shape disappeared through the window, I turned the lights back on. I had a feeling this would be the last time I saw the bookstore in its holiday glory, so I let myself enjoy it, even with my heart in tatters.

The room, once dark and dreary, now looked happy and inviting, as if it held treasures waiting to be discovered, rather than asthma attacks and tripping hazards. It was perfect. And all wrong.

I'd overstepped again, steamrolling past his boundaries without thinking. I could have just hung a few ornaments instead of tackling everything I thought was lacking. He had his reasons for keeping the store as it was. If he'd wanted a new doorbell, he would have installed one. If he'd wanted to sell more books, he would have ordered bestselling titles. I'd assumed too much, like the idiot I was.

If I hadn't been living here, maybe I would've realized it sooner. But I'd already begun thinking of the bookstore as "home," and that made me want to tweak things. On the ship, I'd arranged postcards around the mirror in a desperate attempt to personalize my space and make it a home.

But this isn't your home. It's his workplace.

I wondered how Fredrik lived. Did he own some dusty castle with servants carrying silver trays? His fondness for hideous shelves clearly wasn't about money. If he could keep this store open without selling books, there had to be something else. Investments? Inheritance? Whatever the truth, he was the world's most annoying puzzle, one I couldn't stop trying to solve.

A knock rattled the glass, giving me a start. I peeked out the window and spotted one of my Christmas shop customers, wearing a red beret and a brisk smile, with an oversized tote on her shoulder. I cracked the door.

"Hi! I'm here to see the lights!"

"I'm so sorry," I said. "We closed early. The store's not open for business."

"Can I still peek?"

I hesitated, then gave in. "Alright. Just for a minute."

She perused the shop, eyes wide. "This is something! Can I take photos? I'm Selah Brent, with *The Almanac*. This could be front-page news."

Before I could react, she had pulled out a camera and was clicking away.

"Oh no! You'll need Fredrik's permission," I stammered.

She waved me off. "That's fine. I'll get his sign-off later."

Perfect. I'd let Fredrik disappoint her. He was so good at it.

After she left, I locked the door and stared at the glowing room. The decision settled heavy in my chest. I had to take it all down. It didn't matter how much I loved it. Fredrik didn't, and this was his space.

Maybe I'd ask Selah for a photo, just for myself.

I took a deep breath, then took one last look before dismantling everything. I re-shelved the green books, wrestled the ugly brown bookshelf back into place, blocking the window, and dragged out the ladder to strip down the ceiling lights. My arms ached, and my mood sank. It felt like January. Like Christmas was over.

To console myself, I carried the string lights upstairs and strung them above my bed. When I switched them on, the room glowed soft and warm, and for a second, joy returned. Then the light caught on croissant flakes scattered across the floor. I sighed. I'd deal with that later.

First, I needed air.

I buttoned my coat and crossed the snowy town square to the pink door of Love at First Sip. Eileen poured me a dark roast called *The Heathcliff* and gave me a sharp look.

"You chose the tortured hero," she said. "Do you need to talk?"

"I'm fine." I forced a smile, holding my watery eyes wide so they wouldn't spill.

I couldn't badmouth Fredrik in his own town, no matter how hurt I felt. I'd brought this on myself anyway.

Sensing she'd come over to check on me, I left quickly and climbed Cellular Hill. The climb made my thighs burn and the cold air stung my lungs, but at the top, I was rewarded with a panorama of the inland bay. I counted three ships in the distance, plowing through the freezing water in brilliant sunshine.

A young couple had taken over the gazebo, kissing with more passion than I thought was possible in full winter gear, so I sat on the top step, taking out my phone. The teens paused their make-out session, but stayed, scrolling their phones. Maybe they didn't have anywhere else to go either.

Signal bars lit up on my phone, and I typed a message to Grace.

Hi Grace! I think I messed things up with my neighbor, the grumpy bookstore owner. I tried to be helpful, but I totally overstepped, and now I feel like the biggest idiot. Wish you were here. Wish we were back at sea, going somewhere warm. — Noelle

I HADN'T TOLD Grace I was sleeping above the store. She'd been thrilled to find me a job with accommodations, and I didn't want to sound ungrateful. If it weren't for her, I would have had nowhere to go. Nowhere but back home, back to Spencer. I shuddered.

When our last cruise had ended early, Grace had scored a job in Portland, working at an Asian restaurant. She'd always been better at spotting opportunities and creating them. She would cold call or drop in with her résumé and can-do attitude and find work. I desperately wanted to be like her, but the idea of dropping in unannounced to sell myself to an employer scared me shitless.

HANG IN THERE! We'll be in the Caribbean soon. Working on it xxx —Grace

RELIEF PRICKED MY EYES.

I texted quick reassurances to my mom and Holly, telling them I was fine on the "ship" and sorry to miss Christmas. The lie sat heavy, but I rinsed it down with the last of my coffee and wandered into town.

The Christmas market buzzed on Lobstah Lane. I browsed the handmade soaps, laser-cut town mementos, and knitted scarves, enjoying the atmosphere, then bought some yarn and a hot buttered rum before ducking into the library.

It was quiet there, away from the market. I picked up *The Illustrated History of Hideaway Harbor* and read about the town's Puritan roots. Of course, they were obsessed with Christmas. The more you're told not to celebrate, the harder you go when you can. Maybe that was why I couldn't resist redecorating Fredrik's store. I shared my defiant spirit with the founders of this town.

A white-haired man spotted me lingering over the page about the Locke Reserve. "You should go up there," he urged. "Toss a coin over the Wishing Bridge, see what good it does you."

"Don't badmouth the bridge, Barry!" the young librarian scolded, pushing her cart by with a grin. "I wished for my dream job, and here I am!"

Intrigued, I followed their directions to Locke Reserve. The ornate iron bridge arched over a babbling stream, heavy with snow and hung with dozens of padlocks. I crouched down, browsing the names carved on some of the locks. All these couples who'd been so in love…

Elora & Fredrik.

My breath caught. Fredrik wasn't exactly a common name. Could it be him? Was Elora the wife Felicity had alluded to? How had she died? The questions burned in my mind, but I had to be patient.

The coins at the bottom of the stream glinted in the sun. I threw in one more, fumbling for the right wish. What did I need? Forgiveness? Answers? A new brain?

The coin floated down and hit the pebbled riverbed.

I wish for a place I can decorate to my liking. A place that I can call home.

The words flooded my mind without warning, and I nearly choked on the sudden emotion.

WHEN I RETURNED to the town square, I was met by another holiday event in progress. Fire trucks sporting Christmas decorations. Dogs and their owners in matching Santa outfits and carols blasting from the main stage by the giant Christmas tree. It looked like a parade of sorts.

I weaved through the bustling crowd, smiling at the excited faces.

When I got to the bookstore, I found Felicity in an

armchair, typing on her laptop. She looked up. "There you are!"

"Were you… looking for me?"

"Eileen said you might need a friend. I don't have your phone number!"

"I don't know if it'll help. I only had a signal briefly this morning when I climbed the hill."

"Well, just in case." She thrust her phone at me until I typed it in.

The gesture made my throat tight. I was a visitor in this town. Her brother barely tolerated me. She had no reason to care.

"You put it all back," she said softly, glancing around.

I nodded. "Fredrik was so upset."

"You shouldn't have. He'll get over it. What did he say?"

"Not much. Just… looked like he was in pain."

"He is. But that's no excuse."

I almost asked about Elora but bit my tongue.

"Do you think it's okay if I still sleep upstairs? At least tonight?" My voice wobbled.

Her eyes widened. "Did he tell you to leave?"

"No. But if he's uncomfortable—"

"He's fine! I'll talk to him. Don't you dare go anywhere, okay? Fredrik's not the smoothest guy, but he's hardwired to do the right thing. You need to let him do that. Otherwise, he'll die of shame and self-loathing."

I almost laughed. "Guess we can't let that happen."

"Exactly!" She packed up her laptop. "I have to run. But I'll see you Tuesday."

"Tuesday?"

"Crochet club. Everyone's expecting you."

The wish from the bridge echoed in my chest. Maybe home wasn't a place you decorated. Perhaps it was this feeling. Being known. Being expected.

I SPENT the evening curled in the armchair, devouring the book club's romance novel. I also devoured an eggplant sub I'd bought on the way. It was from Little Italy, the cutest deli I'd discovered hidden in the basement next to the Sip. Fredrik might have been sour, but everything else in this town was delicious. My mood gradually improved, and I didn't even notice when it got dark outside. At some point, fireworks began popping outside the window, casting a festive glow across Fredrik's dark floor. It must have been the grand finale of the parade.

When my head started lolling on my shoulders, I got up and fetched the vacuum cleaner, making sure I left no crumbs behind. While I was still in cleaning mode, I decided to vacuum the bedroom as well.

I dragged the bulky appliance upstairs, plugged it in, and turned it on.

And then everything went dark.

The vacuum cleaner powered down with a sad whistle.

Shit.

I must have blown a fuse. The radiator let out a low hiss and a faint *tick-tick-tick* sound. The heat was evaporating.

Panic clawed my ribs. What now?

After a long and aimless search, I found the fuse box at the end of the hall. It had ancient ceramic fuses and a strip of masking tape with DO NOT TOUCH scrawled on it. My fingers hovered uselessly. Which fuse was which? What if I shocked myself?

Maybe it wasn't worth the risk.

I brushed my teeth and climbed into bed, piling all the blankets I had over myself.

Sometime later, I woke up shivering. My arm had snuck out from under the covers and felt like a refrigerated carrot. I wrapped myself in blankets, waiting for the warmth to return. The room felt like a chest freezer, and the tip of my nose was so cold I had to burrow entirely under the covers. Still, the chill pushed its way through, like an invisible snowman was hugging me.

Bracing myself, I got out of bed and pulled on my winter jacket, woolly hat, and mittens. I'd have to sleep in the Christmas store. It was the only way to survive. But when I went downstairs, I saw that the street outside the window was dark.

Was my fuse box connected to everything around me? It made no sense, but my tired brain was busy connecting dots like a conspiracy theorist. Either way, I had nowhere to go. If the power was out, the Christmas store would be equally cold. Fear gripped my chest as I returned to my bed and crawled under the covers in my winter clothes.

It was going to be a long night.

CHAPTER 18

Fredrik

$\mathcal{I}$'d just finished a bleak dystopian novel and coaxed my fire back to life when the landline rang so loudly that I nearly jumped out of my skin. The ancient thing only ever rang for emergencies or drunks who'd misdialed. Given it was past midnight on Saturday, it could be either.

"What?" I barked into the receiver.

"You need to get to the store."

"Who is this?"

"You know who it is." Felicity's voice was sharp enough to cut steel. "The whole block's out of power on Hideaway Ave."

"Someone strung up too many Christmas lights and blew the grid?" I guessed.

It wouldn't be the first time.

"Duh. That's not why I'm calling." She gave me a second to catch up, like a schoolteacher waiting for the slow kid in class.

"Oh shit. Noelle. She's there, right?"

"Why wouldn't she be? You didn't tell her to leave, did you?"

"No." After the way I'd acted that morning, I wouldn't have blamed her for bolting. But she probably had nowhere else to go.

"I know she's there. It's an old building. You know what that means—"

"Yeah. I'm on my way."

She didn't have to explain to me how cold it was outside and how quickly the inside temperature would drop without the radiators. The building was a hundred years old and leaked so much heat that pigeons had tropical vacations under the eaves.

Adrenaline surged through my veins. I pulled on boots, grabbed my coat, and within minutes, I was on the road. When I arrived in town, I saw my sister was right. Hideaway Ave loomed in eerie darkness, like one side of the town square had disappeared.

I parked, fished a flashlight out of the glove box, and hurried to the store. As I opened the door, I winced at the cool air. It was only marginally warmer than the outside.

I bounded upstairs and knocked. "Noelle?"

"Fredrik?" Her voice was muffled, shaky.

I opened the door and swept the flashlight over the bed. Nothing but a mound of blankets, shifting a little.

"I'm here," a voice said from underneath. "Trying to stay warm. I'm sorry."

"Sorry for what?"

Her woolly hat appeared, followed by her face. She shielded her eyes from the flashlight. "I blew a fuse, I think. I dragged all the lights into this room, and they're old-fashioned bulbs, not LEDs, and then I plugged in the vacuum cleaner and—bam. I've never been good at amp math."

"Amp math?" I stared at her. "What the hell are you talking about?"

She sat up, wrapping the blankets around her like a cape. "I don't even know how your fuse box works. I've never seen anything like it."

Cold dread washed through me. "You didn't touch it, did you? Don't ever touch that thing. It's older than me... It's lethal."

Her eyes widened. "I didn't touch it."

Relief pricked the back of my neck. My ancient FPE panel could absolutely kill someone. I should have given her a safety briefing.

"Why were you even looking at the fuse box?"

Her voice wavered, like she was trying hard not to cry. "Because I thought I caused all this. I mean, I plugged in the vacuum cleaner, and everything went dark. Doesn't that sound like me? Everything I touch turns to shit."

I almost smiled. Almost. "You can't black out a whole street, no matter what you plug in, Noelle."

"You sure? Because I feel cursed."

I could barely see her in the dark, but the way her voice cracked told me she was losing the fight against those tears.

Panic tightened my windpipe. She was staying in my store, and I'd made her feel this way. I was responsible. I had to fix this somehow.

"Thanks for checking on me," she murmured, burrowing deeper under the blankets. "You can go now."

"I'm not leaving you here."

"I'm fine." Her voice was tight and brittle and muffled by the blankets. She wrapped herself like a cigarillo, as if sheer willpower could keep the cold out.

"You're not fine. The temperature's only going to drop. I have a fire going at my house."

The bundle of blankets stilled. Then a small voice piped up. "A real fireplace?"

"No. My house is on fire."

"Smart-ass." She scoffed, but it was softer this time.

"And I have a sauna," I added.

Her head popped out, her eyes widening with interest. "A sauna?"

"The house has Finnish roots."

Her face lit up. "So do I! My grandma was Finnish."

"Then she'd approve. The original owner was a Finn. He built the sauna first, then the house."

"How old is it?"

"Two hundred years." Which was about how old I felt most days.

"I love old houses."

"Perfect. Let's go."

She got up, still hugging herself, shivering so hard her teeth clicked. "I should pack some things."

I stepped back into the hall while she threw a few essentials into a canvas bag. When she emerged, she looked small and fragile, bundled in winter gear but still shaking.

I cranked the car's heaters and seat warmers to the max. She slid into the passenger seat, arms locked around herself, trying to look normal. But the involuntary tremors gave her away.

"It's a short drive," I said.

"All good. You didn't have to—" She broke off as her teeth clattered together.

"Better safe than sorry."

As I steered up toward Locke Heights, I formed a plan. Step one: get her to my house. Step two: get her warm, fast.

I knew what I had to do.

CHAPTER 19

Noelle

So far, Fredrik's house had been shrouded in mystery. I'd pictured a grand old house, but reality still managed to surpass my imagination.

It was a mansion. Bigger than anything I'd ever lived in, or even regularly visited. If this place had Finnish roots, they weren't the cozy kind I associated with my Moomin-mug–collecting grandma.

Faintly lit by two spotlights flanking the iron gate, the house sat farther back from the road than its neighbors. Imposing, beautiful, and lonely.

As Fredrik parked at the front door, another violent shiver rattled through me. I couldn't control the jerks anymore, and I'd stopped trying.

He gave me a hard look. "Let's get you inside."

"I feel a lot better."

"And I'll believe you as soon as you can say that without your teeth clattering."

Holy hell. Why was my body betraying me like this? I felt the cold more easily than most, but I was sitting in a heated car. I should have been fine. Instead, winter had worked its way under my skin and taken over.

Fredrik slipped an arm around my shoulders and guided me to the front door. My tremors had turned me into a hunchback.

"I feel like an old lady being helped across the street by a young man," I joked.

"If it helps, I don't feel like a young man."

The entrance hall was dark and grand, and I kept shaking as we shed our shoes on a rack crowded with work boots and sneakers. My eyes snagged on a shiny new pair of Timberlands.

"Are those yours?" I asked, pointing.

He looked at me, puzzled. "Yeah."

"Why aren't you wearing them?"

I glanced at the pair he'd just taken off. The stitching had come off one, leaving a trail of thread across the floor. The soles were starting to peel off.

Something shadowed his gaze. "They're not my thing."

"What? Non-leaking shoes?"

"Brands."

"Then why buy them?"

I couldn't stop myself; the questions kept firing out, powered by nerves and shivers.

He steered me through a long hallway into a kitchen and dining room that looked like it belonged in a lifestyle magazine: gleaming countertops, wide-plank floors, and a farmhouse table. Everything was polished and beautiful, like a home for a family of seven that had been cleared for the photo shoot.

Fredrik, with his pained frown and his shadowy bookstore, didn't fit the picture at all.

Through a doorway, I glimpsed a living room with moody olive-green couches and a massive stone fireplace, with flames licking against glass doors.

"It's so beautiful," I murmured.

He flicked on the pendant lights, warming the space even more, then guided me to the couch. "Lie down."

I collapsed, still bundled in my jacket and hat. "What about the sauna?"

"You're too cold for the sauna." He wrapped me in a heavy blanket, brisk and serious.

"Too cold for heat? That makes no sense."

"You're showing signs of hypothermia. A sauna could stress your heart."

"I don't have hypothermia! I'm just cold."

"I'm not risking it. You could go into cardiac arrest."

I scoffed, trying to unclench muscles that refused to obey. "My grandma's sauna was mandatory. Like the sweet bread she baked... pulla... and liters of coffee. Nobody ever died."

My words slurred. Exhaustion tugged at me like anesthesia.

He lifted the blanket and pulled off my mittens, examining my hands. His fingers felt hot to my touch. "These are like icicles."

"I'm always cold. It's normal."

Ignoring my protests, he pulled off my boots and

removed my socks. "Oh my God. Your pinky toes... they're white."

I wiggled my toes. "Oh, don't worry. They do that. The blood always comes back. Eventually."

"This has happened before?"

"Sometimes."

He slid a hand under the loose leg of my pajama pants, feeling behind my knee. "You're too cold."

I wasn't sure if the shiver that followed was from the chill or his touch.

Suddenly, he stood up and stripped off his cardigan, shirt, and pants. I watched his clothes pile onto a chair, blinking at his muscled legs, my brain foggy.

"What are you doing?"

"Body heat," he replied, and immediately moved to undress me.

He peeled off the blanket and yanked at the sleeve of my coat, making me feel like a three-year-old girl's Barbie during a wardrobe change. Eventually, the coat came off, along with the sweater. I shivered in my tank top.

"Sorry," he said. "I have to remove some layers for this to work." He paused for a moment, glancing at my pajama pants.

"It's fine," I assured him. "Take off my pants. But could you leave my undies on? Unless you're offering pelvic exams."

His face turned red. "I wasn't going to... I mean..."

"And leave my socks on," I begged. "I need them."

He pulled my socks back on, lowered himself on the couch behind me, and wrapped the blanket over both of us.

"I'm not trying to make you uncomfortable. The safest

way to raise your core temperature is by transferring my body heat to you. We must let your arms and legs warm up slowly to avoid cardiac issues or blood clots."

I was fairly certain my core temperature was normal. My poor circulation was a genetic issue, and my arms and legs would eventually warm up. They always did. But I didn't feel like arguing. Not when his heavy arm landed on me and that woodsy, masculine scent filled my lungs.

Fredrik was spooning me, and for a moment, nothing else mattered. My arms and legs ached as blood began to flow, but I didn't mind the pain. It was overshadowed by the way his body spoke to mine. Like soothing whispers that settled my nerves and promised safety.

He held still, maybe out of respect or awkwardness, making it clear he wasn't going to take advantage of the situation. But I felt his deep inhale against the back of my head, and a breath he released was a little unsteady.

"Thank you," I said.

I wasn't dying of hypothermia, but the way he held me felt lifesaving. Like those hugs from the ladies in the crochet club, it flooded my body with warmth and faith.

He placed his hand on my thigh, then felt behind my knee again. "You're too cold."

I told myself he was assessing my temperature. Yet my inside flooded with warmth that had nothing to do with survival. I counted every part of my body touching his. That hand on my leg, his chest against my back, the arm draped around my shoulder. Each point of contact sizzled with energy.

We were so close, with our entire bodies pressed against each other. Every gust of breath against my neck sent confusing signals to my core, making it throb in anticipation. I was feeling warmer now, and as blood returned to my extremities, it also flooded between my thighs, making me throb. Did he feel it? Did he want me at all? I only needed to arch my back a little, push my bottom back, and—

I froze. That was definitely an erection. And not an emerging kind contained by his boxer shorts. This one poked me right between the butt cheeks, and I gasped.

"Sorry," he whispered. "I think I need new underwear."

He shuffled back and tucked it away, then returned his arm around me.

"What happened to your underwear?" I asked, smothering a grin.

"It's... not supportive."

"Don't tell me they're hand-me-downs from your grandpa."

He huffed a laugh. "Not used. But he did buy them for me. They've got a fly. It gets loose when they wear out."

"A dick flap?"

"Exactly."

I bit my lip. "If only you liked me, we could just skip the underwear. Might be fun."

He stiffened.

"I like you," he said roughly. "I thought that was obvious."

Fear battled curiosity, but curiosity won. I rolled to face him. He angled his hips away, but his arm stayed at my waist.

"Nothing's obvious with you," I said. "Trust me."

"You're going to make me say it, aren't you?"

"Please. I'm feeling fragile."

His eyes caught mine and held my gaze. "You're incredibly sexy, so this is hard for me. Very hard." He raised a meaningful eyebrow. "But I'm trying to do the right thing. Get you warm. Let you sleep."

I yawned right on cue. "I don't mind your erection. I think it's cute."

He scowled. "Erections are not cute. They're inconvenient, embarrassing, and sometimes useful, but never cute."

I giggled. "Yours is as cute as a button. If I had a ribbon, I'd hang it right now."

His glare could have set wood on fire. "You're warm enough if you can talk like that. There's nothing button-like about me."

"Oh no," I teased. "I didn't mean a small button. More like a giant novelty one you'd use at a game show."

He harrumphed, then checked my fingers again. "Yeah. You're better. Go to sleep."

He started to pull away, but panic shot through me. "Don't go."

His voice strained. "I think it's best we're not under the same blanket. But if you want me to stay…"

"I do."

He tucked the blanket tightly around me, creating a barrier between our bodies, then lay down again, hugging me from behind. His restraint made me ache more.

"Is it really the worst thing?" I asked softly. "That something might happen between us?"

His breath stirred my hair. "No. But I need you safe. Tell me if you feel sick, dizzy, anything with your heart. Promise me."

"Okay."

I didn't fully understand his concern, but I felt safe. Cared for. Anchored in a way that made my throat tight.

The tears came out of nowhere. I fought the first wave, but the second swamped me.

"Noelle?" His voice rasped at my neck. "What's wrong?"

"Nothing," I hiccupped. "I'm okay. I'm just…"

But words failed.

He tightened his hold, stroking my hair. "It's okay. Everything's going to be okay."

Gradually, the sobs faded. Through blurry eyes, I watched the flames dance behind the glass doors of the fireplace until they melted into darkness, and sleep carried me away.

I WOKE up to faint daylight seeping in through the windows. Thank God it was Sunday. I didn't have to open the store. I was cocooned under a layer of blankets, blissfully warm, but alone.

I rolled over, browsing the room through dipped eyelids, and suddenly jerked wide awake.

Fredrik *was* here.

He lay on the rug in front of the fireplace, huddled inside a sleeping bag, fast asleep. Red embers still glowed behind the glass. He must have kept the fire going all night. I didn't want to wake him, but I had so many questions.

Why wasn't he sleeping in his bed? Why was his house enormous? Did anyone else live here? Where was the bathroom?

I got up as quietly as I could and tiptoed around his

sleeping form. The polished wood floor felt cool even through my fluffy socks. He was lying on top of a woven rug, which must have been both hard and cold. How could anyone sleep like that?

The bathroom I found down the hall was gorgeous, with emerald-green tiles, a subtle chevron-patterned tile floor, and chrome fixtures. Luxurious but in keeping with the house's historical bones. It reminded me of the first-class lounge on the ship... or Spencer's family estate. I'd loved that house. In hindsight, I loved the estate more than I'd ever loved Spencer.

Lesson learned. I wasn't going to be dazzled by possessions ever again.

Still, I loved this mirror. And the fluffy terracotta towel. And everything else.

Compared to Fredrik's house, the bookstore was a gloomy cave. Which was the real him? The man in threadbare boots surrounded by dusty books, or the one with this quietly spectacular house? Did he come from money? Was he secretly loaded?

I wandered the first floor, careful not to wake him. If he stayed asleep, I could have a quick peek at the rest of the house and figure out what kind of rich he was. Middle-management rich? Richy-rich? Or the worst kind, who called themselves "comfortable"?

Spencer's mom had dropped that line a few times. The gratitude in her quivering voice was always genuine. She believed everyone who didn't have a million dollars in their checking account was painfully uncomfortable.

After ten minutes of tiptoeing around the first floor, I concluded the house was half-renovated. The contrast between the finished and unfinished rooms wasn't stark. It seemed he was restoring the house to its original glory.

There was no evidence of a sauna, though.

Once I'd satisfied my curiosity downstairs, I snuck upstairs. I discovered three more not-yet-renovated bedrooms with yellowing wallpaper, and a bathroom that gave me an idea of what the downstairs one might have looked like before. Off-white and boring. It was also freezing.

"Would you like a tour of my underwear drawer?"

Fredrik's voice made me jump. I slammed the cupboard door. "I... was looking for toilet paper."

"There's toilet paper right there." He pointed at the holder.

I shrugged. "Well... yes. I like to do spot checks. You don't hold a lot of stock."

"How much toilet paper do you need?"

I gave him an indignant look. "I feel safer seeing spare rolls."

"Like these?" He opened a door of a corner cabinet, revealing a stack of toilet paper rolls.

I gave an assessing nod. "Much better."

We both knew I'd been snooping.

"Breakfast?" He nodded at the stairs.

"Do you have coffee?"

"Sure."

He led me to the kitchen, and I admired its high ceiling, paneled windows, and pendant lights glowing over a huge island. It was beautiful, but too pristine, like a showroom.

"This is so gorgeous! I feel like I should move in and spend my life baking pies."

Fredrik gave me a look.

"I won't," I said quickly. "Just a feeling... inspired by your kitchen."

I had an instant urge to add color, even a bowl of fruit or a loud mug, but somehow managed to keep that thought to myself.

I trailed one finger across the counter. Dust clung to my fingertip. "You don't cook much, do you?"

"I live alone. What's the point?"

"What do you mean?" I protested. "You can fry an egg. Make a small pizza. Cook a big batch of curry and freeze it."

His brow furrowed as if I'd proposed he should churn his own butter.

"You want eggs?" He produced a carton of eggs, butter, cheese, and found bread from the freezer, lining them up on the kitchen island.

"Perfect! What do you normally have?"

"Coffee."

"Nothing else?"

"I usually just pick up something on the way to work." He stared at the ingredients as though they'd appeared by sorcery.

My disappointment over the store still simmered in the background, but it was mixing with gratitude. He'd saved me, again. He'd kept me warm all night, worried about my well-being. He deserved a proper, home-cooked breakfast. Moreover, his house deserved to be used. A kitchen like this should smell of butter and sugar and spices, not just exist, gathering dust.

"Can I make eggs?" I asked.

He sagged in visible relief, retreating from the counter. "Make whatever you want."

"Are you sure? What if I... move things?"

He dropped onto a barstool, elbows on the counter, and groaned into his hands. "I'm sorry. I know I've been an asshole."

I froze. "No. I overstepped, but don't worry. I put everything back in the bookstore."

His head lifted. "You put it all back?"

"Yeah. Did you not notice?"

"It was dark." He winced. "Now I feel worse."

Warmth swelled in my chest. I leaned over the island, close enough that my fingertips nearly brushed his. "Fredrik. I mean it. I went too far. And I'm trying hard not to make the same mistake again."

He looked wrecked, sitting there in corduroy slacks and a brown long-sleeved shirt that hugged him in unfair ways. The slice of his muscled forearm that showed made my stomach dip. I wanted to touch it.

I gripped the egg carton instead. "I'm going to open all your drawers until I find a frying pan. Is that okay?"

CHAPTER 20

Fredrik

I was despicable. Instead of helping her feel at home, I'd made her so worried that she'd taken down all the beautiful decorations and was now tiptoeing around my kitchen like she was expecting a slap on the wrist at any moment.

"Please touch and move anything you want," I said. "I mean it. I'm not that picky, I swear. I just have a complicated relationship with Christmas. It was this time of year, you know..." I made a helpless gesture with my hand, and Noelle nodded.

"It's fine."

I watched in silence as she familiarized herself with my kitchen, holding back any instructions so I didn't spook her. After a while, she seemed to relax, and the happy skip in her step returned. Humming a song I didn't recognize, she made scrambled eggs on toast and brewed a pot of coffee.

Seeing her in my kitchen made a lump rise in my throat. There was so much life in her that she filled the entire room with it. For a moment, I wasn't alone or sad or angry. She'd taken over my usual vibe, orchestrating this perfect Sunday morning atmosphere. One I didn't deserve.

When she handed me a plate and a cup, I struggled to find my voice. "Thank you."

"Do you use milk?"

"I don't have milk."

"Black it is," she concluded, clinking her cup with mine. "I'm good either way." She took a sip and grimaced.

"How do you do it?" I asked. "How do you settle into someone else's kitchen... or store? You look so at home."

You make my house feel like a home.

It took her a few seconds to deduce that I wasn't criticizing her. I was marveling at her.

Her smile took on a hint of sadness. "I've been on the move for a while," she said. "Your personal space becomes very small, and everything outside of it is just... facilities."

"I can't even imagine." I shook my head and forked some eggs into my mouth. "This is delicious. It's been a while. My ex... my wife... she didn't cook that much, but she loved to eat out. Sunday brunch, that sort of thing."

"What happened?"

Her question caught me off guard. "With what?"

"Sorry, I didn't mean to pry," she said, looking worried again. "Or maybe I do. But nobody's told me anything, and I can't stop imagining scenarios. Like really weird and horrific ones. If you told me, I could maybe stop scaring myself." She shot me an apologetic look.

It made no sense.

"Are you serious? You've been hanging out with my sister, Eileen, and the rest of the town's busybodies, and nobody has told you about my past?"

She shook her head so hard a piece of egg went flying from her fork. "No! I swear. They're super secretive about it and keep saying it would be best if I heard it from you." Her blush told me the rest.

Of course. The ladies had decided to set us up. It was the only reason anyone in Hideaway Harbor would withhold gossip. The town of true love, blah blah blah.

"You don't have to tell me anything, though!" Noelle rushed to add. "You don't owe me anything. I'm just—"

"Curious," I finished for her.

Her blush intensified, and her gaze briefly dipped to my lips.

"I will try to control my curiosity," she said, her voice a little husky. "I've learned my lesson."

"What lesson was that?"

"That... I tend to freak you out."

Freak me out?

"What do you mean?" I felt defensive.

Her eyes widened in panic. "No! I meant I tend to say the wrong thing. And do the wrong thing. Like I'm doing right now. My brain's not quite right."

She looked alarmed, like she'd done something unfor-givable and had to atone for it. Which, again, made no sense.

I gathered our dishes to put them away, joining her by

the sink. She looked at me like she didn't know whether to flee or cry, and my chest ached. I grabbed her hands to make sure she stayed. "You haven't done anything wrong, Noelle. I struggle with change, but that's my issue. I'm the fucked-up one here, not you."

The tears glistening in her eyes instantly spilled over, and I felt my own misting in response. "Who's told you these lies?" I asked. "Who said your brain's not right? Because I think you're incredibly smart and capable, and you haven't said half the nonsense most people spew on a daily basis."

Her words came out between sniffs and hiccups. "I ask insensitive questions... I can really kill the mood... and embarrass people. Spencer would be giving me this *look*, and I knew I'd done it again."

Okay. Something was finally making sense. In the absence of napkins, I handed her a kitchen towel. She didn't need my help with it, but I wanted so desperately to keep touching her that my hands lingered, tucking strands of her hair behind her ears and using my thumb to catch wayward tears. She didn't push me away.

"I know I'm no picnic," I said. "But this Spencer guy sounds like a gaslighting sociopath."

She looked up, confused. "Why would you say that?"

I let go of her face and took a step back. "It's a way to control someone. Make them feel like they're failing and pose as their savior."

"But... You've never even met Spencer! And I've already made *you* uncomfortable multiple times. Why would you assume there's something wrong with *him*?"

"Well... the gossip seems to be flowing freely in one

direction here because I've seen that article where he talked about you like stolen property. And it seems you're willing to suffer nearly anything, including living illegally at the back of a tiny store, to avoid going back to Bangor and facing him, right? A guy like that can't be good news."

She stared at the stove, frowning. "I'm not scared of him. But I don't want to face everyone. It's too awkward."

I saw the way her shoulders stiffened. She *was* scared. A lot more scared than she wanted me to know.

"Maybe you should be a little scared of him," I said softly. "It sounds like he's looking for you."

A visible shudder went through her, and she grasped the edge of the counter. "It's okay. I'll get back out to sea. He'll never find me."

My throat felt tight. My hand hovered in the air, desperate to touch her. "You can't live like that."

Her eyes were defiant. "Sure, I can. I like it."

She was lying to herself.

"You like being stuck in a floating hotel, occasionally sleeping with the fat, old pirate because of ship goggles?"

She smiled. "Yes. He's an excellent lover. He always takes off his hook before he handles my... business."

"That's considerate. Not mauling a woman is a sign of a great lover. Does he also shower?"

She laughed, but as her amusement fizzled out, her voice turned pensive. "I never slept with anyone on the ship. I only worked. It's great because you don't have to think. Everything is scripted, and you know exactly where to be at any given time. You just follow the program. But it's also tiring and monotonous, and I feel like..."

"Like what?"

"Like I'm not really home. I'm not even fully alive, you know? I'm existing in a vacuum."

"That's sad."

She smiled again. "That's why I love Hideaway Harbor! I can hide here, too, but it feels way more real. People are not passing by, pretending to live here. They *really* live here. There's past, present, and future, all happening in the same place. And everyone cares so much. About everything."

"They do." I sighed. "Hideaway is its own funny ecosystem. People get quite wrapped up in it."

"I've noticed."

I felt like apologizing for whatever she'd experienced so far, but she didn't look weirded out. She looked happy, like she wanted to be part of it.

"They love you here," I said. "They're like vampires when it comes to young blood arriving in town."

"I don't mind." She shrugged, smiling like she was more than happy to feed the vampires. "It's way better than constantly making people uncomfortable."

I shifted a little closer. How could I make her believe she wasn't making me uncomfortable? And even if she was, I probably needed it, like a good gym workout after sitting still. I needed discomfort. I couldn't even begin to describe what it meant to see her here, in my house. Like I'd just woken from a long sleep and suddenly noticed I was still alive, and time was running out.

"I bet I can make *you* way more uncomfortable than you've ever made me." I grinned, raising my eyebrows, and leaned so close that I felt the warmth of her body. "I won't even have to try."

It was a gamble. I held my breath, watching for her face,

ready to retreat if she showed any signs of true discomfort. But if she really thought she was the only one saying or doing the wrong thing, I could put her mind at ease.

Noelle held my gaze for a long moment, her disbelief slowly morphing into fiery excitement. She flashed me a smile she probably intended as wicked. It was adorable. "You're on! No one beats me at awkwardness!"

"Great! Let's heat the sauna."

CHAPTER 21

Noelle

J found it hilarious that Fredrik thought he could make anyone uncomfortable. He was the most reserved guy I'd ever met. Every word out of his mouth was carefully considered, and most of them probably never left his lips. He always paused before speaking.

But the way he smiled at me, presenting this ridiculous challenge, made my entire body vibrate. I knew I was witnessing a rare phenomenon, like one of those flowers that bloomed for only a few minutes at midnight. I couldn't peel my eyes off his pearly white teeth. Had I ever seen him smile before? I couldn't remember. He was gorgeous.

I thought he'd try to embarrass me with words, maybe to make me blush, but he'd chosen a different tactic. The sauna. It was a mistake. I'd grown up with Finnish sauna culture. He couldn't bring out anything that would rattle me.

Half an hour later, I followed him across the snowy backyard. My memories of Finland were set in summer, but the snowy scene felt idyllic and equally Finnish. Maybe even more so.

"Here's the changing room," he said, opening the door to a log building.

The heat hit us at the door, radiating from behind the glass door leading to the sauna. Showers were behind another glass door. The changing room looked traditional, with wooden benches and hooks on the wall, and towels stacked in one corner.

"I'll let you go first," he said, hovering at the doorway. "But you should consider rolling in the snow. It's a tradition. And it's also customary to go to the sauna fully naked."

A laugh bubbled out of me. If he was blushing over that line, I'd already won this contest. "If we're going with tradition, you'll strip right now and join me in there."

"What?"

I pulled off my sweater and tossed it on the bench. "I told you I had a Finnish grandma. Mummi. We visited her in Finland twice. She lived by a lake and had a sauna. It wasn't fancy like this with running water, but she heated it every day. We'd all go in together, naked. I'd swim in the lake naked. I loved it."

He shrugged, dropping the bag he'd been carrying on the bench. "Noted."

With a funny smile on his face, he took off his jacket, then pulled off his sweater and thermal shirt. He had a different energy today. More alert and intense, the corners of his mouth tugging up with ease I hadn't seen before. I stared at his muscled chest, suddenly unsure about my bravado. We were playing chicken and considering how much I wanted to trace the dark hair leading down his stomach, there were worse things I could be than a chicken.

But I couldn't back down. I pulled off my pajama bottoms and tank top, throwing them on top of the sweater. Last night he'd seen me in my lace panties, but that wasn't the full picture. I'd been running low on clean laundry and paired my purple panties with an orange sports bra. A terrible combo if there ever was one. Good thing we were just friends playing a silly game.

Fredrik turned to face the wall, yanking down his corduroys.

"Is my mismatched underwear making you uncomfortable?" I asked.

"What? No!" He angled his body slightly toward me but still wouldn't look at me.

His skin was pale, but his muscles showed signs of use. "Do you work out? Your trapezius is really pronounced." Without thinking, I dragged a finger down his muscled back.

God, stop it, you total perv.

I pulled back my hand, clamping my mouth with it. "This is what I mean. You'll never outdo me in awkwardness."

He laughed. "Jackson drags me to the gym, and I split a lot of firewood. I think your underwear is cute."

He worked hard to force those words out, looking slightly past me, and it made another laugh burst out of me.

"Eyes on me, Fredrik," I said, unhooking my bra. "If you

want to make me uncomfortable, you don't get to be a gentleman. It's time to leer."

His gaze snagged on my bare chest, his face red as a beet. "This is a dangerous game, Noelle. You have no idea..."

"It's a game you will lose," I exclaimed, dropping the bra on the bench and wiggling out of my panties.

I hadn't shaved for a while, adding to my genuine embarrassment. But nobody would beat me in this. I was the queen of awkward.

"Sorry I'm so hairy," I blurted. "It's a great way to keep warm in winter."

Fredrik allowed the briefest glance, coughing into his hand. "It's not like I shaved for this."

"Shall we?" I asked, gesturing at the sauna door.

"Oh. I almost forgot." Fredrik dug into his bag and pulled out a tied-up bundle of something. Branches?

"Is that a *vasta*?" I asked in awe. I remembered the Finnish tradition of using birch branches in a sauna.

"I thought it was a *vihta*. I froze a few of them last summer," he said. "I thought I could make you uncomfortable by suggesting that you beat yourself with birch branches, but I guess that failed, too."

"No. This is amazing." I grabbed it off him and brought the bunch of wet, slightly frozen leaves to my face. "I love the smell."

"We still need to warm it up."

I handed it back to him. Two loose leaves stuck to my chest. As I peeled them off, I noticed his eyes following my hand. At least he wasn't looking at the walls anymore. I spent a moment brushing leaves away, giving him a chance to look. When was the last time he'd even looked at a live woman? He seemed to exist in a sad little world, either alone in the bookstore or in his giant, empty house.

"I told you I could make you uncomfortable." His thick voice caught my attention.

He glanced down and my gaze followed, landing on a huge erection. He gave me a curt nod and covered it with the *vasta*.

"Why do you think I'm uncomfortable?" I asked. "I'm flattered. I mean, if that's for me."

"What do you mean? You're naked." He let out a frustrated sound. "I've never seen anything this hot in my entire life. You have an unfair advantage in making me look like a fool. The least you can do is forfeit the title of the most awkward person in the room."

"Never," I declared. "I'm just as turned on as you are. It's not as obvious, but you can easily confirm it."

I was not backing down. Not now. Not ever. I stepped a little closer. "Look at my dilated pupils." My gaze caught his eyes, noting how dark they were, the deepest evergreen forest. "Check out my nipples." His gaze dipped lower, taking in the hard peaks that tightened further under his stare.

"It's dim here, and a little cold," he said, grabbing the sauna door handle. "We should—"

I yanked his hand off the door handle. "There's one way to confirm, unless you'd rather be a gentleman."

He swallowed hard. "I don't think we need to go that far."

It was cold, but my insides were on fire. "I'm not losing this game, Fredrik."

I didn't even know what the game was anymore. I only

knew we were naked, standing inches apart, and I was slowly dragging his hand down my body. He shifted closer, his breath hot against my forehead.

I guided his hand onto my belly, then lower. As his fingers reached my slit, we both gasped. I kept my chin up, staring at him as I guided him right in. His mouth dropped open, and he made a small, strangled noise as his middle finger dipped in, diving into a pool that ended all arguments.

"Oh my God." He sucked in sharp breaths. "Oh my God."

I'd never done anything this brazen. I'd reached peak embarrassment, and the next step would probably be spontaneous combustion. But he made me brave. I felt so safe with him that I could say and do unimaginable things. Playful, dangerous things.

Fredrik's finger flexed, and he groaned. "You play dirty, Noelle."

"I play to win."

I waited with bated breath as he held still, a battle raging behind his eyes. I wanted this, but I didn't know if he really wanted me. Maybe he just wanted to get through this moment of weakness without making a mistake.

I released his wrist, worried that I was forcing him. His fingers remained, hovering over the most sensitive part of me, not touching. He couldn't take the leap.

Releasing a deep sigh, I turned to open the sauna door.

"Where do you think you're going?" His low growl stopped me cold.

He closed the sauna door and backed me against it, trapping me between his arms. My body pressed on the warm glass, and the bundle of birch leaves hit the floor with a wet thud. "I told you this is a dangerous game. You don't get to back out anymore."

"Why would I?" I batted my eyelashes innocently as desire pooled through me.

The deep, resonant rumble of his voice shot right into my core. "If you want me to be a gentleman, you need to tell me right now. Because I'm not sure I can access that part of myself anymore."

"I like you like this," I said breathlessly. "I like you a little out of control."

He dove for my neck, kissing my collarbone, then dragged his tongue down to my breasts. "You're so perfect," he mumbled before sucking in a nipple.

I'd done it. I'd tapped into the primal part of this man, and it was even better than I'd imagined. He trailed hot kisses down my cool skin, running his hands down my body, exploring every bit of me like he'd never seen anything like it. Worshipping every curve and dip along my skin.

"I'm on the pill," I whispered as he returned to kiss my lips. "I've been tested."

"Me too," he said. "A long time ago. It's been a long time."

"Too long," I said. "Come here."

He aligned the tip of his erection at my opening but held there, moving back and forth ever so slightly. Sparks erupted behind my eyelids. When he pulled away, I moaned. "No. Don't turn into a gentleman now. It's too late."

His mouth curved. "I just want to do this right." He grabbed my waist, lifting me to sit on a nearby bench. "Can I taste you?"

I anchored my toes on the wood floor and my fingers

around the edge of the seat, letting my legs fall open as he fell onto his knees, diving between them. His tongue worked magic, rhythmic and hungry. Circling and teasing, soft and reverent. I wanted to hold back until I saw him lose control, but I couldn't. He'd decided to take care of me, so that was what he did. Gently. Patiently. Like he was still a gentleman who couldn't be anything else.

The scent of birch leaves and hot wood lingered in the air, mixing with something sweet and primal rising from us. He cupped my thighs, holding me in place between his mouth and the wooden seat, and I felt my release building. It was disorienting and beautiful, like too many flavors dancing on your tongue all at once. With every touch, I was transported further from the confusing reality, deeper into a space beyond where nothing else existed. Only me and him, and this moment.

It was a moment I'd barely been brave enough to imagine. Fredrik between my legs, devouring me. How was he so good at this? So precise and careful, yet determined, responding to every little sound I made, making me squirm, then finally applying more pressure, growling like an animal.

I wasn't sure what sent me over the edge, but the release hit me with such force I nearly fell off the bench, every muscle contracting as I rode the wave, finally collapsing forward against his shoulder. It felt so good. So raw. So unfiltered.

When I came to my senses, I reached for him. "I need you."

He pulled me to my feet and against his chest. "What do you want?"

I reached to open the sauna door, breathing in the hot, dry heat. The bottom step was a freestanding stool, so I pushed it aside to make room and hopped onto the middle bench. It wasn't too hot with the door open, and I was sitting at just the right height. "I need you here, Fredrik."

As he stepped in, I spread my thighs, gasping at the size of him.

He aligned himself between my legs, and I felt the tip of him brush my thigh. "Are you sure?"

I wrapped my fingers around him, pulling him closer. "You need this too. Trust me."

When he thrust inside me, I gasped out loud. He filled me so perfectly, so tightly, leaving no room for movement or questions. We held there for a while, breathing heavily, suspended in that sweet ache. He wrapped his palms around me and moved a little. "Does it hurt?"

"No," I whispered, dropping my mouth against his shoulder. His skin tasted salty and sweet. "It's perfect. Give me more."

He pulled back slightly and pumped into me again, sending sparks up my spine. With each thrust, I met him harder, teetering at the edge of the seat, relishing that point of contact and the intense sensation. My body crackled like it held an electric charge. I couldn't hold back, moving with him with wild abandon.

"Noelle. Slow down. I can't—"

He tightened his grip around my bottom, trying to hold still. I felt him pulsing inside me. I could tell he wanted to last longer, but I couldn't hold back any more than he could. Another orgasm was gathering momentum, coiling tighter inside me. I had to move.

"It's okay," I whispered, rolling my hips.

He groaned, and I felt his release erupt inside me. My body followed. I clutched his shoulders and moaned into his chest, shaking uncontrollably, riding the second wave all the way through.

As my brain returned from its journey through the stars, a hazy thought emerged. We'd crossed a bridge we could never uncross, like fastening one of those padlocks and throwing away the key. What did it mean?

After a moment of panting, he pulled away, looking dazed. Fear hit me like a whiplash. Was he going to apologize? Was he going to talk about the future? I wrapped my hands around his neck and pulled him in for a kiss. After a moment's hesitation, he kissed me back, relaxing into it.

"Don't say anything," I whispered quickly. "Please don't say it was a mistake. Let's not think too hard yet, okay?"

"I'm not thinking at all. My brain is mush."

"Good. Because I had two incredible orgasms and that never happens, so I don't want anything to spoil this moment."

"It never happens?" He looked concerned.

"No. Unless I do it myself. And I'm not that good at it."

Truths were slipping out again, my filter completely gone. And now he was looking at me with that unnerving intensity, all soft and warm and open. Like he was about to confess something I wasn't sure I could take. I pulled him closer, burying my face in the crook of his neck. He smelled like birch trees and woodsmoke and sex. I was losing the real game of chicken. I was the chicken. I couldn't meet that gaze.

"That's a shame," he murmured against my cheek. "You deserve thousands."

CHAPTER 22

Fredrik

*S*tay.

Of all the things I wanted to tell her, that one word hovered on my lips, desperate to be released. I *needed* her to stay. The thought of her finishing that temporary job and sailing away was so painful that I had to push it out of my mind.

We barely knew each other, and getting this attached wasn't going to end well for me. Jackson could sleep with someone and move on. I couldn't, which was why I didn't.

The aftereffects of the best sex of my life lingered, making it harder to see reality for what it was. She didn't want to see it either, clinging to me like she was already saying goodbye, climbing on board that ship.

"My wife died," I said.

Her eyes flipped open. "I figured."

"But that's not the whole story."

She nodded, lips pressed together like she was holding back a flood of words. I stroked my thumb over them. "It's okay. I'll tell you, and you can ask all the questions. Whatever pops into that wild, beautiful head." I tapped her temple, and her face relaxed a little.

"I'm so scared I'll offend you."

"Go ahead. It's not the end of the world."

I closed the sauna door, and we climbed onto the top bench. I threw some water onto the stones, and she moaned, inhaling the hot steam with her eyes closed. Maybe it took her back to her childhood. I'd ruin her mood with my story, but I had to get it off my chest. She needed to know, even if I risked her running away for good.

"My wife didn't like living here. We lived by the harbor back then, but she didn't like Hideaway. There wasn't enough going on. She put a lot of effort into her clothes and hair and makeup, and there weren't that many people to show it off to. She was beautiful. I think she needed a bigger audience. So we'd go to Bangor or farther. She loved the theater and figure skating. And shopping."

"She bought those shoes!" Noelle clamped her mouth, looking mortified. "Ignore me."

"You're right. She bought me clothes and dressed me up. I went along with it, but I never felt like myself. Then my grandpa broke his leg, and I spent a lot of time taking care of him at his house. My grandma had died a few years earlier, and he lives in a cabin outside town. Elora hated going there, so she went out with friends while I hung out with my grandpa and his brother, Glenn, who used to own the bookstore. He would come over to help, and we'd talk about books. They were very different. My grandpa was a fisherman, just like my dad. Between them, they've probably read two books, and they're proud of it."

"Really? I thought you'd come from a long line of academics or aristocrats or something."

I had to laugh. "Definitely not."

"But this house… I thought it was a family place. I saw black-and-white photos of guys who totally look like your ancestors."

She must have taken a thorough tour of my house while I slept. My heart skipped at the thought. She wanted to know me.

"It is a family place. It used to belong to my great-uncle Glenn. He was a reader and a businessman. He got wealthy but never married. There was a rumor he was gay, but he never came out, so I don't know. He was private but very smart. We always talked about books."

"What happened to him?"

"He died suddenly. He just fell down and never got up. I found him two days later."

"That's horrible!"

I nodded. "Glenn was old, but it happened so suddenly. Then I found out he'd left me this house and his bookstore. I inherited everything. Until then, we'd been renting a two-bedroom apartment in town. I worked for the family business, handling the books and assisting on fishing trips. My dad expected me to take the reins. I went to college and got my useless English degree, to "get it out of my system," like he said. That's where I met Elora. I think she had a romanticized idea of being a fisherman's wife in a remote coastal town, but then the reality hit, and she wanted out."

"You go out for days, don't you? For lobsters."

"Yeah. It's pretty brutal. To be fair, I didn't want that life either. But I liked being back here. It's home. And I had Glenn and his bookstore, and I spent my spare time there. I never thought I'd inherit it. It didn't even cross my mind."

"That's wild! You have one person in town who gets you, and they suddenly die, and you inherit everything they owned."

I let out a heavy sigh. "I'd rather have someone who gets me than all their stuff. Every time."

"Me too," she said, her voice breaking a little.

The heat was evaporating, so I ladled more water on the stones. Noelle fetched the bundle of birch branches from the changing room floor and heated it over the stove. I took it from her and gently whacked her back with it. She did the same for me, sending a shock wave down my spine. The smell transported me to the summer.

"The money made everything worse," I continued. "Elora wanted to move. She wanted us to sell the bookstore and the house and buy a fancy apartment in Bangor, on Broadway. That last summer, we went to so many open houses."

"Spencer had a place there! I can't imagine you..."

"Neither could I."

"So you found fault with everything?" she guessed.

Did she really know me that well? I nodded.

We sat for a while, breathing through the puff of hot steam. The piles of fresh snow behind the small window were starting to look more and more appealing.

"How did she die?"

The question jolted me. Not because it was insensitive, but because I hadn't landed on an answer that felt true. "She had an aneurysm. It was sudden, just like Glenn. Except she was healthy."

"I'm sorry."

"We'd been fighting, and she ran off to Bangor. I thought she was seeing someone there, but I never found out. I accused her of cheating. I yelled at her, and she stormed out. And then I heard a crash. She'd lost consciousness and driven into the gate."

"That's awful! That's like someone destroying a book you were reading." She stared at the stove. "Like being in the middle of a story and you're holding the only copy, and then poof! It's gone, and you'll never find out how it ends."

I'd gotten condolences up the wazoo and heard every platitude under the sun, yet nobody had come close to voicing my pain. I hadn't told them the whole story, either. You weren't supposed to speak ill of the dead.

"That's exactly how it feels."

She placed her hand on my thigh. We were both covered in sweat now, our faces red from the hot air and steam. "Did you ever try to find out? About the cheating?"

"No. She died the perfect wife. What kind of monster takes that away from someone who can't even defend themselves? And I might have been wrong."

"Did anyone strange come to the funeral?"

A sad smile broke through my inner turmoil. "I didn't notice anyone, but I wasn't looking, either."

Noelle huffed. "You deserve closure! People shouldn't be allowed to die like that and leave all these questions behind. It's not right."

"How would you avoid that? You'd have to die immediately after writing a tell-all memoir."

"But you shouldn't have so many secrets!" She sounded so offended on my behalf that I almost laughed.

"People die and take things to their grave all the time."

"But…"

I leaned my shoulder against hers, feeling lighter. "I'm sure this would be even harder on someone as curious as you."

She buried her face in her hands. "I'm being a total ass right now. I'm sorry. My condolences! But I was expecting a sad story, not this… injustice."

"It is a sad story," I said. "About me."

It was a sad story of how time had stopped for me. How hard it was to try anything. To believe in anything. How I'd become this shell of a man who hid from the world and all the extravagant things that reminded me of Elora. She wasn't here to dress me up and drag me outside, so I never left the house. She wasn't here to tell me how she thought we should spend the money, so I never spent a dime, except on renovations. To honor Glenn by looking after his property. But when it came to what I wanted, I couldn't take action. It felt as if my assets had been frozen because our fight was left unresolved.

"I caused it." The words tumbled out like bubbles rising underwater. "I made her so upset that she burst a blood vessel. She was so angry."

She frowned at me. "It's like you're desperate to take the blame."

"It's true. Anger can spike blood pressure, and that can cause an aneurysm."

"What were you supposed to do? Let her carry on

cheating because she might otherwise burst a blood vessel? Did you know she was at high risk?"

"No. Nobody did."

She shook her head, staring at the sauna stove. "You can't take the blame for that."

"You have no idea what I'm able to blame myself for," I muttered.

I was so hot now that sweat was dripping from my eyebrows.

"You feel like rolling in the snow?" I asked.

She followed me into the changing room. I cracked the door leading outside, making sure no one was in sight. My evergreen hedge was tall and thick, blocking the view to the neighbors' backyards, but there was a tiny chance someone, like my sister or Jackson, had come for a visit. Apparently, my lack of communication occasionally led them to worry that I'd died, so they ventured over uninvited.

The backyard looked empty and quiet, covered in a shiny new layer of snow. I opened the door fully, and Noelle yelped behind me.

"Oh my God, it's arctic. I've only ever gone from the sauna to the lake in the summer."

"The trick is to be quick." I drew a breath and summoned my courage. "Especially you, with your toes and fingers that turn white."

It seemed, with her watching, I had a lot more courage. I launched myself into the nearest bank of snow, rolling over. The cold hit me like an electric shock, but I sat up, forcing a smile. "It's actually refreshing."

Standing in the doorway, naked, her skin glowing pink

and her eyes huge, she was the most beautiful woman I'd ever seen. "I'm a bit scared."

I wasn't feeling the cold quite yet, but I knew it was only a few seconds away. I stood, shaking off clumps of melting snow, and reached out my hand to her. She took it, and I pulled her closer, against my chest.

"You feel nice and cool," she whispered, her breath erupting in clouds of steam. "Can I just roll around on you?"

"Sure."

I was feeling the cold now, but I didn't care. I could tell she wanted to be brave. I led us to another bank of snow.

"I'll lie down first," I said, trying to figure out the best way to ease her in, but she wasn't having it.

"No, I have to just... take a leap."

Noelle drew a breath, closed her eyes, and jumped. At first, she nearly disappeared into the snow, thrashing and squealing. It took me a moment to realize she wasn't excited. She was panicking, struggling to get up. Without thinking, I jumped in, grabbed her by the waist, and yanked her up.

"That was awful," she said, panting and shivering. "I feel like I'm dying."

She clung to me as we walked back into the sauna. Her skin felt freezing against mine. How could anyone get so cold in such a short time?

"This thing you have... the way your fingers and toes looked last night. It's pretty severe, isn't it?" I asked, rubbing her back as we sat on the highest bench and threw more water onto the stones.

She sounded close to tears. "Yeah. It's called Raynaud's. It messes with the circulation in my hands and feet. I get cold easily, and it hurts so much. It feels like I'm being stabbed. My fingers and toes go white, and I have to spend a long time warming up."

"Why didn't you tell me?"

"I didn't want you to worry. And I don't want to be a wuss."

"You're not. You're incredibly brave."

I would have never described being cold the way she did. Something dawned on me. "You must have been in a lot of pain last night?"

"That's just what cold feels like. I think I'm more suited to warmer climates." She tried to smile.

"No kidding."

"But I like the sauna. Here I can finally get warm."

I threw more water onto the stones and pulled her closer. It was stiflingly hot in the sauna now, but her skin still felt cold and clammy. "I promise I'll never ask you to do that again."

"It's okay. I can take the pain."

"But I don't want to cause you pain. I want to heat the sauna and keep the fire going and make sure you're okay, always."

The words rushed out with more meaning than I'd intended, but I didn't want to take them back. Instead, I held her tighter, hot steam burning my lungs.

I was falling for a woman whose body couldn't even take the climate in the place I called home. It was like bringing home an exotic plant I had no idea how to care for. What if she wilted and died like every other plant I'd ever had?

"You grew up in Bangor, right?"

"It's ironic, isn't it? I should have been born in the

Caribbean!" She rubbed her legs. "That's one reason I loved working on the cruise ship. Everyone would be complaining about the heat, but I mostly enjoyed the lack of pain."

"So… you're going back?" I held my breath, feeling like the biggest fool.

Was I expecting her to change her plans because we'd seen each other naked? Because we'd had mind-blowing sex? And why was I assuming it had been mind-blowing for her? We'd both been in desperate need, I knew that. But it didn't mean she was moving in for good.

She looked up, her eyes glowing with hope and sadness and something else. I couldn't read them. I had to wait for the words.

So I waited, with my heart in my throat.

CHAPTER 23

Noelle

as he asking me to stay? Or checking my schedule to see how long we could keep seeing each other? Because I wanted to keep seeing him. I already craved more. But I couldn't think past today or maybe tomorrow.

"I don't know," I said. "I'm waiting to hear from my friend Grace. She's organizing our next gig. I just... go along."

The way he looked at me made my insides twist into a knot. "You don't see a future for yourself on dry land?"

Thinking about staying felt like cracking open a heavy door that hadn't been opened in a long time. If I stopped moving, if I started building something here so close to Bangor, word would eventually get out. Spencer would find me, and I'd have to face everything I'd left behind.

"Do we have to talk about the future?"

He shrugged. "I guess it'll happen, whether we talk about it or not."

"Exactly. We might as well enjoy life and…" My gaze dropped to his crotch. "Each other?"

"So we're together?" He sounded a little wounded. Worried.

"You want to be together?" I looked at him in disbelief.

This man had become my reluctant helper and landlord. And now he wanted a relationship?

He huffed, frustrated. "Yes! I want to be with you, Noelle. Exclusively. Am I not being clear?"

"Not… publicly, though?" I clarified.

He looked conflicted. "I don't like the town knowing my business, if that's what you mean. But that won't stop me from dating you."

"Maybe we can be together on the down-low?"

"I don't think you can do anything on the down-low." A smile warmed his face, and his eyes crinkled at the corners. "And I love that about you."

It was true. I stood out everywhere I went like a multi-colored sore thumb.

I tried to laugh. "Yeah, I'm working on that." I climbed down the steps. "I need a shower."

"Go ahead." He nodded, casting one last look. A weighted one that made my stomach swoop.

I showered, washing my hair with peppermint shampoo I found. I got dressed while Fredrik showered, grateful that I'd managed to pack a change of clothes in the middle of the night. Feeling fresh and relaxed in flowy terracotta pants and a green sweater, I waited for him, combing my unruly hair with my fingers. Our heads wrapped in towels, we crossed the backyard and went back to his house. Fredrik restarted the fire while I made us coffee and searched his pantry for anything to go with it. I found crackers and carried everything to the coffee table in front of the fire.

"You have to tell me if this is not okay," I said. "I'm walking around your house, sticking my head into places... making coffee and eating your stuff. I'm not a very good houseguest. I tend to forget my place. I'm nosy and I want to feel useful. Or maybe I'm just impatient. I don't know. But I'm not good at sitting and waiting and not touching anything." My words tumbled out, my stomach unsettled.

He huffed a sad laugh, closing the fireplace doors. "Does that mean you feel at home? Because that's great. It took me a long time to feel at home here. This was always Glenn's house, and I felt like I was housesitting."

I pulled a face, sipping my coffee. "I don't feel at home anywhere. I've never owned a house, so I don't know how it feels, but in my imagination, it's this grand feeling. Like you're a little bigger than someone without a house. Because your house is an extension of you or something."

He laughed for real now. "The only thing grand about owning a house is the amount of mental energy and money it sucks out of you. Renovating it. Maintaining it. Worrying about anything that might make it depreciate."

I sighed, looking up at the ceiling. "It's so beautiful, though! Everything you've done in here... your uncle would be so proud."

"It's taken me embarrassingly long. I couldn't choose the materials. Or colors. Or anything." He looked away. "Jackson's been helping, but even he gave up on me at some point. And then..."

"Then what?"

"Then I met you. And we finally finished my bathroom."

What?

I sat up, spilling a little coffee on my pants. "You mean the downstairs one with the green tile? The most gorgeous bathroom I've ever seen?"

"You like it?" He joined me on the couch, sitting down slowly as he studied my face, as if to see if I was telling the truth.

I sighed. "I'm not being nice! I love that bathroom. The one upside of not having a filter is that I'm pretty honest."

"Honesty is underrated," he said.

I nuzzled into his side, and he wrapped his arm around me. I felt so safe and relaxed. "Can we stay here all day? Just you and me and the fire?"

He kissed the top of my head. "You can stay as long as you'd like."

Would I be safe right here, with him? Fredrik was a recluse. Who would think of looking for me in this house?

My heart swelling, I climbed onto his lap to straddle him. He kissed me back, running his fingers up my back. I felt his erection between my legs and shivered. He was so good to me. So attentive. Spencer hadn't been a terrible lover, but I'd never wanted him like that. I'd been performing in the bedroom, just like I'd performed for his friends and family.

"I never thought I was that sexual," I said, a little dazed. "I don't usually want it. I have to really focus to get myself in the mood, you know?"

He tilted his head. "With Spencer, you mean?"

"Yeah," I admitted. "I always felt bad that I couldn't be as seductive as he hoped. I'm so spontaneous, and he used to say I should save it for the bedroom. But then I'd feel a bit distant and weird, and I had to... fake it."

Fredrik froze, frowning at me. I tried to kiss him again, but he grabbed my face between his hands. "I know this sounds disingenuous, especially from another guy who's sleeping with you, but your ex is a piece of shit."

"It's true, though. I'm not spontaneous in the bedroom."

"You just seduced me in the sauna, and I'm currently rock hard because you climbed on my lap on the couch in the middle of a serious conversation. So I respectfully disagree."

I smiled at the evidence he laid out. "Of course! We just met. It's all new and hot. But you'll see I'm not... good at it."

"What do you think I'm expecting? And I'm terrible at dirty talk. I can't even flirt. I have no moves."

I drew back, peering at him in confusion. "But you gave me those orgasms! You knew exactly what to do."

He was trying not to look too pleased. "I collect a lot of trivia. Some of it is sex-related."

I stared at him in awe. "You've learned about female pleasure from books, haven't you?"

His gaze flicked sideways. "I may have picked up some of those medical romance novels. They're very detailed."

"Oh my God!" I clasped my mouth.

He didn't seem embarrassed, stroking my hair away from my face, his gaze soft and discerning. "How was your first time with Spencer?"

"I... was drunk," I confessed. "I wasn't brave enough to

go near him, so my friend kept buying drinks. I was impulsive, even forward, but I didn't enjoy it. It's never that much fun when you're wasted."

It had been another performance. My audition, more accurately. With Fredrik, I didn't feel like that. I was finally connected to my own body, not using it to win someone's approval.

"I wouldn't feel like sleeping with someone either if I were constantly scrutinized," he murmured, kissing my neck. "You can't love someone unless you accept who they are. The only person you can change is yourself, and even that's a tall order."

His words relaxed me further, and I melted into his touch. It felt so good. So reverent. Like he was in awe of me, mesmerized by every detail, with no judgment. No expectations. And it was the hottest thing I'd ever experienced.

I peeled off my shirt and tank top, throwing them on the couch. He unhooked my bra and ran his hands over me, groaning. "There's nothing wrong with you, Noelle. Nothing." His voice was husky, and it pooled more heat into my core.

My clit throbbed in anticipation. He might not have been talking dirty, but he was giving me words I desperately needed. Fredrik drew me closer, pinching my nipple between his lips. Starbursts erupted through me, and I rocked against him.

Somehow, we shifted from an upright to a horizontal position, with me lying underneath him on the couch. I fought to get rid of my pants, then my underwear.

"I'm completely nude. In your house," I said, biting back a nervous laugh. "On your couch."

He pulled back, as if noticing the same thing. "So you are!"

"I don't know why I'm laughing, sorry. It's just weird."

"Bad weird? Because this is hands down the hottest thing that's ever happened in this house. Ever."

"How would you know? Maybe they had orgies in here."

He lowered down to kiss my stomach. "Unlikely. But even if they did, it wouldn't be as hot as this." He ran his tongue down my body. "I'm completely drunk on you, Noelle. I've lost all control."

My body responded before my mind even caught up to his words, launching fireworks on every point of contact. His thumbs massaged my thighs as his tongue circled me, teasing and building pressure. I wasn't performing for anyone. I was floating in my little bubble, high on his acceptance, free to focus on every sensation. I felt him there with every breath, kiss, and touch, but he'd stepped into a role that required nothing of me. I tilted my hips, moving with him, riding the wave of pleasure, making incoherent noises he matched with his groans.

When he sensed me getting closer, he pulled back, holding his breath. I was so desperate for him that I nearly learned to levitate. "Please, Fredrik."

He caught my clit with his tongue, and my vision exploded with sparkles. I came apart, shaking against his mouth. Time stopped, and the world vanished for a moment, gifting me a delicious, floating fall, like a snowflake drifting through the sky.

I opened my eyes to his smiling face. My grumpy guy was grinning, watching me. "I love seeing you come," he said matter-of-factly. "I think it's my favorite thing."

I laughed. "It's my favorite thing, too. You wanna see it again?"

I'd never felt this sensitive. This charged. It was a little foreign, but too good to pass up. I pulled him closer, and he yanked down his jeans, finally as naked as I was. The fire crackled behind the glass doors, filling the room with its warm glow. When he filled me, I cried out, my nails digging into his arms as I held on.

"You want on top?" he asked. "I don't mind."

"Maybe," I said. "But I'm so close I—"

It had never happened to me. I'd never come like this, trapped under someone. But I was too far gone. Too sensitive. Maybe we'd both planned to last a little longer, but it wasn't in the cards. I felt him pumping inside me as my body took over in the sweetest release, shaking from head to toe.

"You took me with you," he whispered as we caught our breath. "Next time, I'll last longer."

"It was perfect," I said, still riding the high, my body limp and tender. "I don't like the performance game. How long you're supposed to last or what you're supposed to sound like."

"You're right." He kissed my shoulder, still inside me. "Let's not do that. Next time, I'll sound like a foghorn as I come in my pants."

I chuckled. "Sounds great."

"As long as there's a next time." His voice was thick and tender, and it shot a little arrow straight into my heart.

"We have time," I said gently. I couldn't promise anything more.

He rose onto his forearms, looking at me. His eyes were

the softest I'd ever seen, his voice so vulnerable it sent instant shivers through me. "Noelle. I'm falling for you."

I held my breath against a cocktail of emotions swirling like a sugar-rimmed tornado. Love and desire. Fear and doubt. And an overwhelming sense that everything was about to change.

CHAPTER 24

Fredrik

I waited for her to say something, my heart beating so hard it hurt. I knew it was too early, but if we didn't talk now, when would we? When she was sailing across the Atlantic?

I'd nearly given up when she spoke. "It's scary."

I helped her sit up, and we got dressed in silence. I threw two more logs on the fire and carried our coffee cups back to the kitchen. She joined me, taking a seat across the island.

"Are you angry with me?" she asked.

"No. Why?"

"Oh." She looked genuinely surprised. "I feel like I said something wrong."

"You're right. It's scary. We don't have to decide anything right now."

What else could I say? Nothing like this had happened to me in years. Maybe ever. I knew I was falling hard. I could feel it happening, but I couldn't expect her to follow. I had to pull myself together right now or I'd scare her away. Hell, I was scaring myself with these thoughts. I couldn't blame her for feeling the same.

"You know I ran off from my wedding." She pinned me with a look that was both pained and open. "I called an Uber and never talked to him again. And I still don't know why I did it."

"I think you do," I argued. "Think about it."

She shook her head, her arms resting against the counter like she didn't know who they belonged to. "I wasn't right for him. I know that. But it never stopped me before. We had fights, and then I apologized, and it was... okay. We were okay."

"Do you hear yourself? *You* apologized. Why was it always you?"

Her eyes brimmed with tears. "Yeah, I hear it."

I softened my tone. "What was your last argument about?"

I wasn't a therapist, but if she needed to get something off her chest, I could listen.

She drew a breath, her gaze fixed on the overhead cabinets. "I'd planned this ski trip with Spencer's sister and her friends. And then I found out they'd gone without me. We were drinking one night, throwing around ideas for this trip. I was browsing Airbnb and finding the craziest things, like this entirely pink house. I thought we were planning to go together, but I must have misunderstood. Because two weeks later, I saw it on Instagram. They didn't even tell me they'd booked the trip."

I wondered what all this had to do with Spencer but didn't want to interrupt.

Noelle continued. "I was so hurt, and I wasn't thinking... Heather, his sister, came to see us to talk about the brides-maids' dresses... I hadn't seen her since the trip and said something really careless about how much I loved that pink Airbnb and how I wanted to see it. How I wished they'd invited me." She looked away, wiping a tear off her cheek.

I was no longer following. "But they should have invited you."

She nodded. "I felt like that, but then Spencer explained that they'd thought I was too busy with the wedding and wouldn't have time for it, so they went without me. And then I brought it up and made Heather super uncomfortable. I should have known not to mention it." She groaned. "There are so many unwritten rules, and I'm terrible at them! I make friends, and I get a false sense of security, thinking I can be totally honest with them. And then it backfires. The worst thing with the Alfords was that nobody would tell me I'd messed up. Not until much later. They all just turned a little distant and weird, and kept smiling. I didn't even know Heather was offended until Spencer brought it up later, a day before the wedding."

"That sounds like a high-society thing. Or some sort of sick power play. Maybe both." I shuddered.

She wiped her eyes, and I saw a hint of hope in them. "You really think so?"

"I really think so," I said with conviction. "And I think you understood that, subconsciously. You knew something was off and left to protect yourself. That's a good thing. You have good instincts." I reached across the island and took her hands, squeezing them.

She gave me a sad smile. "Just not good enough to steer clear of him in the first place."

"Well... it's impossible to see all the red flags right away. You're caught up in the romance of it all."

She met my eyes, and her mouth twitched. "Like us, right now?"

"Yeah," I admitted, letting go of her hands. "Although I've been flying my red flags pretty high, so if you haven't noticed anything, that's on you."

"And I've acted like a shortsighted toddler with verbal diarrhea, so if you haven't figured out what I'm like—"

"I love who you are." The words rushed out. I wanted to wrap her in them.

She drew a deep breath, like gathering courage. "I love who you are, too. And maybe I'm not the best at noticing red flags, but I don't see you like that. You're protecting yourself from being hurt. That's normal." Her gaze dipped to my worn flannel. "You care more about your grandpa's feelings than fashion. That's sweet. And you have this connection to Hideaway Harbor... I wish I had that."

She looked so wistful that I almost laughed. "Hideaway Harbor is not hard to connect with. Stay a full year, and you're part of the furniture. After that, leaving would be like escaping a cult."

"That's all I have to do? Survive twelve months?" Her jaw jutted forward, like she was mentally preparing for the challenge.

I lifted a shoulder. "Holiday Hidies can't handle the

shoulder seasons when it's quiet and cold and windy. Only the real Hidies stay."

I circled the kitchen island and took her hand, pulling her through the house to the back door, looking through the window next to it.

I pointed at a shed next to the sauna. "That one is full of firewood. I used to have a chest freezer full of berries, game, and fish. That's fallen to the wayside, but it's what most people do. And then we share what we catch and collect and help those who're struggling. The whole community thing... It can be annoying and invasive, but it's also necessary. It's not like Bangor with all the services. The conditions can be rough. We occasionally experience storms and power cuts and may have to wait for the next delivery truck. The grocer might have empty shelves for a while. We have to pull together to survive."

She nodded. "Makes sense."

"It's not all festivals and fun."

I wanted her to stay, but I was worried she'd make a mistake and end up hating me. Elora had hated the long, quiet winter. She'd hated the nosy townspeople butting their heads into everything, asking her to get involved in their causes. I couldn't lure in another woman without preparing her for the realities of living here. Even if I was terrified she'd decide against it.

"I get it," she said, leaning her shoulder on the door. "You have to split logs and bake your own bread when the grocery truck doesn't arrive. But you have all these events! The Santa Speed Dating and Woolen Sock Running! Have you seen the Christmas calendar? I was just looking at all the appreciation days..."

She went on to detail the town events. Was she even hearing me? Hideaway's events bordered on unhinged, but the weeks between were long.

"I kind of missed the parade yesterday. But I really want to see the sock running and some of the calendar reveals. There's even a Pulla Appreciation Day! You know the Finnish sweet bread with cardamom my grandma used to bake?"

I mustered a smile. Was she expecting me to join her?

Events had never been my thing, not even when I was somewhat happily married. I only got involved when they needed help with something, like erecting yet another market stall or clearing snow from the podium. However, I preferred to help with tasks that were survival-related, such as splitting firewood.

The idea of showing up as a spectator made me a little ill. But as I looked into Noelle's shining eyes, I couldn't tell her that.

"There is a lot going on this time of year," I conceded.

"One day, I want to get involved and not just show up as a tourist, you know?" She looked hopeful, yet uncertain. "On the cruise ship, every time we docked in a harbor, I'd see these amazing, close-knit communities. They waited for the cruise ship and served us to the best of their ability, but we were just passing through. We didn't belong. And I always wondered what the place felt like after we left... what they talked about and how the vibe changed. I wished I could peek behind the curtain."

"There's chaos behind the curtain," I confirmed. "Exhaustion and weird little cliques. Some people talk, others don't. Felicity tends to fill me in, against my will."

She sighed, a dreamy look in her eyes. "I bet it's so different, being part of it. Being known."

If she wanted to be known, I'd make sure everyone in Hideaway knew her. Even if I'd never understand the need to get that involved. You were dragged in against your will either way. I didn't even want to think about what would happen if I were to volunteer.

"Is that why you joined the crochet club?" I asked.

She cocked her head, peering at me from under her lashes. "Kind of. I love that group! But I feel like I want to do more. Give back."

"Be careful what you wish for," I said, pulling her into a hug. "If they get their talons in you, they'll never let go."

Just like me. I'd never let her go.

Letting that thought enter my mind must have triggered the forces of evil. Because that was when the doorbell rang.

Then it rang again.

"It's probably Jackson," I said, moving toward the door.

She grabbed my hand. "Wait! Do we want people to know about us? I mean, maybe some people, but..." Her eyes widened with panic.

"What do you mean?"

"I'm not ready to face Spencer. I don't want him to know where I am. And even Felicity knows who he is. That thing in the paper—"

"She'd never tell him."

"Of course not, but someone else might mention something to someone, and..." She wrung her hands.

I heard my front door open. "Yoohoo!"

"That's my mom," I hissed. "If you don't want this to be public, hide. Now."

Noelle nodded, frantically scanning the room. With no good hiding spots, she dove behind the kitchen island just as Mom appeared.

"Why don't you answer the door?"

She was in full winter gear, with earmuffs over a wool hat and snow boots, her wool socks visible. Mom kept fit by walking everywhere, no matter the weather.

"I was just getting dressed." I adjusted my waistband. "I was in the sauna."

"In the morning?"

"It was a cold night."

Her nose wrinkled. "You're not heating well enough. The hallway is freezing."

"I don't spend time in the hallway."

She tilted her head, giving me that look. "Other people might be more willing to visit if they didn't freeze to death at your doorstep. Or if you even came to the door."

"They know it's open." I tossed another log into the fireplace, more for show than need.

"Fine." Mom softened a little, dropping her bag on the couch. "I need to run something by you."

"Want coffee?" I pulled out a barstool to keep her on the far side of the kitchen island.

Mom wasn't used to being served, but to my relief, she sat. As I circled the counter to the coffee maker, I glanced down and nearly choked.

Noelle had crammed herself into the cupboard under my sink but hadn't managed to close the door all the way. Her hair spilled out of the crack like she'd been left there by the world's sloppiest serial killer.

"What is it?" Mom's eyes narrowed.

I spun back to the machine. "Nothing. Thought I saw a mouse, but it was nothing."

"Do you need your eyes tested? Your dad and I go every year. Your second cousin Andrew has glaucoma. Ida Kallis had surgery last year and said it was a lifesaver. If she lost her eyesight, she'd have to stop with the crafts. Can you imagine?"

"Yeah." She'd probably go nuts. Everyone needed an outlet, whatever it was.

What was mine these days? Reading in the bar? Jerking off in the shower? Trivia nights used to fire me up, training my memory and competing. Now it felt hollow.

"Eileen said you didn't go to her speed dating event." Mom's tone was reproachful. "She was counting on you."

"Really? I haven't gone to any event in... years."

"Well, it's been two years now. We all thought you'd be ready for a bit of interaction."

"Dressing up as Santa and forcing small talk with fifty women isn't *a bit* of interaction—" The coffee machine sputtered and hissed, cutting me off. I let it.

Mom smiled as I handed her a mug. "That's why I came. I found you a date! Just coffee with one lovely lady. That's easy, right?"

I glanced at the cupboard hair fountain, praying there wasn't mouse poop down there. Was the universe testing me?

"Who is it?"

Mom beamed, pulling out her phone. She showed me a picture.

It was Noelle. Fresh-faced in a navy-blue uniform, a neat

braid falling over one shoulder. It must have been a staff photo from the cruise line's website.

"Her name is Noelle. She's very pretty. New in town. I think she's running a little shop near you."

I rubbed my forehead. "Did you ask her? Does she know she's about to go out on a date with me?"

From the corner of my eye, I saw the head in the cupboard shake violently. I stifled a grin.

Mom's gaze sharpened, then she jabbed her finger at me. "Ha! Something's already going on. I knew it!"

"What are you talking about?"

"Eileen told me about her, and we all thought she was perfect for you. Of course I wanted to know how things were going, but your sister wouldn't tell me anything. She's not normally like that." Mom glared at me indignantly.

I rolled my eyes. "I know."

"She kept saying you were being neighborly and told me not to get involved. How can I not get involved? You're my only son. You're miserable."

"I'm not miserable." And for once, I wasn't lying.

Mom studied me, searching my face for cracks. "I almost believe you."

I smiled. No faking this time. "Happy as a clam."

She looked stunned. "Well, great. Can we talk about Christmas arrangements? Felicity's hosting again. Her house is small, but I think we'll fit in somehow, since neither of my children are bringing partners." She cast me desolate look. "Your grandpa is coming, of course. I helped him buy presents online. There's this website that sells locally made... garments."

"Underpants?"

"Yeah." She grimaced.

"Do you need my house? I can heat it up." I didn't know how it was possible to be surprised by your own words, but I was. I didn't even want to take them back. Maybe it was time for me to volunteer for something.

"Are you serious?" Mom gaped at me.

"You need space. I have space." I was already regretting this.

Her grin spread wide as she surveyed the room, already decorating in her mind. "It's going to be perfect! Does this mean you're bringing your girlfriend, then?"

"What girlfriend?"

"Noelle!"

"We're not dating."

She smirked. "Of course you are. I wasn't sure before, but now I know."

"What? Because I'm letting you host Christmas here? I'm not cooking, by the way. All you're getting is the house and some heat."

She just kept smiling. "I can't wait to meet her!"

"You won't. She's only in town for the holidays, and nothing is going on between us. Nothing." I probably sounded too sharp, but I couldn't have her spreading rumors.

Mom raised her hands. "Fine. Have it your way."

"If you want to use my house, you won't spread stories about Noelle and me. Got it?"

She nodded.

"I finally finished the bathroom. You want to see it?"

I had to get her out of here before Noelle gave herself a spinal injury.

CHAPTER 25

Noelle

$\mathcal{I}$ crawled out of the cupboard, feeling like a fool.
There was nothing going on between us?

My brain knew he was protecting our privacy, but my heart whined in protest. Did he have to say it with that much gusto? The craziest thing was that I already liked his mom. She sounded fun.

Bracing my sore back, I tiptoed out of the kitchen. I would have loved this floor plan as a kid because it allowed you to run laps around it. If Fredrik kept his mom in the renovated downstairs bathroom, I could sneak around the other way and go upstairs.

I remembered the stairs being a bit squeaky, so I climbed them, hugging the wall and holding my breath until I made it to the farthest bedroom upstairs. Holy shit, it was cold! I was starting to agree with Fredrik's mom. He really needed to turn on some heaters. The house was too large to stay warm with one fireplace.

After a moment of hopping around and rubbing my arms to keep warm, I heard the front door close, then Fredrik's footsteps on the stairs.

"She's gone," he informed me from the doorway. "Come down and sit by the fire."

I followed him back to the living room and sat on the floor by the fire. He joined me, his knee touching mine.

"I locked the door, by the way," he said. "In case someone else decides to barge in."

"It's okay. Your mom sounds nice."

He looked surprised. "Oh. Yeah, she's nice, but not great with boundaries. I'm sorry she dragged you into it."

"I thought it was cute! She wants us to hook up."

"Hook up?" He looked amused. "If she knew what was happening here, she'd be planning a wedding."

His words took the air out of my lungs, and I fought to push down the immediate panic. This wasn't the Alford family. This wasn't Spencer. It wouldn't go like that. This time, I'd listen to myself and stay in control. I'd enjoy every minute of this extended harbor stay, but I was just visiting. And if I was just visiting, I was safe.

"I feel like I shouldn't have said the word wedding," he said glumly. "Please ignore it. Ignore my family."

I stared into the flames, letting the warmth of the fire seep in. I had to lighten up. I'd seduced him, and we'd had a good time. Why was I making this into more than it was? We could have a fun holiday fling and leave it at that.

I got up. "Should we make lunch?"

I searched his kitchen for anything to cook with and found some eggs, powdered milk and a bag of flour.

"Pancakes or crepes?" I asked.

"You can make both?" He'd joined me at the kitchen island, and his gaze followed my every move.

"Of course! I like crepes with butter and cinnamon."

"I think I have cinnamon. Does it go bad?"

I shrugged. "Don't think so, if it's in a sealed bag."

"Use whatever you can find." He gestured to the kitchen. "Maybe I'll go out and split the rest of the firewood. I got a couple of felled trees from my grandpa's property last week." He nodded at the back door.

"Sure, go ahead!"

I felt a little more relaxed without him hanging around. Without all the hot topics I wasn't ready to touch. We were playing house. His kitchen was so lovely and spacious. A little low on baking supplies and dishes, but I could easily fix that. As I mixed batter and heated his frying pan, I daydreamed about all the ways I could improve the space. How I could make it homier. More colorful. More functional.

Stop. It's not your kitchen.

"Smells amazing!" he called from the door as I was setting the table.

My heart swelled at the praise and the sheer domestic bliss, with the sweet smell of butter and cinnamon saturating the air. How amazing it would be to live like this with someone like him. Someone who looked at me like that, eyes soft with adoration.

Fredrik took off his winter coat and approached me, his arms outstretched. My brain rang little warning bells, but my body was faster, crashing into the warmth of his chest. He was so solid, holding me tight like nothing could get to me.

"You know what I've always wanted to do?" I pulled away with a cheeky smile. "The jump!"

"What's that?"

"You know… running into someone's arms, and they catch you in a spin. Like in *The Notebook* or *Dirty Dancing* or maybe it's more of a koala hold because I'm not much of a dancer. And I might be too heavy."

"No, you're not. Let's go."

He took a step back and spread his arms, his mouth pulling into a lopsided smile. I backed all the way to the far wall, then ran and jumped into his arms, wrapping my legs around his body. He caught me in a kiss, holding me off the floor, spinning us around until I felt dizzy, and the kiss dissolved into laughter.

"You're really playing into my housewife fantasy right now," I said, giggling into his chest as he lowered my feet to the floor.

"I thought it was my fantasy." His voice was thick.

"Can we play house for the day and not talk about the future?" I asked, my face still nuzzled into his shirt, my every nerve soothed by his steady heartbeat.

I wasn't asking him. I was asking myself. Could I, for once, suppress that part of my brain that sputtered dangerous, half-cooked thoughts and enjoy the moment? Especially as we were on borrowed time.

"Okay." His voice held a hint of sadness as he stroked my hair, placing a kiss on my forehead. "Let's play house."

We ate and cleaned up, then got dressed and pushed the

snow off his property, getting so sweaty that we had to shower again.

TWO HOURS LATER, we were snuggled up on his couch, watching *The Pelican Brief*.

"I can't believe you have a VHS player," I said when the movie stopped for an ad break. An actual ad break from fifteen years ago, featuring Cadbury's drumming gorilla ad. "And I can't believe you've recorded this off the TV."

Fredrik laughed. "I know. When Uncle Glenn gave me this player, everyone else was updating from DVD to Blu-ray. My parents had thrown out their VHS player a long time ago, but I kept my tapes. Everyone thought I was nuts."

"You like well-worn things," I said matter-of-factly. "I get it. A tape that's been used many times has these little imperfections." I pointed at the distortion on the edge of the image. "No two copies are the same. Each has its own unique damage. Like a signature."

He shook his head, looking at me all soft and funny. "You make it sound a lot better than my high school classmates. But you're right. I think that's what makes us truly unique. The damages we take. It's a lovely way of looking at the trauma and hang-ups."

"Are you still hung up on Elora?" The question slipped out, and I tensed. This was exactly what I was not supposed to talk about. The heavy stuff.

Fredrik didn't seem tense. He leaned back, arms behind his head. "No. I mean, she's gone. There's nothing to hang on to. But I still couldn't imagine myself with anyone else. Not until I met you."

My heart did a little flip and a jump. This was my fault. I'd opened the door to a conversation I couldn't handle. "We've only just met."

He sat up, paused the movie, and took my hands in his. My heart pounded so loudly I could barely hear his soft voice. "You woke me from a coma. I was existing, not living. I saw no future ahead of me. You've changed everything, Noelle. This isn't a fling for me. It's not an affair or a bit of fun. Maybe it is that for you?" His eyes glossed. "You've satisfied your curiosity. But for me, this is huge."

My throat clogged up with tears, too. I'd end up hurting him so much. I'd end up hurting myself. "It *is* huge! I wasn't expecting or planning or… I don't know what to do with this. I love being here with you. I love everything about today. But I'm scared."

His grip on my hands tightened. "What can we not conquer? When you find someone who makes you feel alive, you do anything, right?"

Panic joined the swelling sensations in my chest. I wanted to give him everything. But I'd end up giving him the other side of me, too. The weird looks and the rumors. All the unfinished business. The shame.

"Do you really want the whole town knowing about us, though?"

Doing anything in public wasn't his thing. Maybe that was our common ground.

His eyes glazed with defiance. "You don't want to be seen with me?"

"Of course I do! But I thought it might be nice to keep this between us, at least for a little while before we let the whole town in. It's a bit overwhelming, and I still don't know what my future holds. I don't have a job here beyond the holidays, and I don't—"

"You can stay if you want to! Stay with me. It's not a problem."

His gaze was boring holes into me. I looked away. "I can't mooch off you for everything! I can't be a charity case. I dropped out of college. Working on the cruise lines is the only real job experience I have. I'm good at it. When I'm out there, I'm safe and relaxed and not worrying…"

He dropped my hands and stood, his tone sharper. "Do you really like it that much? Being constantly on the move and wearing the same uniform every day? I've seen you get excited about so many things here. Either you're lying to yourself or you're lying to me!"

"About what?" I asked in a small voice.

"I think you want to stay and build a home. Be known. Be loved. Wear your outrageous colors and do your crafts. Be yourself."

I don't deserve that.

I wanted everything he described so badly my heart ached, but that nagging voice was like a pin that pricked my ballooning dreams. I couldn't fall in love like nothing had happened. I'd already failed at it and hurt everyone.

I pulled my knees to my chest, gazing up at his looming height. "I can be myself on the ship. My home fits into a suitcase. I'm fine."

His eyes filled with disappointment. "You're still lying."

"Spencer is looking for me," I countered. "If he wants revenge, I don't want you or anyone else caught in the crosshairs."

At least that was true.

"I don't care if he shows up! I'm not scared of him. You've built this guy into some demigod and live your life around avoiding him. That's never going to work. You need to confront him. Get it over with. We can drive there right now!"

He pulled his car keys out of his pocket and looked at me expectantly, like he'd suggested a fun road trip.

"What?" My heart thumped so hard that I felt dizzy.

He was right, yet I knew with deep certainty that I couldn't do it. Not yet. I hadn't just humiliated Spencer. I'd humiliated my own family. Everyone.

If I went back...

"I can't, Fredrik. I'm sorry," I finally said, hugging my legs so tightly it hurt.

He groaned, sagging back onto the couch, fingers rubbing his forehead. "Okay. Okay."

We sat there for a moment, catching our breath and trying to see a way forward.

Finally, he stood. "Get your coat. I'll drive you back to the store."

"You're kicking me out?" Tears ran down my cheeks.

I'd lost him. I hadn't been brave enough. And now the perfect day was over.

"I can't get involved with someone who's not available. I'm not looking for a hookup. If I was, I'd go to Bangor with Jackson or something. I can't..." I saw the pain in his eyes.

I forced myself up from the couch. "Thank you for rescuing me. Thank you for the sauna. For playing house. I'll never forget you."

Then I gathered my things and followed him to the door, my legs shaking so much I could barely walk.

CHAPTER 26

Noelle

We drove in silence, with the heater blasting. Despite the heat, every muscle in my body was rigid, my fingers curled into tight fists, fighting the pain flooding through me. I desperately wanted to go back in time. I wanted to find a way through that conversation that produced a different outcome. One where we stayed together.

What should I have said?

I knew he wanted to be with me. He didn't want this to be over. But he was right. I wasn't over Spencer. I was carrying wounds that stood between us, making it impossible to give him the reassurance and commitment he needed. And maybe he needed more of it because of his past. His wife had chosen someone else and somewhere else. That had to hurt. It must have eroded his confidence.

We each had our own scratches and distortions, like those old VHS tapes.

When he parked outside the bookstore, I halted, turning to look at him. "Come inside. I want to show you something."

"What?"

"Please?"

I expected him to refuse, but he killed the engine and followed me to the door. Cold wind whipped us with snowflakes that melted on my neck, mixing with the cold sweat I was already producing. I didn't want this to end. I didn't want to lose the connection between us. But I couldn't promise him something I wasn't sure about. I'd already broken a promise, and it still haunted me.

Was there any way around this?

Despite having no plan, I took his hand and pulled him into the store, all the way to the armchairs. I was desperate, improvising.

"You put everything back the way it was," he noted, browsing the store. "Except for the doorbell."

"I'll do that, too. I just need to get Jackson—"

"Don't. I like the new one." His eyes softened, and it gave me hope.

I took a step closer. "If you're sure?"

He nodded. "What did you want to show me?"

I took a breath, meeting his gaze. He'd called my bluff. "Nothing. I just wanted to hold onto you. I know it's wrong, but I don't know anyone else in this town. Not really. I need you to be my friend." My voice came out shaky, alarmed. "Please."

I was losing him, and I couldn't handle it.

He swallowed. "Of course."

"It's true. I'm scared of Spencer. I know I have to face him at some point. But I can't do it yet."

"So you'd rather... sail away?" The hurt in his voice made my throat tighter.

"I don't know. I don't know what to do."

He grabbed my wrists. "Don't go. Move in with me. We'll lock the door and..." His words faded to uncertainty, and I saw the doubt in his eyes.

We couldn't keep hiding. Not here. Not together.

"I know," I said quietly. "Whatever we do in this town is everybody's business. But I don't want to lose you. Not when I'm still here. It's too painful."

He frowned. "What do you propose we do?"

We stood for a moment, examining each other with a mix of hope and fear. Was there a way forward? Could we go back to being friends? Just friends, nothing more? My arms ached to touch him again. How hard would it be to keep my hands off him? I already missed him even though he was right here, breathing the same air.

I stepped so close my hands landed on his chest, and my mouth was an inch from his. I could feel he wanted me, even if he was fighting himself. "We go back to being friends."

He drew a quick breath. "Just friends?"

I was standing so close to him now, and memories of every touch and moment we'd shared flooded my mind. I wanted his hands on me. We were good together. So good, that never touching him again felt inconceivable. Absurd.

"Yeah. Very close friends," I said, my heart pounding. "Bosom buddies."

If I didn't act now, I'd lose him. I peeled off my sweater and threw it over the armchair, then tugged off my undershirt and unhooked my bra.

"Bosom," he repeated, staring at my bare chest, his mouth ajar.

I bit back a smile. "I think it's the safest. Since you don't want to get involved with someone... temporary. This way, you won't have to."

"O...kay." His breath was heavy, his gaze lingering on my skin, barely visiting my eyes. "This bosom buddy thing... what exactly is involved?"

"We spend time together."

He was pressed flush against me now, regarding me with cautious wonder. "Can I spend the whole time between your legs?"

My clit pulsed in response to his words, and my back curved. We held there for a moment, his erection pressing into my thigh, his hot breath on my neck. He was arguing with himself, holding still. Would he leave me here, naked and alone?

"Fredrik," I whispered. "I know I'm playing dirty, but I don't want to give you up. I can't. Please don't leave me here." My throat tightened at the thought.

He pulled back, running his fingers through his messy hair, his eyes full of conflict. "You're going to break my heart." I held my breath as he swallowed, then exhaled in surrender. "But I can't say no. My dick would never forgive me."

His rueful smile made my heart melt into a puddle. The words might have been crude, but they felt like the sweetest thing. The hottest thing. A promise.

"I think my pussy would hold a grudge, too. It's quickly becoming your biggest fan."

"Fuck, Noelle. You talk dirty."

He helped me out of my pants and pushed me into the armchair. I reached to unbutton his jeans and freed his hard-on, but he wouldn't let me go on. Instead, he lowered between my thighs again. As his lips found my sensitive flesh, I let out a shaky whimper. His touch was magic. Soft, teasing, and surprising. It ebbed and flowed through me like a current, accumulating sensations that I could barely handle. He teased me through my panties, then pulled them aside. With each lick and stroke, I shivered from head to toe. I wanted to hold on, but I couldn't. The sensation built and built until I grabbed the chair, letting out a broken gasp as my body dissolved under a crashing, hot-sweet wave of pleasure. I held there for a moment, letting it wash through me.

"Should we test how sturdy your chair is?" I asked, getting to my feet.

"It's pretty sturdy."

He gave me a sly smile and helped me to sit on the back of the chair. I wrapped my arms around his neck and held on tight as he drove into me. I was teetering on the edge in more ways than one, and each thrust built more pressure in my core, taking me closer.

"Harder," I grunted, and he complied, his hands gripping my buttocks as he pushed into me, again and again.

He needed this. I could sense the immense relief as he came. I felt his release pumping inside me, and it sent me over the edge. I came apart, my arms tight around his neck, holding on to him in more ways than one.

Staying friends made sense. We could protect ourselves and avoid complications. But I couldn't keep away from this man. He made me feel better than I'd ever felt with anyone. Other people could keep their babbling brooks. My happy place was right here, with my legs wrapped around him, his heartbeat pounding through me. How could I ever be happy again without him?

CHAPTER 27

Fredrik

I was supposed to stay away from this woman, not fuck her in the middle of my workplace.

"Now what?" I asked as I helped her down from the armchair I'd probably have to torch. "We're... friends?"

Obviously, I couldn't be just friends with her. Not if she ever took her shirt off. Not if she even looked at me like that. I would fall every time.

Her arms still around my neck, she pressed her naked body against mine. "Friends with benefits?"

I sighed into her hair, my hands tracing the curves of her back. She was unbearably hot and beautiful. Touching her felt like winning the lottery without buying a ticket. I could no longer protect myself from hurt. I only wanted to stay with her.

"Okay," I said. "What kind of benefits are we talking about?"

I already knew I'd take anything she was willing to offer and would accept any terms. I'd sign the contract blindfolded.

Noelle smiled, picking up her clothes and dressing as she spoke. "We see each other at your place or here or anywhere private that works out? And we do this... or something else we both enjoy."

"And do you have any other friends enjoying similar benefits?" I tried to keep my voice light, but even I could hear the jealousy.

"No! Of course not. I hope you don't, either?"

I almost laughed at her uncertain expression. As if I had multiple ladies on rotation. I couldn't think of anyone else. She'd snuck in and filled my entire world. My eyes followed her wherever she went, and my cock was constantly hard as I thought of her. If this was what friends with benefits felt like, I must have misunderstood the concept.

"There's no room for anyone else in my mind," I replied truthfully.

If she thought I was pathetic, at least I wasn't misrepresenting myself. Other than hiding the true degree of my obsession. It made no sense to feel this way after knowing someone for such a short time. Maybe it was the sudden influx of sex hormones. My body wasn't used to them.

Noelle pulled her sweater over her head, and two glistening eyes appeared, framed by mussed hair. "That is the sweetest thing anyone's..." She took a deep breath and made an emotional noise as she crashed into my chest, wrapping her arms around me.

She mumbled the rest of that sentence, holding on tight. The hug lasted for a long time. With every inhale of her scent, I felt weaker and stronger at the same time. I didn't want to let go, and it seemed neither did she. I wondered if other people in friends-with-benefits relationships were acting like this. This was the exact opposite of casual.

Eventually, I let her go and walked her upstairs. I didn't want to leave her there, but at least the power was back on. The room felt warmer.

"Do you think it'll blow the fuse if I turn these on?" She gestured at the ridiculous pile of Christmas lights covering the window.

"Should be fine. But I think they'd look better downstairs. You know, where they were."

"You're not changing your mind!" She laughed, a little incredulous. "I just took everything down."

I shrugged. "Up to you."

I felt different. Maybe my store could look different, too. I scooped her waist and pulled her closer, full of wonder that I could do so. That I was allowed to touch her. She sighed, relaxing into me like she belonged right there.

Still, her eyes held a hint of rebellion. "I'm keeping the lights up here. Otherwise, it's too much too soon. Friends with benefits don't decorate each other's houses. Or workplaces."

"Okay. Can I get a list of dos and don'ts? It'd be really helpful."

She glanced at the ceiling, thinking. "They do hang out, I think. Because friends do that."

"And what are the benefits, exactly?"

She blushed, her teeth skating over her lower lip. "Anything we both enjoy? Just no couple stuff."

"What's couple stuff?"

Her smile morphed into confusion. "Umm... hand holding? Or anything else only a couple would do."

"What, like joint bank accounts? Co-owning a turtle?"

"A turtle sounds amazing! But yeah, I guess."

My phone rang, and I pulled it out of my pocket. "It's Jackson."

That was weird.

I was about to ignore the call, but Noelle grabbed my wrist. "You need to take it."

"Why?"

"Because friends don't blow off other friends."

I stared at the phone, a little alarmed. Jackson never called. Most people didn't. "But he and I have no benefits."

"Ha ha! You have a signal, which means it's a good day in Hideaway! Don't take that for granted."

She urged me into the hallway, and I finally answered the call.

"What's up?"

"Teddy?" Jackson's voice was full of wonder. "Did you really pick up your phone?"

"Why are you calling?"

"I'm channeling my inner boomer. I watched *Taken* the other day, and people just looked cooler having real phone calls. Like, urgent ones on a tiny slide phone."

"What's the urgency?"

The line crackled as he laughed. "Nothing. I just wanted to catch up. Are you home?"

"No, but..." Was I going back home? Was that what a

friend-who-didn't-blow-off-other-friends would do? I'd figure this out.

"Bookstore?" he guessed.

"Yeah. I can come home—"

"Let's meet at Kippis? My treat."

I cringed at the idea. Not because anything was wrong with the small corner bar. I just didn't want to go out in public, not unless I could hide behind a book and pretend other people didn't exist.

Which, I now realized, I wouldn't have to do with Noelle. I could just hook up, quietly, and not worry about any of that. No pointless outings, expensive meals, or other couple friends to entertain.

How had I landed such an amazing deal?

"THAT'S THE WORST DEAL EVER!"

Jackson's hand flexed like it wanted to bitch-slap me.

We'd secured a small table by the window overlooking the street. It was a picture-perfect scene, complete with Christmas lights and floating snowflakes, both of which I was uncharacteristically appreciating on this fine night. And for some inexplicable reason, my best friend was glaring at me.

"Why? You do it all the time." I sipped my beer.

He groaned. "Yeah. Sure. I have. And it can be fun if you're the type. Which you're not."

"How do you know?" I managed to sound hurt.

"Because you have to keep emotions out of it. You have to set clear rules and boundaries."

"We did!"

He shook his head. "No, you didn't. You can't."

"Why not?"

"Because you're involved up to your eyeballs. Because you're in love with her. Because she's falling for you. Take your pick."

"Earlier, you told me I should have a fling. You said it's great because she's only in town for a short time. No hassle. She's still going to get on the next ship and sail away."

"And you're okay with that?" He gave me a long, hard look, and I covered my flinch by taking a long swig of beer. "Didn't think so," he concluded.

The tourists at the neighboring table watched the scene behind the window, hypnotized. The snow was falling more heavily now, and the wind was picking up, obscuring visibility. Where they saw a photo opportunity, I saw hazards. I saw a never-ending labor camp of snow being pushed and scraped. Noelle had no idea. She was one of those tourists.

"Maybe she'll change her mind. Maybe she'll... stay."

"To be your fuck buddy?"

"It was her idea!"

Jackson put down his beer and took a deep breath. "I know I'm not any sort of authority on commitment or relationships, but lately, I've been thinking I want more. I don't know what exactly it'll look like, but I'm done with the hookups. I deleted Tinder."

"Seriously?"

He looked exactly like I remembered, dressed and styled for the cover of *GQ*, but there was a hint of pain and uncertainty in his eyes I didn't remember seeing before. He'd always been the incorrigible charmer who didn't let life get him down. The one who saw the silver lining in the worst tragedy. Even mine.

"Yeah. I think I wanna grow up. Be worthy of someone's primary cell number. Not the dirty little secret."

"Sounds good. Is that why you called? Is something... going on?" I narrowed my eyes.

Jackson looked surprised. "No. I mean, not yet. I'm working on it." He looked like he wanted to say something else, but changed his mind.

The door slammed as the tourists left, their phones held high as they photographed the flurry of snow swirling around the string lights of Main Street, holding onto their hats. Their enthusiasm made me think of Noelle. Everything made me think of her.

"Like I said, I'm still working on this, but you're already that guy, Teddy. You're a commitment junkie. Premium husband material. Which makes me think you're fooling yourself."

I took another gulp of liquid encouragement, keeping my gaze out the window. "I know what you mean, and I did that at first. I came on too strong, and I freaked her out. We nearly broke up before it even started. But you know what? I hate relationship stuff. Going to concerts and restaurants and endless public outings that you have to shower and dress up for. Clearing drawers and watching them take over your space and move everything... fill your windowsills and counter space with pointless crap. Cushions everywhere! Pretending to like their family and friends... it's dreadful."

"Do you know her family or friends?"

"No, but..."

"So you're talking about Elle?"

He'd never called Elora by her real name, and she'd hated it.

"Well, you can't choose your family, so the chances are—"

"The chances are that your severely introverted ass won't enjoy any social interaction that involves more than two people. That doesn't mean her family is awful."

I tilted my head, accepting his assessment. "Yeah."

"And if that's your reasoning… that this arrangement will let you off the hook and you don't have to suffer through dinner parties or double dates, then you're an idiot."

"Well, that's how it works, doesn't it?" I insisted. "Friends don't make friends sit through family dinners or cousins' weddings. Friends don't make friends throw out perfectly functional bookshelves."

"For fuck's sake! That bookshelf needs to go. I can't believe she put it all back. Nobody should be enabling you like that."

"That's the thing! We're friends, so she respects my wishes. She's not trying to change me."

The more I thought about it, the better it sounded. Maybe I could be this guy. Perhaps I could, for once, not be the commitment junkie or whatever Jackson was talking about. What good had that ever brought to my life? For the past two years, I'd battled with my commitment to a dead woman.

"She's not trying to change you because she can see it's futile. You're not making room in your life. You're not really open to a relationship."

"What? I told her I wanted her to stay. She's scared of

her ex. That's why she wants to get back on the ship. She won't confront the guy."

"Why do you think she's scared of him?"

I shrugged. "He's rich and famous or something. I don't know."

He gave me a long, unnerving look. "I read the article. I saw your sister reading it on her phone the other day. She looked so... rapt, so I took a peek. She tried to stop me but..." He lifted a shoulder, looking a little ashamed but mostly pleased with himself. "It was an enlightening piece of journalism. That guy is unhinged. Jealous with delusions of grandeur. And he's looking for her. If he finds her with another guy, she better hope that guy's a fighter. If I were her, I'd go for a protective bodyguard type. Not an antisocial bookstore owner who freaks out over a bit of tinsel."

I cringed. "I didn't freak out. I'm just not the biggest fan—"

"She messaged me about the doorbell, and I'm not fucking changing it back."

I held up a hand. "You don't have to. I overreacted. But that's what's so great about this friends-with-benefits thing. She's not trying to change me or upend my life."

Jackson sighed. "I can't believe I'm telling you this, but you get what you put in. If you don't make room in your life, she's not going to stay."

"I've made room! She's living in my store. She's staying in my house. She can have as many rooms as she wants!"

"But she can't touch or change anything?"

"She made pancakes! She opened every cupboard. When my mom came for a visit, she squeezed herself into one of them." I clamped my mouth, realizing what I'd admitted to.

"You're hiding her from your mother?" Jackson rubbed his forehead, groaning with frustration. "I can't even... I thought I was the one with commitment issues, but I guess we've gone through some kind of role reversal."

"I don't have commitment issues," I insisted. I was starting to hate the sound of my own voice.

Jackson was right. I'd happily shoved Noelle into a cupboard and told my mom nothing was going on between us. She wanted to feel part of something, and I'd excluded her from the first family member who walked in. She'd gone along with it, but *I* shouldn't have.

"Either way," I continued, unable to stop. "Friends don't need to worry about commitment."

Jackson gave me a sad smile. "No, they don't. Say they get a job in another town or on a cruise ship? They can just take off. Adios. And the way you're falling for this girl... the way she's weaving herself into your life. She lives in your store. She's friends with your sister. She's real tight with your niece. Apparently, Eileen has a photo of her in her dream journal, next to yours. She's not some casual hookup you can just forget. And if you do, someone else in this town will kindly remind you."

My gut pulled itself into a knot as I considered his words. He was right. I'd be torn to pieces. But did I have a choice? I couldn't force her to stay with me, and I was too weak to turn her down. Whatever she was willing to give me, I'd lap it up for as long as it was there. If that made me pathetic, so be it. I'd been pathetic long before.

"I can't stop her from making friends. That's what she's like. She connects with everyone, and she has this dreamy idea of what it's like to live here. You and I both know it won't last. Even if she decided to stay, she's not a small-town girl. She'll get bored and leave. Maybe this friends-with-benefits thing is the best we can do."

"You're basing this on Elle. She didn't want to stay. She ran off with…" He looked away, clearing his throat. "Noelle is not the same person. She's not Elle!" Jackson looked up in shock. "Holy shit! She's No-elle! Even her name is making a point." He stuck out his arm. "I know you can't tell with all these layers, but I swear I have goose bumps."

I scoffed a laugh, shaking my head at the weird coincidence. But something about his words gave me pause. "Wait. You said Elora ran off with… with whom?"

Jackson looked mortified. "I didn't mean to… It was just a rumor. I don't know if it's true."

My skin was hot and cold. "Who?"

"Someone said she was seeing the editor in chief of the local paper in Bangor, but I don't know if that's true."

My chest felt so tight I could barely breathe. "Mr. Tillard? Her fifty-year-old boss?"

Jackson softened his tone, sounding more like he'd done for the past couple of years, walking on eggshells like everyone else. "I didn't want to tell you since it might not be true, and well… does it matter anymore? I'm sorry."

"It's okay." I was saying it to myself. "Honestly."

I gave him a reassuring nod. I didn't want him to lose the earlier honesty. I needed the tough love, not the careful platitudes used with grieving people.

"It's better," I said decisively. "Because I had no proof. Not even a rumor. I only had a suspicion, and she accused me of being paranoid. And then she was gone, and what kind of monster accuses a dead woman of cheating?"

Jackson laughed a little, and I relaxed.

"She traveled to Bangor every week. She told me that guy, Greg, loved her work and was going to give her a column or something. That's why she wanted to move there. That's why she wanted to sell the house. Maybe she was in love with him."

The words tumbled out of me with unexpected calm and clarity. I'd been blaming myself for our marriage falling apart. For her death. For everything. I was disagreeable. Antisocial. Annoying. But maybe there was more to it.

The worst thing about death was the silence. I couldn't get the truth out of her. We couldn't reconcile or even properly break up. Her last words were frozen in time. *You're like a fucking octogenarian!* she'd screamed, gathering her things and throwing them into a suitcase. *I refuse to live this small, pathetic life! There's nothing for me here, but you don't care. You don't care if I'm happy!*

Maybe Jackson was right. I was a commitment junkie. Even after she collapsed and never woke up, I wanted to work things out. I needed to make sense of her. Of us. But I was ghosted, in a literal sense, without any chance of closure. The dead offered nothing but silence. And as much as I abhorred socializing, I didn't thrive in silence. My brain went around in circles, always ending up in the same spot. Guilt.

Jackson held still as a statue, the beer dangling from his fingertips. "Do you... want to talk about it?"

"Maybe I do."

CHAPTER 28

Noelle

"*N*oelle, dear. You don't even have a kitchen."

Ida's words brought me back to reality, and I lowered my raised hand. It was Tuesday night, and the crochet club was about to begin. Minutes earlier, Ida had burst in, bearing news. Her daughter had gone into labor a month early, so she was leaving town and wouldn't be around for her Christmas Calendar event.

Which was the Pulla Appreciation Day.

"But I've been really, really looking forward to it." My voice wobbled, and I set down my half-crocheted Santa hat. "My grandmother was Finnish, and when we visited her, we'd eat so much pulla! I even have my grandma's recipe. She gave it to us just before she died."

Ida offered me a comforting smile. "Oh, trust me.

There's no one else I'd rather hand this over to. But you'd need a kitchen. A big one."

"Then mine's out," Felicity said.

Erica shot me an apologetic look. "I'm quite busy too, but maybe we can find a day that works?"

I couldn't ask her. It sounded like she was baking for half the town already. Lola was running late, and Deidre's kitchen was probably being used to make lotions. Eileen had arrived with her assistant, Lucy, a gorgeous woman in her twenties with long, curly hair. I'd seen her in the café. Yesterday, they had a special on cappuccinos, a really good special, and the line was out the door. They must have both been exhausted. I couldn't bother any of these people with my kitchen issues.

I caught Kailee's eye, and she mouthed Fredrik's name, giving me the push I needed.

"I'll ask Fredrik!"

He had a huge, unused kitchen. And we were friends. What was one more benefit?

I'd overslept that morning, after a night of wandering the town, doing my good deeds, and had only seen him in passing as I rushed to open my store. He'd brought me a sandwich for lunch, though, and we'd agreed to meet for dinner tomorrow night. I couldn't wait. My store was busy, yet the hours felt longer than ever. Sweet and agonizing, with a hint of underlying fear.

If I fell for him, I'd ruin everything. Even if Spencer stayed out of it, I'd mess it up. I'd change his surroundings, get too involved, and freak him out. I'd become that girl again who slipped into someone else's life and lost sight of herself. Instead of Spencer, I'd be molding myself to

Fredrik. I'd live in his house and drive his car and worry about his reactions. How was that any different?

If I had any hope of navigating this, I had to stick to our agreement. We were friends. And friends didn't rearrange friends' kitchens.

But maybe I could use his kitchen, very discreetly, when he wasn't there.

"Do you think we could have it at my store? Maybe right outside if the weather's okay?" I asked Ida.

"It would have to be outside. You can't fit more than five people inside," Kailee pointed out.

Ida tilted her head, peering at the ceiling, her crochet-hook hand moving independently from the rest of her body. "Well, it's just hot drinks and pulla. If we got some trestle tables..."

"I have four," Felicity inserted. "And a van to transport them."

"That'd be perfect!" I clapped my hands.

"Your store is tiny," Ida cautioned. "You'd be spilling over to block the entrance to other stores."

She was right. But would Fredrik be okay with us using the outside of his store? I couldn't ask him that. I could spill over to the other side, in front of the empty real estate office they were still renovating.

"You sure you can get Fredrik onboard?" Deidre asked. "I saw you had to take down the lights."

"I loved that window display!" Erica echoed. "Shame it didn't last."

I swallowed. Of course they'd all seen it. "Yeah. He took it pretty hard, so I decided it was best to pull back."

Erica raised her crochet hook. "Honey. If that's his reaction when you touched his store… how do you think he's going to react if you take over his home kitchen?"

"He doesn't even use that kitchen! Everything has a thick layer of dust." The words slipped out before I could stop them.

A huge, dreamy smile spread across Eileen's face. "You've been to his house?"

They were all staring at me, grinning like lunatics. Before I could respond, Felicity jumped in. "He took you in on Saturday night, right? I called him about the power cut. Jackson messaged me about the whole block being dark and asked if you were still staying in the Christmas store."

"Yeah," I said, grateful for the explanation. "It was a really cold night. Thank God Fredrik has a sauna."

The word instantly triggered an X-rated memory, making my face burn.

"Sauna?" Felicity raised an eyebrow.

"Love is in the air!" Eileen clutched her chest. "I had a feeling about this."

I didn't know what to say. They all leaned in, watching as my face got hotter and hotter.

"Wait? What have I missed?" Felicity demanded. "Are you two…?"

I turned to her, suddenly worried. She was his sister. What was she going to say? "A little bit since Saturday. Or technically Sunday."

The entire table erupted in cheers. I held my breath, watching Felicity. She looked emotional, equal parts happy and sad.

"I really hope it works out," she finally said. "I hope we get to keep you."

My stomach clenched. "We haven't talked about the future."

I couldn't exactly tell them about our friends-with-benefits deal. This was the haven'town of true love'—I'd seen the slogan on *The Almanac*. They'd chase me out with pitchforks.

"I bet Fredrik is already planning a proposal," Eileen said firmly. "He's not the casual type."

"Eileen! Can we not?" Felicity shot her a look. "They haven't even been on a date." She turned to me. "Have you?"

I shook my head, my face on fire. "We talked about going to the Harbor Tree Lighting on Saturday. I've never seen a Christmas tree made from lobster traps before."

Even that was a panic-fueled lie I shouldn't have told. What if it ended up in that gossip column in *The Almanac*?

"Can we... keep this between us?" I asked, catching everyone's gaze. "It's very new, and I'm worried about him. If there's too much pressure or expectations..."

Awkward silence filled the room. Finally, Erica spoke. "Oh, honey. It's Hideaway Harbor. How would you keep something like this a secret?"

As she spoke, the door opened, launching a tinny melody of "Jingle Bells." "Keep what a secret?" Lola asked, heaving her purse on the table.

"That Noelle and Uncle Fredrik are doing it," Kailee supplied.

"They're in love!" Eileen amended.

I held my breath, waiting for the doorbell to finish its musical number. I'd sold it to Eileen, not realizing how annoying it was. Lucy's face told me she was quite over hearing it hundreds of times a day.

"I won't say anything," Felicity promised. "But people are so nosy... they are already talking about seeing you two buying whoopie pies. It was in the last *Almanac*."

"What?" My pulse jumped. "Do you think Fredrik's seen it?"

Felicity gave me a wry smile. "Are you asking if I read it to him against his will?"

Of course. Fredrik didn't consume gossip.

Eileen smiled reassuringly. "Don't worry! Everyone's moved on to talking about the Santa Speed Dating disaster." She winked at Lucy, who looked furious. "And soon they'll move on to something else."

"What disaster?" Ida asked.

"Beard lice," Felicity summed up. "False alarm, though."

"We were sabotaged," Lucy added.

The doorbell went off again, and we all turned. A wiry young guy with a clown-worthy head of curly red hair stepped in. "Hello, ladies! Am I late?"

"Hi, Ralph!" Eileen called, echoed by the others.

"It is seven fifteen," Ida told him, straightening her crocheted vest. "And I have to leave early tonight. I'm catching a six o'clock bus tomorrow morning."

Ralph smiled, undeterred. "Oh, surely you have time to teach me all that you know before then!" He wedged an extra chair between Kailee and me, then peeled off his puffer jacket, whipping us both with his sleeves. "I read about these guys who started knitting woolly hats, and it became a million-dollar business."

"We're not knitting, we're crocheting," Kailee corrected.

Ralph waved his hand. "That'll be my point of difference!"

"And it would take me years to teach you everything I know," Ida grumbled. She handed Ralph a hook and a roll of yarn. "But I'll do what I can in half an hour."

"I'm a fast learner!" Ralph assured us and promptly dropped the roll, looking alarmed as it unraveled across the floor.

Kailee fetched it, but he barely noticed her. Instead, he turned to me. "Hey, you're the girl from the Christmas shop!" His grin spread wide. "How would you like to go out with Hideaway Harbor's most eligible bachelor?"

"You mean Dr. Handsome?" Lola teased.

"I wouldn't mind," Deidre agreed. "I tried to go back for my annual checkup, but apparently, he was too busy. Too busy with his receptionist, I bet. She's gatekeeping him."

"How many annual checkups can you have in a year?" Felicity muttered.

Ralph ignored them, jerking two thumbs at himself. "Forget the doctor! You are looking at this year's Larry the *Lobstah*!"

Felicity's hand flew over her mouth, but a very unlady-like snort still escaped. The others tried harder to hide their amusement.

"Larry the *Lobstah* is the town mascot," Lola clarified, biting back a grin. "He looks... spectacular. Another great reason to come to the Harbor Tree Lighting. Larry will be there."

"Don't mind them, dear," Erica said soothingly, smiling at Ralph. "You'll do a wonderful job."

"You will! You have just the right coloring!" Eileen added, without a hint of irony.

Ralph turned back to me with that goofy grin. "So how

about it? Drinks at The Shore Thing after Tree Lighting? I think my mom would really like you. She loves peachy colors."

I glanced down at my peach sweater, mortified. "I... I'm not sure I'll—"

"Back off! She's spoken for," Felicity cut in.

Ralph frowned. "By who?"

"By whom," Ida corrected.

"Are you sure?" Deidre frowned. "I would've said who. Whom sounds pretentious."

"I agree," Erica said. "It's like hence. Makes you sound highfalutin."

They were trying to distract Ralph like you would a toddler, but he wasn't buying it.

"Are you really seeing someone?" he asked me under his breath.

I opened my mouth, but Kailee beat me to it. "She's seeing Uncle Teddy, okay? Stop harassing her! Can't you see she's not interested?"

She grabbed her jacket and bolted, her eyes glossy.

"What just happened?" Ralph stared after her as we all listened to "Jingle Bells" for the tenth time.

"I think she likes you," Eileen suggested.

"No!" I scrambled. Even if it was true, Kailee didn't need her feelings broadcast. "She's just... passionate."

"Either way, she's fifteen and way too good for you." Felicity glared at Ralph, already pulling out her phone to message her daughter.

Ralph raised his hands. "Understood." Then he turned back to me. "So you're dating the old man?"

"He's one year older than you," Felicity shot back. "And

they're trying to keep a low profile, so..." She cast me a worried look.

"I'd really appreciate it if you didn't tell anyone," I said, heart in my throat.

Ralph leaned back like a cat with a gallon of cream. "You want me to keep a secret? In Hideaway Harbor?"

"Only for a little while. Till Christmas."

"And what's in it for me?"

"Shush, you big baby!" Erica snapped. "You'll do it because you're a decent person."

Ralph threw his arms wide, nearly tipping his chair. "Relax! I'll keep your secret. Just looking for a sweetener. Drinks after Tree Lighting?" He threw me another hopeful look. "If I'm seen with a pretty girl, my stock will go up. I'll leave after one drink, you watch me go... Look sad."

"You really think that'll help you with the ladies?" Felicity gawked.

"Works for Jackson."

Red blotches rose on Felicity's cheeks. "So does throwing money around."

"Oh, Ralph," Deidre sighed. "The real problem is this air of desperation. You need to cleanse your aura. I have just the thing. Come by tomorrow—"

"I'm not trying another tea. The last one gave me the trots, and my tennis serve didn't improve at all!"

Deidre pouted. "I told you, it improves your *focus*. You still need to practice."

"And speaking of practice." Ida gave him a stern look, handing him the hook he'd already dropped. "Let's get started."

For the next half hour, Ida taught Ralph his first slipknot. We chatted about the week's reading, ate cookies, and drank tea while Ralph proudly produced a loopy chain.

"There," he announced, wiping his forehead. "Always good to get the MVP out quickly. Fail early, pivot fast. I've actually had another idea…" He pocketed the rest of the cookies, tipped his chin at us, and strutted out.

"And… that's Ralph," Felicity summed up as the door closed.

"What's an MVP?" Ida asked.

"Minimum viable product," Lola explained, holding up his sad chain of yarn. "And this ain't it."

I laughed with the others until realization hit. I couldn't let Ralph leave. Not before I made sure he wouldn't spill our secret.

I grabbed my coat and rushed outside. "Hey! Can we talk?"

He was scraping frost from the window of his vintage Dodge with his ID card.

"She's not a bar leaner," he said reproachfully as I rested against the car.

I straightened. "Sorry."

"But I'll take you to a bar you can lean on all you like." He winked.

"Nice segue." I mustered a smile.

"You think I'm a joke?" His face fell.

"No." I fished a credit card from my pocket and joined him in scraping. "How did it freeze like this? You were here less than an hour."

"I ran out of gas two days ago and had to leave it." He nudged a gas canister by his foot.

Ah. That made more sense.

"You know everyone's jealous of my hair." He ran his fingers through his curls. "Guys are getting perms left and right. I have the real deal. I'm thinking of getting a mohawk. Maybe a mullet. Some speed stripes. The mayor won't let me till after the lobster gig, but then…"

He looked up, gauging my reaction. Did he really think a mullet was the difference between me wanting to date him or not?

"You're lucky," I said. "Perms are expensive."

His grin returned. "Right? Mine's like money in the bank. Who wouldn't back this investment?" He gestured to his tall, lanky form, dressed in an oversized puffer jacket and baggy jeans.

I wasn't sure Ralph understood much about business or how banks worked, but I appreciated his entrepreneurial spirit.

"You're a catch." I smiled. "Just like lobster."

He sighed. "The problem with small towns is that you're not allowed to reinvent yourself. Everyone remembers you from the day you were born. Every mistake. Every awkward phase. They typecast you before you even start. I need freedom! We only have one life."

"Sure. I get that." I met his gaze. "Look, if you think it'll help, I'll go out for one drink. But you have to promise you won't tell anyone about Fredrik and me. No one. Not your mom, not your sister, not another date—"

"Okay, okay." He held up his hands. "The Shore Thing, next Saturday after Tree Lighting?"

"I'll be there." He pocketed his ID card, and we shook hands.

"Wear something sexy."

"Nope."

"Fine."

He slid into his car and drove away, leaving me standing in the cold, my heart racing. What had I just agreed to?

CHAPTER 29

Fredrik

"You have a date with Ralph?" I tried not to raise my voice, but it came out loud regardless. "Ralph Peabody?"

"Larry the *Lobstah*, actually." Noelle picked up another clementine slice and popped it into her mouth. "It's just a fake date to boost his social standing."

It was Saturday morning, and she'd asked me to meet her for breakfast at the closed Christmas store since, as she put it, it'd be on "her turf."

I couldn't say I totally understood, but anywhere she wanted to meet was fine with me. She'd been so busy I'd barely seen her for the past couple of days and was starting to spiral. I worried she was keeping something from me, and I hoped to God it wasn't about her next cruise assignment.

Now I wasn't sure this Ralph news was any better.

"But, why?" I asked, trying to find a more comfortable sitting position.

Noelle had managed to fit a picnic blanket on the floor between two shelves, and the racks of Christmas crap dug into my back.

"I'm just dating him to throw everyone off the scent about us, okay? It's all fake."

"Does *he* know that? He's not the sharpest tool in the shed. Or the junkyard."

"He knows," she insisted. "He promised to stay quiet about us, and he's kept his word all week. There was nothing in *The Almanac*. I checked! And now I have to keep my word." She took a sip of her coffee.

"He's blackmailing you?" Now I was definitely shouting. "That is not okay!"

"We made a deal." She gave me a stern look. "It'll take twenty minutes. We'll meet at The Shore Thing after he's done with the lobster gig. We have one drink, he walks out, I pout for five minutes, then leave. It's no big deal."

"Why do you have to pout?"

She side-eyed me like I was a bit slow. "Because I'm sad I lost my chance with the town mascot."

"That's what he's asking?"

What kind of sick game was that halfwit playing?

I tried to calm down. I had no right to act this jealous or possessive. She'd set up this beautiful breakfast for me. She was hanging out with me. The air smelled of citrus, baked goods, and plastic. Noelle had bought every fruit and yogurt the Hideaway Grocer stocked and picked up fresh crois-sants from the bakery.

I'd brought the coffees, lovingly made by Eileen. According to Noelle, she knew about us but had been sworn to secrecy. Watching her try to act normal was quite entertaining, like watching those aliens in *Men in Black*.

Noelle cast me a beseeching look. "Please don't make a big deal about this. We're friends, remember?"

I couldn't match the lightness of her tone. "If it's not a big deal, why didn't you tell me about it earlier? And how does he know about us in the first place?"

She bit her lip, her gaze flicking about like she was searching for words. "He was at the crochet club. Did I not mention that?"

"I don't think you did."

Why did she look so guilty? What was Ralph really getting out of this? A dry hump? A muscle in my jaw ticked, and my hand tightened into a fist.

"Oh yeah. He popped in with this business idea but then changed his mind. He seems... special. Felicity said he was tested, and he's not on the spectrum. But maybe he's on the far end of *another* spectrum that hasn't been discovered yet?"

"Like the IQ spectrum?"

"Don't be mean! He's just looking for his place in the world."

I sighed. "Aren't we all?"

She smiled her gorgeous smile, the one that always turned my insides into jelly. "Thanks for understanding. I just want to keep our secret safe."

I wasn't jealous of Ralph or afraid she'd run away with him. I was angry with myself. Why had I agreed to this? It should have been me going out for drinks with her. Holding hands with her. Pulling her into a kiss and holding her close, in private *and* in public.

But just like her and Ralph, we'd made a deal. We were hiding for a reason. I couldn't ask her to go public with me, especially at an event that was documented for the town social channels, *The Almanac,* and possibly other news media. Hideaway Harbor was the go-to destination for feel-good filler stories, and the Harbor Tree Lighting was one of their annual favorites. Like the dropping of the ball in New York, only tiny and cute and lobster-themed. The chance of her getting photographed was pretty high.

"It's later today, isn't it?" I glanced at my watch.

"Yeah. But you don't have to go, don't worry!"

"My sister is going with Kailee. And I think Jackson will be there."

That was another odd thing. Jackson hanging out in Hideaway on the weekend, with no date. He'd asked me to meet him there, and I'd told him he had a better chance of inviting Felicity, who we all knew hated his guts.

Noelle finished her coffee and started cleaning up. "Trust me. I know how you feel about these things. *Nobody* is expecting you."

"I think I'll go," I said. "I don't want to miss Santa. Or Larry the *Lobstah.*"

Or Ralph on a date with my woman, my brain added, and that ticking in my jaw intensified.

"Are you serious?" She cast me a suspicious once-over.

"We're friends, right? Friends hang out together in public. No hand holding. Just… hanging out. You, me, Felicity, Kailee, Jackson."

And the rest of the town.

Noelle was still looking at me, eyes narrowed, but I could see the excitement shining through, like sun peeking behind clouds. She loved this shit. Silly small-town events. Christmas lights. For a moment, it didn't matter how I felt about any of it. It only mattered that she was happy.

LATER THAT DAY, we were driving to the harbor, her head resting against my wheel-holding arm, so deep asleep that she bounced around like a rag doll every time I made a turn.

She'd slept poorly again. She didn't talk about it, but I could tell. And I didn't want to wake her. I didn't want to break contact. Ever. Not even in public.

This was going to be hard.

I snatched the last available parking spot along Main Street, and she missed my perfect parallel parking.

"Where are we?" she asked, blinking her sleepy eyes.

We'd spent the day on the road. I'd driven her up to the mountains, to the historic lookout with expansive views over the town. We'd wandered around Locke Estate, visiting the museum. We'd even made it to the lighthouse to learn the history of the late lighthouse keeper's dog, Skippy. Noelle had a soft spot for the joint town pet and kept taking photos on her phone. It made me nervous. She was acting like a tourist, and tourists always left. Still, I felt compelled to show her everything. If she found enough to love in this town, maybe she'd stay.

"It's a short stroll to the harbor," I said. "Do you feel up for it?"

She rubbed her eyes. "Yes! All good now. Thanks for the snooze."

I discreetly brushed her drool off my sleeve. "No problem."

We got out of the car, wrapping ourselves in woolly hats, scarves, and mittens, ready for the icy wind. It was already getting dark.

"Do we need to feed the meter?" she asked, gesturing at the ancient machine.

I shook my head. "Only if you're a tourist."

"What? They know everyone's cars or something?"

I joined her on the sidewalk and nearly grabbed her waist, then remembered our deal. We'd been alone all day, and I'd touched her whenever I felt like it, which seemed to be every two seconds. "The parking lots aren't monitored. We only collect the coins tourists put in."

She chuckled. "I love that."

On the way to the harbor, we passed the post office, and Noelle lingered at the small red mailbox by the door. "Letters to Santa!" she exclaimed, her eyes glowing with excitement. "I love it. I love the post office, too. I got to know the postmistress—"

"Lumi?"

"Yes! She said someone crashed into the town sign the night of the snowstorm. You remember the night you went out for drinks with Jackson and the weather turned really wild? They nearly hit Skippy."

Of course, I remembered that night. I'd fought my way across the stormy town square late that night, a little drunk, and curled up next to her on the single bed, holding her so tight. She'd assured me friends with benefits could crash with each other. That it was okay to spoon all night, especially as I was in no condition to drive home. And in the morning, I'd slid my hand between her legs...

"Skippy is fine," she said, cutting off my sexy highlight reel. "I heard he got attacked by a cat at the other tree lighting, but this lawyer who's helping Audrey from Making Whoopie took him to the vet for a full check-up."

How did she know all this? She'd been here for a couple of weeks and knew more about what was going on in Hideaway than I did.

We joined the steady stream of people headed for the harbor. The Christmas lights glowed against the pink evening sky. The freezing ocean mirrored the pinks with deeper shades of purple, and gentle snowflakes floated over the scenery. I heard Noelle's sharp intake of breath as she took in the view.

"How is this place like a postcard?"

"With good timing." I couldn't downplay it, though. Hideaway was beautiful, and every time she noticed it, I received a new dose of hope.

We wandered along the pier, weaving through excited tourists, looking for Felicity and Kailee. Just when I was about to take out my phone and try my luck, I noticed my sister. She'd already found Jackson, and I could see daggers flying between them. Or were they sparks? I had never considered the possibility, but now it seemed like the obvious answer. How blind had I been?

"I don't want you speaking in the vicinity of my daughter!" Felicity hissed. "Not a word about your overnight trips or what you did on top of... whom, or what. You hear me?"

Jackson let out a frustrated laugh. "Chill! It's not a

euphemism. I literally didn't sleep last night. I tossed and turned. I started bingeing this show on Netflix. It had vampires—"

"Wait, you stayed home? Why? Are you sick?" She took a step backward. "Two of my staff called in sick this morning, and someone took the medicinal honey and antivirals I had in my van, so now I'm screwed if I get it."

"You need to lock that stuff down! Why do you let people steal from you?"

"I should be able to trust them," she grumbled.

"No. Instead of protecting what's yours, you leave your stuff lying around and then play victim."

"I can't lock them out! We all use that van. Our equipment is—"

"What seems to be the problem?" I asked, stepping so close I was practically between them.

Laced with sexual tension or not, their bickering could ruin this outing for all of us. That is, if I didn't ruin it first. I wasn't sure which one was more likely, but I was on guard. I could tell how important tonight was for Noelle. How much she wanted to be part of everything.

Noelle's head whipped from side to side, a big white pompom on the top of her woolly hat bouncing as she scanned the crowd. She seemed to spot familiar faces everywhere, even people I'd never met before, grinning and waving excitedly at each one. How did she know this many people?

I was still not feeling great about her date with Ralph, but I pushed the thought out of my mind and focused on the scene. The crowd cheered as the old fishing boat appeared on the horizon, cruising toward the harbor. After a while, we could make out Santa. Next to him, Larry the *Lobstah* waved at us with his floppy orange claws. There was something hilarious about his haphazard movements, coupled with his tall, gangly frame. So this was my competition?

Noelle clapped, joining the kids chanting "Santa." Even my sister forgot her argument with Jackson and shouted along. Kailee wandered ahead of us for a better view. Maybe she wanted to get closer to Ralph. Why couldn't she be into boys her own age? Like the two youngsters currently behind us, trying to shove snow down each other's coats, screaming in high-pitched voices.

Well, maybe that was why.

When the boat tooted its horn, even the teenagers stopped messing around and paid attention. As the antique vessel made it to the harbor, the noise swelled to a deafening roar. I hadn't attended this event in years. Had it always been this loud?

"What's happening?" Noelle asked, rising to her tippy-toes to see over an older lady's shoulder. "Why am I not taller?"

I knew one of the lobster fishermen would be driving the boat, but I realized someone else was with him—a woman. That was all I saw before another tourist pushed in front of me, blocking my view.

"I don't know," I said, taking a step back to keep a healthy distance.

I didn't need to see anything. I could just stand here, maybe close my eyes and try to enter my happy place. I just had to block out the "Santa Claus Is Coming to Town" blasting from a nearby speaker.

"They're kissing!" Noelle informed me, grinning from ear to ear.

She'd snuck through the wall of older ladies to have a look, making her way back by ducking under someone's armpit.

"Who? Santa and Larry?"

She laughed. "No. The captain and a pretty woman on his boat. Everyone is going nuts over it. I really want the full story!"

"I'm sure it'll be in the next *Almanac*."

I couldn't have cared less. I wanted to kiss her, not watch other people do what I couldn't.

"You're right! I'll look it up."

She was genuinely excited about the town gossip rag.

"Look!" She pointed at something moving behind a porta-potty.

It was Skippy. He didn't usually join outdoor events unless it was nice and warm. But here he was, watching the tree lighting. Noelle pulled us closer to pet the dog, and we found a better view of the wharf. Larry the *Lobstah* and Santa were approaching the vaguely Christmas-tree-shaped construction of lobster traps wrapped in ropes and Christmas lights. Another lobster sat at the top—that one a lot less lively than one containing Ralph, who soon tripped over in his ill-fitting costume, breaking his fall with his foam claws. Santa nearly went down as well but corrected at the last minute and landed next to the lobster trap tree. Everyone cheered.

I snuck glances at Noelle, drinking in her excitement. I hadn't felt an ounce of it for so long. I couldn't feel it over two grown men in homemade costumes or a pile of fishing gear wrapped with string lights. But when Noelle's face lit up like a Christmas tree, I felt that. I felt *her* excitement, and my mood shifted. I wasn't here to pretend I was okay. I was here for her, and that was enough.

As the festivities fizzled out, darkness had fallen. The wind had a salty bite to it, but it seemed most people were not quite ready to return home. Many headed to the bars and restaurants along the wharf or grabbed hot drinks to stay warm. Christmas music still played in the background, and spirits were high. We followed Felicity to the nearest stand selling hot buttered rum and took our place in the line.

"You must try this. It's divine!" she told Noelle.

I didn't even notice Ralph until a huge foam claw landed on my shoulder.

"Oh, sorry!" He pivoted and whacked Jackson with the other one.

He adjusted the claws and grinned at Noelle. "You ready?"

"Are you?" she asked. "You don't want to change first?"

He'd ditched the lobster head, but the claws and long tail were still attached.

Ralph shook his head. "Nah, I'm good. I'll take the claws off when we get inside."

Kailee gave them both a sharp look. "Everyone's going to know you guys are faking."

"Shh! Don't announce it," Ralph hissed back. "This is my one chance. I don't have the looks or the bank account"—he shot a side-eye at Jackson and me—"but tonight, I'm Larry the *Lobstah*, and I have a hot date. Unless you're about to cancel on me. In that case, I might just... spread the word about you-know-what." His eyebrows wiggled.

Noelle scanned our group. "Pretty sure all of these guys already know. Jackson?"

"Know what?" Jackson mumbled, not looking up from his phone.

"You know about me and Noelle," I said flatly.

He nodded, briefly glancing up from his screen.

"How do you even have service?" Felicity demanded. "Mine's been garbage all day."

Jackson smirked. "Want a hotspot? Step closer to the heat." He spread his arms.

She glared. "Does that actually work on anyone?"

"You'd be surprised."

I ignored them, stepping between Noelle and Ralph. "I don't appreciate blackmail. And what's your evidence, exactly? You heard a rumor. Doesn't make it true."

Ralph leaned in, looking smug. "Well... I was walking past the bookstore on Sunday night. Ran out of gas. Turns out there's a leak in my tank. Anyway, I saw movement in the window..."

"No!" Noelle groaned.

Kailee and Felicity leaned closer.

"You two hooked up in the bookstore?" Felicity gaped at me.

Jackson finally put his phone away. "Wait, what?"

"We must've been too close to the window!" Noelle covered her face.

"Where did you do it? Against the door?" Felicity squeaked.

"Against the window?" Jackson grinned.

"No! On the armchair!" Noelle yelped, then slapped her hand over her mouth. "Somebody shut me up!"

"Oh, my God! The slot machine!" Felicity stared at her, equally shocked and entertained.

I narrowed my eyes at Ralph. "It was dark. The bookshelf blocks the window. You didn't see anything."

His smirk grew. "Didn't have to. I saw your car parked outside. Thought you were working late. Then Kailee said Noelle's been living there, so I put two and two together."

"No, you didn't!" Felicity shot back. "You got it out of her at crochet club. But you still played it pretty well." She turned to Noelle. "Since now everybody knows about your... armchair activities."

Ralph's grin spread even wider, like he'd just realized his leverage. "Exactly. What's to stop me from dropping a little anonymous tip? Signed, Larry the *Lobstah*."

I stared at him. The fool didn't understand what "anonymous" meant but had still managed to play us. I wanted to grab him by the foam tail and toss him into the harbor, but I caught Noelle's panicked look. I couldn't blow our cover.

"She's not my girlfriend," I said. "She can go out with whoever she wants."

Why wasn't she my girlfriend?

Noelle forced a grin. "That's right. Nothing going on here. No stories for *The Almanac*. But I promised the lobster one drink, so..." She gestured toward the bar.

"Good thing it's not a private venue," I muttered. "I'm suddenly in the mood for chowder."

Ralph looked horrified. "He's not coming with us."

"No, he's not," Noelle confirmed quickly.

But I followed anyway.

"Way to look totally sane and not at all like a jealous boyfriend," Jackson murmured behind me.

"I want chowder," I insisted. "I'm not joining them at the bar."

"In that case, I'll sit with you," he said, still eyeing me like I was unstable.

"Keep him twenty feet away," Ralph ordered Jackson.

When we reached the bar, I realized that Felicity and Kailee had also tagged along.

"What?" Felicity snapped when I looked at her. "The whole town's going to be watching. I want a front row seat."

Noelle sighed, opening the door for Ralph, who was struggling to wedge his claws through the handle. "I guess we're all going in, then."

CHAPTER 30

Noelle

I had a feeling Ralph struggled with units of distance because I wanted my current lover at least twenty *miles* away from any date I was on. Even if it was a fake date.

Aside from being fake, this was also the most public date I'd ever been on. I'd noticed several people taking photos on their cell phones, and one casually walking by holding a Polaroid camera. Fredrik had taken his usual corner table, a good fifty feet from us, but I could feel his eyes on me.

Why was he making this so difficult?

I sipped my mulled wine, nodding at Ralph's long-winded story of how he might make a good private detective and why he might consider this as a future career path.

"I know most of them are ex-cops, but maybe there's room for one slightly unconventional one? It's all about marketing, isn't it? Finding the right angle. Like, what makes you stand out? If I were psychic, that'd be a piece of cake. Maybe I could allude to that without saying it. Like... he's very astute, often mistaken for being psychic..."

Was he talking about himself in the third person?

"You're right. Marketing is probably the hard part. I can't imagine there'd be that much private detective work available in a small town."

"I could expand to the neighboring towns," he mused, taking a sip of his matching drink.

He'd told me it would look better if we ordered the same thing, like we were totally in sync. Which we totally were.

"What are you looking for in a woman?" I asked him, desperate to change the subject. "Other than peach-colored clothing?"

He laughed. "Oh, yeah. My mom's crazy about the color peach. We have peach curtains and bedspreads and towels. Everything. I figured she'd like a girl who was wearing peach."

"You want someone who gets along with your mom?"

"Well, I have a sweet deal. I'm not going to move out anytime soon. So I guess they would have to get along."

"Makes sense."

"And she should be hot. A total smoke show. Like high heels and a dress. No offense."

I suppressed my amusement, glancing at my loose-knit sweater. "That's okay. I didn't bring the smoke machine."

"You're funny, though. That's good, too." He reached across the bar to touch my hand.

Despite the general noise level and Christmas music, I could practically feel Fredrik gasp across the room.

Well, he'd agreed to this. He'd just have to deal with it. I pulled my hand away from Ralph's grasp, trying to look like I wasn't rejecting him and only adjusting myself on the barstool. I rested my elbow on the bar and smiled. "Do you know how many people are staring at us right now?"

"At least ten," Ralph replied without missing a beat. "It's working."

"How much longer do you want to keep going?"

"Maybe five minutes," he said.

We kept talking about potential hairstyles for him until he informed me it was time for him to make his exit. I sighed with relief.

And that was when it happened.

Ralph stood, reaching for a hug. As I slid off my stool to meet him, he stumbled over his tail and pitched forward, hands first. Without the foam claws, his bare palms landed squarely on my chest.

"Whoa—" I staggered back, trying to steady him, but he grabbed at my neckline for balance, yanking my sweater down as he flailed. My ass hit the barstool, knocking it over with a clatter. I braced for Ralph to crash to the floor.

He didn't.

Fredrik had him by the scruff of his costume, holding him upright like he weighed nothing. His voice cracked like a whip. "What the hell are you doing?"

Ralph's eyes went wide. "Nothing! It was an accident—"

Fredrik's fist cut him off. One sharp crack to the face, and Ralph folded, sprawling on the floor like a rag doll.

"No!" I screamed, rushing forward. "He's just clumsy. He didn't mean—"

Fredrik's hand clamped around my arm. "You're coming

with me." He yanked me toward the door, not slowing even as people turned to stare. Camera flashes popped at the edge of my periphery—God, we were being recorded.

The cold outside slapped me awake. I tried to twist myself free. "Stop! I'm not going anywhere until I know he's okay—"

"He's fine. That ridiculous costume cushioned his fall. He'll have a black eye, and I'll apologize later. But right now, I need you to come with me."

Even furious, his tone carried a strange calm. He still wouldn't release me.

"Are you seriously manhandling me right now?" I snapped.

His face went red, and his expression shifted, as if he was suddenly sobering up. He let go of my arm. "I'm sorry. I've never done anything like this. You can go, if you want. I'm sorry."

Fury stormed through me. "For fuck's sake! You sucker punch my date and drag me outside, and now you're going soft? Finish what you started!"

"Finish?" He glanced back at the bar door, baffled. "You want me to kill him?"

I nodded toward Main Street. "No! I want you to take me to your car. Tie me up and fuck me like you mean it. Or are you telling me I inspire just enough caveman instinct to punch the guy, but not to steal the woman?"

His eyes blazed. "Is that what you want?"

"Is that what a caveman asks?"

I saw something shift again behind his eyes. I was giving him permission. Daring him. He threw a firm arm around my shoulders, steering me down the sidewalk. People were still watching. Whispering. But I didn't care. His claim on me felt fierce and solid. I loved it.

We drove in silence. At first, I thought he'd dump me at the bookstore, but he kept going, turning toward his house.

My phone found reception somewhere along the way and pinged with messages.

> Felicity: I think your secret's out.

> Kailee: I've never seen Uncle Teddy like that! That was so sick.

> Lola: You have to explain this video I just saw on the town group chat. By the way, your bra is showing, but don't worry, no nipple, and the red lace looks amazing.

I pressed the phone to my chest, mortified. "There's already a video online. Everyone's seen my underwear."

"I'm sorry," Fredrik said hoarsely. "I wasn't fast enough."

"It wasn't your job to stop it."

"I should have stopped it earlier. I should never have let you go out with him."

"We're just friends—"

"No, we're not. We're obviously not." His head bowed. "I can't do this. I couldn't even watch you with him."

He parked in front of his house. The lone yard light painted him in silver and shadow. He looked broken.

"Okay," I said, heart hammering. "What do you want, then? To be my possessive boyfriend?"

His head jerked up, green eyes searching mine.

"You're loving this, aren't you?"

"A little," I admitted. Embarrassing, yes, but true. No one

had ever looked at me like that, like I was worth fighting for. Worth losing control over.

Once we were inside, he started a fire. We sat shoulder to shoulder on the rug, peeling bark for kindling. His voice was low and rough. "Now you know. I'm not a friends-with-benefits guy. I'm the sucker who falls hard and gets his heart broken."

I stroked his worn jacket sleeve. "I'm falling for you too. I don't know what it means, but we'll figure it out. Don't ask me to promise—"

"Maybe we just see how it goes?" His eyes lifted, suddenly bright with hope. "Because right now, there's no one else I'd rather be with."

Heat swelled through me. "Same here. And if it makes any difference... you're not a sucker. You're brave and passionate."

His mouth curved, gaze darkening. "Like a caveman ruled by his limbic brain?"

"Then I'm just as bad because it turns me on."

Something sparked in his eyes. He pushed me onto my back, his weight solid above me. "What did you want me to do? Tie you up and fuck you like I mean it?" The words sounded strange on his lips, like his body rejected them.

I smiled. "Could you? Pretty please?"

"You... delinquent," he whispered, his voice tender and eyes liquid with emotion.

He pinned my wrists above my head and lowered down to kiss my neck. My breath hitched, and heat rushed through me.

Maybe we'd both get our hearts broken, but this moment was worth any future pain. I was mesmerized by his transformation. From all the arguments and agreements to this moment of surrender. A leap of faith. I wanted this moment more than I cared about what came after. The future was probably fucked anyway, and it felt good to narrow my vision. It was just us, lying on a rug by the fire, his weight on top of me, his eyes soft and playful as he took his time. I was desperate for him. Desperate to feel as close as I could, with nothing between us.

For the rest of the night, we didn't check our phones. We didn't discuss the videos, photos, or what was happening in the town chat or on the internet. Maybe we both wanted to escape and feel intact, for as long as we still could. The fallout of that night's events was already in motion. I knew it. He knew it. It was as inevitable as the snow coming from the sky. But we still had time. We could still play house a little while longer.

Early the following morning, when I woke up in his bed, my leg wrapped around him, I remembered something.

"Fredrik. Fredrik." I nudged his side.

"What?" He pulled me into him, kissing my forehead.

"Can I use your kitchen to make fifteen pounds of pulla?"

CHAPTER 31

Fredrik

She'd really meant it. Noelle had bought giant sacks of flour and sugar, enough butter to clog a thousand arteries, and turned my kitchen into a commercial bakery. She'd called her sister on the landline to confirm the family recipe and borrowed a commercial-grade mixer from someone I didn't even know.

"I promise I won't get in your way! I'll bake when you're not around, and we'll host this thing outside the Christmas store so that it won't affect the bookstore," she said, trying in vain to hide her mountain of supplies.

"It's okay," I assured her. "It's temporary anyway."

I wasn't even sure I cared if it was permanent. I loved the smell of cinnamon and cardamom that drifted through the house. I loved her. Those words had started sneaking into my mind at random moments, filling my chest with a glow.

She was everything I hadn't known I was missing. And the more she threw herself into town events, the more hope built in me.

Maybe she'd stay. I couldn't be everything to another person, but perhaps she'd find whatever she needed in Hideaway Harbor.

So far, I'd kept my thoughts to myself. Jackson was right. Pushing her to make a choice or handing out ultimatums was not the answer. She was scared and unable to see the life we could have together, the one I now saw glimpses of.

I needed her to relax in my home. She wouldn't even slide a bottle of lotion into the bedroom drawer I'd cleared for her but kept her things in two canvas bags for what she called our "sleepovers".

I only had myself to blame. My knee-jerk reaction to her store makeover, plus that stupid friends-with-benefits agreement, must've convinced her I couldn't handle even a nightstand out of place. Or maybe she was already planning her exit, and I was too blind to see it.

The thought terrified me, but I wouldn't let it ruin what we had. Forcing answers was never going to work. I had to be patient.

We led very different lives that somehow fit together perfectly. While I pushed snow, split logs and sat in my armchair re-reading an old book, she'd crocheted Santa hats for the caroling event, and weird-looking vaginas for the adult toy store. But whenever we were in the same room, we gravitated together. If I lay on the couch, she climbed on top of me. If she stood in the kitchen, I snuck up to hug her from behind. I couldn't get enough of her.

She never pushed me to join her at any event, but I came

along anyway, to see her delight and excitement. We'd celebrated the day school was out with Kailee, taking her out for hot chocolates at the Sip. I even joined Noelle at the caroling event and the Woolen Sock Run. I had to admit, Hideaway Harbor put on some entertaining functions. The more I showed up, the easier it felt, even with the long looks from the locals.

I knew there were videos online. Rumors were circulating. But so far, nothing had come of it, and we were happy in our bubble, stealing every available moment to be together, keeping each other warm at night.

And now Noelle was ready for Pulla Appreciation Day with fifteen baskets of sweet Finnish cardamom bread—braided loaves and rolls she'd baked all night. My kitchen had never been that hot. When her boss said no to hosting the event at the Christmas store, I offered to host it outside my bookstore instead. Technically, her store had to stay open according to her contract, but since Kailee had already finished school, she could manage it for the day.

"You don't have to do that," Noelle told me as I gathered a stack of baskets to load them into the car. "Being able to use your kitchen is enough."

"Don't be silly." I shoved the front door open with my shoulder. "It'll be faster this way."

When we reached the bookstore, my sister was already waiting with trestle tables. The morning sun was bright, but darker clouds loomed on the horizon. I hoped they stayed back.

Noelle ran ahead to greet Felicity, helping her unload the van. I carried baskets, but she insisted I could leave once the setup was done. She was still worried about forcing me into uncomfortable situations, but she didn't understand that I was no longer the same man I'd been when we met. I could barely remember what life felt like before she showed up. Ten days with her, and I had no comfort zone to return to. She was my comfort zone.

I lingered inside the bookstore, watching through the window as she arranged pulla and thermoses of hot drinks on the red tablecloths flapping in the wind. The Christmas calendar admin, Miriam, carted in her oversized calendar, and soon people began arriving. Usually, these calendar events were hosted inside businesses, so they'd get extra sales. Noelle's setup was nonsensical. She was serving free food on the sidewalk, all paid for out of her own pocket, to people who would grab it and then wander off.

I felt a flash of anger on her behalf. Didn't they realize how hard she'd worked? How much she'd spent? They weren't even looking at her and at the beautiful table she'd set up, their noses held up high.

It took me a moment to realize they weren't ignoring the baking—they were looking at the sky. The storm had rolled in fast. A burst of hail pelted the tables.

I rushed outside, flinging the door open so hard it smacked an old man's shoulder. "Noelle! Let's move it all inside!"

Noelle's eyes went wide, then she nodded, springing into action. Felicity and Miriam joined, and together we managed to save the baskets of pulla. The tablecloths took the worst hit, but they'd dry quickly.

Inside, we faced a new problem: there was no space.

People kept coming anyway, piling in between the bookshelves like sardines.

Jackson stumbled in, brushing ice from his coat. "You could've moved some shelves to make room."

"It was supposed to be outside!" Felicity snapped. "Did you not notice the weather change?"

He shrugged. "It was in the forecast, if you know where to look."

We compromised by clearing my checkout counter and wedging another table beside it. Miriam set up her giant calendar by the armchairs, waiting to rip the page at ten o'clock. It was crowded as hell, but at least people weren't being pummeled by ice bullets.

Noelle joined me behind the counter. "I'm sorry," she whispered. "You don't have to be here. You can go upstairs. This will be over soon."

She wore an emerald-green dress under her fluffy peach jacket, her long braid unraveling as damp strands clung to her temples. She looked sweet and wild, the way she'd looked like in the sauna, and my heart swelled. I was in over my head.

"It's okay." I slipped a hand under her jacket, pulling her closer for a second. "Do what you need to do. I'll stay out of the way."

I retreated toward the back with Jackson, leaving the women to handle the counter. More people kept arriving. I heard a language that definitely wasn't English. Probably the Finns she'd told me about, who always traveled from miles away for pulla. Noelle had worried about impressing them, but the blond ladies dropping harsh consonants wasn't the main act.

"It's Brody King," someone hissed.

Sure enough, the Hollywood star himself stood in the middle of my bookstore, surrounded by eager fans. I knew he was from Hideaway and remembered him vaguely from my school days, but he hadn't shown his face here in years. Why now?

Was he here for pulla, too?

Across the store, Noelle's eyes locked on mine, shell-shocked. She mouthed something I couldn't decipher. We all waited for Miriam to ceremoniously rip the calendar page for December 20th, declaring it was five days until Christmas.

The air grew thick with the smell of baking, layered with perfume and bad breath. Paper plates and cups piled up on my bookshelves even though Noelle hustled around with a trash bag. The crowd around Brody grew louder. Why had I ever balked at a few Christmas decorations? This was objectively far worse.

When Brody and his entourage finally left, I exhaled in relief. Little did I know that the true disaster was still walking toward my door.

A man in a tailored wool coat and leather gloves stepped in. My gaze snapped to his face, and my chest seized.

Spencer Alford. Same self-important air and glossy helmet hair I remembered from the article.

He scanned the room and brushed past me without a flicker of recognition.

Where was Noelle?

I spotted her crouched near the brown bookshelf, picking up another napkin someone had tossed like my store was a trash can.

Spencer zeroed in on her like a hunter on his target, and I surged forward. Whether on legs or pure adrenaline, I wasn't sure, but I had to get there. I had to protect her.

Noelle jumped up to stand, grasping the bookshelf as she laid eyes on him. "Spence! What are you doing here?"

CHAPTER 32

Noelle

$\mathcal{I}$'d imagined this moment a thousand times. First, I'd imagined him acting benevolently, waving off my apologies and saying he was happier now. That everything was fine. And then I'd read the article. After that, I hadn't been able to imagine anything at all. Nothing past that first moment of recognition, and my overwhelming urge to run away.

Now I felt the urge, right on cue, but my feet remained frozen against Fredrik's wooden floor, my hand anchored on his ugly bookshelf.

Spencer clicked his tongue at me with a mix of reproach and satisfaction. "Noelle Clarke. You have no idea what you put me through. What a fool you've made of me."

"I... I..." I couldn't form a sentence, but Spencer didn't need my words.

He stepped closer and pulled me into a suffocating hug. "Oh, Noelle. Thank God I finally found you!"

He said it theatrically, as if he were performing for an audience. Sudden panic got my limbs moving, and I wriggled out of his arms, spotting the camera guy behind him, holding up a phone.

Then I saw Fredrik. He dove at Spencer, grabbing the lapels of his coat and backing him up against the bookshelf. "You need to get out," he hissed. "Right now."

Spencer recoiled, his hands raised and his mouth twisted as if he were being touched by a leper. "What is your problem, man? She's my fiancée! I've been looking for her for a year. She needs help."

"She needs nothing from you." He let go of Spencer's coat but stood between us.

Spencer angled toward me, his voice softening. "Noelle, baby... who's this guy?"

A crowd of people had gathered around us, munching on pulla. I shot an alarmed look at Fredrik, shaking my head in warning. It was one thing to punch Ralph, who had nothing to his name. But if he did something to Spencer... I was too scared to even think about the consequences.

Spencer glanced at his broad-shouldered friend filming the scene. "I'm here for Noelle. No trouble." He edged past Fredrik and offered me his arm. "Come on, baby. Let's go. You can tell me all about your small-town adventures on the way back. I'm not mad. We'll get you the help you need, and everything will be okay, I promise. Everyone's so worried about you."

He gave me a sad smile, his eyes slanted in concern. It

was the perfect performance. So perfect. But I'd already seen behind the curtain.

I found my voice. "I'm not leaving with you."

My eyes snapped to Fredrik. I didn't mean to linger, but I was drowning, and he was my life preserver. Just holding his gaze settled the storm inside me, filling me with quiet faith.

That was my worst mistake. Spencer followed my gaze, reading me like an open book. "This homeless guy is your little side hustle? Noelle? Seriously?"

I was supposed to spare Fredrik from this drama. Instead, I was pulling him into the epicenter of it.

"You don't know him," I spat, my jaw tense.

"I can *see* him." Spencer turned to examine Fredrik like he was on display in a boutique, and he wasn't impressed.

I knew what he meant. In his cardigan and corduroys, his hair a little too long and jaw uns, Fredrik looked as unkempt as ever. Yet my heart somersaulted. He was my home. The only reason I didn't *feel* homeless even though I was. Everything else around me turned into white noise, and I stepped closer.

"I'm so sorry."

His arms opened, ready to catch me. I nearly melted into him. But Spencer slid between us, addressing Fredrik. "No offense, but she's using you. If you knew her, you'd understand." He turned to me. "Fine, Noelle. You've made your point. You're not shallow. You see this diamond in the rough or whatever. It's very cute. We'll make a donation to whichever halfway house he's staying at. We'll make sure he's okay. But let's take you out of here first. You seem so tense. Your hair's a mess. Look at your nails! I'll book you a weekend at a spa and a personal shopper. I'll get you a good therapist. Let me help."

Fury brewed in my gut. "He's not homeless, you moron! And I'd rather be homeless myself than one of your fucking assets!"

Spencer looked confused, like I'd deviated from a script we'd agreed upon. "What assets? Come on, Noelle. Let's go."

I gathered all my courage and stepped so close he could hear my whisper. "I'm not going back. Not now. Not ever. I'm sorry I didn't leave you earlier. I let it go on for too long. But we were never good together. You made me feel like I was broken. And I kept apologizing, like everything was my fault. And you never admitted fault. You never apologized."

He looked perplexed. "What would I apologize for?"

I heaved a sigh, closing my eyes. Exactly. He believed he was justified in everything he said and did. He didn't second-guess himself or worry about other people's feelings. That was who he was, and it had taken me this long to see it.

From the corner of my eye, I saw Fredrik's fingers closing into a fist. I could tell he was holding back, letting me have my say. But I could almost see the steam puffing out of his ears. I had to get Spencer out of here. I had to de-escalate.

But it was too late. Spencer, clocking that he wasn't going to get his way, launched at Fredrik. "Good luck with this one. She's after the easy life, you know? She wants the house and the car and the jewelry. But watch out. She'll run away with it and leave you wondering what happened. She'll mess with your head."

"What the hell did I take from you?" I yelled, and then I remembered.

The ring. I'd run off with the ring. Not on purpose, but still. By the time I'd been hiding at my sister's apartment, planning my exit, it was too late. Holly had taken it from me, promising to "take care of it." What had she done?

Spencer ignored me, his eyes on Fredrik. "But I guess you have nothing to give her anyway, so you don't have to worry about that."

"I don't worry about that," Fredrik replied.

"She's going to keep running, you know? I thought I could convince her to get some help, but I can see now that she's too damaged. You and your silly little town are a pit stop for her. Trust me. I know her. She'll use you for free lodging. She'll plan parties... then she'll move on."

My heart sank. Was that who I was? I'd relied on Spencer for everything. He'd convinced me to quit my job at The Gap, so I had no income. I'd been a financial burden. I still was. I squeezed my eyes shut, trying to repel the picture he'd painted.

And that was when it happened.

"You fucking snake!" Fredrik hissed.

I heard a struggle, then opened my eyes to see them crash against the big ugly bookshelf. It toppled on them with a splintering crack, spilling its contents across the floor.

Chaos erupted. People screamed and pushed as they tried to get out of the door. I didn't care about them. I only needed Fredrik to be okay.

Jackson shoved the loose shelves aside and pulled

Fredrik to his feet. He leaned heavily on another bookcase, wincing.

Spencer stayed down, clutching his side and moaning. "You ingrate! I'll sue you for everything you have. I'll make you regret the day you were born."

Tears blurred my vision. I'd done this. I'd brought him here. I'd brought destruction into Hideaway Harbor and onto the man I loved.

Fredrik hobbled toward me, holding his side, pain etched on his face. "Noelle—"

"I'm so sorry," I sobbed. "I'm sorry."

And then I turned and ran.

CHAPTER 33

Noelle

I burst out the door into the icy air, my breath coming in frantic gasps. The hail had stopped, but the sidewalks were crunchy, dark clouds still hanging low.

Fredrik didn't follow me outside. He must have been too hurt to move. I didn't know where to go, but my legs carried me to the Christmas store, the only place that still felt like mine. I could lock the door, hide, and think.

But someone was already there. A small figure crouched by the entrance, bundled in a white wool hat and beige coat with a small suitcase next to her. When she lifted her head, relief flooded me.

"Grace! What are you doing here?"

"Oh, thank God! I couldn't find you!" She leaped up and

hugged me tight. "I thought, if I waited here long enough, you'd show up. You live here, right?"

I took a deep breath, trying to push down the tears that welled behind my eyes. Too much was happening today with no time to process any of it. I could feel the telltale signs of an anxiety attack in my gut.

Maybe it was good that I wasn't alone. Grace would understand.

I unlocked the door, and we piled inside.

"It's so small!" Grace spun around, peering at the half-empty shelves.

I was supposed to keep the store open for another two days, but I had little left to sell, and now I couldn't even stomach the idea of opening my doors for business.

"It's been lovely," I assured her. "Absolutely perfect. Thank you so much!"

Grace took one look at my face, and I knew she wasn't buying a word I said. She marched into the back room and surveyed the tiny bed and table. "Okay. This is not an apartment, and you clearly haven't been staying here. What's the deal?"

I sat on the bed, making the springs shriek. "I'm sorry I didn't tell you. It's not a big deal, and I didn't want you to worry. Mr. Young told me I couldn't live here, so I've been staying in Fredrik's bookstore. He has a room upstairs. And a bathroom. To be honest, I've been staying in his house, too. He's been so nice…"

"Wait… why are you crying? What happened?"

I couldn't hold it together anymore. My body shook as I fought to draw in enough oxygen between the wails. Grace sat next to me, muttering about how awful the bed was.

"I… I was just there and…" Between sniffs and hiccups, I told the story of the Pulla Appreciation Day and how I'd been seeing Fredrik, first as friends with benefits and then as something more.

"And now I can't even face him," I finished. "I caused this awful scene, and Spencer is going to sue him. He'll destroy him. But maybe, if I go far away again and break all contact, he'll lose interest in Fredrik. He's only going after him to punish me."

Grace listened, rubbing her hand up and down the back of my fluffy coat like she was comforting a bunny rabbit. "You're in love with this guy?"

"Did I say that?"

"Oh. I feel like you said that."

At this point, it was probably written across my forehead, because it was true. I was desperately in love with him, even if I hadn't been brave enough to say it out loud.

"If I really love him, I have to fix this," I said. "I need to call Spencer… let him know I'm not with Fredrik. That he has nothing to do with this, and I'm going away. I need him to turn his anger at me, not him."

Grace looked at me like I was losing it. "Why? That guy sounds crazy."

"That's what I mean! I can't let him go after Fredrik. Maybe if I get far away from here—"

"Well, if that's what you want, I have good news!" She smiled, pulling a brochure out of her pocket. Palm trees and white sand. "I got us a gig! That's why I'm here. You weren't answering your emails, and we need to get to Bar Harbor this weekend to board the ship on Monday."

"This weekend, as in… Christmas?"

"Yeah. The cruise leaves the day after Christmas, and they have a huge New Year's party planned. It's really last minute. Two servers pulled out, and they need replacements."

"We'd be serving cocktails?"

A huge smile spread across her face. "In a tropical climate."

"I'm supposed to keep the store open for two more days. But I don't have anywhere to live. I can't go back to Fredrik."

Grace cast a disapproving look at the storage room. "I'm not happy with Uncle In-soo! He let me think you had a place to stay, not a daybed! Don't worry about him. Don't worry about the store. Just close it and we can go."

"How do we get out of here? Do you have a car?"

Grace's mouth twisted. "No. A friend gave me a boat ride. But there are buses, right?"

My anxiety amped up a little more. "I don't know! This place is so inaccessible."

Grace took out her phone and, to my amazement, did an internet search.

"You're getting a signal? Mine hasn't worked once! I always have to climb the hill outside of town. That's why I haven't replied to your emails." I offered her my useless phone as proof.

"It's okay," she said, browsing the local bus company's website. "There's a bus leaving today at twelve and then one on Friday."

I glanced at the clock on my screen. "It's already eleven! And I don't have my things. Everything is in Fredrik's store and in his house. I'd have to go back…" I blocked one nostril to stop myself from hyperventilating.

Grace squeezed me into a side hug. "It's okay. Breathe. We can stay here until Friday. It'll be like… camping."

"Camping?"

"Yeah. I'll get some camping gear, and we'll stay here in this store. We'll cover the windows and put up a sign that says we're closed for the season, then enjoy some yummy food, wine, and puzzles. Just hang out here. Get you over this heartbreak."

I sucked in a breath through my one nostril, trying to settle my cries. She was so good at this. Always looking at the upside and finding a solution. I wanted to be like her, not this wobbly mess.

"And how do we go to the bathroom?" I asked.

"Hmm… is there a gym? A gas station?"

"Not very close. I still have the key to Fredrik's store, though. I don't think he'll sleep there, so maybe we can pop in at night when he's away. And during the day, we'll figure something out."

Grace raised her eyebrows. "Let's make a copy of the key and return it. That way, he'll think you're not coming back and won't be sitting there waiting. Because it sounds like he… might do that."

I nodded. It was a terrible yet necessary plan that made me feel sick to my stomach. I didn't want to run away. Never seeing Fredrik again was the worst punishment I could imagine. And it was exactly what I deserved.

"Okay," I said. "I'm in."

If I really loved him, I'd save him from the fallout of my mistakes.

CHAPTER 34

Fredrik

"She can't have left!" I shouted, trying to get up from the bed Felicity and Jackson had imprisoned me in.

I'd been examined by the town doctor, then harassed by half the town after they brought me home to rest my fractured rib. Eileen and her friends had visited one by one, carrying pies and gingerbread, asking endless questions about Noelle and me, as well as about the handsome doctor in charge of my care. Thankfully, my mom and Felicity had taken over receiving them, sparing me from most of the inane conversation.

And now, I was staring at a photo of a CLOSED sign on The Christmas Wonderland window, papered over with pages of the latest *Almanac*, featuring stories about me punching the town mascot and, of course, the Christmas lights in my store. I'd bartered with the reporter, trading a short interview on my complicated relationship with Christmas in exchange for them keeping Spencer's name and face out of their publication. He didn't deserve any publicity—positive or negative—especially if he was planning to sue me.

Jackson took his phone away. "I don't know where she is. I'm just telling you that the shop is closed."

"I need to get there." I tried to get out of bed, but Felicity stopped me, shooting Jackson a furious look. "Are you trying to make him worse? Why does he need to know about the store? If Noelle decides to run off, there's nothing he can do about it anyway. Two buses left yesterday. She could have been on either of them."

"Does he not deserve to know?" Jackson asked, folding his arms. "If it were me... if I were head over heels for someone and actively looking for them, I'd be pretty pissed if my closest friend or sister was keeping things from me."

He emphasized the word *sister*, meeting Felicity's gaze head-on.

"Wait, what have you not told me?" I demanded.

Felicity chewed her lip, looking torn. Finally, she cleared her throat. "I went in this morning to clean the bookstore, and she'd taken her things. All gone. The key was on the counter." She dug into her pocket and handed me Noelle's spare key.

"No note?" My voice cracked.

She shook her head. "Sorry."

"She wouldn't leave without saying goodbye," I insisted, wanting so badly to believe my own words. "She wouldn't just... leave."

They both gave me a sorry look.

"What?" I shouted. "She loves me. I love her. We belong together, and we both know it."

"Look at you!" Jackson grinned. "What happened to friends with benefits? You were so happy you didn't have to worry about commitment or meeting her friends and family."

He was a true multitasker, simultaneously poking fun at me and scandalizing my sister.

"Please tell me you didn't say that!" Felicity directed her fury at me, and I swallowed hard.

"She suggested it, but it didn't last long. I mean, I got so jealous I punched Ralph." I tried to hang my head, but the pain flared in my chest, and I had to raise my chin again.

"Why would she suggest something that stupid?" Felicity huffed in disappointment. "I thought you guys were endgame, not some stupid hookup."

"We are!" I whacked the bottle of pain pills off my nightstand.

As Felicity bent to pick it up, and Jackson focused on staring at her ass, I rolled out of bed, pressing a pillow to my chest.

If I avoided unnecessary movement, especially twisting, I was fine. I could walk. And I had to get to my store. I had to find the note. If she'd really left, there must have been a note.

"Three days of full bed rest, you idiot!" my loving sister screamed as I hobbled out of the room and out of her reach.

I knocked over a heavy hat rack on my way to the door, blocking the hallway. It bought me five extra seconds, which was enough to make it to my car and lock the doors before my self-appointed home health nurses caught up. Unfortunately, the windshield was frozen solid, so I couldn't drive anywhere.

I started the engine and cracked the window, peering at Felicity's disapproving face. "I'll just wait for it to thaw."

"How environmental of you."

"What do you think you'll find?" Jackson asked, sidling up next to her. "I showed you the store. She gave you the key. She's not hiding anything... right?" He glanced at Felicity, who sighed.

"No! If I had any clue where she was, I'd tell you! I want you guys to work it out. I also want to kill that rich dude."

"Say the word. I'll make it look like an accident," Jackson offered.

Felicity gave him a tired huff. "Let's spare the world you as an assassin."

"Can you guys stop the foreplay and help me with the window? Then I promise I'll open the doors, and you can come along to babysit me as much as you like."

Jackson coughed, and Felicity looked at her shoes. "Yeah, fine," she muttered, buttoning her coat and taking the scraper I passed through the window gap. "But I'm driving."

Something was definitely going on between them, but I didn't have time to worry about it. Not now. They cleared the windshield, and I kept my promise, moving into the passenger seat.

As we entered the town center, I scanned the streets for any sign of her. The town was crowded with tourists, but there was nobody in a fluffy peach coat. Nobody who looked like her. Making Whoopie looked unusually busy, with a small crowd spilling into the street.

"Can we check that out?" I asked.

Felicity shrugged, parking illegally across the sidewalk. "Jackson would love to investigate."

"No problem, your majesty." My best friend climbed out of the back seat to see what was going on.

I took my opportunity. "What is going on between you two?"

Felicity looked indignant. "Nothing!"

"Well, then something's going on with him. He told me he deleted Tinder."

"Probably just ran out of space for all the other dating apps," my sister grumbled, but I could tell she was listening. Processing.

"No, I think he's serious. It's weird."

"Well, he won't be getting serious with me."

"Why do you hate him so much?"

She stared out the window, her brows drawn. "I don't hate him. He's just... the epitome of all the guys I'm trying to keep my daughter away from. The kind who'd just use her, you know? The kind who won't even remember..."

I nodded. Just like Kailee's dad, who couldn't handle responsibility. Who ran at the sight of the first dirty diaper. "Yeah, fine. Well, can you hold off biting his head off until I find Noelle and marry her? I know he's not perfect, but he's my oldest friend, and I want him to be the best man at my wedding."

"Your wedding to the runaway bride who ran away before you even proposed to her?" Felicity looked at me like she was reasoning with a toddler.

"Who said relationships are easy?"

Her face softened into a smile. She wasn't a hugger, but

she patted my shoulder with tears in her eyes. "Honestly, I'm so happy to see you moving on."

And that was when I realized I'd changed. I'd *really* changed. Even with my desperation to find Noelle, I felt more alive than I had in years. Life had high stakes again. It had meaning. And I was ready for it.

"It's just a party for Audrey. Noelle's not there," Jackson reported, hopping back in the car. "I checked the Sip, too. Eileen said she vanished. Didn't come to the crochet club, but some random Korean girl did."

"Korean girl?" My pulse kicked up. "When? Last night?"

"Yeah, she just turned up at the meeting to buy yarn. Said she'd heard about them from a friend but apparently didn't know Noelle."

Noelle had told me about her friend who got her the Christmas store job. Grace! She'd never mentioned her nationality, but I was fairly sure her boss had been Korean. Maybe Grace was, too.

"Let's go," I said.

We drove to the bookstore, crawling past The Christmas Wonderland. No lights inside. The window was entirely covered with pages from *The Almanac*. Why paper them so thoroughly, and why now? The season wasn't even over. Who would renovate during the busiest week of the year?

"Stop!" I told my sister. "I need to get closer."

"I checked the door. It's locked," Jackson said, but he got out and helped me out of the car anyway.

We tested the door and examined the window for gaps. There was no way to see inside. Getting a closer look at the town paper, I browsed the story of me hitting Ralph and the one about my store. They painted a picture of a deeply troubled man. Jealous, possessive, and allergic to change. I bristled. Could I really blame Noelle for running? On paper, I sounded worse than her ex-fiancé.

"I just wanted to let you know it's cute. The whole being in love and delusional thing. Adorable." Jackson patted me on the back. "I much prefer this to the walking zombie. Even if it's, what, the seventh stage of grief?"

"I thought grief only had five stages."

"I guess you're more advanced, my man."

I shook my head at him and pressed my ear to the door. Delusional or not, I didn't care. "I hear something. Like music."

Something faint, rhythmic. Christmas carols.

Jackson moved me aside and listened. "Could be coming from next door. Or upstairs."

"Or from that back room!"

"Sure." He looked at me with compassion and pity.

We walked to the bookstore, and I unlocked it, bracing myself for the chaos we'd left behind. But Felicity had already cleared the broken shelf and stacked the books by the wall. Otherwise, everything looked the same. Crowded, dark, and ugly. Suddenly, I saw what Noelle had seen. Why she'd wanted to add lights and decorations.

She'd been right. And she was the only hope my business had. I was running out of cash. If I didn't want to close shop, I needed her. Every part of my life needed Noelle's magic touch.

Bracing my ribs, I climbed upstairs and checked the office she'd been sleeping in. The bed was made, the desk clean. The Christmas lights still hung in the window, but she'd left nothing else behind. No clues. No sign she'd ever been here.

Was I delusional? Clinging to baseless hope? I wandered down the hall into the bathroom, praying for a miracle. A Christmas miracle.

And there it was. A damp towel. Hanging on the rack, far too wet to be two days old.

She'd been here. Maybe last night or perhaps this morning. I held the towel to my face, tears stinging my eyes. It smelled of berries and vanilla. Of her.

If she was hiding in her store and using my bathroom, I had hope.

But first, I had to take my reformed philanderer friend's advice and make room in my life. Not just a little. A lot of room.

I hurried downstairs, ignoring the way my ribs ached. "Guys. I need your help."

CHAPTER 35

Noelle

"I think you need to hydrate," Grace told me, handing me the bottle of water I'd been avoiding.

"His car is still out there, and I already need to pee." I carefully closed the gap I'd peeled into the papered window and sat back on our picnic blanket, picking up my crocheting.

I'd already made five little elves, complete with fluffy gray beards made from unspun yarn Grace had scored for me from the local craft shop. I was getting a little crazy in my self-imposed house arrest, but Christmas was coming, and I'd decided to create as many gifts as I could. I'd drop them off before getting on the bus on Friday. Or rather, Grace would.

I loved that my nightly wanderings had started the lore

about a Christmas elf, and I didn't want to break the illusion by revealing myself. But I'd still chosen to crochet elves. I couldn't help it. Maybe they would help the people of Hideaway Harbor keep the myth alive.

The night before, Grace had acted as my substitute elf, dropping off Santa hats for the snowmen I'd made earlier for the schoolyard and the library entrance. I'd even made her check the café steps for ice buildup.

Grace was gifted at sourcing things and had quickly transformed the little shop into a makeshift pillow fort, complete with camping mattresses and a portable hot plate. It was all very dangerous and illegal, and would have been so much fun, had I not been the worst camping buddy in the history of camping.

It was Thursday night, and something had been happening in the bookstore all day. Felicity's van stood outside, the window was covered with cardboard, and the noise they were making carried through the wall. Needless to say, we hadn't been able to use the bookstore bathroom.

I'd snuck out earlier to use the bathroom at the library, which was now closed. If Fredrik never left the bookstore, I'd have to venture out into the night to a bar or a restaurant and risk being recognized. The library had been so quiet that I'd been able to sneak in and out without bumping into anyone. It probably helped that I had borrowed Grace's beige jacket.

As well as needing to pee, I was desperately curious. What was Fredrik doing to his store? Was he selling it to cover his legal fees? I needed him to leave so I could use my secret spare key and take a peek.

When I was ready to burst, I finally heard the engine. I

peeked through a tiny gap in the window and saw his car driving away. Finally!

I grabbed the key and ran through the darkness, letting myself into the bookstore.

I didn't want to turn on the lights, but even in the faint glow of streetlamps and Christmas lights from the street, I could tell something dramatic was happening.

The store was empty. The shelves were gone. There were boxes along the wall, maybe housing the books. The desk and the armchairs were gone. Drop cloths ran across the floor and buckets of paint stood by the back wall. He was selling!

My throat clogged with tears, but my bladder wouldn't let me stop for any longer, so I continued upstairs. Once I was done using the bathroom, I decided to take a quick shower as well. When would I have that opportunity again? I could only hope Fredrik didn't notice a towel missing. I'd have to take it with me.

Afterward, I dressed up and wrapped my hair into a towel turban, taking a quick look at my old bedroom on the way. It still had furniture, but the desk had been moved to the side, and a big cardboard box stood next to it.

I snuck a little closer, trying to see if it had any writing on it. Perhaps I could just open a flap and take a peek inside.

The lights flicked on.

"I knew I could count on your curiosity."

I jumped, letting out a choked cry, and turned around, my heart pounding. Fredrik leaned on the doorframe, breathing heavily. He looked on the verge of tears—or maybe just in pain.

My body jerked, ready to run, but he'd blocked the only

entrance. So I stood there, frozen, a thousand confusing thoughts crashing through my brain.

"I'm sorry," I said. "I'm trying to get him off your back. I have a plan, I promise. I'll lead him away from you. I'll make a deal with him if I have to. I won't let him destroy you."

"What are you talking about? Nobody is destroying me."

Was he playing dumb?

"Spencer! He said he'll sue you, and I know he means it. But don't worry. I'm leaving, and I'll lead him away from you."

"He won't sue me." Fredrik took a step closer, and I saw my opening.

I charged past him and down the stairs. I had to get out, right now. I wasn't strong enough to stay away from him. I'd destroy his life. My eyes blurred with tears, but I made it across the floor and to the front door, fumbling with the lock.

I heard him cursing on the stairs. "Please, Noelle... I have a broken rib." He groaned in pain, and I stopped.

He was coming after me. If I ran, he'd follow. He'd puncture his lung or pass out or something.

I couldn't let that happen.

I leaned against the door, catching my breath, listening to his slow footsteps. With the dramatic lighting, it could have been a scene from a horror film, but all I felt was compassion. He was hurt. Was it because of Spencer? Because of me.

When he reached me, he pinned me against the door. My heartbeat skyrocketed, and my body flooded with something warm and debilitating, like a drug. I couldn't move at all.

"I'm going to hold you like this until I catch my breath… and we sort this out," he grumbled into my ear, his breath choppy. My knees felt soft, no longer supporting my weight. Despite his pain, he was holding me upright. "You're a bit of a flight risk."

I wanted desperately to dive into his arms and stay there. But it was selfish and wrong. "I can't let Spencer ruin your life. I can't."

"He won't sue me. He has zero evidence. He wasn't hurt, either. The doc checked us both. He's fine. I have a fractured rib, so if anyone should sue, it's me."

My hand hovered over his chest without my permission. I wanted to take his pain. "Fredrik. I'm so sorry."

"It's not your fault. I did this. Well, me and the bookshelf I should have torched long ago."

"But…" I rubbed my forehead, causing the towel turban to unravel. "Spencer had a camera guy! They filmed the whole thing."

"It was some dude he recruited off the street. And Jackson took his phone before anything happened, so all he recorded was himself saying obnoxious things." He leaned in, his breath heavy and fast. It was making me dizzy. "Noelle. I'm not going to let him hurt either of us."

"But… there were lots of people. Eyewitnesses." My breathing matched his—erratic and labored—even though my ribs were fine.

"For some reason, nobody feels like testifying," he said.

"How do you know? Spencer will contact each one and offer an obscene amount of money. He'll get to them." Tears burned the back of my throat. I wanted to believe him, but my experience told me otherwise. I'd heard

Spencer talking about his legal victories, people he'd "taken down".

"Felicity talked to everyone. She says it's all good, and I trust her. Apparently, a lot of people didn't see what really happened. They were too busy eating your pulla. Which was excellent."

I smiled a little. There was still a hint of cinnamon in the air, and it transported me into his kitchen. Into all the moments we'd shared.

I sighed. "I'm so glad you found me."

Fredrik grabbed the towel that hung loosely over my shoulder. "I'm so glad your store doesn't have a bathroom. That you had to come here. That you needed something from me."

Spencer's earlier words wormed their way into my head and words tumbled out. "It's true what Spencer said. I was living at his expense. I even ran off with his ring. Not on purpose, but I did. I cost him a lot."

He shook his head. "He's a dick, and you're the most generous person I know. I could give you everything I own, and still feel like I'm in your debt."

His eyes were so kind, his voice soft like a caress. But I wasn't done getting things off my chest. "I gave that ring to my sister. She said she'd take care of it, but it turns out she sold it to buy blankets for the homeless. Apparently, she got a lot of blankets."

Now that I could tap into Grace's internet, I'd been talking to my sister every day.

"That's the best use for his money I can imagine." Fredrik swiped a strand of damp hair off my face. "I wish you'd taken more than a ring."

His eyes glistened, reflecting the fairy lights outside. He looked nothing like when I'd first met him. There was a fighting spirit in him. A hope. I wanted to inhale it. I was so tired of running and hiding. So exhausted of living in fear. And here he was, bruised and battered, yet waiting to catch me. Waiting for me to come around.

My chest felt tight. "I'm sorry I ran."

"It's okay. I figured you didn't go far, so I waited."

His words stole air from my lungs. "You knew where I was?"

He smiled. "I had a hunch."

His eyes were dark as the night, lingering on my face, adoring me. Even after everything I'd put him through, Fredrik looked at me like I was some kind of miracle, and it broke me.

"I thought I had to leave. I thought it was the only way to save you."

He caught me when the tears burst out, securing me against his chest. There was the heartbeat that made me feel whole. There it was, pounding through me, finding a rhythm with my own.

"You already saved me." He stroked my hair, his fingernails grazing my neck. "And you don't have to run. Ever again. I promise."

He held me as I cried, letting all the stress and fear melt away and wet the collar of his cardigan. It had a mustard-yellow diamond pattern that looked antiquated in the best way.

What would it be like to stop running? To stay here.

"I don't have a job anymore," I muttered into his chest. "I

have to go with Grace and take that job on the cruise ship. We're leaving tomorrow."

"What if you had another job?" he whispered into my ear.

"Another job?"

"I heard of a bookstore that's looking for a store manager. It's a tough job, though. You need to redecorate and create a new business plan. The place is a bit tired, and it's not doing well. It's in desperate need of a refresh. New paint. New books. New merch. A whole new setup. The owner really wants some color. Do you know anyone suitable?"

I pulled away to look him in the eye. "What are you talking about?"

He took a deep breath. "I'm stepping away. I've brought Felicity and Jackson on board as business advisors. We had an honest chat yesterday, and they told me I need to hire someone to run this store. It was probably the first time I'd ever heard them agree on something. And they're right. I'm the reason this business is failing, and I don't want it to fail. For Uncle Glenn's sake. It's his legacy. I suppose I was the closest thing to a son and the only one he could talk books with, so he thought I could replace him, but I couldn't. He was outgoing and flamboyant, and I'm... you know."

I nodded. "And what are you going to do?"

"Something I should have done a long time ago. Get a proper internet connection and sell rare books online. Maybe start writing again. I used to enjoy that." There was a lightness to him and a hint of excitement.

"No dealing with people?" I smiled.

"You know how much I enjoy that." He raised a brow.

It sounded like a huge pivot, but it also made sense.

"So do you know anyone?" he asked. "The job comes with an apartment. Not a fancy one, but you'll have a kitchenette once I've installed some cupboards."

So that's what was in the box upstairs?

"How can you afford to pay anyone? You said the business is failing."

He looked a little flustered. "I'm really hoping I find someone who values the free accommodation perk and accepts minimum wage, plus shares and bonuses. I have a draft agreement on my laptop if you're interested?"

"You know I'm pathologically curious," I said tentatively. "But you shouldn't hire someone you're sleeping with. That's messy."

"Noelle. I'm trying to make room for you. I want you to have a real, sustainable, long-term foothold in this town."

"But what if we break up? Then I'd lose my job *and* my home."

"No! It's all in the contract. Two years to start with. I can't hire you or fire you without Felicity and Jackson anyway. I know it's awkward, but we'll keep it clear and separate. If you have any terms or conditions, we can add them before you sign."

My heart raced like I'd been running. "Fredrik! This is totally crazy! You know that, right?"

"I want you to stay, but I don't want you to worry about being a burden or mooching off me or anything like that. I don't feel like that, but I know you do, so—"

"So you're creating a job for me?"

"I'm just trying to fix things."

"Fredrik, please. I have a job. I'm leaving tomorrow, and I'll be gone for eight months. It's all set up."

"But it's Christmas! You can't leave before Christmas."

"Why not? That was the plan all—"

"Because your family is coming over!"

I froze. "What do you mean, my family? My parents don't even know where I am."

I watched his Adam's apple bob as he swallowed. "They do now. I invited your sister over for Christmas, and she thought we should tell them and invite them too. I mean, Spencer already knows where you are. Why would you keep on hiding? I'm heating the house. There's enough room for everyone."

"You invited them here without asking me?" My voice crept up in shock. "When?"

"Yesterday." He looked down at the floor. "I would have asked you, but..."

"I was talking to my parents, telling them I'm out on a cruise ship. You made me a liar!"

"Well..."

Okay. I was a liar, but something about what he'd done felt wrong. "You can't do this, Fredrik. You can't just fix things and expect me to fall in line. I thought I had to get away, so I made plans with Grace. She's my best friend. What would I tell her?"

Fredrik captured my face between his hands, speaking in a soft, low voice. "You tell her that there's a hopeless man in a small town who can't go on without you, who needs you so desperately he's doing stupid things his friend warned him about."

"Jackson thought this was stupid?"

"He said inviting your family was risky and presumptuous. But it's Christmas, and I know you miss them."

"What if I'd left already? Would you carry on spending Christmas with my family?"

He looked guilty. "I kind of have the whole town on a lookout. They know Grace and report back to me whenever either of you goes anywhere."

I frowned. "But we've been really careful."

"It's Hideaway Harbor. This is the most fun they've had in ages. I have three detailed reports from different people on how you went into the library to use the bathroom. Did you think I was going to let you sneak out? I'm in love with you, Noelle. If you go, you'll take everything... you'll take all the colors with you."

My heart glowed in all the colors, my tongue lost for words. "You're in love with me?"

"Hopelessly, head over heels and toes and all my internal organs. Since the day I agreed to be your friend with benefits. Which probably explains why I was so terrible at it."

"We were both terrible at it. I wanted to make you jealous. I wanted to make you admit it because I..." I swallowed against the truth that tried to push its way out of me.

Lifting my chin, he brushed our lips together like a gentle promise. "Please, stay."

He was offering me a choice I thought I'd lost. Could I take it?

CHAPTER 36

Fredrik

$\mathcal{I}$ held my fingers under her chin, holding my breath. She'd come into my life like a lightning bolt of sunshine and color. Would she go and take it all away?

"What's holding you back?" I asked, trying to swallow the terror I felt.

"So you can fix it?" Her eyebrows gathered in concern. "You can't fix everything, Fredrik. Some things, you just have to accept."

I thought I'd needed to fix the circumstances, remove every obstacle out of her way so she'd stay. But she had doubts. If I pushed harder, she'd run. I could feel it. Maybe we'd gone about this all wrong, playing house and pretending tomorrow wasn't coming. And of course, inviting her family behind her back, which in hindsight was incredibly stupid.

We were both woefully unprepared for the real world. Me, the socially inept hermit, and her, the restless spirit, only in town for the holidays. We weren't compatible. This was another woman I couldn't hold on to. If I guilted her into staying, I'd end up killing her, just like I'd killed Elora.

Steeling myself, I let go of her and opened the front door. "Okay, go. I'll cancel plans with your family. I'm being selfish. I'm holding on to you because I need you. But I don't want you to stay because of that."

I waited, closing my eyes so I didn't have to see her walk away. I didn't want that memory. She took the door handle from me. The cold air from the street hit me, sending a chill to my bones. Finally, I heard the door close, and I opened my eyes.

She hadn't left.

She stood right in front of me, looking up in earnest. "You know I'll probably mess up your life. You'll have to deal with a lot."

My chest ached at the sudden hope. "I'd rather have your issues than go on without you. Even if I *only* had your issues."

"You don't mean that." She shook her head, unbelieving. But I saw my own hope reflecting in her eyes.

"I do."

She wrapped her arms around my neck. "You can have kisses with the issues."

Her lips found mine. Searching. Discovering. I grabbed her waist and pulled her into a deep kiss. She softened against me, and I softened my hold.

Eventually, she pulled back, her mouth curving a little. "And I'm going to need to review that employment contract."

I turned around to get my laptop, but she grabbed my cardigan. "Not right now, you silly man. First, I need you to come upstairs with me. We have to talk about that bed. I mean, I'm dating this guy. He's pretty tall and has these big wood-chopping muscles, and I'm afraid that bed is not big enough for us. I'm flexible on the kitchen, but I'm going to need at least a queen. Otherwise, I can't even consider this job offer. Because I'm so in love with him, I want to stay with him every night. Sometimes, it's not practical to stay at his place, you know? He might have to stay over."

Relief flooded every nook of my body. My heart glowed like it was made of light. "You're so in love with him, huh?"

She took my hand and pulled me toward the stairs. "I hope that doesn't make me a bad hire because I'll be daydreaming about him and will probably get so distracted, I'll order way too many romance books."

"I heard your employer is very laid-back and under-standing. He knows what it's like. All those hormones."

"Exactly! It's insane." She skipped up the stairs, turning around to wait for me. "Oh my God! Are you okay? Can you even walk?"

I held the banister, trying to breathe through the pain. "Walk, yes. Just struggling a bit with stairs."

My chest ached so much I could barely speak. I'd already been up those stairs once and survived. But I must have angered my body, and it was fighting back.

She scurried back down to where I stood, her eyes watery. "I'm so sorry! I didn't think. You need to rest. Does it hurt more when you're sitting or standing? What about lying down?"

"I'm fine with sitting and standing. And I can lie down, but I need to avoid too much movement."

I leaned on the wall, trying to find a somewhat comfortable angle. I didn't want her to see how much pain I was in. If I could have made it up the stairs without passing out, I would have. I wanted nothing more than to lay her down on that bed and give her everything. She deserved so much better than this.

"You really need help," she said thoughtfully, placing a hand gently on my chest. "How did you drive here?"

"I... snuck out. Felicity and Jackson have been taking turns watching me, but today, they were busy working, so I promised I'd stay home. If I move slowly, I'm okay. I just need to rest for a bit, and I can drive home."

"I'll drive you home! I need to call Felicity and find out what your doctor's orders are."

"No, it's fine. I can—"

"Fredrik!" Her eyes burned with passion. "I want to take care of you. I *want* to be needed, not just a nice-to-have."

She looked so happy and hopeful, like this was what she'd been looking for, a man who couldn't get up the stairs.

"You are absolutely vital. An essential element that sustains life on the planet. Or at least within my rib cage."

She let out an easy laugh. "Good."

"And please take over all this Christmas stuff. I can't handle it. I don't know what your family is expecting, and it's stressing me out so much I'm having nightmares."

She chuckled. "I can't believe you invited everyone to your house. You don't even like people."

"I like you. And I know I can't have you without accepting everything that comes with it. Your past, your present, and your future."

"If that's from one of your Russian classics, I might consider putting some on my TBR."

"Well, according to Dostoevsky, to love is to suffer, so maybe you want to stick to romance."

Smiling, she took my hand and led me to the door. Slowly. Gently. "You're suffering for love right now. Does it make you feel connected to the 19th-century greats?"

I scoffed. "I just feel sore and stupid."

She locked the door behind us, then handed me the key. "I'm sorry I copied this. Grace thought it might sell the idea that we'd left town, but we still needed to use the bathroom. It was a stupid plan."

"It worked, until I found your damp towel."

"Ha! I thought we were being so careful." She gestured at the Christmas store. "I have to go tell Grace. She'll be worried sick. I left for a bathroom trip, and I've been away for a long time."

"Of course. You go ahead. I'll catch up."

She wouldn't leave my side. "No. It's slippery out here, and you're disabled."

My chest felt hot, but it wasn't from the broken rib. It was the emotion building up and boiling over. Because I'd never felt this. Elora hadn't been the nurturing type. She'd been stimulating and fun, but not someone you'd lean on. I'd been trying to support her and make her happy. I'd tried so hard. But I'd never had someone like this in my life. Someone who drew joy from being needed. Being helpful.

Noelle opened the door to her shop and poked her head in. "Grace! It's me. I have news!"

I heard a female voice say something inside, and Noelle pulled me into the store, closing the door behind us.

A small light was set up on a picnic blanket in the middle of the floor. The entire shop had been turned into a small indoor camp, with mattresses and pillows, a portable hot plate, and bottles of water. How on earth did they cook without running water? The whole setup made me think of a zombie apocalypse, with the last remaining humans hiding in abandoned buildings.

Grace was a small, bright-eyed Korean woman with long black hair and a sophisticated white-and-beige outfit. Nothing about her said "zombie apocalypse."

"This is Fredrik," Noelle told her, then turned to me. "And this is my friend Grace."

She shook my hand, her eyes assessing me. "She's in love with you."

"Good," I said. "I'm in love with her."

Grace turned to Noelle, her eyes a little sad. "You're not coming with me after all?"

Noelle burst into tears. "Please don't hate me! I'm messing you around, and you came all the way here."

"It's okay." She nodded, her eyes cast down.

I pulled Noelle into my arms.

"Do you have to leave right away?" I asked Grace. "Can you stay for Christmas?"

"I have to get to Bar Harbor for Sunday, and no buses are going because it's Christmas. The last one leaves tomorrow. And I have to find someone else to take Noelle's place. They're expecting two servers."

Noelle tensed against me, wiping her eyes. "What if you can't find anyone? Do you lose your job?"

She shrugged and pulled out her phone. "Let's see what they say. I'll message them now. We'll probably hear back tomorrow."

"Don't worry about the bus. Noelle can take my car and drive you. I'd do it myself, but I'm not supposed to drive at the moment. Get your things. You're coming to my house. I don't want anyone sleeping in here. This is depressing."

"Oh, Grace, please! It'll be so nice!" Noelle cast a pleading look at her friend. "His house is huge."

Grace raised her eyebrows. "I guess I should check you out. Make sure you're good enough for her."

"Absolutely," I agreed.

Great. Now I'd invited her parents, her sister, *and* her best friend. I was starting to worry there wasn't enough snow-pushing in the world to save me from all the awkward peopling this Christmas, especially when I wasn't allowed to do anything strenuous.

We bundled into the car, Grace sliding into the back seat. On the way to my house, my phone pinged. Noelle was driving, so I checked the message.

> Jackson: You need firewood or fire starters? We're clearing a tree that fell on the road, and there's a lot here.

"What is it?" Noelle asked.

I relayed the message to her, and she perked up.

"Do they have pine cones? We've been looking at craft tutorials with Grace, and there was one for pine cone fire starters. They burn in beautiful colors!"

"I don't know. Do you want me to ask?"

"Yes! If I'm staying here, I want to drop off Christmas presents for everyone! I've been making things, but I don't have enough, and those pine cones would make such cute gifts."

"What do you need for them?"

"Beeswax, I think. Maybe some colors." Her shoulders sagged as she slowed down to turn toward the road leading to Locke Heights. "Not the easiest things to source, I guess. Forget about it."

"Jackson uses beeswax for restoring wood. He'd have lots of it."

"Really?"

I loved the excitement on her face. I'd do anything to keep it there.

> Fredrik: Please bring small twigs and as many pine cones as possible, as well as beeswax. Pretty please.
>
> Jackson: Two pleases? Is this for a woman?
>
> Fredrik: How did you know? [tongue-out emoji]
>
> Jackson: What? Did she crawl out of her hiding place? Did you close the deal?
>
> Fredrik: She's with me, and we're driving to my place. Need pine cones and beeswax, stat. She wants to make fire starters. [eye-roll emoji]
>
> Jackson: I'll make it happen.

"He'll bring everything," I told Noelle.

"So far, so good," said Grace from the back seat.

Noelle gave me a cautious sideways look. "You know we'll be taking over your kitchen and probably ruining a perfectly fine cooking pot or something. And then I'll need your help driving around, dropping them off. I don't know where anyone lives."

"That's okay."

She'd be in my house, making it feel like a home. If that meant she'd open the door to a hundred other people I had to tolerate, it was still worth it. She was worth it.

CHAPTER 37

Noelle

"You ready to go?" I asked, tying a ribbon around the last bunch of kindling and attaching it to a bag of wax-coated pine cones. "We should drop these off before we go shopping."

We were all up well before sunrise, having barely slept, and still had a lot to do before our families arrived for Christmas Eve dinner, including baking more pulla. Grace leaned on the kitchen island next to me, making a shopping list.

We'd somehow managed to warm up the cones in his oven so they opened and melted the wax without destroying anything, but the general mess was still evident all around us.

"Are you adding a note?" Fredrik asked, admiring the row of pretty packages.

I shook my head. "Why?"

He smiled like I was being funny. "What if they're not home? They won't know it's from you."

"You can use these." Grace handed me a stack of gift tags.

I let out a nervous laugh. I was so used to doing my good deeds in the dead of night that it felt more natural that way. Putting my name on a card felt icky, like I was expecting something in return: recognition, praise, something.

"It's okay." I scrunched up my nose, feeling awkward. "I'll just write 'Happy Holidays' or something."

"Or..." Fredrik leaned across the island, a subtle smile on his lips. "You could write 'Happy Holidays from the Hideaway Elf.'"

My eyes flew wide open. "The... what?"

Grace giggled. "I think he knows your secret."

I stared at him in disbelief. "But... how?"

Fredrik took one of the gift tags, turning it in his hands. "Remember how I had the whole town on the lookout, reporting to me on your whereabouts?"

"Yeah. But I didn't do anything in the last two nights."

"No, but your friend did."

I exchanged a look with Grace, who shrugged. "He's not too dumb, this one."

I folded my arms. "How do you know she wasn't just playing the copycat elf on behalf of whoever the mysterious person is..."

"The mysterious person who has insomnia from sleeping in terrible beds and falls asleep in the middle of the day? Who really loves this town and constantly goes the extra mile trying to make everyone happy?"

I hid my face behind my hands. "You knew?"

"I had my suspicions."

"I didn't want anyone to know," I whispered.

He circled the island, grabbed my wrists, and gently pulled them away from my face. "I know everyone loves a good piece of lore around here, and your elf has given them endless enjoyment, but you don't have to do good things in secret. We all want to know you. I love knowing it's you."

I blinked away tears, feeling like I'd just stepped into bright sunlight and was burning to a crisp. Yet I was okay. I was okay to be seen by him.

"Please don't tell anyone else," I asked. "I'll sign the cards as the Hideaway Elf, and we'll let the kids enjoy thinking there's an elf walking around at night. What's the harm in that?"

"No harm." He smiled, placing a kiss on my forehead. "I'll go get the car ready. Unless the elf put a blanket over the windshield last night because I forgot."

I smiled back. "The elf may have also forgotten, sorry."

We drove around for the rest of the morning, sneaking to people's doors to drop off Christmas gifts without being noticed. Good thing it was still dark outside. When the sun finally rose and the shops opened, we headed to the town center to do our shopping. Last-minute shoppers buzzed up and down Main Street, the scents of hot-buttered rum, peppermint, and gingerbread filling the air, and carols played in every shop.

"ARE you sure you're okay with this?" I asked as I set my handmade centerpiece in the middle of his dining table.

"It's a table," he said. "I don't care what you put on it."

"No, I mean this whole thing. Inviting my family. And your family! They're going to meet, you know?"

He laughed. "Yes, I've considered that possibility, given that we gave them the same timeframe and address."

It was Christmas Eve, and Fredrik's house had been transformed into something festive and homey. Grace had worked with me all day, preparing the bedrooms and ensuring we had enough chairs, linens, dishes, and toilet paper. Felicity had helped, lending extra items and her favorite cleaning cloths.

Uncle Glenn had obviously been an entertainer, and we discovered many items in his old storage shed. Fredrik knew little about the contents of his own house but told us we were welcome to use anything we found.

Time was running out, so I had to take him at his word, even if I still felt nervous about changing his environment. But I couldn't help but feel the excitement building as I found the missing pieces, and the house began to look more and more welcoming. I was enjoying myself, swept up in the sights, sounds, and scents of the Christmas season.

I had easy access to decorations, and since Fredrik had given his blessing, I couldn't resist completing the makeover with some lights and tinsel. I'd thought it was too late to get a tree, but Felicity had scored a small one at the last minute from Pine & Dandy, a Christmas tree farm run by her friend. Kailee decorated it while Grace and I baked more pulla and Finnish gingerbread—another recipe from Grandma that my sister had kindly sent me. Fredrik's mom and Felicity had insisted on bringing the dinner.

Holly sent updates on the way, assuring me our parents

didn't seem angry with me but rather relieved and happy we'd all be together for Christmas.

Grace's phone pinged, and I glanced at the screen.

> Holly: Stopped at the lookout. This town is
> so cute!

Fredrik had already ordered me a new SIM card from another phone carrier. Apparently, other people in town at least got a signal every now and then, and there was no reason for my life to be extra difficult. I was so used to difficult that I barely noticed, but I had to admit it sounded nice.

"My family is at the lookout," I told Fredrik. "How far is it? Twenty minutes?"

"Maybe thirty in this weather." He peeked out the window. His voice was calm, but I could see the tension in his freshly shaved jaw. Maybe it had been there all along, under the scruff. Earlier, he'd asked what he should wear, but I'd refused to play stylist. I just wanted him comfortable. In the end, he'd settled on flannel and jeans.

Snow was falling again, covering the freshly cleared driveway under a white blanket. It was late afternoon, with a couple of hours of daylight left.

"The rooms are ready," Grace announced from the doorway, with all the efficiency of someone who regularly handled thirty cabins per day on a cruise ship. "And I wrapped our presents. They're under the tree."

"Oh my God! Thank you!" I'd forgotten about the elves I'd created and other last-minute presents we'd scored from town.

Grace hadn't done any crafts, but she'd bought gifts for everyone. I'd told her not to worry about it, but she wouldn't listen. I understood. She felt like she was impos-ing. I'd begged her to stay, for my sake. I needed my friend, and I hated the idea of not seeing her for the next eight months. She was the reason I was here in the first place. I had Grace to thank for my life being the way it was right now. Instead of lying to my family and hiding over the holi-days, we'd be together, celebrating.

I could tell Grace was warming up to Hideaway Harbor. She loved the coffee at the Sip, whoopie pies from the bakery, and the lotions from Tonic Room. Apparently, the specialty blend Deidre made had instantly cured a rash on her hands. I suspected her hands were simply healing on their own now that she'd left her restaurant job and was no longer married to an industrial dishwasher. But she seemed happy and loved exploring the shops, which might have been why our hiding-in-plain-sight plan had been so unsuc-cessful.

"I'm so glad you're here," I told my friend, joining her by the beautiful Christmas tree and giving her a side hug.

She glanced over her shoulder at Fredrik, who was moving toward the door.

"I'll… check something." He nodded at the hallway and left.

My stomach twisted. "Does he look really uncomfort-able?" I asked Grace.

She looked nonplussed. "Kind of. But he also looks at you like he's captured a unicorn—"

"And doesn't know what to do with it?" I finished for her. "Do you think I'm crazy for even thinking of staying here? I'm supposed to be independent and build a life for myself, not get tangled up with another guy."

Grace gave me a long, compassionate look. "I don't know what went down with Spencer. You never really told me. But I got a sense that you were ashamed or scared. I don't know. All I know is that you didn't talk about him like people talk about exes. Something was weird about it, like he had this hold over you. And I get that you felt safe on the ship, but you weren't really moving on. You never wanted to talk about the guys there or meet up after work. You just sat in the cabin with your Kindle."

"Wait! What do you mean? We worked long hours! You didn't go out either."

"I tried to, but you had zero interest in anything, so…"

"I thought you didn't, either. Ship goggles and all that."

"I know! It's terrible. But I always wondered why you didn't have a crush on anyone. I wondered what that Spencer guy had done to you."

I closed my eyes, rubbing my forehead as the realization took hold. I hadn't been open to anything. I hadn't allowed myself to even look at someone else.

"I'm sorry I was such a lame friend."

Grace let out a bubbly laugh. "I'm not mad at you! You saved me from a lot of embarrassment. I saw Eric in Bar Harbor last week, and he's not nearly as cute as I thought he was on the ship! I'm so glad we didn't go out that one night."

"But it's true! I was such a bore. I never did anything with the crew."

"And look at you now!" Grace smiled, gesturing at the house around us. "That's the point I was trying to make. You're different here. Like you were pastel before, and now you're in full color."

I bit my lip. "Are you sure it's not the wardrobe?"

"It's the whole package," she assured me. "Someone told me there's something in the water here, and whatever it is, I want some. Because you guys are disgustingly happy. I mean, your man's not a people person, but he's so in love with you it's a bit sickening." She made a gagging motion with her fingers and laughed. "Just kidding. I'm jealous."

The sound of the front door gave us a start, and we held still, hearing multiple voices. I recognized Felicity's happy chatter and Fredrik's grunts. His family had arrived right before mine.

"Do I look okay?" I asked Grace, brushing the front of my emerald-green dress. It was the nicest thing I owned.

"Adorable. Go!" She pushed me ahead toward the hallway.

"Noelle!" Fredrik's mom yelped my name, thrusting two oven dishes into Felicity's arms so she could hug me.

From the corner of my eye, I saw Kailee rolling her eyes.

"Mrs.... Hagberg," I said awkwardly, drawing in a lungful of her perfume.

"Call me Stella. And that's Hans." She released me and cast a look over her shoulder at her husband, a shorter, stockier version of Fredrik with long strands of gray hair sticking out from under a thick wool hat.

He cleared his throat. "Merry Christmas."

"Merry Christmas! Come in. Can I get you a drink?"

Fredrik grabbed my arm. "Relax. You don't have to..."

His dad gave him a measured look. "I'm not a big drinker, but I wouldn't mind a glass of something stiff right now."

"Can I have some?" Kailee asked.

I ignored her, nodding at her grandfather. "I think we

have gin. If we move quickly, you'll have time to finish a glass before my parents arrive and my dad starts talking to you about fire safety in old buildings." I flashed them both an apologetic smile.

Hans looked at the ceiling. "Well, I've told Fredrik many times, these colonial buildings don't have enough fire-resistant barriers. It's all good and well to fit out a new kitchen or bathrooms, but if you don't update the wiring..." He lifted an eyebrow at his son, who rolled his eyes at me.

Maybe he'd get along fine with my dad.

"What is your mom like?" Stella asked me as I helped her and Felicity carry the food into the kitchen.

"According to my sister, she is currently into something called 'death cleaning.'"

"Oh!" Stella's eyes widened. "Is she in ill health?"

I wanted to slap myself. Choose happy, safe subjects! How many times had I heard that in the Alford house?

"No! She's very well," I replied. "It's a figure of speech."

"Oh, I know that! It's like a Swedish thing," Felicity said, turning on the oven. "Where's your friend?"

I looked around for Grace and found her standing quietly by the Christmas tree. We'd all walked past her without even noticing. I was the worst hostess ever.

My face burning, I fetched my friend, and we joined them at the kitchen island. Felicity and Stella didn't seem bothered by my patchy social skills, so I tried to relax, focusing on the party preparations.

By the time my family rang the doorbell, the table was set, and the smell of oyster stew, turkey, and mashed potatoes wafted in the air, mixing with gingerbread and cinnamon.

I rushed to the door, suddenly shaking from head to toe. I'd deceived my parents for weeks. I'd humiliated them, running off and leaving them to deal with the aftermath. The word "sorry" hovered on my lips, but I didn't have time to utter it before Mom wrapped me into the tightest hug of my life, then Dad and Holly piled on. I could barely breathe, but the tears flowed regardless.

As we separated, I saw tears in their eyes. The cold air blasted us through the open doorway, so I led them inside and closed the door.

Mom sniffed, untying her pink scarf. "It's so good to see you! That call from Fredrik was the best thing that's happened all year. I'm so relieved you're on dry land and... happy?"

I nodded, my throat too clogged for words.

"I told them about Spencer's visit," Holly said, unbuttoning her heavy parka to reveal a pair of overalls. She brushed her short hair off her face, smiling.

She knew how to dress for herself, not the male gaze. I'd been taking inspiration from her ever since I'd left Spencer.

"Well, you look great," Mom concluded, taking in my emerald-green knit dress and candy cane–patterned stockings.

It was my only dress, showing off more cleavage than anything else I owned, and I was wearing it entirely for Fredrik.

"I thought that man had half a spine," Dad grumbled. "If a woman leaves you at the altar, it doesn't mean she's lost her marbles! Maybe she doesn't want to marry you. The Alfords have too much money. It's messed with their heads."

"We thought he handled it poorly," Mom said diplomatically. "It tells us a lot about his character."

Relief poured through me. "I'm sorry I let it go that far. I should have called it off much earlier. I should have never agreed to marry him!"

Mom handed me a tissue, then took over another task that was probably mine—hanging their coats on the rack. "It's okay. You're a bit of a people pleaser, like me. It's hard for us to say no."

I shook my head. "A people pleaser with no filter! I kept embarrassing them at fancy events. I never fit into that world."

Dad nudged Mom. "Are you saying you married me because it's hard for you to say 'no'?"

Mom chuckled. "You take after your father. Only filter he has is the one in his car."

"What about the dryer, vacuum cleaner, range hood…"

"Case in point," Holly confirmed.

Mom ushered us inside. "Now, let's meet this new beau of yours."

I realized Fredrik stood quietly at the end of the hallway, giving us space. His face looked friendly enough, but his arms hung awkwardly like he didn't know what to do with them. I grabbed the closest limb and pulled him forward. "Mom, Dad, Holly… this is Fredrik Hagberg. He owns the bookstore in town."

Everyone shook hands, and we advanced into the living room to meet Fredrik's parents, Felicity, Kailee, and Grace. Fredrik thrust drinks into everyone's hands, including one finger of gin for Kailee. Even my mom, who was usually at ease, downed hers quickly. Nervous energy vibrated across the room.

"I can help you with your luggage and show you to your rooms," Grace suggested to my parents in her hospitality voice. "Then I think it's dinnertime."

I'd never been more grateful for my friend. While I'd loved planning the party, baking, and preparing for it, I was not ready for this part. Flashbacks of dinner parties at the Alford mansion played on repeat in the back of my mind, reminding me of all the potential missteps, looming like land mines around me.

I told myself I was being irrational. This was family. There was no fancy social protocol or delicate pecking order I was supposed to adhere to.

But despite my best efforts to calm down, by the time we sat down for dinner, I was in knots. The conversation sounded stilted. Everyone was polite, but we were all practically strangers. What if they didn't find anything in common? What if his parents hated mine, or the other way around?

Thankfully, the food was delicious, momentarily distracting me from my thoughts.

When it was time for dessert, Fredrik stood, groaning. "I apologize. I have a fractured rib, and I need to take my meds and do certain breathing exercises. Doctor's orders. I'll join you later." He glanced at Felicity, then at me.

"Noelle can help you," Felicity said, gathering dirty plates in the crook of her arm. "I need to heat the apple pie."

I shot up and followed Fredrik down the hall into his bedroom.

CHAPTER 38

Noelle

Fredrik closed the door behind us, taking my shoulders. "Breathe. Relax."

"Aren't you the one supposed to be doing breathing exercises?"

"Yes. But I'm not as critical as you." He fixed me with a concerned stare. "If you get any more anxious, you'll self-combust during dessert. There'll be little pieces of Noelle scattered across my sister's apple pie, and she'll be quite upset."

He placed his fingers under my lower jaw, feeling my racing pulse.

So I was a little tense. "I want this to go well. Because if our families don't get along—"

"Then they don't. Then we limit contact. But so far, everyone's fine."

Everyone except me, I thought. I was the one making them uncomfortable. That was why he'd pulled me aside. I was failing, again.

"I've tried to hold my tongue so I don't offend anyone or ruin anything." I drew in a shuddering breath, gazing at him in panic. "But I'm still the problem."

Maybe dating with benefits was the best I could ever have. A secret relationship with no public component. No families.

He held my face, leaning on me so we stumbled backward against the door. "Noelle. You have to hear me. I didn't drag you away to tell you off. I brought you here so I could help you relax. I love you. I want you to feel at ease, especially with family. Especially at Christmas." He sighed so loudly it was almost a growl. "What this Spencer guy did to you... I should have broken his jaw!"

"Are you saying you held back?"

The muscle in his jaw twitched. "I did. And I know hurting him won't fix anything. But I still feel like I should have taken a proper swing."

Sandwiched between the door and his warm body was my current favorite place in the universe. With every breath, I felt more grounded. Protected. And desired.

He leaned closer, still holding those fingers against the soft hollow of my neck, observing each heartbeat. My pulse was settling, but I wasn't that mellow. His mouth hovered an inch above mine, and desire surged through me. We hadn't had a moment alone since he'd found me in the bookstore. He'd fallen asleep upright, propped up with pillows and dosed with pain meds, and I'd stayed up late to prepare the next day's party with Grace.

"You know this door is locked, right? And nobody is coming to find us."

"How do you know?"

"Because I made a deal with Felicity that she'd take care of them if I needed a moment. I wasn't sure if you'd need a moment, too, but I think she figured that out."

His lips landed on mine, and I melted into that kiss. No part of me held back. I opened up, meeting his tongue, moaning out of sheer need. He hiked up my dress, and his hand brushed up my thigh, cupping my ass. "You have no idea how much I've wanted this. How much I've thought about this."

"But your rib…" I lost all words as that hand reached in, his fingers grazing my delicate flesh through the thick stockings.

Damn stockings. I was dressed like one of the elves I'd crocheted.

"Don't worry about my ribs," he grunted, pressing his erection against my throbbing clit.

I loved seeing him in flannel. It channeled some kind of lumberjack sexual energy I found irresistible. He kissed me again, his tongue as desperate as our bodies to get closer and not leave any air between us. My excitement built, turning into a deep, throbbing need.

He couldn't lift me, though, and I knew lying down made his chest hurt.

"How would you like an ass print on that antique dresser of yours?" I asked as we came up for breath.

I glanced at the old piece of furniture, which seemed the perfect height.

"Put a bow on it, and it'll be the best Christmas present I've ever had."

Before he could make a move, I slid out of his reach, wiggled out of my stockings and panties, and hopped up on the dresser. I didn't have to wait for him. Before I could lift the hem of my dress, he stood between my thighs, rolling it up for me. "You're doing all the work."

"I care about your health." I smiled, popping the button on his jeans.

He took over undressing. The hard-on that sprang free was so impressive I blinked at it, frozen for a second. The flannel shirt split on each side of it like theater curtains.

"I'm actually desperate for you," he said. "I was scared for a minute there that I'd come in my pants."

"You can still sound like a foghorn if you want." I bit my lip.

I'd never seen anyone that far gone. That much in need. There was something so hot and beautiful about it. So vulnerable. Yet he held back, trying to crouch down to take care of me.

"No. Stand up. Use your fingers," I said firmly.

I was already so charged that a breath could have sent me over the edge. As his fingers circled me, my breath turned into gasps, and I grabbed the edge of the dresser. Forget ass prints. This dresser would need to be treated for hot liquid stains.

"More," I murmured. "A little closer."

He made the circles smaller, gently brushing over my clit. I shook from head to toe.

"Pressure."

"Oh my God. Noelle. You're so wet."

I couldn't believe I was telling him what to do.

"Now," I told him. "I need you now."

I raised my knees, and he thrust into me. I wrapped my legs around his waist and breathed through the sensation. The fullness. The pressure. It was perfect, and it was doing its thing. I tilted my hips, and he followed my lead, pumping into me, making sparkles erupt behind my eyelids like thousands of Christmas lights. I was coming. I was coming so hard I lost all sense of time and place. I didn't know who I was anymore, and it didn't matter.

I was happy and secure and one with the universe. I was home.

He groaned, and I felt his orgasm inside me as he held me, shaking. I clung to him, my whole body pulsing in sync with his. He didn't let go. He didn't rush me. And as we held there, I felt my pulse gradually slowing down until I was almost sleepy.

"I love you so much," he whispered into my hair.

"I love you too." I sniffed, swallowing a sudden ball of tears in my throat. "Don't lift me," I warned him, sliding off the dresser.

He raised his arms. "I also love it when you take charge."

I met his drowsy, adoring eyes and smiled back, feeling a little different. A little bolder. A bit more like myself. Like I'd been as a child, secure in my soul. When doing your best was enough for a gold star. When I knew I was adored, just as I was.

We cleaned up and got dressed, but I left the dresser the way it was. So what if someone figured out we were having sex? I was happy, and I wasn't hiding anymore.

"I feel better," I said as I smoothed my hair in front of his mirror. "Way more relaxed. What kind of sorcery was that?"

He chuckled. "The accidental kind, I suppose. I'm just a man who's been thinking about your pussy all day."

"Wow." I cocked an eyebrow, feeling a little flustered. "Where's that fancy English degree now?"

"Void," he said. "I've been reduced to a blabbering puddle of need."

"With a horny caveman vocabulary?"

He laughed, drawing me into his arms. "Yep. Only three thoughts in rotation. Must protect my woman. Must keep her fed and happy. Must fill her with my seed. Must reproduce."

A shiver ran through me. "That was four."

"Oops." He grinned.

"Do you want kids?" The question slipped out in my usual style, bypassing all retrofitted filters.

"We can talk about that later."

"No. What if it's a dealbreaker? I... I..." I had to be brave enough to tell him. "I want to be a mom. It's important. I don't want to wait forever, either. I'm sorry—"

He silenced me with his fingers, shaking his head. "Do not apologize. It was the one thing we fought about the most with Elora. She didn't want kids, and it drove us apart." He sighed, looking out the window. "This is good. We should talk about it. I'm so used to avoiding that subject to maintain peace. But you're right. It's important."

"She didn't want kids, but you..." I held my breath.

He met my gaze, his eyes full of conviction. "Whenever you're ready."

I sighed as another piece of our puzzle clicked into place. "Not yet," I said firmly. "But I'll let you know."

When we walked down the hallway, I heard squeals of laughter. We found everyone sitting by the fire with drinks in hand, talking animatedly. All the seats were taken, with Kailee and Grace on the rug in front of the fire.

Felicity raised her glass of mulled cider. "There's still some apple pie left. I put the ice cream back in the freezer."

"Thank you."

I tried to wipe the guilty look off my face, but as we walked past her, she grabbed my arm, grinning. "Those breathing exercises are truly amazing! You both look so much better."

"Yeah, they're great." My face flushed.

"I haven't done breathing exercises with anyone in a long time." She downed her drink and sighed. "I miss them."

"Oh! Jackson said he'd come by tonight to drop off a present," Fredrik told her.

Felicity's eyes narrowed. "And what made you think of him?"

Fredrik shrugged. "I don't know. Maybe the fact that you were thinking of him. I was having a psychic moment."

"I don't have a present for him," Felicity spat out and returned to the rest of the party.

"Is there something going on between them?" I asked Fredrik.

He looked as baffled as I felt. "It's... something."

We'd just finished our desserts when the doorbell rang.

"I'll get it." Felicity headed to the front door with a full-blown frown.

"Jackson's going to get a dose of Christmas spirit," Fredrik whispered, following his sister.

My curiosity bubbling up in full force, I shadowed them, standing back in the hallway.

I heard Jackson's cheery voice from the door. "Merrrrry Christmas!!"

"What the fuck are you wearing?" Felicity asked.

I edged a little closer to get a peek at his outfit. It was a Santa costume, but with a red velvet coat several sizes too small, revealing most of his muscled, bare chest.

"It's Christmas tomorrow. My clothes are entirely appropriate. And... this is for you." He handed her something the size of a microwave in golden gift wrap.

"What?"

"Nothing for me?" Fredrik asked. I could hear the smile in his voice.

"I'm dressed as a slutty Santa. You don't want what's in my bag."

"I don't think I want it either," Felicity grumbled.

"No. Open it!" Jackson pleaded. "And can we do it inside? The snow is getting into my underwear."

They closed the door, and Felicity tore open the package, gasping in shock. "Is this a... safe?"

"It's really easy to use. Choose a code, program it in, and don't tell anyone. No one will ever take your stuff again. I can also bolt it into your van if needed."

I'd never seen Felicity speechless. To be precise, I didn't see her face from where I was standing, but the silence that followed was potent.

"Thank you," she finally uttered.

Jackson waved his hand, wished us all happy holidays,

and left. I ran to Felicity, taking the heavy safe from her before Fredrik did something stupid and gentlemanly.

"You weren't expecting this?" I lowered the gift onto the hall table, giving her a moment to gather her wits.

"No," she said. "I don't know what game he's playing."

"I think… he's hoping to do some breathing exercises with you."

Fredrik caught my eye, looking half alarmed, half excited, probably thinking of what we'd been doing.

Felicity blew a forceful breath. "Well, I won't be exercising with him anytime soon."

We watched her stomp down the hallway.

"I think they'd be great together. What's her problem?" I asked Fredrik.

"They go way back. It's complicated."

"I get that it's weird for you. Your best friend and your sister. But something's clearly going on. Wouldn't it be better if they were… um… breathing together and not killing each other?"

Fredrik turned to me, and the conflicted expression on his face shifted into pure joy. "I don't know. But is it bedtime yet? I think I'll need to do my exercises again very soon. Doctor's orders."

I stepped so close I was flush against his chest. "Doctors may give orders, but I'll be your nurse carrying them out. You'll do exactly as I say."

He smiled so widely my heart ached. "You're my every fantasy wrapped up in one candy cane package, Noelle. Anything you say goes."

"Then I say, let's sneak out right now. I can help you heat the sauna."

"I do need help with that." He gave me a meaningful look. "You know I'm not allowed to carry firewood."

We put on our boots, coats, and wool hats, and hurried through the living room to the back door, grinning very tellingly at our families.

"We'll just go heat the sauna," Fredrik told them.

"I'll carry the firewood," I announced, biting back on my smile. "Because he's not allowed."

"Have fun!" Felicity gave us a knowing look, lifting a huge glass of wine. "It's a great place for breathing exercises."

"You have a sauna?" My mom sat up, ecstatic.

"Sure do. It'll take about half an hour to heat," Fredrik said.

"Or maybe forty-five minutes," I blurted, my face hot.

Holly grinned. "In forty-five minutes, you'll heat it twice."

Fredrik coughed into his sleeve, diving behind my back to open the door.

"Don't use protection!" my dad yelled. "I want grandkids while my knees are still good for walking."

They all burst out in laughter, and I skipped out the door Fredrik was holding for me, feeling lighter than air. The fresh snow sparkled under starlight, and my breath sent out smoke signals into the sky. Not even the freezing cold could get to me. I was living my own Christmas miracle, and there was nowhere else I'd rather be.

NEW YEAR'S DAY

Fredrik

W e were up bright and early, watching a leathery older man in swimming trunks lower himself into a hole in the ice and disappear. He reappeared soon enough and was helped up by Larry the *Lobstah* and a woman wearing a dress that could have featured in a period drama. The crowd cheered.

I hadn't even known my hometown put on an event like this every year. I wasn't sure I needed this in my life, but being with Noelle meant that I stood here, figuratively freezing my balls off as I watched others literally do the same. She didn't drag me into every single thing, but so far, if she asked twice, peering at me with those huge brown eyes, I caved. Whatever the pointless activity, at least I got to stare at her excited face. Last night at the New Year's Eve Town Dance, she'd also worn a sexy little dress that made it impossible to keep my eyes on her face even half the time. I didn't think I called the event frivolous or pointless even once.

"Ralph looks steadier on his feet," Noelle remarked. "I heard they altered his costume so he could take bigger steps."

"His mom took it in around the shoulders and made those slits on the sides," Felicity confirmed.

She'd joined us, along with Noelle's friend Grace, who'd decided to stay a little longer. Thanks to the weekend we'd spent together in my house, my sister had discovered her cleaning background and impeccable work ethic and hired her on the spot. She was currently living in my upstairs bedroom and insisted on paying rent.

I joked that I'd gotten a two-for-one deal, but in the last week, the actual head count had been higher on most days. Felicity visited all the time, seamlessly mixing business with pleasure as she oriented Grace to her job. Jackson also hung around, possibly to bump into my sister. My mom had taken a keen interest, popping over with the flimsiest excuse to chat with Noelle and Grace. She didn't even seem to need me in the room, which suited me fine.

"I can't believe they just walk around in swimsuits in the middle of winter!" Grace hugged a steaming mug of hot chocolate, visibly shocked.

"It's tradition," Noelle said, as if that explained everything. Maybe it did, at least in this town.

"Anyone seen Jackson?" I asked. "He said he'd be here."

Felicity hid behind her own steaming mug, looking away. "He says a lot of things."

"Maybe he overslept," Noelle suggested. "He'll regret it

later, because this is the most epic way to kick off the new year!"

She nuzzled into my side, and I wrapped my arm around her.

I loved her. She changed a little every day, showing more confidence and courage while doubting herself a little less. The woman I'd met had been beautiful, but this one was gorgeous. She was less fearful and more openly herself. Spontaneous and excitable. Curious and clever. And often unfiltered. But she laughed at herself more and apologized a little less, which I considered progress.

I could only hope I was making progress, too. Not freaking out over the smallest change or withdrawing in the face of conflict. My house was changing, but it was mainly evolving for the better.

The swimmers were escorted away, and the crowd dispersed. We followed Felicity and Grace toward our cars, but I sensed Noelle's reluctance. She never wanted to be the first to leave.

"Red snappers!" She pointed at a hot dog stand. "I haven't had these in years."

"Not what the great Alford family served for dinner?"

She pulled a face. "Imagine if they had!"

"I'm sure it would have been quite the scandal." Felicity snickered. "You guys go get hot dogs. I promised I'd give Grace a tour of our office."

We waved goodbye and joined the line at the stand.

Despite the mention of her ex-boyfriend, Noelle seemed relaxed. I'd decided it was best to talk about her past and the Alfords. I wanted to share everything, with no forbidden topics or buried secrets. I was done living that way. The more I'd tried to avoid the painful things, the more they festered and gained strength. Noelle had shown me a different way. She'd brought everything to the surface. She'd exposed my deepest secrets to sunlight and helped me move on. If I helped her do the same, we had a hope of making this work.

So far, Spencer hadn't sued me or anyone else. I'd heard through the grapevine (called Felicity) that his business was being investigated for abusing workers' rights and employment contracts, so maybe he was otherwise occupied. Based on everything I'd learned about him, I would have bet he was guilty. People who routinely manipulated their significant others didn't make the greatest employers.

We bought two red snappers and ambled back to the pier to eat them. The swimming was over, but Ralph hung around, still in his costume. He seemed happiest when dressed up as a lobster these days. Maybe he'd finally found his calling. If only someone paid for his services. Noelle waved at him, grinning. He waved back, giving me a dirty look, which I deserved.

I'd apologized, but I expected him to hold a grudge for a while, even if the bruise around his eye had already faded.

"Wait! Wait!" a deep, out-of-breath voice called from behind us, and we turned around.

It was Wayne, one of Eileen's regulars. He leaned his hands on his knees to catch his breath. "You youngsters keep running."

"I'm sorry! We didn't hear you." Noelle peered at him with concern. "Are you okay?"

Wayne looked over his shoulder, confirming we were alone. "I need to talk to you."

"Me?" I asked.

"No, your girlfriend."

"What?" Noelle blinked at him, confused.

"Yes. You. The Hideaway Elf. Whatever your name is."

Noelle's cheeks matched the pink hot dog in her hands. "What?"

"Don't you deny it. I saw you on my security camera." He scoffed.

"Camera? Where?" I demanded, suddenly uneasy.

Wayne yanked up the collar of his coat to shield himself from the cold wind, or maybe my questions. "I was worried about Eileen. A stranger using her tools at night…"

"To make her steps safer," I clarified. "How is that something to worry about?"

"Well, Eileen keeps leaving that iron scraper outside. It's for the elf, she says. And even if your girlfriend's not up to anything unsavory, someone else might not be as nice."

"What the heck are you implying?"

He was starting to piss me off, but Noelle grabbed my raised hand, smiling like she'd won a contest. "He wants to be the elf," she told me. "For Eileen." She grinned at me, her eyebrows doing a silly dance.

Wayne withdrew deeper inside his collar like a turtle. "I'd do it if she let me. If no one else was poking around at night. Be safer that way," he grumbled. "I'd bring my own tools."

Noelle nodded enthusiastically. "I promise I won't go near the café, if you promise you won't tell anyone it was me."

"Alright."

He took Noelle's outstretched hand and gave her an

awkward handshake, then wandered off to where he'd come from.

"So... Wayne and Eileen?" I was gradually catching up.

Noelle sighed in a way that reminded me of Eileen herself. "I know! Isn't it romantic?"

"What? Him installing a secret camera at her business?"

She laughed. "He had to get rid of the elf so Eileen would need him! Poor guy. If I'd known, I would have never touched those steps."

"Why wasn't he doing it before, though? I think you gave him the idea."

Her eyes sparkled. "You're right. That's perfect! I really hope they get together."

"Really? He's a cantankerous old fart, and Eileen's..."

"A sunny romantic?" She looked at me, silently chuckling. "It's a match made in heaven!"

"Ah." Just like us. Maybe Eileen could see through that prickly exterior, just like Noelle had seen through mine.

We finished our hot dogs, and I noticed Noelle's lips were turning blue. As much as she loved the outdoor events, her body had its limits. When she began hopping in one spot to keep her blood circulating, I decided it was time for us to return to the car.

"Can we stop at the bookstore?" she asked as we walked back toward Main Street. "I want to take some photos."

It was still early days, but Noelle had already begun planning the new store. She wanted to keep the name but expand its meaning. Hard to Find would not only stock rare editions of old classics. It would have lesser-known indie hits, mixed with special editions of bestsellers and exclusive merchandise she wanted to organize with the authors. It was a good plan. If anyone could pull it off, it was her. I'd assume a supporting role, as hands-off as possible.

To be clear, I was planning to keep my hands on her, but off the business. Not that I could help hearing about it, as she rambled on about displays, signings, and mailing lists. Apparently, I should have been doing about a thousand and one things as a bookseller that had nothing to do with sitting behind a desk and reading.

I parked in front of the store, and she unlocked the door with her master key. She'd officially accepted my job offer and was now officially living in this building. But since Grace had decided to stay, she wanted to stay with her friend, so it made sense that we all lived under the same roof.

I loved having her in my house, but I also wanted her to have her own place. Being with me had to be a choice she made freely, not because she had nowhere else to go.

"I think we should make this the feature wall," she said, pointing at the back wall. "What about a neon sign... 'Hard Dicks to Find' and romance titles featured on little shelves?"

I neutralized my expression. She was not sucking me into this. No matter how out there her ideas were, they'd still be better than my inaction. It took me a few seconds to realize she was kidding.

"Come on! I told you I'm not getting involved," I said as she doubled over, laughing. "And considering the romance readers in this town, that's not even a bad idea. I can name several women who'd line up with their credit cards."

"Fine. I hear you. I'll think about a... better term." She hiccupped, framing her first shot.

Uncle Glenn would have loved her, I thought as I walked

behind her, trying to stay out of the photos she snapped. He would have been thrilled to know Noelle and happy that I'd found someone who shone where I didn't.

When she was done with the photos, I pulled her into my arms, noting that my chest no longer twinged in pain. I was healing.

"I'm so glad you bounced into my life," I whispered into her hair. "With your fluffy baby chick coat and your makeup brush and your cactus."

She grinned, and her eyes caught the sun, turning it into two glowing stars. "How else was I going to get your attention?"

And she was right. That was what it took for me to look up from my book and take notice. She was exactly what I needed, and she'd burst into my life exactly the way I needed. I might have been one of the few people who knew there was no Hideaway Elf, yet I was the one who now believed in miracles.

CHRISTMAS AT HIDEAWAY HARBOR SERIES

The Holiday Hate-Off by Angela Casella

The Holiday Fakers by Evie Alexander

The Holiday Whoopie by Sara L. Hudson

The Holiday Post by L.B. Dunbar

The Holiday Grump by Enni Amanda

[You are here]

All books are interconnected standalones and can be read in any order.

More about Hideaway Harbor:

www.hideawayharborbooks.com

WANT MORE OF
NOELLE AND FREDRIK?

Join my mailing list and download a free bonus epilogue!

https://BookHip.com/DCBHDWJ

Falling Slowly is part of the **Cozy Creek Collection** of small-town standalones. It is a steamy, full-length romantic comedy. It's a boss-to-lovers, autumn-inspired romance with a golden retriever hero who falls first. Each book in the series is a complete stand alone with a happily ever after.

Available on KindleUnlimited
And as ebook, paperback, hardcover, and audiobook

ACKNOWLEDGMENTS

Hideaway Harbor wouldn't exist without my dear author friend, Evie Alexander. She's a talented powerhouse who moved from idea to execution so fast my head spun. I hung on, because I could see her brilliance and our shared vision taking shape.

I've adored Evie's books and followed her career for years. She's in the UK; I'm in New Zealand. That didn't stop our late-night/early-morning meetups or the steady friendship that grew from them. We haven't met in person yet, but I hope we will—in Maine, ideally—somewhere that looks like the world we built together. A pink café or a chowder house. I'm not picky.

Though I grew up in Finland, I can't take credit for all the Finnish flavors in Hideaway Harbor. Yes, I insisted on sauna and pulla (cardamom buns). But "Kippis" (Finnish for cheers) for the corner bar was Angela's stroke of genius, and Evie championed woolen-sock running, a sport that's newer to Finland than my childhood staples of cross-country skiing and ice hockey.

Huge thanks to Angela Casella, L.B. Dunbar, and Sara L. Hudson for jumping aboard and making Hideaway Harbor truly special. I've learned so much from each of you.

As always, endless gratitude to my husband, who not only supports my wild writing life but also built our series website (<u>www.hideawayharborbooks.com</u>). He's a gem and inspires every hero I write.

Thank you, Mom, for first telling me about woolen-sock running and for sending us to the sauna with a beautiful 'vasta' on our last visit. We enjoyed Finland in June this year, cold as it was. And thank you, Dad, for introducing me to Dostoevsky long ago. I did love *Crime and Punishment*, even if I still write romance.

ALSO BY ENNI AMANDA

A Tiny House on Wheels (2019)

Coffee on Waihi Beach (2020)

Christmas in July (novella) (2021)

LOVE NEW ZEALAND SERIES

Nest or Invest (2021)

Hidden Gem (2021)

Night and Day (2022)

LOVE ISTANBUL SERIES

My Lucky Star (2023)

My Turkish Fling (2024)

COZY CREEK COLLECTION

Falling Slowly (2024)

Falling Madly (2025)

You can find all of Enni's books and more information on her
website: **enniamanda.com**

Photo by Aini Räisänen. Pulla by Riitta Hallman.

PULLA RECIPE

INGREDIENTS

Dough

- 1 cup (2 sticks / 8 oz / 225 g) unsalted butter
- 2 cups (500 ml) whole milk
- 2 packets (4½ tsp / 14 g) active dry yeast
- ¾ cup (150 g) granulated sugar
- 2 Tbsp coarsely ground cardamom (or to taste)
- 1 Tbsp vanilla sugar **or** 1½ tsp vanilla extract
- 1½ tsp salt
- 1 large egg
- About 6 to 6½ cups (750–800 g) all-purpose flour

For brushing

- 1 egg, lightly beaten

Topping

- Pearl sugar (Swedish pearl sugar or crushed sugar cubes)

INSTRUCTIONS

1. Melt the butter: In a small saucepan or microwave, melt the butter. Set aside to cool slightly.

2. Warm the milk: Heat the milk until it's warm to the touch (about 100°F / 37°C). If using active dry yeast, aim for 105–110°F (40–43°C). Don't overheat — too hot milk will kill the yeast.

3. Activate the yeast: Pour the warm milk into a large mixing bowl or the bowl of a stand mixer. Stir in the yeast until dissolved. Let sit for a few minutes until it starts to bubble slightly.

4. Add sugar and spices: Stir in the sugar, cardamom, vanilla sugar (or extract), and salt.

5. Add the egg: Beat in the egg until combined.

6. Add flour: Begin adding the flour, about half at first, mixing with a whisk or wooden spoon until smooth and airy.

Switch to a dough hook or knead by hand, adding more flour a little at a time until a soft dough forms. It should still be slightly tacky but not sticky.

7. Add the melted butter: When about two-thirds of the flour has been added, pour in the melted butter and knead it in well. Continue adding the remaining flour as needed — you may not need all of it. The dough should be soft and elastic, not stiff or dry.

8. Knead the dough: Knead for about 10 minutes, by hand or in a mixer, until the dough is smooth and stretchy. (If you pull off a small piece and stretch it gently, it should form a thin "windowpane" without tearing easily.)

9. First rise: Cover the bowl with a clean kitchen towel and let rise in a warm, draft-free place for about 45 minutes, or until doubled in size. (A turned-off microwave or slightly warm oven works well.)

10 Shape the rolls: Turn the dough onto a lightly floured surface. Divide it in half for easier handling. Roll each half into a log and cut into 12 even pieces (about 24 rolls total). Shape each piece into a smooth ball by rolling it between your palms or against the work surface.

11. Second rise: Place the rolls on parchment-lined baking sheets, leaving space between them. Cover with a towel and let rise for at least 20 minutes, until puffy.

12. Brush and decorate: Gently brush each roll with beaten egg. Sprinkle generously with pearl sugar.

13. Bake: Bake in a preheated 400°F (200°C) oven for 8–15 minutes, depending on the size of your rolls and your oven. Smaller rolls take about 10–12 minutes. They're ready when golden brown on top.

14. Cool and enjoy: Transfer to a wire rack to cool slightly. Serve warm or at room temperature with coffee or tea.

Notes

- **Storage:** Keep in an airtight container for up to 3 days, or freeze up to 2 months. Warm briefly before serving.
- **Variations:** Use this same dough for braids, or Finnish cinnamon rolls (korvapuusti).

Happy baking!